UNSPOKEN
IRONIES

Peter Boxall

ISBN: 9798410557573

For Grace

PROLOGUE; DETECTIVE INSPECTOR MIKE GRIFFIN

'Yes ma'am, of course.' Mike Griffin responded to his DCI thinking, 'get off my fucking back', as he padded across the wooden floor from the kitchen in his black socks admiring his recently acquired 4th floor Penthouse apartment, a significant step up from his previous flats. Dodging the unopened packing cases dotted around the open plan living area he made his way to the contemporary walnut dining table where piles of folders awaited his attention. His left hand held his phone to his ear listening to his boss's demands, in his right an empty wine glass and a bottle of New Zealand Merlot. The blue jacket of his top-of-the-range off-the-peg blue suit slung over a leather sofa along with one of his many non-descript silk ties. His trusty aging black brogues parked at the front door. 'Absolutely ma'am, but with due respect.' Griffin placed the bottle and glass on a dark blue place mat and lowered himself onto one of the six matching leather chairs looking out over the majestic Epping Forest with central London in the distance through a full-length window. Dusk approached, a hazy sunset over to his right. 'Sorry, yes, as I said I'm on it, in fact they're my priority tonight ma'am.' With a little dexterity he twisted the cap off the bottle whilst not releasing the phone. 'Okay, tomorrow.' He placed the phone on the table with a sigh and poured a large slug of wine into the glass, raising it to his lips, pondering where to start or whether he could be arsed, the call ending without any pleasantries. 'Yes ma'am, no ma'am, three fucking sacks full ma'am,' he said to himself looking at files that all needed his attention, paperwork was not a strength, in his book enough had been written and discussed but he was still being harassed by the pen pushers for facts and figures and his DCI was pressing for staff appraisals, plus more info into a lingering, pain in the arse internal inquiry into the finances of his ex-DS.

A survey of colleagues past and present would garner that Detective Inspector Mike Griffin was an all-round nice guy, if you were on his side, if not, he liked to think that he was fair copper. A stocky 5' 9" in his early 40s with likeable features, handsome for no particular reason. Respected throughout the force, a man of self-pride and little ego, and what he hoped was a good sense of humour, Griffin allowed his results and the respect of those who worked with him to speak for themselves. The New Zealand Merlot you would think a kickback to his upbringing in Hamilton on the North Island. Not so, arriving in England in his early teens, when his academic parents sought pastures new, the liking of their wines was a recent thing, supplementing his second love, a good pint of real ale. New Zealand had introduced him to his first love, rugby union and the All Blacks, a sport that he had a passion for, playing to a relatively high level, now coaching locally when the pressures of work allowed.

This permanent move away from New Scotland Yard was an integral part of Griffin's embryonic mid-life strategy and a desire to ensure that his private life matched his professional one, far too frequently neglected in his past. His relationship with Veronica, universally known as Ronni or Ron, the popular landlady of The Cobblers, the local boozer, needed handling with care to avoid her slipping from his grasp like so many in the past.

Since moving to this patch around eighteen months ago, a leafy suburb with a reputation for a criminal underbelly, his workload had been a demanding cocktail of anguish, frustration and despair, coupled with a fair element of success and inevitably some failures. The files were full of cases. Some of which were done and dusted awaiting trial, others were dead and buried, literally. Then there were those that irritated and infuriated, likely to remain dormant unless something significant occurred. One large folder sat alone, an unresolved case that he feared he would take to his grave.

These had been unprecedented times in this slice of suburbia. Murders and a questionable suicide of sorts, a wealthy accountant to the celebrities of the criminal world, found face down in his swimming pool. No note, but remnants of blister packs and empty Champagne bottles on a table beside the pool. A pissed trip the likely cause, or was he pushed? The wealthy accountant could have been leaving a happy family if his wife, Stephanie a lady gangster, just out from a ten-stretch, and son had not been killed in an explosion that transpired to be a deliberate act. A blast that took out a wing of Blue Skies House, the renowned local retirement home, just a couple of hundred metres away from where he was sitting.

A gas engineer, a journalist, an architect, a builder, and the owner of the Home among those who became embroiled all sorts of shenanigans. A couple of them in the wrong place at the wrong time, all ending up on a cold slab in the police's mortuary. The truth was that none of them were totally innocent and in Griffin's eyes they had all broken the law in some way, although even he admitted a few of them were unlucky to lose their lives for their misdemeanours. The downside for the DI was the mountain of paperwork it generated.

There were a few who dodged the net as it swept the pond. Some escaped these shores to pastures new, others simply ducked the radar. With his superiors more than happy with the headcount there had been no urgency to follow up these loose strands. Not for Griffin, a criminal was a criminal in his book, he joined the force to solve crime and feel the collar of those responsible, not to tick boxes.

Those he would like to interrogate included Geoff, a serial peddler of hooky goods, and Henry Wilton-Brook, a dodgy vicar. Both having gone AWOL, although there had been a sighting of them running a bar together in Phuket. The Right Reverend had a CV that made West Ham winning the Premiership seem believable, a piece of fiction that had secured him the enviable gig at St Vincent's, an impressive 200 year old church just across the road on top of the hill. Mandy Fisher, a young, full of ideas vicar with a colourful past had replaced him and was proving to be very popular in the community. Then there were the two owners of the pub next door to the retirement home, The Bootmakers Arms, known to all as The Cobblers, home to the local riff-raff. In the DI's book the 'City Slickers' as he referred to them, were just too squeaky clean. He couldn't be too heavy handed though with Ronni managing the pub.

The catalyst for much of the spike in crime was an unresolved case, details of which filled the largest and oldest file on the table that he pulled towards him and patted in an despised old friend sort of way, taking a glug of wine as he opened the grubby beige cardboard file with 'Spanish Gold' scrawled across the front. A high profile bullion raid. Sixteen gold bars stolen a dozen years ago from the ultra-secure, impregnable vault of Banco Catalan, a Spanish bank with a fine reputation in The City of London. Value of the gold? North of five million. A haul that literally floated out of their secure basement down the Victorian sewers of Ye Olde London Town, never to be seen again. What should have been a simple open and shut case had been far from that, the ingots once again slipping from his grasp nine months previous. Griffin found it hard reading, pushing the file away. Having written down nothing his mind wandered onto the other crimes that had occurred during the past eighteen months. The worst of which was an extremely ugly case that involved many innocent vulnerable women all aggressively violated by Andy Nash, a late twenties marketing executive at the aforementioned exclusive Blue Skies House, a retirement home for the rich. Previously a well-liked playboy character in the locality Nash was convicted of multiple rapes. One of which was Prisha, the popular receptionist at the Home. Nash being exposed by a lady that Griffin admired, Margaret, an eighty year old resident who Prisha confided in, a respected lady who had had her own unpleasant confrontation with Nash. With Prisha going public many other ghastly accusations flooded in. Once apprehended Nash was immediately sectioned, and his trial fast tracked. Inevitably he was found guilty and locked up in a secure psychiatric unit, supposedly for the rest of his life, unless, as Griffin feared the do-gooders with their rehab in the community ideals had their say. The case left a nasty taste in the mouths of locals and Griffin was relieved to get Nash put away as he knew there were many vigilantes out there looking for retribution. In Griffin's book Andy Nash was the worst of all the scum, pushing the file away with venom he took another large gulp of his wine.

Calming down Griffin gazed out of the window, the sun had set, darkness spread over the ancient woodland, in the distance the lights of the capital sparkled. The truth was he thrived on being busy and the pressure that came with it. Police work would never be a walk in the park, he had not signed up for an easy life. Many warned Griffin that his move out of the Met may be a backward step, to date this proved to be the opposite. He was happy with his lot, and of course there was Ronni to think of, a relationship that he must not make a pigs ear of. The intercom buzzed interrupting his thoughts.

Griffin got to his feet and pressed the button. 'Hello.'

'Mr Mike, Chutney Ali's.'

'Hi, yes fourth floor thanks.'

CHAPTER ONE ~ A few days later

Griffin perched on the edge of his desk watching his two detectives amble into his office. 'Good to see you both looking so bright and bushy tailed,'

DS Lucy Mantel and DC Nimra Shimra both sipping at their hot drinks, took the two chairs available in the organised but not fussy office. The only items of personal note a few bits of the force's rugby memorabilia, tucked away in a discreet corner on a shelf.

'Don't look too bad yourself boss, quiet night?' Mantel asked. 'So what's with the seven thirty meet?'

'Thank you Luce. We're off to church,' Griffin replied with a smile.

'Sorry?' Mantel asked. 'Did I need to book the armed response guys?'

'Don't worry, it's just for a quiet chat and hopefully not a sermon. I guessed that at eight o'clock the coffee will be brewing at the Vicarage, but primarily I don't want to draw too much attention to our visit.'

'Why the church then?'

'I hear the new Vicar is looking for new parishioners.'

Mantel looked at her boss with never shrinking intrigue, knowing that one of the pluses of working for him was that you could never second guess him. A minus being that you had to put up with a sense of humour that he alone appreciated. 'Ha bloody ha. Not another hunch about the gold is it? Mandy Jarvis is not like that old Wilton-Brook, who, even I admit with hindsight, was simply too much of a complete wanker.' DS Mantel was not one to mince her words.

New to CID Nimra sat with her arms folded, still to get in tune with the banter. 'So sir, as Lucy asked, why the church?

'Something has come up about her past and I have been asked to get some clarification. It's a little off the normal agenda and sensitive amongst those who should be obeyed,' Griffin responded pointing upwards.

'What God?'

'No Luce, although they sometimes think they are, our hierarchy, they'll be no need to take any notes on this one.'

Mantel stood and stretched. A trim, netball playing, 5'5" natural blond who thrived on manipulating political correctness to its full. An ambitious female, who didn't mind adopting tactics that ensured that the doors to her sex remained fully open, a little envious of Nimra for holding the ethnic card. 'And, just to confirm, even if this has nothing to do with the gold the bling and is long, long gone. So we can write it off.'

'Yes, yes Luce, we've listened to your scratched vinyl on many occasions, but this has nothing to do with the gold,' Griffin said giving his DS a knowing look. 'This is an internal matter, our Reverend Mandy Jarvis was previously an escort, some would say prostitute.'

'That's not a problem sir, is it?' Nimra asked folding her arms a little tighter. Mid-twenties, attractive, and if she wanted it, a long and successful career in the force ahead of her, and ambition was certainly something that Nimra didn't lack. Another, like her idol and colleague Lucy Mantel, who was prepared to exploit the current politically correct environment to her advantage. 'This is the 21st century. Surely anyone can see the light.'

'Quite Nimra, we all can, from whatever position, but it's not what she's done, it's who she done it with that's the issue,' Griffin replied with a smile. 'Oh, and this is just between us. Not for spreading round the station. My bollocks would be very much on the line if this meeting got out. A few years back intelligence, a much-maligned word around here, dug up a client list that included a number of our top brass. Upstairs now wants to ensure that her sermons don't include reference to one of our braided bunch. I want the two of you to lead the discussion. I'll brief you more in the car. We're three handed because it's off the record and I want no misunderstandings. Oh, and suffice to say whiplash and bondage are not going to useful lines of communication.' Mantel and Nimra giving their boss their best 'you are such a dinosaur' looks as they went to grab their jackets from their desks.

'Bollocks, have you seen this?' Griffin called after them. 'Andy Nash done a bunk overnight from his supposed secure unit.'

Nimra admired the tastefully decorated high-ceiling drawing room in St Vincent's vicarage as the Reverend returned with a tray of coffees and extras, including a large plate of assorted biscuits that caught the eye. 'Nice place. The houses the police provide are certainly not like this.'

'Thank you, perk of the job I suppose although it is rather large for me,' Mandy replied handing out the mugs. 'Now, how can I help you? Biscuit anyone?'

'It's slightly awkward, but as you are well aware the church needs to make checks on your cv, in particular after the last appointment and these were obviously fine,' Mantel said assuming the lead role as agreed on their short journey, with Griffin and Nimra taking a garibaldi and a bourbon. 'At the same time, our intelligence is always keeping a check on the movement of individuals that have been flagged up in the past.'

Mandy Jarvis a generally perky attractive lady in her mid-thirties, shifted uneasily in her chair, unsure as to whether this would be a new revelation. Straightening her cassock and looking intently at the sergeant.

'So, your name has come up in relation to your past occupation,' Mantel continued surprisingly a little nervous herself having seen the Vicar's reaction. Not too pleased with her boss's decision to delegate the meeting. Griffin gazing down at his mug, while Nimra looked Mandy in the eye. 'Now, don't worry, you have done absolutely nothing wrong and this is simply an off the record chat to make you aware of what is on record. Facts that I am sure you are totally aware of.'

'Quite, and it's all in the past.' Mandy replied taking a sip of coffee, more at ease knowing the reason for this unexpected early visit, hence the hastily slipped on cassock, it being close at hand when the doorbell rang out, requiring very little else under it, today nothing at all, apart from plain black satin pumps. A smile spread across Mandy's face in an attempt to counter the unease she could feel in the room. 'As they say, it all happened before I saw the light.'

'See. I told you so,' Nimra said glancing at her colleagues. 'Sorry vicar, please continue.'

'Mandy, please. Yes, I did have a high-profile client list that included a number of your colleagues. Discretion though, I can assure you, has always been a by-word, now even more so, as you can imagine. You will no doubt have noted that it was one of yours, or should I say their wife, that spilled the beans. I suppose that was my day of reckoning. You could say that I now have another flock to look after.'

'Yes, quite,' Mantel continued warming to the vicar, whilst really not seeing the point of the visit. 'As I said we just wanted you to know that we are aware. We'll leave you our cards in case anyone bothers you, and please don't hesitate to call.'

'As I said it was a few years back now and I can assure you that it is all well behind me. A few of the media had their fun at the time, but hey, c'est la vie, I'm now looking forward to my time here at St Vincent's, but thank you for coming it's been reassuring.'

*

'Our holier than thou Vicar wasn't being totally straight with us,' Griffin said as they returned to their car, the 200 year old church resplendent behind them.

Mantel stopped by the car. 'Sorry?'

'Apologies but I left a bit out of the brief. This was simply meant to be a warning shot. Hoping she'd get the hint of what we are aware of.'

'You're aware of it, we're not. Aware of what?' a perplexed Mantel asked. 'Come on boss.'

'Sorry, but I didn't want it to influence your chat with her. Our Mandy is still having an affair. Nothing much we can do though as they are both consenting adults.'

'So, who is it?' Nimra asked. 'That's if we can ask?'

'Not a problem Nim, Superintendent James Hawes from Hertfordshire our neighbouring force. Who, as you know, leads most of the joint operations and is often seen around the station, he's still shagging our new vicar.'

'Leads with his dick, is the word in the locker room,' Mantel quipped zapping the car lock.

*

Griffin stood in front of a white wipe board in his office that he had attempted to clean, smeared impressions from past cases remained. 'Look, I think we've exhausted the Superintendent's liaison with our Mandy Jarvis.' His two subordinates smiled having enjoyed the early morning distraction from their day-to-day enquiries. 'And as I said this stays with us and those upstairs who need to know. Obviously, those who surf the web can find out her history, but let's try to keep this particular issue to ourselves, especially what we discussed in the car. I've always said that ladies minds are far filthier, I doubt I will ever be able to get the image of them going at it in the pulpit with their uniforms on out of my mind, so thank you for that Lucy. One final question for you both, which occupation was Mandy's cassock bought for? Was it before or, as Nimra and the vicar said, when she saw the light?'

'Didn't see any stains,' Mantel said nonchalantly clasping a warm soya milk.

'Please Luce'

'So boss, enough of whiplash Mandy, who I must say I liked, Andy Nash?'

'Right. Now Nimra I know that this is a little personal. But I'm hoping you're okay to handle it.'

Nimra picked up her carton of coffee, a straight white with sugar and looked her new DI in the eye. 'Thank you. I'll be fine. It won't be a problem sir I can assure you.' Her grip on the carboard cup tightened.

Griffin stuck a recent head and shoulder photo of Nash on the board. 'I know we are all pretty familiar with this guy, but I suggest that I swiftly run through who Andy Nash is and what he's about, so we all sing from the same hymn sheet.' Griffin paused and took a sip of his large espresso. 'Andy Nash, a 29-year-old womaniser. Pretty boy around town, at least he was. Head of Marketing at Blue Skies House, the retirement home that received a five-star rating from a top Sunday glossy magazine, with fees to match. An establishment that has attracted media attention for the wrong reasons. Experiencing considerable upheaval since the explosion rocked it a few months back. Nash's father, Jonny, a Director of the Home, was one of five who lost their lives. We know that Nash was at it before this so it could never be used as a reason. The blast was originally deemed to be an accident, now proved to be an orchestrated gas fault. The rogue gas engineer was murdered by his accomplices, Blue Skies owner's wife, Julie, and one of her lovers, a senior police officer, DCI Countney, our old boss. Tom, the gas engineer, apparently getting too greedy with his blackmailing. Julie and Countney are now both on remand for their misdemeanours. The scenario was all part of the gold fiasco which we won't dwell on. Now, we have no link between Andy Nash and the gold but, especially for you Nimra, I thought it was worth running through all of this as Blue Skies House was heavily involved, and Nash was employed there. Who knows we may have missed something, but I don't think so, although there's always a chance.' Nimra nodded. 'Thank you sir.' She had only recently moved from uniform, so unlike Mantel had not been directly involved in the case. 'Right more specifically about Nash,' Griffin continued. 'In amongst the whole debacle complaints were made of him from two totally different individuals. Prisha, one of the receptionists at the Home, accused and subsequently proved that she was raped late one night in the dining room. Sharing her details with you Nimra, her close friend, and this helped to bring him in. The other came from Margaret, who Prisha had also confided in, an 80 year old resident, who alleged that the high as a kite Andy Nash had requested oral sex at a quiz afternoon. These were the Dambusters, many other accusations flooded in. Nash was swiftly brought to trial and sentenced. Pleading a sex addiction, more bullshit in my book, he was sectioned and placed in what was supposed to be a secure psychiatric facility. Now he's on the run. Just for the record, and of no particular consequence and as we all know Prisha, somewhat ironically, was promoted to Head of Marketing Nash's old position. Oh, and Margaret is still a resident, a right plucky old bird, I like her a lot. So, I think that covers it. Your thoughts please.'

'Nash was very much a local guy. His family were from round here,' Nimra said calmly, inwardly visualising what she could achieve with two grubby house bricks. 'So is he likely to return home?'

'I would hope not,' Mantel interjected. 'It was well publicised, and I would suggest that fifty percent or more of the local population will be looking around for a couple of bricks to administer retribution.' The DS viciously clapped her hands making her DI look up. Nimra allowing herself a smile, sketched a realistic picture of two bricks and two bollocks on her pad, an artistic talent that was largely wasted.

'Quite, I don't think there will be many who will have time for him round here,' Griffin said. 'But who knows he could be drinking champagne, watching footie on Sky in someone's house whilst we talk.'

'More likely a porn channel. I suppose we could call it Operation Castration. It rhymes, well nearly,' Mantel quipped sipping her drink, her colleagues remaining silent. 'Okay not funny. At least it would be poignant.'

'Let's remember,' Nimra said with a serious edge. 'He's a dangerous bloke who raped many women, and when his medication runs out could become very desperate.'

Griffin pointed at the photo on the board. 'You're totally right Nimra. Don't forget this guy was none too happy about going down. Reckoning that it was all consensual and that drugs were a mitigating factor. All fucking bullshit in my book. Plus, he felt his admittance to being a sex addict would help him. Bollocks again and as you said Nimra, he's just a fucking dangerous nutter,' an agitated Griffin said grabbing his jacket hanging off his chair. 'Okay Luce, you and me to Blue Skies to have a chat with Mr Ravi Patel to see if he's heard anything, this will not be welcomed news. Nimra, probably best for you to coordinate getting his details out and I suggest you keep in close contact with Prisha. Uniform need to keep her and his other victims under check. After Blue Skies we'll have a chat with Andy's uncle Rodney and Ellie Richmond, my new neighbours, they are literally just across the landing. If there's time Luce, I'll give you a tour.'

*

Griffin and Mantel stood a little uneasily whilst admiring the reception of Blue Skies House. An area that was back to its magnificent best. Opulent decor; chandelier, gilt mirrors, Chesterfield chairs, with two antique mahogany desks. On an ornate casual table four crystal glasses and a jug of water refreshed hourly, along with a silver ice bucket. A large flat screen television, broadcasting a news channel, thankfully without reference to Nash. Sandra one of three very efficient receptionists had acknowledged them from behind her desk. Immaculately turned out as always, her smile though was shallow, clearly showing that news of Nash's absconding had reached the Home.

'Inspector, Sergeant, so pleased to see you.' Mr Ravi Patel a portly, engaging individual came down the wide staircase and greeted them. Smartly dressed in a blue suit and colourful tie, his accent clipped Anglo Asian Queen's English. The new owner had a concerned look on his 55-year-old round face, a clear demonstration of a furrowed brow replacing his normal friendly look. 'Please this way.'

The detectives followed Ravi towards his office. 'Not noticed the artwork before Mr Patel,' Griffin said admiring the abstract pieces hung beside the staircase. 'I like them.'

'Yes, I inherited them. A local artist called Pete I believe,' Ravi replied not wishing to dwell on small talk. 'Now come in please and take a seat.'

Griffin and Mantel sat on black leather chairs in front of Mr Patel's expansive desk in a splendid office with views over the manicured gardens. Refreshments had not been offered by the normally hospitable host who they could tell was rattled by developments. Ravi told them what he had heard, all of which was sketchy and added nothing to what they already knew. There were no sightings nor contact that he knew of.

'Well Inspector I have employed the services of a discreet security company. They will work alongside and supplement my concierges. Just to add a presence,' Ravi continued. 'Although I really cannot believe that he would have the audacity to show his face round here.'

'We'd like to think not,' Griffin replied. 'However, it is not unusual for criminals to return to the scene of their crimes. And yes, added vigilance is what we would recommend. And we will ensure that there are extra patrols in the area. Oh, and my DC, Nimra Shimra, will be keeping a close eye on Prisha.'

Ravi's stubby fingers shuffled papers for no apparent reason. 'Yes, I heard that they were close. Thank you that will be reassuring not just to Prisha, but also the staff who have already expressed concern. Now if you will excuse me, I have said that I will give the residents and staff an update after this meeting. There is already an uneasy atmosphere and quite rightly so. I need to give them some reassurance.'

*

'Well for the sake of the residents and the staff boss, we need to track down Andy Nash as soon as possible. You could cut through the tension,' Mantel said opening her car door in the car park bathed in sunshine. 'Where to now?'

'You won't need a sat nav for this one,' Griffin replied climbing in. 'Just a couple of blocks down the road, I'll show you. There's a gated carpark. As we've got half an hour I'll give you a shifty of the new pad. '

'It was good to see the vicar in the lounge playing cards with the residents, probably offering reassurances.'

'I'm pleased you said that she was playing cards and not handing them out.'

*

'Very nice boss,' Mantel said admiring both the apartment and its view. 'A bit of a change in direction for you though. Nothing to do with a certain landlady down the road?'

'Not directly but may have had some bearing,' Griffin replied lounging on one of the two leather sofas. 'Never thought I'd say it, but I really enjoy it out here. I know that you've found it hard to adjust.'

Mantel waved towards the city out of the window. 'Just a bit quiet. Not the guts of that place,' Mantel had worked for Griffin for a few years and followed him out of central London at his request, a career move that she could not resist. Work wise it had gone well, it was just that in her heart she was a city girl. This recent promotion to sergeant would probably satisfy her ambitions for a while, but she could see herself seeking a move back when the opportunity presented itself. 'I'm not sure if I'm cut out for anything other than urban.'

'I can see your point, but I'm at a very different stage of my career. And you have to remember my upbringing was all about the great outdoors in New Zealand.'

'So what you're saying is that you're getting old?'

'Easy. Any fears that this would be a quiet backwater have been totally squashed. You have to admit it couldn't have been busier and more intriguing,' Griffin replied. 'Then as I say there's the great outdoors, there must be something in my genes. You point towards the bright lights of the city. For me it's the forest that has been a big plus point.'

'What Epping Forest, home to flashers and corpses.'

'Very funny. A walk through there really clears the mind. Quite unlike a stroll along grimy, polluted streets packed with irritated people.'

'Blimey, mid-life crisis and all that. So, this is it then, no other places to lay your hat. Well unless you include your lady friend, conveniently placed on your doorstep.'

'Let's just see, shall we,' Griffin replied again recognizing that Veronica figured in his thoughts more than others in his past. 'Right, Rod and Ellie are just across the landing, the blue door.'

*

'Here you go a neighbourly brew Inspector,' Rod Nash said handing out mugs of tea. 'Welcome to Hawthorn Towers.'

'It's going to have to be Mike as we're such close neighbours Rod, that's if it's okay with me calling you that. This place is virtually the same as mine just flipped over.'

'Sounds good to me Mike. Yes, the block is symmetrical. Sorry, Ellie's been called to a staff meeting at Blue Skies, I guess to get an update on what we're about to discuss,' Rod replied, an archetypal local builder, except he was no longer, having retired a few years back when his wife died, moving into this apartment and hanging up his spirit level. Volunteering to return to the fray when his bother Jonny was killed in the blast at Blue Skies House where he oversaw the rebuilding, admitting that he thoroughly enjoyed being back at the coalface. This was also when his relationship with Ellie Richmond, Director of Nursing, Matron to most at Blue Skies House blossomed, a partnership that had not only flourished but was about to bear fruit, a sprog imminent. 'So, Andy's done a bunk has he. What a twat.'

'Quite, heard nothing then?'

'Don't think he'd come running to me. Never his favourite Uncle. No particular reason. Just that I didn't spoil him. He never liked getting his hands dirty when he came on site. Thought he may turn out to be a fucking queer at one point. Another character assignation that I fucked up. Oops, sorry dear.'

'No worries, the dear is probably more insulting,' Mantel replied engaged by the straight-talking Rodney, a lean 58 year old, having avoided the beer and butty belly that plagued so many fellow builders.

'Sorry again, a little patronising. I'm old school love, sorry, Sergeant. Ellie's not keen on my language either, especially at home. Not sure where I picked it up? Building sites are such tame places,' Rod said with a mischievous look as he sipped his tea. 'So, no sighting then and as I say he's not holed up in the en-suite.'

'Didn't expect him to be,' Griffin replied passing his card. 'Look anything or anybody you can think of please call. To be honest we've very little to go on.'

'Don't worry Mike I will, I can just knock on your door.'

*

'Don't know either of them well, in fact hardly at all,' Mantel said in the car park beneath the apartments. 'But it is a real feel good story to come out of the Blue Skies mess, probably the only one. That's unless you're the one who got away with the gold that is.'

Griffin gave his DS a sideways glance. 'Please don't remind me about the gold and those who have benefited. But yes, even I can see the good side of it. And old Rod, word had it that he thought he was a Jaffa. Fingers crossed for the baby. Right, back to base to see what Nimra has got for us. Young Nash in custody? Or is that hoping for a little too much?'

*

'Right, you fucking idiot, how stupid are you?' Rod yelled. 'I told you to never come here. And that's fucking why. How would I explain it. I'd fucking forgotten they were coming round. You're just lucky that they didn't have a snoop around when my back was turned or ask to go to the bleeding loo. Jesus I was shitting myself, thought I'd have a fucking heart attack. I just hope you've filled your cacks. Right, you need to get out and fucking fast. You cannot be here when Ellie gets back, that's for fucking sure.'

*

Veronica gently smashed, if you can do that, a basket of poppadum's. 'So, what are you having Mr Griffin? Something spicy, or are you saving that for later?'

Griffin delved into the poppadum pieces. 'My, we are frisky tonight.'

'Long day with an audit. Or should I say, another fucking audit. Sorry, pardon my French,' Veronica replied, hand to mouth having scooped up some onion salad. The savvy landlady of The Cobblers public house was relishing quality time with the often elusive DI. Leaving her assistant to handle the chucking out and locking up.

'Counting their pennies? My grandmother always said look after the pounds and the pennies would sort themselves out. Or something like that.'

'The other way round I think, and I don't know that Freddie and Glenn know what pennies are,' Veronica replied referring to her bosses, the owners of The Cobblers and three other public houses, self-made City of London multis. Their finances currently a little stretched by the proposed redevelopment of the pub and an unforeseen spending binge by their previous builder. An undetected drug addict who spiralled out of control and managed to spend near on three hundred grand in the blink of an eye, in the process murdering a journalist posing as a builder who had rubbed him up the wrong way. Now on remand, unlikely to see another hod for many years. Freddie and Glenn both agreed that you couldn't make it up, unless you looked at their bank balance.

'Any sign of the development restarting?'

'All systems should be go. I think they found another few bob down the back of the sofa. But there's been a huge problem in finding a builder.'

'Sign of the times. Especially if you've had your fingers burnt as they have. Ultra-cautious I would suggest. I know I would be, especially with their money, although there's no chance of that on a DI's salary. Suitable kosher builders will have full order books. It's not a small job.'

'At least with the building on hold many of the old regulars have returned and you mentioned kosher, the old Jewish piano is pretty busy.'

'None of your punters up for the job?'

'Ha-ha. It already looks like a wild west saloon, what with all the cowboys who drink in there. A boutique hotel with a few death traps thrown in, not quite the USP they were looking for. So, come on what are you having and any news on Nash?' Veronica asked glancing at the menu as Bollywood muzak wafted over them. 'Dansak, bhindi, Pilau rice and a plain naan for me.'

'Jalfrezi and Bombay's for me. Share your rice and naan?'

'Fine by me, I asked around the bar and there was zilch as far as Andy Nash was concerned. Although there were some mutterings that he would be very stupid to show his face round here.'

Griffin put the menu down and returned to the poppadum's. 'Someone must know. Could well have done a bunk out of the country. The ports weren't on alert, in fact I'm not sure they are now. Shit, I hope someone's sorted that. Upstairs don't appear too bothered and with the way things are they probably won't think it's a problem until he commits a statistic and a box requires ticking. Find him, send him back job done. Modern policing eh. For me it feels personal.'

'I can't believe that, surely it's a worry…Oh, here's Sam,' Veronica responded as the jovial, squat, Head Waiter approached.

'Good evening to my favourite couple. Always so good to see you both. Our favourite ten o'clock regulars who aren't pissed,' Sam said smiling. Like many he had a soft spot for Veronica, an attractive thirty-something brunette, who maintained her trim five feet and a few inches figure with the vigour's of running a pub, man-handling the barrels and crates of wine, along with sex as frequently as circumstances allowed, which after a concerning lull had picked up with her relationship with the Inspector. 'Now what will it be?' Sam continued. 'No, wait, don't tell me. Chicken Dansak, Chicken Jalfrezi and the usual sides. And a top up of drinks?'

Sam was the top man, with a memory that should see him on Mastermind, although a specialist subject of, 'the culinary choices of the customers at Chutney Ali's', may be a little narrow. A cousin of the owners, Sam ran the show, never appearing to take any time off from what was regarded as the exclusive Indian in the locality. Frequented by the area's high and mighty in all walks of life, plus a few of the local lowlifes. 'Yes please and you always do that, we must be so boring,' Griffin said handing over his menu. 'Don't know why I bother with this.' Sam took the menus without replying, smiled knowingly and headed for the pan crashing, shouty kitchen behind the kick-marked swinging door.

'Oh, before I forget, you have got the quiz in your diary?' Veronica asked. 'It's just that Julian from the Hospice is getting really excited, so I really want a good turnout and a decent donation. Your team sorted?'

'Yep, all in hand,' Griffin replied making a mental note to sort it out.

'So, back to Andy Nash,' Veronica said scooping a small amount of lime pickle.

'Look, it was a very local issue and history says that many return to the scenes of their crimes.'

'He wouldn't dare. Would he? I know of many who would be digging out a couple of old bricks to do the deed.'

'That's exactly what Lucy said,' Griffin replied sitting back and sipping his ice cold Cobra lager. 'I think you should have a word with the guys. I know there are plenty of lumps in the pub who will look after you. But that's only if they're in. You have quiet times and I'm sure that Nash is aware of that.'

'You suggesting a bouncer at The Cobblers?'

'Not exactly. But as Mr Patel said to me earlier some discreet security. Remember this guy's a nutter. And that's official.'

'Putting it like that perhaps I will have a word with the Freddie and Glenn. I'll give them a call with your thoughts.'

CHAPTER TWO

'So, Lil, as I was saying before I was so rudely interrupted by that creep Les Chandler,' Veronica said returning to her mug of tea on a table in the empty Cobblers public house having just taken a landline call from a crisp rep. 'Listen to this, he was offering an unbeatable deal on their new line, 'Crushed Avocado on Toast', I mean what the fuck, I've told him that unless it's Ready Salted, Cheese 'n' Onion or Salt and Vinegar, it won't float in here. He's so fucking infuriating, he just doesn't listen.'

'Letchy Les, as fresh as his crisps,' Lily quipped, a late twenties attractive blond, Veronica's assistant sipping her tea. Lily was her own woman, whilst not discouraging those who saw her as Veronica's protégé, a boss she had much respect for. 'He makes me creep.'

'Married with three, I hear.'

'A dib dobbie in my book.'

'Quite. Look I've had a chat with the guys about the Andy Nash situation.'

'I've got my bricks ready for him,' Lily responded viciously slapping her hands together. 'And they'll be a long queue behind me wanting to dish out some of the same. Although there won't be any left after I've finished with him.'

Veronica smiled at Lily's forthrightness, one of the reasons for giving her the job, running The Cobblers was not something for a shrinking violet. 'Quite, well they agreed with Mike's advice that we should have some discreet muscle about the place.'

'Do I get to interview them?' Lily asked with a cheeky smile.

'Easy Tiger. No I've done it via a specialist agency on the internet that Glenn gave me. The first one should be arriving at any time and we don't want them to melt in. Tell everyone who they are. They are meant to be a deterrent, especially when we're quiet,' Veronica said glancing up at the pub's large clock; ten twenty-nine, a minute ahead of the unofficial opening time, eleven the official one.

Lily went behind the bar and looked in the ornate mirror behind the spirit bottles, running her fingers through her shoulder length hair. 'Better prepare myself then, don't want to disappoint.'

'And I deliberately went for a looker to not blend in with the locals.'

'Oooh, you're such a bitch Ron. Look out, stand by your beds so to speak,' Lily said as the main door rattled.

'Please don't faint on me,' Veronica replied with the door opening.

'What, Reuben?' He'd struggle to open a packet of Les's crisps.'

'Morning Rueben. Usual?' Veronica asked, discreetly mouthing 'fuck off' in Lily's direction.

'Morning ladies, yes please,' Reuben responded, a non-descript chap in slacks and sweater, settling onto a stool as the door opened again. Two young guys in dark blue sweatshirts with distinctive Telecom logos bowled in.

'Two lagers please darling.'

'Certainly,' Lily replied. Although 'darling' was pretty standard when ordering a pint in The Cobblers, it did stop Lily and her fellow barmaids loathing it. Despite this Lily could not help but admire the eye candy ahead of her.

The rickety side door opened and a burly unshaven chap in a weathered brown leather jacket, who could be just out of casting, hustled in and glanced round the bar. 'Can I help you?' Veronica enquired, guessing that this may be the extra security.

'Veronica?' replied a surprisingly quiet voice.

'That's me, you must be Ian?'

'No Greg,' he said brandishing an ID card. 'I switched with Ian. Didn't they phone?'

'No, but it doesn't matter. Here let's take a seat. Nice to meet you by the way.'

'Likewise Veronica.'

'Ron or Ronni please.'

'Recruiting a barman?' Reuben asked, as nosy as ever, sipping his lager. 'Won't go down well in here.'

'Not quite Reuben,' Lily replied adjusting items on the bar, admiring her new colleague, the Telecom guys having moved away to a table. 'Look I've been told to spread this around. He's here to keep an eye out in case Andy Nash makes an appearance.

'Oh yeh. Word is that he's out and could be heading this way.'

'Really.'

*

Griffin handed out a hot soya milk and a flat white to his detectives, then placed his strong black on the vacant desk beside him.

'Nice surprise boss. Thank you. Your birthday or are we getting the sack?' Mantel asked sipping her soya through the little hole in the lid.

'I'm just a nice guy Luce.' The banter between her DI and DS prompting Nimra to smile.

Mantel held up an empty page in her notepad. 'So boss, Andy Nash, here's the reported sightings, he's vanished.'

'He can't just vanish, he's not Paul Daniels,' Griffin said with the main office bustling around them. 'He simply can't just vanish. Come on, I need some help, I'm getting flak.'

'Paul Daniels did.'

'Sorry?'

'He vanished. He died.'

'Sorry, did he? Look he's out there somewhere, Nash not Paul Daniels. I just had a call from Ronni saying that word on the street is that he's heading back home.'

'The source?' Nimra asked.

'One of the regulars.'

'Sound then?'

'Very perceptive Nim,' Griffin replied. 'But it's all we've got. Not only do we not know where he is, we don't know why he escaped. Need to chat with his handlers at the oh, so fucking secure unit and see if he mentioned anything or anyone. You two take a trip out there first thing. See if you can glean anything more than they've told the local guys. I'll take whatever you can get.'

*

'So, is this your way of making a confession James?' the Right Reverend Mandy Jarvis asked, her cassock pulled up round her waist, bent over the tomb of Lord Hall, gripping its ornate brass fittings deep in the cool crypt of St Vincent's. The door locked from the inside.

'Never bothered with that crap Mandy, what have I to confess to,' replied the well-spoken, partially out of uniform, Superintendent James Hawes, enjoying an unscheduled late afternoon rendezvous with his theology tutor.

'I know this is not your patch, but have you heard anything about this Andy Nash?' the vicar asked. 'Just that a lot of people are very concerned.'

'Only that we are all keeping an eye out for him,' replied the happily married father of two. 'Sounds like an unscrupulous sort to me.'

*

'Time gentlemen please,' Veronica announced looking towards three stragglers at one end of the bar. 'And that means you lot.'

Begrudgingly the remnants of pints bought just as the bell sounded were downed. 'Night Ron,' said the three Richards brothers.

'Night guys,' Veronica replied straightening her red silk blouse and turning towards Griffin at the other end of the bar sat on 'Geoff's Stool'. 'They never just sup up and go like normal people, always require a little encouragement.'

'Never caused any real trouble, have they?' Griffin asked, who always made a point of sitting on this stool when free, on which the regulars had a brass plaque made and fixed it to its back:

Geoff woz here

So woz his bag

This referred to Geoff Rous and his steady stream of popular hooky goods deriving from London's West End that were always available from his popular Poundland laundry bag that sat obediently at his feet.

'They're on the cusp I reckon those Richards boys. Odd little wrist slap, as with most of them. Give the place a tinder box feel. Not saying that's not pretty much standard round here. Another?'

'Go on then just the one, actually a half, thanks, early start again tomorrow,' Griffin said glancing at his watch. 'The Richards are on our radar. You joining me?'

'Yeh, why not, just a small one as it seems that I will be alone again tonight. I take it they have history with you lot?' Veronica asked as she poured the beer and a real G 'n' T for herself; not one from the landlady's H2O 'gin' bottle.

'Sorry but some of us have work to do tomorrow,' Griffin continued as Veronica settled onto a barstool and brushed non-existent specs from her tailored blue 'capri' trousers. They've had plenty of cautions, pretty minor stuff, with some time inside and that's all the family. Moved around the country over the years. Usually get an intake of breadth whenever we ask anything about the Richards family.'

'How long have they been around here now?'

'A few months. If you remember they arrived under the radar in that period after the gold debacle. Strange move from the Nottingham area. Some social services bollocks was mooted, the usual cop-out. Probably goes deeper if their files are anything to go by. Get the re-development back on track and that will push them away from here,' Griffin said

27

looking round the once quaint country pub now in much need of some tlc. Rustic in age, not trendy, a honeypot for many who have had the constabulary's attention. The pub's rural selling point was that it butted onto the glorious Epping Forest, making it a walker's haven. It's refurbishment into a boutique dining room with rooms had been approved and partially started to the rear until funds had dried up. With that now resolved, the search was on for a reliable builder to get it back on track.

'At the moment we are just keeping a quiet eye on the whole Richards family,' Griffin continued looking towards the now closed door. 'They've sold some gear and there's a little bit of drugs. Not enough to warrant pulling them in when there could be something bigger in the future. Although the last time I used that strategy I seem to remember I ended up with a crate full of eggs on my face.'

'I don't particularly warm to them, although they're generally polite, but not charming like most of the wrong-uns round here and their banter is pretty boring, again not like the rest of them. Some of the guys in here can have me cracking up, they really should be on the stage, perhaps we should get them an audition with that Britain's Got Talent show. Not the Richards family, they're just not in sync with this area's brand of humour. Don't seem to get on with many of the others. No reason to ban them, they spend and certainly no drugs, at least in here. As you know they'd be out if I caught them,' Veronica said in the forthright voice that Griffin and the regulars knew only too well. 'Live on the Harding, don't they?'

'Yep, they were given a five-bedroom jobby, previously an Officer's house,' Griffin replied tapping a bar mat recalling the scenario. The Hardy Estate was an old RAF base, closed and redeployed as social housing in the seventies, named after a local World War II spitfire pilot. In Griffin's view, 'homes for heroes' turned into 'homes with hassle', a reputation that had not subsided with time. The initial cash payment to turn it into a housing estate and the subsequent hand-outs for accepting the country's waif and strays too enticing for councils to turn down over the years. The Richards supposedly received preferential housing because of their younger sister and her two pre-school children, that the grandparents said that they cared for when their daughter was out at work. All a touch of

Hans Christian in Griffin's book, but the authorities bought the story. 'It doesn't seem right when so many with legit needs, kids and all that, are desperate for somewhere to live.'

Out in the car park Roger, David and Larry Richards, otherwise known as Roj, Davy and Larry, jumped into their aging red Corsa. There was little between them in age and brains, remaining dependent on mum and dad. They fired up the motor to head back along the tree lined roads to the Hardy Estate, a semi-rural setting, very different from the urban grime they had previously inhabited. Griffin smiled as he heard the Corsa shift gravel speeding out of the carpark. 'Amazingly none of them are banned from driving or they certainly wouldn't be getting into that.'

'Don't suppose that's insured though and why are you suddenly looking so smug? Shouldn't you have at least questioned them before they drove off?'

'Policing ain't that straight forward Ron. My view, as you know, is that there are the goodies and there's the baddies and why should the goodies suffer for the baddies. Anyway I'm off duty. I stop them out there and they haven't got insurance, then I'll have all the paperwork to do and the other shit that comes with it. Them, well, they'd get a warning, maybe a fine that they don't pay and told to not be naughty boys, then they'll call a cab and go home. While I'm down the station for a few hours. This way it's all in a day's work and they get the hassle and all it took from me was a call when I arrived, that I followed-up just now.'

'Sorry, I don't understand you've lost me, they've driven off in a potentially dodgy car.'

'Ah, that is the calculated risk. But those are the decisions we're paid to make. Obviously, I hope that they don't get into an accident and I doubt they will. It's less than a mile up the road.'

'It's a bit further than that and there's Epping town between here and the Hardy that they'll go through.'

'They won't get any further than the Dukes Arms, trust me,' Griffin said referring to the roundabout in the forest a mile away, that used to have the Dukes Arms pub on the junction, now semi-derelict awaiting a saviour.

'Sorry, still lost.'

'Uniform will be waiting to greet them. Then I'm not sure how they are going to get home from there, generally not a great signal at the Duke's, and fingers crossed there isn't one tonight, so calling a cab could be tricky?'

'That's just sneaky. They won't be happy with you.'

'Don't think they know me. Anyway, it's a routine check, others will be being pulled in. Just that they're keeping an eye out for a red Corsa with three oiks on board, so they don't do a bunk. What it all means is that uniform, the goodies, will be happy to have something meaningful to do and the Richards boys, the baddies, get all the shit. Simples,' Griffin said finishing his drink. 'Right, sorry again, seven o'clock in the station.'

'I get it all now,' Veronica said sliding off the stool to collect the three empty pint glasses at the far and of the bar. 'Seven o'clock, well it's probably best you do go to your own bed. Oh, and Greg the security guy from the agency started today, he went just before you walked in probably passed him in the carpark, said he could go when I knew you were coming. Really nice guy, I think Lil's will be having a sniff, although I reckon my brother may have more of a chance.'

CHAPTER THREE

Finally settled in Jenny Roberts office waiting for the Chief Psychiatric Nurse, Mantel and Nimra laughed and reflected on the draconian security measures that had taken up to nearly an hour. Considering whether these were the norm or hastily implemented after Andy Nash checked out? Ahead of them a tray with four fine white with a discreet gold inlay pattern bone china cups and saucers, milk and sugar, with matching tea pot, disappointing for both, no biscuits. Neither of them had visited a psychiatric establishment such as this before and were relieved that the screams they had been goaded to believed would fill the corridors had not materialized.

Softish furnishings, bright non-offensive paintings gave the office a feely touchy ambiance. In addition to where they sat there was a round table with six desk style chairs, no actual desk which took up most of the remaining floor space. Around the walls many closed and supposedly locked cabinets. All neat, tidy and uniformed, obviously designed to be non-threatening.

'I'm just pleased that I wasn't trying to smuggle in any drugs up the old jasksie,' Mantel said. 'Although Anton the blond guy doing the check was more than welcome.'

'Lucy please. Although it does make you thankful for disposable gloves,' Nimra said leaning forward. 'Tea darling?'

'Absolutely.'

'Shit,' Nimra exclaimed spilling some tea onto the tray. 'Don't know about you, but there's something strange about this place.'

'Something strange, was that some kind of joke? Thank you darling,' Mantel said lifting her tea with her pinkie outstretched. 'I tell you what, if this level of security was in place when Nash done his flip, then he definitely tunnelled out.'

'Does make you wonder,' Nimra said spotting two casually dressed, late thirtyish looking individuals, one male, one female approaching through the glass windows. 'I think this may be them.'

'Remember, it's Andy Nash and who he might have had contact with, not where he hid the earth from the tunnel that we're here for,' Mantel said smiling as the door opened.

The detectives stood, greetings exchanged, and more tea poured. Pleasantries continued, largely about the journey, although Jenny's assistant remained silent. The spillage went unmentioned.

'So,' Mantel said, having had enough of the niceties, wishing to bring some order to proceedings. 'We are here about find out more about Andy Nash and not details of his actual escape.'

'Technically I suppose you could call it that,' Jenny Roberts replied, an attractive lady in smart casual attire, probably, with closer examination in her early forties. Although, ten years either way could also be on the mark. Jenny was the big cheese at the Rotherfield Secure Psychiatric Unit. A facility based on the edge of a modern housing estate, a suburb of Rotherfield, a once small village. The thousands of new builds meant that its village green and church, dating back to Norman times, were engulfed. The independent shops closed, the out of town hyper-market thriving. The plus for visitors was that this gated compound had plenty of parking. For the inmates none of the soothing surrounds of the long gone Victorian institutions. An exercise yard the size of two netball courts and a neat small garden with benches replaced acres of rolling tranquil grounds. Jenny, first names being important, was renowned in the field of psychiatric care, having had many clinical papers published. Her reputation as a manager though, according to the information they could glean, could be summed up in one word: Flaky.

'Whatever it may be termed as, an escape or absconding, Andy Nash is at large. It is our job to find him and bring him in before he commits any further crimes. What we would like from you is any information that will make our task easier.'

'You do know that patient confidentiality is of paramount importance,' interjected the previously quiet, serious looking Iain Swift, Assistant Chief Psychiatric Nurse. Early thirties, with a shabby chic casual look, known to be an arsehole by anyone in the police force who had dealings with him. A paid-up leftie who lived by the rule book when it suited.

Mantel, briefed for this, smiled through gritted teeth. 'This patient is technically not your patient now, as you allowed him to get out. Andy Nash is, in our eyes, simply a criminal at large. And further to that, a potentially very dangerous one at that. A person who has raped at the very least ten ladies, not noted for asking them politely. So, we would appreciate your full co-operation before he commits another rape whilst on day release from here. So if you have a problem with any of that Mr Swift please air it now.'

Nimra resisted getting to her feet and applauding.

'Yes, of course sergeant,' Jenny said looking towards her number two. A person that she had little time for, having had virtually no say in his appointment nearly a year previous. 'Of course, Iain and I will be only too pleased to fully co-operate with you.'

Swift said nothing further, simply glared at Mantel and crossed his legs looking as if he was having a personal hissy-fit. He had worked the system since qualifying as a Psychiatric Nurse, climbing the greasy pole with consummate political correctness ease. He came to Rotherfield with a reputation of never being around, enrolling for every off-site course he could justify, which amounted to more days away than on site. Ticking boxes to slide through the pay grades.

'Thank you, that will be appreciated,' Mantel said with a quick glance at Swift before refocussing on Jenny, pleased to have regained the upper ground. 'The names of everyone he had contact with will be required. Whether staff, inmates, visitors, ancillary staff, anyone. Did he have contact with anyone else? A telephone, computer, social media, skype, zoom, anything. We need to build some sort of profile of his time in here to help us find him. Just to let you know, at present we have no sightings.'

'Okay,' Jenny replied scribbling on a notepad. 'You'll have to give us a little time'

'Sure, but hours, not days would be appreciated. We'll call later. I don't need to reiterate how serious this is.'

Jenny knew only too well how serious this case was, her superiors had been on her back ever since Nash's disappearance was discovered.

Occurring on a shift when Iain Swift held the keys. Many questions remained unanswered internally, and the heat was on her. A non-confrontational sort, Jenny was at the end of her tether covering her colleague's shoddy work practices. Perhaps this was the time to remove the burden and to allow him to explain his actions for himself. Something that to date he appeared expert in side-stepping. She would be in line for a severe bollocking as the person in ultimate charge, disciplinary action a distinct possibility. What the fuck though, she was reaching the end of the road when it came to Swift. She should have acted sooner but put it down to him being new to their procedures. Never questioning that her own ability to manage may be the root of the problem. Time passed and his questionable work ethics were allowed to develop. She had absolutely no allegiance to Swift and if push came to shove, reluctantly, she could seek refuge in the private sector. 'What I will say,' Jenny replied visibly taking a deep breath. 'Is that Andy Nash was Iain's case and he had developed a personal interest.' With this Swift looked towards his boss. Not endearingly, a look of concern swept across him. 'I have had a lot on my plate, so it has been Iain who has largely monitored Andy's care. Yes, I am in overall charge but this has been Iain's case,' Jenny continued, not wishing to be seen to be passing the buck, which she knew she was. 'I think that Iain will be the best point of liaison on this and that he will be able to answer all of your questions and provide all the help that you need. Won't you Iain?'

'Well, yes. Yes. Of course,' Swift replied none-too-convincingly, uncrossing his legs and leaning forward, glancing at Jenny and looking particularly ill at ease with her unexpected and out of character shift in responsibility.

'Excellent,' Mantel replied inwardly thinking 'shit' as she had wanted to deal with Jenny, believing that Swift may present hurdles. Perhaps he would come good on this one? She had her reservations though, aware of how the Assistant Chief Psychiatric Nurse had shifted in his seat when told that he would be the focal point. They needed information though, and quickly, Nash was out there, somewhere, so they had to hope that Swift would deliver. Deciding that there was no point dwelling here any longer, listening to what were obvious internal issues Mantel closed the meeting. She couldn't wait to hear Nimra's observations of Swift. 'Okay we'll be off, we'll call later this afternoon.'…

…'Totally fucking agree,' Nimra responded animatedly in the car park. 'Shifty as hell. I'm looking forward to delving into the background of our shitty Iain Swift.'

*

'Thanks for that,' Swift said pouring hot water onto his 'Artisan Herbal' tea bag in his 'Live Life' mug in the unit's functional kitchen, forcibly returning the kettle to its housing.

'What's that Iain?' Jenny replied pouring herself a glass of tap water, eager to maintain the stance she had adopted with the police officers.

'Dropping me in it. Especially when you know the workload I've got.'

'I certainly do and that you have more courses booked,' Jenny responded her glass to her lips, turning to face her subordinate. 'Which will mean that all this work, that you have so willingly taken on, will, as always, be shifted onto someone else's lap. Probably mine.'

'Who upset you this morning?'

'Nobody Iain, it's just that I've decided that I've enough to do without having to nanny you. As far as Andy Nash is concerned you were here. You must know what happened. I mean you two had become quite buddies. I just think that the answers they require will be better coming from you.'

Swift didn't reply, squeezing his tea bag into his mug before throwing it in the swing top bin. Departing without even a glance in his boss's direction.

CHAPTER FOUR

'I have news,' Griffin exclaimed, gesticulating towards Mantel and Nimra from his office door.

'What's that sir?' Nimra asked acknowledging his appearance.

'You beauty,' Mantel exclaimed closing her call and turning from her desk. 'Sorry, what was that boss?'

'We've had a possible sighting of Nash.'

'Excellent, some progress,' Nimra said. 'Where?'

'The forest.'

Mantel looked sceptically at her DI. 'I hope it's not what I suspect.'

Griffin crossed his arms, Nimra giving Mantel a quizzical look. 'Knowing you as well as I do, I would suspect that you are spot on. So go on, let's see if you are.'

'Well if I'm right I suppose the forest is better than Waitrose.'

'Correct, although there would have been cameras and maybe a security guard.'

'And young children and grannies.'

'What?' Nimra asked frustrated to be missing the point. 'You two speak with forked tongues.'

'He's been flashing, exposing one's self,' Mantel responded flapping her arms, giving a demonstration without having seen one in the flesh, so to speak.

'Oh, I see,' Nimra replied, the penny dropping. 'Now I understand the Waitrose bit.'

'Dark Donkey Jacket, blue or black and a beanie. The witness is pretty convinced that it is Nash having known of him from old. She had followed the story and heard that he'd got out. Said her dog went wild.'

'Obviously likes a bit of sausage,' Mantel quipped. 'So, is she definite, definite, it's Nash?'

'Well, not definite, definite, as you say. Don't think she had a long look at his face before the dog chased him off.'

Nimra looked from Mantel to her DI. 'If it is a positive sighting then that confirms that he is back in the area.'

'And the negative is that it confirms that he is back in the area,' Griffin said. 'I'd hoped he'd be spotted in Thailand rather than the forest.'

'Is she giving a statement?' Nimra asked.

'No need for a photo fit,' Mantel smiled, Griffin raising an eyebrow. 'Was it far into the woods?'

'No, just a matter of a few hundred yards behind the Cobblers, pleased I got Ronni to hire those guys. Bit close to home. We need to step up. As I've said he really concerns me,' Griffin said. 'So, what was your call about Luce, it sounded positive?'

'A delightful guy called Angelo Romero. Sexy Med accent, Spanish if I was pressed.'

'Oh yes, if pressed eh?' Nimra said with a knowing look. 'Shame that we didn't meet him this morning.'

'Yes, he was apologetic, had a dentist appointment.'

Griffin leant against the door frame.' And, sorry who is this dashing matador?'

'The PA to Jenny Roberts at Rotherfield.'

'Who you saw this morning and you were going to get round to filling me in on.'

'Yes, sorry, of course boss,' Mantel said consulting her notebook. 'Well, Romero was calling off the record.'

'For fucks sake Luce, cut to the chase.'

'Sorry, well it appears that Romero is no friend of our Iain Swift.'

'Iain Swift?' Griffin enquired, starting to simmer with his sergeant.

'Assistant Psychiatric Nurse who Nimra thinks is a bit of a bullshitter,' Mantel said before noticing the look that Nimra gave her. 'Okay we both did, and an arse-hole to boot. Well it appears that our Mr Swift is partial to a bit of porn on his PC.'

'That's not exactly hold the fucking front page Luce. Shock, horror, office worker views porn on his PC,' Griffin exclaimed hands now on head. 'I just hope that there is an addendum to this and that I am going to like it.'

'Romero has clocked Swift sharing this, the pornography, with Nash on more than one occasion.'

'Not exactly what you'd read in the psychiatric care coaching manual for sex addicts, is it?' Griffin suggested. 'Which of you two is digging out this Iain Swift?'

'Me,' Nimra replied. 'Give me just a little bit longer and I reckon a whole load will come flooding in. Those I've been able to speak to have not been very complimentary.'

'Well, sooner rather than later would be appreciated. I reckon we need to pull him in and ask our Mr Swift a few questions about his viewing habits,' Griffin said making to return to his office. 'Although what bearing it has on Nash's whereabouts I'm not sure.'

'I agree, but let's see what Nimra gets,' Mantel replied following her boss into his office. 'And I'm due to call him anytime soon, in fact, I'll call him now. He should have feedback and answers following our meeting. It'll be interesting to see what he has for us.'

CHAPTER FIVE

Griffin ambled towards the bar in The Anchor, a delightful, thatched country pub in the heart of the Hertfordshire countryside, having passed through an extensive redundant beer garden and industrial bar-b-q, with views over polytunnels, spawned over the past few decades in previously decaying fields. Rammed with petunias, marigolds and other highly coloured all year round annuals. Inside the Inn, low beams, flagstones and brass trinkets; a cleaner's bugbear. Not a one-armed bandit in sight. Griffin suspected the ladies and gents had smelly toiletries, scrubbed tiled walls and disposable hand towels. A perfect environment for middle England to snort away undetected. He glanced at his watch, pleased to not be too late, looking around for a lady of the description she had given; 'blond, 5'3", wearing a blue blouse, probably drinking a G'n'T', modestly no mention of weight nor looks. As nobody immediately jumped out, he ordered himself a pint of local cask bitter then turned back towards the oak tables. In a quiet corner, a lady smiled in his direction. Either his luck was in or this attractive blond was Jenny Roberts. Seven pm midweek out in the sticks Griffin went with the latter and took the considered gamble to smile back. With no negative response in return Griffin made an approach. The lady stood and held out her hand. 'Detective Inspector Griffin?'

'Correct,' Griffin replied. 'Jenny Roberts?'

'Also correct,' Jenny said resuming her seat and not taking her eyes off Griffin as he noisily scraped out a chair. 'Thanks for coming at such short notice.'

'No problem. This is very current, so any information is more than welcome. Just not quite sure why the cloak and dagger stuff when you saw my officers earlier?' Griffin asked with curiosity, before taking an elongated sip of his ale.

'I'm sorry Inspector, but I would like this to be off the record. I hope that's not a problem?' Jenny replied taking a nervous sip. She had reflected on the day's events whilst waiting for Griffin's arrival, and her newfound desire to stand up for herself. Googling DS Mantel's superior, from experience a Detective Inspector was a good level to deal with, they were the doers in a police force. Not shackled with the bureaucracy that comes with extra braiding, generally able to act on their own instincts.

'No problem at this stage. And you don't mind if I call you Jenny, and it's Mike? Now, what did you want to tell me?' Griffin replied adopting a friendly, welcoming persona whilst getting to the point. When the personal call came through requesting this meeting Griffin had reacted enthusiastically. He had an inkling that Jenny Roberts had something of significance to say. Meaning, frustratingly having to once again call off assisting with the rugby coaching at Burlingham, the local independent school, so often taking a backseat to the demands of being a police officer.

'As you are aware Andy Nash is a patient of mine. However, as your colleagues have probably told you his case was largely handled by my colleague and assistant, Iain Swift,' Jenny said twisting her twizzler around a slice of lemon. Today felt like she was negotiating stepping-stones away from her comfort zone through potentially deep waters. Each step as uncertain as the previous one.

'Yes, they fully briefed me on your meeting,' Griffin replied having finally received a rushed update of this morning's meeting from Mantel and Nimra before he left the station. Ironically interrupted when Mantel got her call returned by Swift, leaving Nimra to complete the briefing out into the car park.

'Well as you can imagine, ours is a very sensitive area. Our patients may be convicted criminals, but they still have rights to patient confidentiality. What is reported, written down or not, hearsay, or simply logged in here,' Jenny said pointing to the side of her head and taking a drink. 'If not initially recorded, it will still be stored for future use, the building of a profile on or off the record is so important. Always a contentious issue, both with us practitioners and those in the corridors of power. I'm sure that you have to balance similar dilemmas.'

Griffin nodded and smiled, he couldn't agree more, to reveal or not to reveal was a frequent question, choosing to remain quiet to let Jenny pour out what she had to say under her own steam.

'So, Nash and Iain developed a strong relationship over a very short period of time. Positive in many ways. But. And this is where it may become a little more sensitive, I've always let Iain have a free rein, I have enough to deal with. We have a couple of patients who have, at least on paper, worse profiles than Nash. Far worse, if you were to go by the rule book,' Jenny paused, almost visibly taking an intake of breath, finishing her drink.

Griffin sensed a few moments to take stock may be of benefit. 'Another?'

'Please. Just a tonic though. Driving.'

Griffin returned and placed the hi-ball in front of Jenny, noting that she appeared to have not moved a muscle whilst he was away, staring across the bar. 'Here you go. Now, where were we?'

'Thank you. Yes, right. So, I have obviously kept a professional eye on everything. As I do with all cases. Well, in the past week, possibly longer, Nash's reading habits have changed rather dramatically. From largely football related to asking Iain for bios of notorious criminals. A request that Iain has fulfilled.'

'When you say notorious criminals…'

'Murderers,' Jenny replied looking Griffin in the eye. 'As I said, he's not the worst we have or have had, nor that I've had to deal with, but he's always made me slightly uneasy, which is unusual for me. Whereas with most you discover that their actions to draw of a line in the sand, with Andy Nash I never got that feeling. His remonstrations of innocence, when so plainly guilty, I felt indicated unfinished business. Now, I may be very, very wrong, but with him no longer having the protection of the unit, it is a worry.'

Griffin looked at Jenny Roberts and saw a concerned woman. A professional, laboured by her profession's expectations and personal complexities, trying to exorcise previously harboured thoughts. Nash's absconding and his change in reading habits prior to this had given her this impetus. Griffin knew from personal experience that sometimes events can take you on a tangent that is difficult to recover from. Griffin decided to not disclose the off the record chat he had with Nash's

Barrister in the aftermath of the trial, where he also expressed the same worrying concerns that Nash had unfinished business that he refused to let go. Of some surprise to Griffin was that Jenny made no mention of pornography, and if honest this revelation did not warrant a meeting, especially nearly an hour's drive away, there were underlying issues at the Rotherfield Psychiatric Unit. There was something very shallow about Jenny Roberts that didn't particularly endear her to him.

*

'Look Sis, do you really think that you should be out there wandering about the forest?'

'The area's been swarming with police. Don't think that he'd be that foolish,' Veronica replied talking into her phone, kicking loose twigs with her flowery Converse pumps as she meandered through a clearing in the forest beside her pub, with the light starting to fade she had donned a gilet to fend off the chilly evening air.

'Yeh, but from what I've read he's a complete nutter,' Stephen replied at the other end of the line from his Hertfordshire home.

'Look, little, oh so caring bruv. In one pocket I've pepper spray for his boat, in the other Ralgex for his bollocks. So as the scouts say, I'm prepared. And before he's able to get away my screams would alert the guys smoking outside the pub who would be here in seconds.'

'Still sounds dangerous.'

'Have no fear, although I do sense from Mike that this is moving up their agenda, especially the longer he's at large. If it was him flashing his bits he has lifted the bar. That's if it was him which I doubt. He'd be foolish exposing them in my book, I'd keep them well hidden, there's more than a few round here who have nasty plans for them. Look, Mike should be in later; I'll get an update.'

'Okay but stay safe. I like the extra security bit. Tell me, how are the owners at the moment?' Stephen asked changing tact. 'Redevelopment back on? Last time you mentioned Glenn you said that he had perked up a bit and that he may have filled his extra-marital void.'

'Well funny you should say that,' Veronica said starting to head back. 'My trusted spy has news on that front.'

'Oh yes, tell me more, would this be the lovely Lily?' Stephen asked, referring to his sister's assistant, a lady who, if he wasn't otherwise inclined he would certainly have been interested in.

'Correct. Well, she was in The Foresters Arms to meet up with her Inspector Bazzer and Annie, the oh so discreet Landlady, just happened to let it slip that one of our owners had been in the night before and had taken the best room. Lil didn't let it rest there and probed further, knowing that Lucy Mantel was no longer on his agenda. And she came up trumps.'

'So, was it Glenn?'

'Yes, our own Mr Friar.'

'So, not alone?'

'Nope.'

'Who then?'

'Who, times two.'

'You're kidding.'

'Both known locally.'

'You're fucking kidding.'

'Yep. Look I need to go,' Veronica replied with the pub in sight, knowing that her brother would be pulling his carefully styled hair out.

'Sis, please. You cannot leave me like this. You know how I thrive on your gossip. What will I write in my 'Lighter Shades of Pink' blog?'

'Two Asian beauties. Let's leave it at that. Text me with your thoughts. Speak tomorrow. Love you.' Veronica closed the call, smiled, pocketed her mobile and strode back to The Cobblers hoping that that Griffin would be in, Nash was top of the social media agenda and she needed some facts to offset against the rumour mill that was spiralling out of control.

CHAPTER SIX

Griffin breezed into the bristling CID office, where there always appeared to more people than space available. His two detectives animated in their chatter. 'Morning ladies, cat and cream springs to mind.' To be honest he was upbeat after an excellent night on the first floor, not literally, at The Cobblers, and a full English to set up the day. 'I take it that you have something to bring to an otherwise bare table. Please come in and show me what you've got.'

Mantel smiled as she handed her DI a sheet of A4 as he slipped into his chair. 'Nothing definitive.' A sound night's sleep alone in her apartment had recharged her batteries, the top of the range mattress doing its job.

'But definitely of interest,' Nimra continued following in and passing over page of notes having had a conversation with Mantel. A little jaded after another frisky night with her best friend and their new man .

'So, mine is the answers to the questions we posed at our meeting at Rotherfield yesterday,' Mantel said pointing at the page from her chair then smoothing the black suit she had chosen for the day. 'It would appear that Nash led the life of a monk. A combination of those three wise monkeys; see no evil, hear no evil, speak no evil. Don't see why he was locked up. Doing a bunk he's done the right thing for society. Making it a better and safer place for us all, by re-joining us he has brought his outstanding moral scruples to this nasty old world we all live in.'

Griffin threw a knowing glance in his DS's direction as he read the information. 'No phone, no inward calls. No TV, apart from sport. Just an avid reader of all things football. No mention of anything else. Particular about his diet, that's good to hear. Liked fresh veg and fish. Was he resurrected at Easter?'

'Quite, oh, there is a phone registered to him but apparently not used inside. I'm having it checked out. Let's not forget this is the world of Andy Nash, seen through the eyes of Iain Swift.'

'Yes. Iain Swift quite. So Nimra let's see what you've found out about this psychiatric nurse.'

'A paid-up member of everything you would want to be paid up to if you were that way inclined, politically that is,' Nimra responded in jeans and sneakers, her jet-black hair tied firmly back, having left herself no time to wash it. 'An activist at Uni, then manoeuvres himself through and up the public sector. Single, living alone. Flat near the unit, but also owns an attractive looking apartment in central London that must be worth a few bob.'

Griffin pointed to a particular line on the sheet. 'I see that he had a spell working at the Scrubs.'

'Another brief spell that he was moved on from. Sorry promoted.'

'Just that I've got a mate, Rob Sidwell. He's a Prison Warden up at Bradwell. You must remember him Luce,' Griffin said, Mantel shrugging her shoulders in response. 'His mum was looking at Blue Skies House. Don't know what happened to that.'

'Ah yes, I do remember something about Bradwell Prison and you knowing someone there.'

'Anyway, he was at Wormwood Scrubs around this time, it's where I first met him, good guy. I'll give him a call. Perhaps I'll meet up and catch up. Always good to get the gossip and inside track from the frontline prison service. And there's a chance he knew Swift.'

'It would be interesting to get an inside track,' Nimra said. 'To date not a good word to be had. Admittedly all are from the work side of his life. Yet to discover any friends, if he has any. Also, I'm looking into any political allegiances.'

'Okay, all good stuff. Well done. But reality is apart from the one dubious sighting we remain in the dark as to where Nash is holed out.' Griffin put his hands behind his head. 'I think we need to have a chat with this Swift regarding his pornographic habits. I'm sure there's more there. Fancy a ride Luce, from what the two of you have been going on about it sounds like there's a couple of blokes for you to check out.'

*

'Thanks for seeing us Mr Swift,' Griffin said sitting down next to Mantel in the clinical meeting room at the Rotherfield Secure Psychiatric Unit, with refreshments from the vending machine in the staffroom. The fine china crockery apparently the preserve of Jenny Roberts and her VIP guests. Mantel making a mental note that security procedures were far less intense than on her previous visit. Disappointed to be frisked by an efficient brunette lady, not Anton, and no sign of the boss's PA. Opposite was Iain Swift less shabby chic than last time, today in cargo trousers and an open neck chequered shirt with his sleeves rolled up. Mantel pondered whether this was of any significance.

'Not a problem,' Swift replied looking at the two detectives with a supposedly sincere look that didn't quite cut it. 'How can I help you? I thought we'd covered most things in our chat on the phone.'

Griffin took a sip of his tea looking directly at the Assistant Psychiatric Nurse already not liking what he was seeing. 'It's just a quickie and a bit of clarification on a matter.' The agreed strategy was for Griffin to maintain eye contact, whilst Mantel looked for other mannerisms in response to her boss's questioning.

The room had a different feel to Jenny's feely-touchy office. This was a stark space, no doubt used for strategic thought and the occasional bollocking. No pot plants, simple abstract art in muted colours. Industrial lighting that was not subtle.

'Fine by me, fire away,' Swift responded. Mantel noting the rubbing of thumbnails on Swift's tightly clasped hands.

'Pornography, do you indulge?'

'What has this to do with anything?'

'Please answer the question Mr Swift, it's pretty simple.'

'Occasionally, who doesn't?'

'Do you ever look at pornography on a computer here in the unit?'

Mantel was unsure as to whether Swift's knuckles could get any whiter.

'As I said, occasionally.'

'Is that allowed Mr Swift?' Griffin asked maintaining a direct approach, encouraged to date that Swift had chosen not to lie.

'You know it's not, but what's the harm?' Swift said trying to remain nonchalant.

'Mr Swift, you more than most, must know that pornography and sex offenders don't mix.'

'None of the patients see it, I'm not that foolish.'

'Quite. Well that's your opinion, this was just to let you know that our computer experts ran checks on the systems here and found a considerable amount of access to hardcore sites using your password,' Griffin replied lying, the tech guys had yet to do a thorough check, gambling from experience that Swift would be unlikely to question this as he would be starting to worry, and specific details would be rolling into one. 'Now, you are an adult and we can't stop you indulging in your own time. Although it will no doubt warrant an internal warning for doing it on the premises with company property. We just wanted you to know that we know what you get up to. Our guys are now going through anything related to Andy Nash, so no doubt we will be back in touch.'

Swift sat in silence, sensibly choosing to not dig a bigger hole. Wise enough to appreciate a warning shot and hope that it was just a slapped wrist.

'And whilst we're here, could you please give us a list of the non-football books that you provided for Nash. Those that you failed to mention to DS Mantel in your telephone conversation.'

Swift's emotions dived. The techies finding the porn he could understand, albeit sloppy on his part and a little annoying, the books though, who had been talking? 'Yes, of course. Sorry, didn't I mention them?'

'Thank you. And we'd like that list before we go please. We'll take a look round while you're putting it together if that's okay. Oh, and finally,' Griffin said getting to his feet. 'Do you have any knowledge of the whereabouts of Andy Nash?'

'Absolutely not.'

Having successfully navigated the security to exit the building, Griffin and Mantel walked towards their car. 'Well what do you think boss. Does he know? When you asked about Nash's whereabouts, he definitely reached for the Andrex.'

'Quite, get the tech guys on it and let's get this porn he's been sharing with Nash,' Griffin said zapping his car lock. 'Shame we didn't have the proof now so we could have brought him in. We will though, as soon as we have the evidence. Then it'll be time for some WD40 on those thumb screws. It wouldn't surprise me if that was his.'

Mantel looked at the black Mercedes Sports her boss was pointing at, parked across two 'Staff Only' bays. 'Probably,'

'Come on, enough of that wanker, you can tell me about the books Nash has been reading, quite a little list.'

'If we have a good run I might get to netball for once.'

'Traffic permitting should be back within the hour.'

*

Nimra exited the pharmacy, pleased to have a late opening one so handy, her subscription in its paper bag tucked into her black and white leather shoulder bag. With the sun low in the sky she pulled out her shades and looked at her reflection in the chemist's window, adjusting her glasses. Behind her, a young, apparently bearded guy passed on the other side of the road with a dark Donkey jacket slung over his shoulder, wearing a beanie despite the upturn in temperature...the penny dropped. She turned; the chap was now a couple of shops down looking at designer clothes. Nimra edged smoothly and quickly down her side of the street. Eager to remain undetected, she continued to track the Donkey jacket in the reflection in the shop windows, first a gift shop then a travel agent. Eager to get ahead and a different view. The jacket moved on, now appearing to make a call on their mobile. Eyes focussed on her prey Nimra narrowly avoided a rubbish bin and a lamp post. When her prey halted at a shoe shop, Nimra nipped down the road and crossed it to be in a position to come back towards him. She found herself looking into a launderette. Puzzled customers looked out at her. She turned to see the Donkey jacket disappear down an alleyway. Knowing the area Nimra walked at pace across the road, down four shops to the smart Italian restaurant. She knew that they had a car park to the rear with access to the road at the back, where the alley would emerge. Passing swiftly through the empty car park Nimra remembered a 'bad hair day' baseball cap in her bag. Rummaging on the move, she lobbed it on her head and pulled it down. The road at the back was residential, largely highly sought-after turn of the last century terraces. Looking around she caught sight of the Donkey jacket, moving away from her towards the High Road. Nimra ambled at pace to get within thirty metres, when suddenly he stopped to light a cigarette. Nimra was still unable to get a positive sighting and took the executive decision to cross the road and keep going, she could find no reason to stop. Should she call it in? Dressed in jeans, sneakers, shades and 'Love Is…' baseball cap she should blend in. That was if there was anyone one else in the road, which there wasn't. Evenings in suburbia; time for bathing, dinner and TV. Having passed him Nimra paused and took out her mobile, using it as a mirror to look over her shoulder. She was now alone in the road. The Donkey jacket had gone. Vanished into thin air or one of the houses. Or the cul-de-sac that led into the forest. Or back up the alleyway. Nimra gave a theatrical stomp and quietly screamed, 'bullocks'. She would never know whether the Donkey jacket with the beanie was Andy Nash. She hadn't even taken a photo. This would have to be her secret.

CHAPTER SEVEN

'Is the DI in?' Nimra asked smartly turned out in a dark blue suit and white blouse. Her hair washed and stylishly held back with a diamanté clip.

'Nope. He's up in Northamptonshire seeing that Prison Warden,' Mantel replied, glancing up at her colleague whilst tapping away at her keyboard. 'All okay?'

Nimra placed her bag beside her desk, having not slept. Tossing and turning over yesterday's potential sighting of Nash and her failure to deal with it. Finally deciding to come clean, now thwarted by the DI not being in the office. 'Yeh, fine.' Should she confide in Mantel? Perhaps that was the better option, although one that she had dismissed at regular intervals throughout the night. Nimra grabbed her 'Love Is..' mug from her desk. 'Soya?'

*

'Rob is this the same pub?' Griffin asked as Rob Sidwell placed a foaming pint of cask ale on a beer mat ahead of him. 'Thanks, it just seems so different from my last visit when it was fizzy beer and sticky floors.'

Rob took a sip of his beer. 'Cheers. Yep, The Bradwell Arms, now the chicest place in town.'

'Cheers, and quite a lady, I take it she's in charge.'

'Yes, Chantel's done wonders. Got the brewery to give it a 'Changing Rooms' style makeover and here we are. From a clapped out back street boozer to this,' Sidwell replied, a barrel chested, cropped hair, forty something divorcee, dressed in jeans and a navy blue polo shirt, leaning back in admiration.

'The last time I came in here the landlord was a John Hardwell. Had he been found in the canal, or was that still to happen?'

'Can't really remember the timeline. What a fucking arsehole he was.'

''Yeh, knowing that I was coming up I took a look at his file. What they found on his computer was mind boggling. If you just take your Prison, every sort of detail imaginable, payroll down to inside leg measurements.

Roll that out, then, well. A real hyper-hacker. The guy had files on files,' Griffin said enjoying his pint. 'But of course he tried it on just too much and got his comeuppance. Mixing with the fucking low life in this world can have nasty consequences. One of which is ending up face down in the Grand Union. Did you have much to do with his shady side?'

Sidwell listened to Griffin's question knowing that he was going to have to lie as he recalled his experiences with the ex-landlord, thankfully a distant memory. Hardwell, a journeyman pub manager, perpetrated to be a dark web super guru, rather than the run of the mill hacker that he was. Hardwell had assured Sidwell and his two colleagues that he could help them in their belief that they knew the whereabouts of sixteen bars of dodgy gold and how, as they say, they could have had it away on their toes. All of which was totally unknown to his old mate Griffin. The gold in question being the as yet unfound haul of gold bars from a Spanish bank in The City of London a dozen years previous, a case that remained on Griffin's agenda. Sidwell and his chums foolishly saw it as a healthy addition to their pension pots. Their plans, albeit sketchy and with holes, were ambushed by the ex-landlord and his attempt to muscle in. His clumsy and arrogant approach at least enabled the prison officers, with a sigh of relief, to return to their day jobs. Their fingers so nearly burnt. The greedy, naive publican came unstuck when he pushed his luck and tried to bluff it out with the notorious, violent and elusive serial criminal, Terry 'Teflon' Albert, who, once again escaped the clutches of the law, hence the nickname. The landlord's demise meant that Stilwell and his fellow prison workers avoided being implicated at all. 'No, I probably know less than you about what he go up to.'

The warden and Griffin had become friends a few years back, when Sidwell was doing a lengthy stint at Wormwood Scrubs. As a warden not an inmate. A friendship that had continued, if largely at a distance. It was a coincidence that their paths had crossed with the gold. Both unaware of each other's respective interests, Griffin still oblivious to his chum's close brush with criminality.

The murder of Bradwell Arms landlord proved to be a welcome change for all, except him, at the pub in the shadow of the prison. Chantel arrived at the pub with a small pot of money for re-development. The bar received a deep clean and make-over; a retro look back to its 60s origins. The jukebox an immediate success. The small kitchen upgraded to provide agreeable retro pub grub, scampi in a basket going down a storm. The revamped pub was never banged out but then nowhere was in Bradwell, but there had been success of sorts and a decent clientele. Largely unknown was that Chantel had a close relationship with Charlie Hobbs, great, great grandchild of Herbert Hobbs founder of the local brewery, Hobbs & Co., a Director of the company and deemed responsible for their return to more prosperous times.

Griffin's stomach rumbled, breakfast having been missed. 'Is the food any good? The chef looks as perky as the landlady.'

'Good pub grub thoroughly recommend it,' Sidwell replied sensing an 'expenses' lunch, a bonus on a day off with the prison's staff canteen not accessible. 'Tracey and Chantel are joined at the hip. Although I haven't been upstairs, from all accounts they have a really nice place up there.'

'Really...Look, let's get something to eat, my shout, then we can get down to why I'm here. As I said on the phone, I've a couple of things to discuss.'

*

Mantel rose from her seat and moved round the table to give Nimra a great big hug. 'Look, I can assure you this is nothing in the whole scheme of things. I've done far worse.'

'Are you sure?'

None of the other customers batted an eyelid. The outpouring of emotions were common in 'The Old Boy and His Stool', the police station's 'local', less than fifty metres from the front door. A refuge for those feeling the strain of police life. A place for celebration when a result was achieved. Recognized as a no-go zone for disagreements. A run of the mill pub serving good everyday food with perhaps the biggest range of nuts and crisps in the country, although never verified by the Guinness Book of Records. The optics coming alive later in the day when stress levels needed easing.

'Look you don't even know if it was Nash. To be honest Nimra it is very unlikely, especially still with the donkey jacket. I don't think even he's that stupid. Look, if you like I'll have a word with the boss,' Mantel said her arm still round the DC's shoulders. 'Now I suggest we finish these then go and pay Iain Swift a visit. Did you see the contents of his computer?'

'Yes, I took a look this morning' Nimra replied appreciating Mantel's comments managing a slight smile. 'I thought I was broad minded, but.'

'Quite, some extraordinary positions, not my scene at all. You.'

'Oh yeh, can't get enough of all that masochism,' Nimra responded nonchalantly. 'Doesn't the DI want to pick up Swift?'

'Nope. I cleared it with him and he's more than happy for us to go and to start the questioning. Said he'll catch up when he gets back. Anyway, we need to get a move on, this quiz starts at eight, doesn't it? Don't want to be letting the boss's floozie down, do we.'

*

Griffin wiped his mouth with his red paper napkin, chucking it on the empty plate that he had pushed to one side. 'Well that was an excellent steak and kidney pie. The chef is obviously very capable.'

'You'd like to think so,' a grinning Sidwell replied, having demolished his gammon with pineapple.

Griffin took out his notebook. 'Right Iain Swift. I believe you worked with him at the Scrubs. Give it to me straight, having met him I already have my own thoughts on him.'

'I don't think you'll be disappointed with my opinion.'

'Go on, in three words.'

'Okay. Obnoxious, fucking arrogant and slightly weird.'

'That's four or five, but I'll let you have it. So why?'

'Well, he was only young. I think he'd had a couple of other junior posts. Never been in a prison before, as far as I know. Certainly nothing like the Scrubs if he had. But he came in as if he knew it all. Chucked the rule book around, without apparently referring to it when it suited him. Caused a lot of upset and irritation. But as you know shit won't stick on these individuals. The lady we have over the road doing his job couldn't be more chalk and cheese, she listens.'

'Okay, so we're both on the same page as to his character. What about how he got on with others, in particular prisoners?'

'Well funny you should ask that. The reason for him moving on was familiarisation, and that's not with colleagues.'

'In what way? Thank you,' Griffin said as the plates were removed by the chef. 'That was absolutely wonderful. I'll have to come again.'

Tracey smiled. 'Thank you. We look forward to seeing you again.'

'Easy detective,' Sidwell grinned as the chef departed. 'Get to the back of the queue.'

'In what way was he over familiar with the prisoners?'

'Well he insisted on one to one interviews. Obviously they were cuffed, but still, us wardens didn't like it one bit. We just had to watch from the outside.'

'Was it just him and them or did he have his laptop with him?'

'That's the crunch. Our Governor at the time was so wet that he needed squeezing out at home time. He was persuaded that his laptop and the psychiatric tests on it were essential to the treatment. I mean what the fuck. Essential my arse.'

'Sorry, what was the problem?' Griffin asked a little surprised by the usually laidback Sidwell's sudden show of emotion.

'Now I'm a man of the world Mike and admit to having looked at some porn over time. But with Swift it was pretty hard stuff and it seemed to be his screen saver.'

'Yes, we've downloaded some very interesting material from his work hard drive. He doesn't appear to know how to cover his tracks. Hate to think what we'd find on his personal one. So, what happened?'

'Well it had to happen. He said it was an error, but we'd been suspicious for some time. He just seemed too popular. At first, we couldn't see his screen, which I know was a little naive. Then one of the guys altered a camera angle without Swift knowing. Bingo, low and behold.'

'Why wasn't he sacked?'

'As I said a combination of him saying oohps and a liberal Governor. It was suggested that he may be better placed elsewhere. Moving on quickly to a better paid, higher grade placement in, would you believe it, a young offenders institute.'

'You couldn't make it up, but it happens so often. Was he chummy with anyone in the Scrubs?'

'Far from it, a loner. Seemed to thrive on alienating himself. Although he was always excusing himself for calls and infuriatingly, always texting or whatever in meetings. From what I remember he was rarely in, always on some course. Managed to wind most of us up when he was in.'

'So, a black mark on his record?'

'What do you think?'

'Point taken. This is all great stuff. My team are interviewing him later. As I said this is all in conjunction with a rapist who's jumped a secure unit where Swift was in charge on the shift when he absconded. As I am sure you can tell, like you, I don't like him. Bit of a wet wanker,' Griffin said getting to his feet. 'Enough of Swift. I'll get a round in then you can tell me all about Roger and David Richards who I believe checked in with you a few months back.'

*

'Well that's great to know Rob, if a little disappointing,' Griffin said having received the lowdown on two of the Richards boys and their time spent separately at Bradwell. Apparently model prisoners, much to Griffin's dismay. He had hoped to add to his file on them for the day when inevitably he brought them and other members of their family in. 'Sorry but I need to get the train back. Three-line whip for a charity quiz night tonight. This has been extremely useful.'

'Before you go Mike, I just had a thought. The Richards boys' father, Larry isn't it?'

'Yep, what about him?'

'Well I'm pretty sure that he was in the Scrubs when Swift and I were there.'

CHAPTER EIGHT

Regular quizzers were joined by others wishing to contribute their minds and money to a fantastic local cause, and The Cobblers was buzzing every table taken. Whereas the weekly quiz nights had a competitive, some would say serious edge, tonight was all about paying your entry fee and enjoying yourself. Not the usual tenner per team, tonight ten pounds per person. 'Custard's Last Stand', the frequent winners of the regular quiz, usually a pretty dour group of journeyman quizzers, laughed and joked. Julian, the owner of 'Stairway', the local children's hospice, the benefactor sitting with his team in anticipation, was delighted with the turnout. Lily and Veronica hoped to raise well over the six hundred pounds entrance fees, possibly substantially more if the auction matched the buoyant mood.

Bob, the quizmaster busied himself in the corner. Checking the questions on his laptop and that his PA system was fully operational. Unknown to most this large jovial chap had baulked at Veronica's request, 'to do a free one for charity'. Only subsiding when free drinks and a taxi were thrown in, this really irked her, but it was too late to find a replacement. She already had her concerns about him. Yes, he was probably the best at delivering quizzes in the area, but she had been deciding whether it was worth a change. Prompted a couple of weeks back when she took him over a drink, only to notice that he had failed to close the screen on his laptop showing hard-core porn, which if honest hadn't surprised her.

Veronica stood at the end of the bar admiring the scene as Lily passed by. 'What a great turnout Lils.'

'Yep. Fantastic, isn't it,' her assistant replied, on a high with her idea coming to fruition. 'We should raise loads.'

Fifteen teams of four were due to compete. There was a handsome trophy to be won that would no doubt become sought after if this became an annual event. Not your usual piece of over-priced shiny plastic tat, a friend of Julian's had produced a bespoke piece of art; a forefinger pressed thoughtfully against lips, sculptured in oak from the forest, mounted on a plinth with enough space for yearly additions. Veronica hoped that her two teams of regulars would win as it would look good on one of the shelves behind the bar, unfortunately both teams were already knocking it back, her slim hopes disappearing as fast as the ale.

Veronica mooched around the tables with a beer mug collecting the entrance fees. Ensuring that all had enough pens, distributing the answer sheet with the warm-up question; 'Name the last twelve British Prime Ministers?' Reaffirming Veronica's thoughts that the trophy would not be gracing the bar. 'Bazzer, good to see you. Going it alone?' Veronica enquired standing by the table reserved for the local constabulary where Inspector Barry 'Bazzer' Hargreaves sat alone and supped his pint.

'Well you know what these sleuths are like Ron,' Bazzer responded with a smile, Veronica noting that he avoided eye contact with Lily as she passed the table. 'They're probably here, but undercover. Secret Squirrel and all that.'

'Oh yes, I never thought of that,' Veronica replied laughing. 'Mike said that it might be tight. The girls should be here though.' With that the main doors swung open and befitting a spaghetti western the three detectives breezed into the saloon. Griffin raised his hand to acknowledge Veronica and Bazzer, asking his colleague via sign language whether he wanted a refill, receiving a positive silent response.

'I suppose better late than never for our three amigos,' Veronica said laughing, a friendly tap on Bazzer's shoulder before moving onto another table.

'Evening ladies pleased you could make it, I was starting to feel like Billy no mates,' Bazzer said smiling as Mantel and Nimra approached.

Griffin removed his jacket. 'Some of us have work to do and to put in a full shift.'

'You okay Mike, you look a little flushed.'

'Brisk walk from the station, their idea,' Griffin replied taking a long sup of his pint. 'Right eyes down, think it's about to start. Come on team, we're going to win this. And come on Luce, dish the crisps.'

'Good evening everyone and welcome to this very special Stairway quiz night.' Bob's radio trained voice projected from the black speaker in front of his small table.

With proceedings underway and only a few disinterested regulars to serve until the break, Veronica, Lily and their fellow barmaids, Marti, Angie and Georgie, gathered around a quiz sheet, not being an official team they agreed that all evidence of their efforts should be shredded.

'So come on ladies, who would your money be on?' Veronica asked of her gathering as they pondered over the first question about capital cities; to place them from north to south.

'Well 'Custard's Last Stand' must be favourites,' Marti said an attractive, trim, thirty something brunette.

'Yeh, but the Church team have to be up there surely,' Lily chipped in. 'Don't bright people go to church and the new vicar's a bit of an unknown. I really like her.'

'What about the police team. You must have some inside info there Ron?' Georgie added, an attractive, small, non-natural blond, a single mother, albeit well-financed in her divorce, with two prep school children, who kept her First in mathematics to herself.

'It's all smoke and mirrors with detectives, I can assure you. But if you want my expert insider knowledge on them, they will be in the running until half time then they'll get pissed and fall away. For me it's the Blue Skies team.'

'Oo yes, a bit of a dream team,' Lily replied looking over to a table with a considerable breadth of knowledge. 'I mean despite Prisha pulling out, they've got Ellie's medical background. Rod on anything building and DIY which may include architecture. Then Sam, concierges know everything don't they, and of course Robbie for everything cooking.' This was Robbie Jones, the exceedingly popular chef, soon to be, 'TV Celebrity Chef', who they hoped had brought some goodies from the studio for the auction.

'Agreed,' Veronica said. 'The residents shouldn't be ruled out either, years of experiences there and they may not get quite so sloshed as the others.'

'I wouldn't count on that, I think they'd had a couple before they came over,' Lily responded. 'And of course there's the Hospice team. Although going home with their own trophy is that allowed?

'So to sum it up,' Angi said. 'They've all got a chance.'

Marti grinned and made to serve a customer. 'One thing for certain, it wouldn't have been us.'

So engrossed was everyone that the face at the window went unnoticed. Having a team of police officers on the premises it had seemed fine to send the security guy home.

The evening rattled on. At halfway the Custard's and St Vincent's were vying for top spot. The police were knocking at the door, so to speak, but as predicted the drink had started to flow. The pub's owners, Freddie Bone and Glenn Friar made an appearance during the second half, having dodged the invitation to form a team, absolutely delighted with the positive publicity that this would generate, a welcomed change…

…Veronica stood at the bar with the results sheet to hand, the quiz and auction completed, alongside her Julian holding the trophy, sporting a lubricated smile. She tapped a glass with a spoon. 'Ladies and gentlemen please, Bob has totted up the scores and has given me the results. Now bearing in mind that he's been on free drinks all night, this may be a complete work of fiction.' Much laughter, to which Bob raised his glass. 'I hope that you will agree with me that the night has been a tremendous success,' Veronica continued. 'Not sure yet of the final total but I can assure you that it will be well over a thousand pounds. And that's all down to your generosity. With a special thanks to all our auction donors, in particular, Robbie. I'm not sure what his producers will say when they return to their studio and find it stripped bare. So, let's give yourselves a round of applause and here's to next year.'

Veronica ran through the scores from the bottom up. 'So that leaves me with the final two. There could still be a steward's as to how 'Custard's Last Stand' managed to balls it up. But hey-ho that's how it goes. Right, the result, that I've just given away, the winners are the 'St Vincent's Vanguard'. Congratulations St Vincent's, please come up and accept the trophy.'

Applause filled the bar as the team, led by Mandy Jarvis, the Vanguard team rose modestly to their feet and made to collect the handsome prize. Inwardly the Vicar wanted celebratory high-fives and to run round the pub waving her blouse above her head but decided that it was probably no befitting her position.

*

Veronica pulled back the duvet to let her naked body slide into bed. 'Well a right result, even if I say so myself.' The adrenalin still flowed more than an hour after the culmination of the quiz., unfortunately, Griffin had gone back to his own place, so her words were lost, his redundant pillow all that was left to cuddle.

*

'Night Luce,' Nimra said as she opened her front door.

'Night Nimra, bright and breezy in the morning' replied Mantel heading off towards her own apartment wondering whether the night-cap at Griffin's new pad was such a good idea. Yes, it was on the way home, so why not? But coming fifth in the quiz, was that a real reason to celebrate? And not a decent bloke in sight for the whole evening. Bazzer probably heading the field. Although he's not only married, his spare time was taken up shagging Lily. Glenn's late appearance was a little awkward. Although his business partner, Freddie, now there's a thought? With her head full of unlikely permutations, she strolled contented down the nostalgically lit shopping street towards her home.

Checking her locks then climbing the stairs to her small flat over the Opticians, Nimra pondered the questions that had eluded them. In particular, why their score was so much worse in the second half? Flicking a light on, she dumped her bag and kicked off her shoes, a poor choice for walking, and took the couple of strides to the kitchenette for a glass of water, assessing that size of home probably equated to rank, with the DI's being so much more spacious. Reaching to open the cupboard above the sink a strong arm grabbed her around the throat. A gloved hand covered her mouth. She attempted and failed to bite it. Kicking out, arms flailing, dragging her backwards into her unlit bedroom, being aggressively thrust onto her double bed. A masked face pinned her down. About to scream a hand shoved something in her mouth. For all she knew it could be a pair of her own knickers, they had her fragrance. This split second, where the hand was released, allowed Nimra to unleash a left hook that Tyson Fury would be proud of. She caught her attacker's head flush, he toppled off of her with the unexpected force. Nimra slid off the bed and grabbed the baseball bat she kept for such occasions from under her bed. On her knees she swung with all her might at the shaken figure, sitting uninvited on her bed. Connecting big time with the rib cage. A scream of pain accompanied cracking bones. The mask was now skewwhiff, but poor light obscured any chance of identification; Nimra had her suspicions though. Did she try to apprehend or be thankful if they escaped? Desperate to avoid hand-to-hand combat.

'You fucking bastard!' Nimra screamed aiming another blow as her assailant made to get off the bed. Missing, as they made for the door. Getting to her feet, another swing, crashing across the back of their knees. They buckled. Cuffs? In her bag? Her attacker hobbled the couple of steps towards the stairs. Another blow would send him down them. 'Shit.' Nimra exclaimed as she tripped; bag found. Hurried limping steps could be heard descending the stairs. Locks rattled. The front door opened, then slammed. More footsteps could be heard shuffling at speed up the street.

Nimra lay panting on the floor next to the bag and shoes she had abandoned by her bedroom door, rummaging in her bag for her phone. Not to call it in, but to warn Mantel who she hoped had reached home.

CHAPTER NINE

'Yo Nimra,' Griffin exclaimed offering a high five on entering the never quiet CID office. 'I thought I told you to go straight home.'

'I did, just that there was an unexpected guest waiting for me.'

'Did they bring chocolates and flowers? Must admit I didn't have you down for a bit of the rough stuff.'

Nimra glanced at her boss and grinned whilst Mantel smiled a sleepy smile, she and Nimra had been in the office all night. As expected, the search of the area had found nothing. Nimra refusing a trip to A&E.

Griffin put his arm round his DC. 'Seriously Nimra, it's so good to see that you're okay. I hear that they've got no DNA.'

'He was wearing gloves and I didn't get the chance to get my nails into him or to grab his hair, to be honest I wasn't really thinking about that.'

'Well if we haven't got it, we haven't got it. I suppose the guys at your flat could still come up with something.'

'Nice to think so sir, but I doubt it, I reckon he was ultra-careful not to leave anything.'

'I suppose it could have been someone else, a chancer high on drugs?'

'Do you really think so boss?' Mantel asked.

'No, from what Nim said it has all the signs of being Nash, which makes him even more dangerous. We need to step everything up. Did you know Nash before?'

'Not really, only in passing,' Nimra replied. 'Without the photos I may not have recognized him, obviously Prisha knew him, but, no, our paths hardly crossed, not my sort, thankfully, thought too much of himself.'

'So you've got nothing else?'

'Nope, it all happened so quick, it was dark, I even had problems telling the guys what the mask looked like, I just thought it was Nash. In fact I'm not even sure if I got the mask right.'

'Fair enough, it must have been fucking horrendous. It's got upstairs jumping, which means fire being breathed down my neck, which is great and means they're interested. Right who's getting the coffees in?' Griffin said making for his office. 'I want to know what Iain Swift had to say for himself. Oh and if possible let's keep Nimra's attack to ourselves, it might be useful to see if and where it leaks from.'...

...Griffin tapped a biro firmly on his desk, having listened to his detectives the espresso long gone. 'So quite rightly you let him off with a caution. If we locked up everyone who viewed hard-core porn, well...'

'Look boss, he didn't flinch at any of the stuff, arrogant bastard in my book,' Mantel replied. 'We just couldn't find anything to link him to Nash's whereabouts and thought he would be of more use out there where if he does know something he's liable to make a slip. But I really don't think that he'd want to be involved. He's got grander ideas for himself on the political stage and he's a bit of a wimp.'

'Yep, with you on that. He obviously wasn't going back to the unit if you didn't provide transport.'

'No, the cheeky fucker, thanked us for bringing him in as he was planning to stay in his apartment up town. Think he went off to the tube,' Mantel said twisting the biro in her hand. 'He's just one of those people who've got 'irritating prick' running through them like a stick of rock.'

'This apartment up town?' What have we got on that Nimra?'

'All paid up and above board from my initial searches.'

'Family money?'

'Certainly would appear that way. Mother and father lawyers. Both now retired.'

'Ah yes, come to think of it I have recollections of The Right Honourable Swifts. He was a right fucking pain in the arse. Always dragged out cases to max his fees. Looking for loopholes rather than justice. Can see where their Iain got his principles from. If I'm right I think the mother traded under her maiden name and was no better. Can just see them round the kitchen table counting the cash and gloating about who they got off. Dig a bit deeper Nimra, although I don't think it's going to find us Nash and that's where our cupboard remains bare. If we don't find him soon I'll get warrants for Swift and Roberts places. She's not out of the equation with the aiding and abetting.'

Nimra made to leave. 'Anything else sir?'

'No. Hang on, I've just got this through,' Griffin said looking at his phone. 'The identikit guys are ready for you.'

'Sir?'

'Yeh, they've looked at your statement and have a number of masks for you to identify. I'm not kidding look, you probably got the same mail,' Griffin replied smiling and showing Nimra his screen. 'Luce, whilst Nimra is onto that, let's pay Rod Nash another visit. As far as we know, he is Andy's only family. We may have missed something. Make out that you want the loo and have a shifty...'

'Sorry?'

'Shifty. I'll keep Rod talking. You just never know.'

*

'Yeh, it was a real success. Just finished tallying it up. £1,300 give or take. Julian at the Hospice should be chuffed, it will help soothe the hangover I reckon he's got,' Veronica said phone to her ear, sat on a bench in the morning sun outside the pub, its unofficial opening imminent, early stragglers could be expected at any time.

'That sounds like a good reason for a celebration,' Stephen replied. 'Lunch, dinner? Out here, up town, even round there, your choice?'

'Sounds good to me. I need a change. Not sure if the Detective Inspector is going cold on me.'

'Oh, why do you say that? It sounded so promising.'

'Work has crept up again. He's always very busy. Early meetings, late-night rendezvouses. Perhaps it's just me.'

'Come on sis. Dating a copper is never going to be straightforward, especially one like Mike.'

'Yeh, you're probably right. Don't think I'd like a PC Plod. Let's get a date in the diary, sooner than later. I need some fun. Oh, and I sacked Bob this morning.'

'What Bob the quizmaster.'

'He just irritated me too much. Took the piss last night with the amount of free booze he had. Be good for a change. Know any quiz people?'

'Err, no. I must admit what you told me about the hard-core on his laptop was not right.'

'Oh, and that's the other thing I wanted to ask. Last night's winners were the local church. They've got a new vicar after that dodgy one done a bunk. Mandy Jarvis, could you check her out, there's just something familiar about her, you know, when Dan was alive. I'm sure I've come across her before.'

*

'Here you go, sorry no soya' Griffin said passing Mantel a mug of hot water. 'I really don't think he's had any contact.'

'Agreed,' Mantel replied from the dining table in Griffin's apartment, placing the hot mug on a coaster. 'Managed to have a snoop round the bedrooms. No signs. All very tidy. Ellie Richmond is obviously a tidy bunny, nothing out of place. Don't think she'd be party to it anyway. Actually, I wasn't sure what I was looking for, a Donkey jacket or beanie?'

'This is becoming more fucking frustrating by the hour,' Griffin said leaning against a kitchen unit. Their chat with Rod Nash proving fruitless. 'Right get onto the tech guys. Get them looking into this dark web, you never know. He must be communicating with someone, there may be a deep dark forum for escaped nutters.'

*

'Ye-hahs' filled the air in the elegant 'ballroom' at the centre of Blue Skies House, accompanied by the twanging of guitar strings and the deep voice of 'Tone', the country and western singer with roots from the deep south; Peckham, London SE15. The aging Tony Baker, celebrated performer, at least on the Old People's Homes circuit, with his vintage, much loved Gretsch guitar, accompanied by what looked to be a pre-war Amp. Tone wooed his audience building them up to a line-dancing country frenzy, ably assisted with a Jack Daniels or two to sooth his vocal cords. An hour and a half of 'Applejacks' should ensure that all got a good night's sleep.

'Wow, this is great,' the Reverend Mandy Jarvis said, having decided to spread her herself around her corner of the Bishop's diocese.

'This your first one then?' Prisha asked clapping along as the room reverberated with foot stamping.

'I've done line dancing, but this is special. Good to get the staff involved,' Mandy replied having accepted a bourbon from the crooner's personal bottle, suspecting that the old guy may have taken a fancy to her. From previous experiences she knew that there was an attraction with a dog collar.

'Yes, Robbie absolutely loves it, always makes time to get involved. I suppose it's because he's also from the deep south.'

'Didn't realise he was an American, I mean the Welsh accent?'

'Correct, so perceptive Mandy' exclaimed Prisha laughing. 'Deepest south Wales.'

On her couple of previous visits Mandy had marvelled at the Retirement Home. The explosion and the distressing times that came hand in hand, were now a thing of the distant past for most of the Residents; Blue Skies House was back to its best. The old house had coped with much change since being built at the end of the 1800's. Initially a palatial home for Lord Hall, local landowner, whose tomb was the finest in St Vincent's crypt. Around fifty years later according to local folklore in the 1930s the house was owned by the notorious gangster Richard 'Dick' Anvil, who ruled his criminal empire from here. Often referred to as the then modern-day Dick Turpin, the highwayman who had pillaged along the roads through Epping Forest in the early 1700s. Both Dicks taking from the rich and not giving to the poor. Dick Anvil being shot dead in a shoot-out following a failed heist in the City of London in 1936. His resting place was not a tomb in St Vincent's, Anvil had a simple plot in a nearby cemetery, where fittingly his close neighbours were Kray twins. The house changed hands over the next few decades, sidestepping the Luftwaffe's efforts. In the early seventies it became the much sought after Forest Edge Prep School. Cosmetically the school was a fine establishment, initially with an academic reputation to match. Fraud of some magnitude saw it close down without notice. Jack and Sheila Bromsworth, the Headmaster and Chair of Governors respectively, making off with the fees, a not inconsiderable amount, never to be heard of again. The building, initially resembling the Marie Celeste, was left to go to rack and ruin. A decade later unknown developers set about turning it into a top end boutique hotel. A short-lived project that was secretly fronted by the now owners of The Cobblers. They had a change of heart and bought the hostelry next door, and its three sister pubs. Enter the larger than life Benny 'BJ' Johnson. Converting the partially developed site into the majestic Blue Skies House. Running it for six years up until his death in the fatal explosion.

The new owner, Ravi Patel, a local businessman with fingers in many pies, stood by the entrance to the ballroom with a large smile on his face, the Andy Nash situation temporarily pushed aside. He was accompanied by a tall, elegant lady, dressed in designer blue suit and cream blouse, set off with discreet jewellery and black heels.

Prisha looked across the room to where her boss and his guest, the local MP, Suzanne Holder were engaged in animated conversation. 'Excellent, she said she'd pop in, what a star.'

It was common knowledge that Suzanne Holder was a recovering alcoholic, and as a fresh-minded new member of Parliament she had received sympathetic press. This proved to be the perfect foil for her early adult life, before politics. The 'Red Tops' and social media yet to discover that, under a different name, she was an occasional centre fold and escort, apparently to pay her University bills

The Vicar glanced towards the recent additions to the shindig. 'Prisha, I'm so sorry, but I must be off,' Mandy said, hastily finishing her JD and putting the glass down.

'Oh, that's a shame. Have you met with our local MP?'

'Oh yes, many times. Look I'll let you go and chat with her. Just remembered that there's a sermon I need to finish off.'

With that the Reverend Jarvis slipped out of the door beside her. Prisha, a little bemused made her way across the room to say hello to her boss and his guest. Nobody noticed the vicar leaving nor the face at a side window.

*

With side and central lights switched on, it being dusk outside, Mandy Jarvis, in trackies and sweatshirt sat crossed legged on the floor in one of the spare bedrooms in the Vicarage. Leaning against a substantial old wooden double bed, dotted around her sealed carboard boxes. Beside her one with its lid open. To her other side a large glass of Merlot. On her lap a deep red photo album with pre-digital images from her early adult years. She didn't have a vast collection of photographs nor a lot of memorabilia. Selfies had yet to be invented and, more poignantly, her 'partners' at the time would have been adverse to publicity or giving her trinkets to remember them by.

There was one particular snap that she sought. She knew that she hadn't thrown it away, unlike so much else. This was a rare publicity shot that she had sneaked into, where she was one of a crowd of say fifteen to twenty. A gathering of some notable faces in the world of the Home Office. Not just those who had made it, but also a couple climbing quickly through the ranks. Stars of the future in the Civil Service now regularly seen as spokesmen on the news channels.

Frustrated, she put the closed album down in front of her on the carpeted floor and took a swig of her wine. Her stomach rumbled, there was a slab of cheese in the fridge but not a lot else. Taking a royal blue album from the box she opened it up. Hallelujah! On the first page beaming up at her was the photo. Immediately memories flooded back of what was not only a drug and drink fuelled evening but also a nice little earner that had held her in good stead over the years. And yes, there she was. Mandy laughed to herself, as always, she had her hands full. On this occasion it wasn't a glass, although Mandy knew for certain there would have been one close by. It was the crotch of the gentleman whose arm was round her, always making Mandy smile as no one else appeared to notice it. This was Suzie Bellford, a fellow hooker, who like Mandy had seen the light and resurrected herself in public life. These were the days before her failed marriage to Tony Holder, whose name she kept, a Corgi approved gas engineer, an old mucker of them both, who classically ditched Suzie for a housewife whose boiler he had serviced.

The Reverend had much admiration for the MP but was fully aware that they both had secrets that required preserving. They never fell out, just drifted apart. With Mandy based in her constituency it would be tricky to avoid meeting as they would no doubt come together at local events. At their last clandestine meet, quite a few years back they had established that they could not allow the media to link them to events of yesteryear, recognizing though that there was a hack out there with their names on their agenda. Whereas Mandy had come clean to a less than pure background, albeit severely watered down, Suzie had kept it under wraps. A strategy that Mandy believed would inevitably end in tears.

Drinking her wine and feeling hungrier Mandy smiled at the photograph and the stories she could tell. With yet another rumble Mandy decided that it was time to be imaginative with the cheese.

*

Griffin smeared mango chutney on a poppadum. 'So, Luce, we've got the dark web guys coming back to us first thing. That lot are so secretive and sensitive, more than a little weird,'

'It's a weird world that they work in, not a lot of natural light,' Mantel replied a little cynically, sipping at her Cobra lager as gentle Bollywood music played in the restaurant. 'But yep, until then we have to wait.'

'And we've no news on the fucker in my flat?' Nimra said munching on a poppadum. 'I just hope the wanker's got some severe bruising.'

'So, is that the extent of your love life Nimra?' Griffin enquired grabbing his beer.

'Nope. Got an address book full of film producers and aging DJs. Not all have their own front door key though. By the way, I got the landlord to fix that dodgy back window. Boy did I tear him off a strip. Shaking in his fucking boots by the time I'd finished with him, the shyster. Worth it though, got three months free rent,' Nimra replied smugly. 'What about your love life sir?'

'It's enough for me just satisfying Veronica so to speak,' Griffin said leaning back. 'With this job it's so difficult to find quality time.'

'If you don't mind me saying boss, make time,' Mantel said finishing her pint. 'Don't get complacent. It's all very well keeping her wanting. It's when she goes wanting elsewhere that the problems start.'

Griffin pointed a piece of poppadum at his DS, aware of his failings in the relationship stakes. 'Point taken and noted Luce. What about you? It's general knowledge round the station that the old lover got the heave ho a few months back.'

'Well,' Mantel said tapping her nose. 'That's for me to know.'

'So, nobody then,' Griffin replied. Nimra smiled and tucked into the lime pickle.

'Yep, in one. Anything decent and available is taken, probably have more luck on eBay.'

'Plenty of geezers at The Cobblers who think they're god's gifts. What about the Richards' boys'?

'Ha fucking ha. They can't even spell conversation.'

'Just trying to think laterally,' Griffin said glancing round the restaurant. 'What about this Tinder app?'

'Please,' Nimra retorted. 'We're just fine being single. I can assure you that I'm getting my share and I'm sure Lucy's not struggling either.'

'Yep, all fine on that front,' Mantel replied thinking that sex had been a bit thin on the ground since dumping Glenn Friar. 'Anyway, no-one is better than some creep. Right, here's the food, so here endeth the dating forum moderated by New Zealand's answer to Dear Deidre.'

'Well if you were on the lookout, I bet Sam's got a few guys that he can put you in touch with,' Griffin retorted.

'Did I hear my name?' Sam asked serving up, a young waiter arriving with Nimra's sizzling Chicken Shaslik on a wooden platter.

'Just saying Sam that you must know of loads of single guys for these ladies,' Griffin continued a little mischievously, placing a white linen napkin on his lap. 'I mean all these waiters you employ.'

'No comment Mr Griffin, please enjoy your meal,' Sam replied leaving the table tapping his round tray and grinning from ear to ear.

'Do you think that's a yes boss? Not sure that I can rustle up the dodgy passport. Anyway, there's just one bloke we need to find at the moment. I cannot believe the wall of silence we're getting.'

CHAPTER TEN

The ramblers were thoroughly enjoying the fine weather. The group of seven from Blue Skies House, kitted out appropriately, had strolled the pleasant distance through the delightful forest to the 'bikers' tea hut. An institution tucked away amongst the web of small roads that criss-cross the nearly 6,000 acres of former royal forest, where if you visited at weekends and Bank Holidays you could be confronted by literally hundreds of bikers converging for a cup of choice. Preening themselves in front of their gleaming machines, enjoying animated chat about motorbikes and their open road experiences. Today the tea hut had been relatively quiet when the walkers on their regular jaunt enjoyed an old-fashioned brew. One of their party indulging in a bacon roll out of the prying eyes of the synagogue. 'What the Rabbi can't see...' being their defence.

Five of the trekkers were residents, accompanied as usual by a Concierge, today Sam had the pleasurable task. Also on board was Eddie, ex-SAS, one of the 'discreet' security outfit. The conversation had flowed, matters flora and fauna receiving educated responses from a knowledgeable bunch of horticulturists as they strolled through the magnificent woodland. For all this, it was Andy Nash that dominated. All, with the exception of Eddie had known him well when was employed at the House. And if pushed, they all liked him, that was until the whole scenario turned extremely murky. The chatter was similar to any conversation you tuned into in the area. The wall of Chinese whispers regarding his whereabouts extended further than the Great Wall. With each and every discussion reaching the same conclusion; nobody had a clue, but everyone had their own ideas.

'I'm so sorry ladies,' Reginald said a portly, well-spoken chap with wire rimmed glasses that gave him the look of Captain Mainwaring, hence his nickname.

'Yes, Captain,' Alice replied in her headmistress way. As prim in the forest, as she was in the dining room. 'Don't tell us, another pee? We're not far from being back, can't it wait?'

'Fraid not, sorry.'

'Well as always Captain watch out for those brambles and nettles,' Margaret giggled. 'Remember, if you do get stung rub it with a dock leaf.'

'It'll have to be a bleeding small dock leaf,' Don replied, an upright ex-services sort.

'Ha, bleeding, ha. Haven't you got any new lines Don,' Reginald called over his shoulder as he submerged into the undergrowth, the party setting themselves up as strategic lookouts. Reality was that Don had forgotten most of what he had said throughout the morning.

'Cows,' Trevor shouted, an ex-market trader, his thick black hair benefitting from the Brylcreem look of a bygone day. The cry of cows not as unlikely as it may sound in the ancient woods. Local farmers having very old rights to graze their cows, more than those with tents who wrongly thought they could freely camp in the forest.

'You're fucking joking.' The panicked reply from within.

'Captain, language please.'

Trevor nonchalantly pulled on his cigarette. 'Only kidding.'

'Bastard.'

'Come on Captain,' Alice demanded hands on hips.

'Holy Shit...' Reginald reappeared, flustered, his feet catching in the brambles, struggling with his fly, having not fully completed the task in hand. 'There's a bleeding dead body in there.'

*

Jeeps and other 4x4 vehicles owned by the forest authorities were parked alongside those of the police force. Blue lights oscillating to warn those close and far. Blue and white tape strung from tree to tree, some distance away from where Reginald had found the body. He and his fellow walkers removed from the now not so idyllic piece of countryside, safely back at Blue Skies House. Statements taken; strong drinks provided. Reginald, the only one of residents to see the body, particularly shaken. Ex-SAS Eddie, a man of few words, had assumed control after taking a look at the corpse. Calling the emergency services, ensuring that a decent distance was kept, and the crime scene remained secured. Amongst the bushes and trees it had been difficult to erect a tent to protect the victim and provide enough space for the examination to commence. Eddie's survival training proving useful. Forensics and medics were now inside, doing what forensics and medics do.

Griffin stood, hands in pockets, looking around the scene. The area eerily quiet, rustling amongst the undergrowth the prominent noise as everyone went about their assignments. It was noted with some envy that the forest rangers appeared better prepared with their thermos flasks. Rumour had it that there were sexual connotations. The unspoken fear being that Nash had struck and in doing so had upped the ante by some margin.

'It doesn't look like the usual body in the woods scenario,' Griffin said as Mantel and Nimra joined him. 'Most, as we all know are a quick drive out of town and low-and-behold they come across the forest. Pull over with all good intentions to take the body deep into the woods. Bottle it and dump it as quick as possible before wheel spinning back into town. Then they're surprised that we find the body so easily. This from all accounts was committed elsewhere, but they really did try to hide it. This is at least three hundred metres from the pub and the road. That's quite a carry or drag.'

'Yeh, the doc says sometime yesterday evening for time of death. He's going to come back with something more accurate,' Mantel replied. 'He thinks twenty something, female obviously, white. Raped then probably strangled.'

'Yeh. They didn't want this one found that's for sure. At least not as quick as we have. They hid it pretty well. Don't think they reckoned on our Reginald taking a pee here, especially him going in so deep to not be seen by the ladies,' Griffin said scuffing his shoes on the ground, dislodging twigs and leaves. 'If he's now murdering, it's unfortunately confirming my fears. We need to find Nash quickly.'

'We're checking with the identification of the body sir,' Nimra replied looking at her notepad, feeling extremely sorry for the lady as thoughts of her own attack flooded back. 'Nothing so far. No belongings probably disposed of them at the scene of the murder. It'll take prints to find out who she is. Interesting to see where she's from, she had an eastern European look about her.'

'At least this one's got fingers, remember that one where they'd been cut off and teeth removed. They identified him, nothing gets past those guys. Right, let's get on it and as they say on the telly, no stone unturned,' Griffin said making back towards the Cobblers car park where a makeshift operations unit had been set up. 'The murder guys will be here soon, and it will be out of our hands, but I want to be able to handover a watertight file. But before that let's get a drink, you look like you need one Nimra.'

'Yes, thanks. So, if it is Nash, he'll no longer be our case?' Nimra asked with more than a hint of disappointment in her question.

'Fraid so. It's all above my pay grade. The 'Murders 'R' Us' boys, or MIT to give it the current title, will take over all aspects and will be moving in. Very frustrating I know. So, as I said, you both make sure that your notes are up to date.'

'This is Deja fucking vu Lils,' Veronica said frantically serving customers. The pub's potholed car park filled to overflowing. The verges of the adjacent country roads dangerously jammed. A horse rider had already been in to complain and from experience Veronica expected more of the same. 'It doesn't take them long to get wind of it. I recognize a few of them from last year's fun and games.

The explosion and other events in and around the area had made The Cobblers a media focal point. Good for takings, if not a lot else. Today's discovery had already made the news. A media helicopter hovered. Journos and associated technicians, a thirsty bunch, convening in the pub.

'The vultures have re-landed,' Lily replied rushing around to stay ahead of demand 'I've asked the girls to come in and give us a hand.'

Veronica kicked at the near empty crisp boxes below the bar. 'Good idea, well done. With hindsight I should have stocked up with crisps,' Currently crisps and nuts, with the occasional bag of pork scratchings, being the extent of the pub's lunch menu. 'This ain't good news Lils. Like Mike. I'm very worried about Andy Nash.'

'I think we all are,' Lily replied with a concerned look over her shoulder at her boss and friend.

'Mike, nice surprise, just talking about you' Veronica said as the DI reached the end of the bar.

Griffin slid onto a stool. 'Just needed a pint to get my head round this,'

'Lucy, Nimra, twice in a week?' said Veronica greeting the detectives

'What will it be ladies?' Griffin asked as his pint was placed in front of him.

'White wine please boss,' Mantel said grabbing a vacant stool.

'Same please sir.'

Griffin pulled out a twenty-pound note and slapped his hands palm down flat on the bar in exasperation.

'On me,' Veronica said serving the ladies. 'We're looking to you guys to find him.'

'I can assure you Ron that we will get the bastard,' Mantel replied with a steely gaze.

'Yep, definitely,' Griffin said supping his pint. 'Every uniformed officer will be on the streets. Got a feeling that it is going to be a long night ahead for many. The boss has said she wants to see me, hence the pint. She's going to want news that I haven't got. Any crisps?'

*

'Yes ma'am. I quite understand. I can see how it looks,' Griffin said sitting is his boss's soleless office, much like most of the station, a space bereft of anything personal. 'I can assure you that I'm not withholding information.'

'There is no need for flippancy Inspector,' DCI Nicola Fairmead retorted in a rough Lancashire brogue.

'None intended ma'am. It's just that I can't tell you something that I don't know.'

'Intelligence on the street, you must have some. What's it saying?'

'The same as me.'

'There must be someone who knows something or someone,' Fairmead responded rising from her chair to her full five feet ten inches and moving over to a window that had a decent view of the forest, a rarity in this building. Strategically built to house terrorists in the late 1970s, dug into a hill to limit access. At a time when the health and wellbeing of those working in it figured low on the requirements. Many rooms without natural light. Those with failing to take advantage of the potential stunning vistas. For a police station in a leafy suburb, next to a stunning piece of green belt this development had managed to be an architectural cock-up of some proportions. 'Right, let's get back to this supposed secure psychiatric unit. I don't like what I hear about this Iain Swift's attitude. His boss, Jenny Roberts, you say that she's been helpful. Well not fucking helpful enough in my book. Uncle Rod, you're one hundred percent sure he's clean? Old mates, whoever they are, check them out again. I want results Inspector. I'm being harangued.'

Griffin looked on, reflecting on his boss's utterances; 'stating the bleeding obvious' sprang to mind. His encounters with his relatively new DCI had been both limited and generally at arm's length. Doing what needed to be done and what was asked of him. Fairmead came with a reputation as a no nonsense northerner. Humble beginnings, first to University from her family and all that. Worked the streets as a bobby in Lancashire, her home county. Then the sluice gates opened in the politically correct world of modern policing. The next few years for her must of felt like being in a kayak on the rapids as she sailed at speed through the ranks. Griffin could never fathom out why those promoted beyond DI rapidly forgot the basics as far as nicking criminals, and all that they had signed up for. If he ever got that extra pip on his shoulder Griffin was determined to stick with his principles. He hoped that this would not be long in coming. Next time an opportunity came up he would put himself forward, which wasn't on the table prior to Fairmead's arrival, and if he was honest he wasn't up for it at the time anyway. Griffin had heard that she was a stop gap appointment to replace the previously disgraced DCI and that she would not be around for long, at least he hoped so. She sought a move back up north, which would no doubt be found. Griffin pondered that if she were at least a little bit attractive it would give him something to fantasise about as she droned on. Angular, rake thin and an aggressive short haircut didn't tick any of his boxes.

'Yes ma'am, I'm on it. Is there anything else?'

Griffin metaphorically shrugged his shoulders as he jogged down the stairs to the sanctuary of his office, with no new ideas forthcoming, what else was he supposed to do other than what he was already doing?

CHAPTER ELEVEN

The Cobblers could have resided in inner city London, it had the feel of a traditional Eastend boozer, it was not what you would expect to find in a semi-rural setting. No thatch nor quirky nooks and crannies, a substantial cube of a brick built building. It had never been anything other than a public house, built as one in the late 1800s. Its ornate original cornices harboured smoke from generations of colourful history. Nicotine beige remained the prominent colour on the ceiling and walls. When built it would have been completely rural. A stopping point out of London, the stable block visible in sepia photographs long demolished. Detached from the then very small village by three quarters of a mile or so of largely farmland. The building that is now Blue Skies House and a few foresters' cottagers being its near neighbours, with St Vincent's Church up on the hill halfway between the town and the pub.

A considerable cellar for barrels of fine cask ales, and more than enough storage for the excess nuts and crisps, when ordered, spreading beneath. The steps down not the trickiest, but extreme care should be taken after a drink or two and certainly not with heels as Veronica can verify.

A substantial three-sided bar dominated the ground floor, with a small, cramped office tucked behind it. To the rear a spacious, largely redundant kitchen, its dated appliances rarely fired up, a sandwich buffet offered at a stretch. With such basic catering Veronica found it hard to fathom out the pub's popularity for wakes. Over three decades ago, long before being known as The Cobblers, The Bootmaker's Arms was a forerunner for quality pub meals. Patrons travelling from far and wide to sample their menu, an era without the internet and social media to spread the word. The redevelopment should see the return of culinary glory to the building.

Screens showing predominantly sports, horseracing in particular, a must have. An infrequently used dart board remains, memories of a team as distant as those of food, old trophies gather dust in a small cabinet. Tucked in a far corner a blast from the past, a popular bar billiards table. Somewhat surprisingly the pub has just the one equivalent of the old one-armed bandit. The locals, despite many being gamblers, voted to restrict them and that it be muted. A talking, drinking and watching sports establishment, with more than a hint of wheeler-dealing thrown in.

In the middle of the building a well-worn wooden staircase rose to the first floor. Here the living space, that Veronica has made little impression on in her time, awaits refurbishment. A tired kitchen stroke diner, basic bathroom and separate toilet, and three large and airy bedrooms, all with wonderful views. Spread across the front of the pub a substantial lounge. A beige carpet and large flat screen TV the only recent changes. The television prominent between two large sash windows looking out over the car park.

With the redevelopment the physicality would remain, but The Cobblers would disappear as an old fashioned boozer.

Barefooted and blouse untucked, with the pub safely locked up, Veronica carried two glasses and a bottle of Merlot into the lounge and placed them on the table. 'So, you decided against an all-nighter down the station,'

'Yep, decided that a change of environment would serve me better. Don't get me wrong the worker ants are hard at it,' Griffin replied, jacketless, tie thrown over the arm of a chair, perched on the edge of a sofa next to Veronica. 'We're waiting for lab reports that we should have first thing. No need to be a hero just sitting at your desk tapping away whilst falling asleep. This could be a long haul. Anyway I'm not in charge of the murder investigation.'

'Well as much as I'm pleased to see you here. It is a very worrying time for everyone.'

'I can totally understand that. But it would be extremely unusual for him to strike again so soon and so close. Cheers,' Griffin said taking his wine and settling back.

'Yes, cheers. Yeh, I suppose you're right, just that this can be a bit of a big, lonely place at times. Don't get me wrong it's great to come up her and shut the door after a busy session. It's just these are strange times,' Veronica replied pushing herself deep into the cushions clasping her glass.

'I'd love to say that I'd move in and keep guard, but I can't guarantee when I'd be here, and they'd probably be the times when you'd most want me,' Griffin said with genuine concern.

'Hey, look at us, so negative. You'll have him locked up tomorrow.'

'Here's hoping,' Griffin replied none too convincingly. 'Got to find the bastard first. Look what about Lily?'

'What about Lily?'

'Well she must feel the same at night. Alone in her flat isn't she? She must have the same thoughts as you.'

'You're right, what an excellent idea Inspector. Why didn't we think of that? No wonder you're a detective. I'll ask her in the morning, bit late to call now. Anyway, she's not alone tonight, off on one of her romantic liaisons with Bazzer at The Foresters. It would be good for both of us and wouldn't stop you visiting.'

'Exactly. So, that's hopefully sorted then.' Griffin clinked his glass with Veronica. 'I'd feel a lot better about it too.'

'Yes, it's a strange scenario. It's just not knowing where he is that is so scary. Fancy some crisps? I stashed a couple of packets away.' Veronica nipped downstairs to recover the last couple of packs she had set aside for herself, desperate for a delivery to arrive before re-opening. As Griffin checked his phone for any news, he contemplated Mantel's wise words at Chutney Ali's. If honest this was the prime reason for being here. He liked Veronica a lot and that troubled him. Unlike his day job, relationships did not come easy to him. His default to date was to make excuses to prevent it progressing, so much easier than confronting anything tricky. He knew that this had to change if he didn't want to lose her. It was time to pull up his big boy pants. There would not be a conveyor belt of Veronicas, he was extremely lucky to have found her. To let her go now would be foolish.

Veronica returned, lobbing a bag of salt and vinegar in Griffin's direction. 'There you go, don't say that I don't treat you. These are like gold dust.' The quietness of the night smashed by a couple of racers, possibly joyriders, tearing up The High Road beyond the windows. 'Wallies. So, come on, what else is news?'

'Well as you know a circus is coming to town.'

'A circus? Don't you mean a funfair?'

'Sorry, yes, minor difference.'

'What a bleeding big tent?'

'Okay, okay. Easy mistake. A funfair is coming to town, bringing with it waltzers, dodgems, coconut shy's and a spike in crime.'

'Oh, you kill joy. All those children so excited on the rides. And the candy floss.'

'Heaven for fucking pick-pocketers,' Griffin continued gesticulating at Veronica. 'The local oiks riding on the shirttails of the reputations of fairground workers and their gypsy backgrounds. Don't get me wrong travellers are often a law unto themselves, but they're not all bad. The locals rogues use it as an excuse to go on a petty crime spree.'

'We must remember that old adage that a goldfish is for life and not just a summer's evening. And don't forget the high quality prizes you might win whilst eating a dodgy hot dog. You're right a great night out will be had by all.'

'Exactly, as always you're so right. At least circuses don't come with quite the same baggage. They may be travellers of a kind, but they bring different beliefs. Maybe it's the artistic angle.'

Veronica finger licked the last morsel of crisp and put the empty packet on the table. 'And now animals are banned, circuses are just like a pop-up theatre show, circ-du-whatever in a tent.'

'That's a neat way of looking at them.'

'So, I take it you're not a fan of funfairs and won't be donning your 'kiss me quick' hat.'

'That's the seaside isn't it?'

'All the same in my book.'

Griffin, his crisps long gone, topped up their glasses. 'You don't sound much of a fan either. It's not going to help the Nash situation. Resources will have to be deployed in and around the fair, although I suppose they will be eyes and ears on the ground. All I'd say is prepare yourself for an influx of the local dregs.'

'So Inspector, you and your team are going to be busy bunnies,' Veronica said leaning back with her refreshed glass. 'Oh, and just to help your mood.'

'What mood? I'm not in a mood, far from it,' a playfully indignant Griffin replied.

'You know what I mean. Although this may change that. I overheard the Richards family talking in the bar with some excitement about the fair coming to town.'

'See, it's a fucking honeypot. The air will not only be filled with the aroma of fried onions. If they think we can enforce a smoking ban at these things, well...'

'Quite, and from what I could hear they're planning some sort of re-union, you know like that Friends Reunited, if that's still going.'

Griffin with a smile, took the landlady's glass and placed it back on the table. 'Enough. You're winding me up,' He pulled her towards him. 'It's time for us to have all the fun of the fair.'

CHAPTER TWELVE

'I thought this oh so fucking deep, dark, black web was meant to hold the secrets to everything. Only accessible to the great and dodgy. TV cops spend the whole show knocking on doors, then this dark web thing produces the answer, they lock 'em up and job fucking done,' Griffin exasperated and agitated exclaimed. His night of passion and the full English a distant memory as he looked at the report on his screen. 'They've told me that there's nothing specific on our Andy fucking Nash.'

'It's surprising,' Mantel replied standing alongside Nimra in the DI's office, both unsure as to how to respond without further agitating their boss. 'We can be pretty sure that the Andy Nash they've highlighted is him.'

'Oh yeh, it's him alright, there's a lovely fucking photo and profile. Oh, don't get me wrong it's very detailed. But according to this he's done nothing untoward on the internet, which in my book is a load of bollocks. I just don't believe it,' Griffin said turning from his screen.

'He must be using other identities boss,' Mantel replied, herself disappointed by the report. Nimra choosing to keep stum.

'Stating the bleeding obvious sergeant. I've got a boss going fucking ape upstairs. What I need is answers.'

'Sorry, yes, you're right boss,' Mantel responded immediately annoyed with herself for not offering something constructive. In this mood the boss did not need aggravating, and pacifying was not in his dictionary. Generally when he called her sergeant she knew that the touch paper was lit. She needed to be pro-active. What to do though? 'Right I'll get back onto them, there may be another level.'

'You do that. Get onto it now, then powder your nose or whatever you do, then we're off,' Griffin said turning back to his screen and calling up personnel files as Mantel left the room. Nimra turned to join her, eager to leave. 'Now Nimra, best behaviour today please and get some information for me please.'

'Yes sir, I'll try,' the DC replied edging out of the office.

'Hang on guys,' Griffin said appearing at his door as Nimra made to leave for the ladies. 'They're saying that they've got nothing to say it's Nash. Early doors, but at the moment it's DNA free which is a right fucker, so there's even more reason for everyone to be extra vigilant and for us to find the bastard.'

*

DC Nimra Shimra could not help herself grinning despite the boss's tantrum. The ladies in the locker room were envious, and she was happy to be the focus of their envy. An away day with Detective Constable Kevin Henshall to the Rotherfield secure psychiatric unit to re-interview the staff would not be an arduous task. Henshall being the most recent arrival at the station on his promotion into the ranks of detective. Previously a bobby in rural Yorkshire, now assigned to DI Griffin to bolster his team. The son of a Nottinghamshire farmer, the 27-year-old was a brute of a man. 6' 6" and just as wide, currently in possession of the No. 8 jersey in the British Police rugby union team. His arrival yesterday at Forest Edge station caused a social media frenzy, anguish in Yorkshire, anticipation in the suburbs. His first day should have been a whirlwind, with a murder coming so early in his placement, however, HR ensured that he was embroiled in procedure.

Griffin was more than happy to take the rugby player under his wing, pleased to have adopted such a highly regarded young officer, teaming him with Nimra early on gave him the opportunity to ask the questions that he wouldn't ask of him. Nimra more than happy to oblige, promising her colleagues that she would handle him carefully as she left the locker room. The 'me-too movement' alive and kicking, the males seeking protection.

Blue eyed and single with a reputation of being the perfect English gentleman, not a bad word could be heard of him, although on the rugby field it was a different matter. Crossing the white line Kevin Henshall was one of the most ferocious players to don the shirt. Fair but brutal was the consensus. Nimra calculated that the drive there and back to the unit would give her a head start over the competition in the station.

*

Mantel sipped at her warm soya milk and looked out through the windscreen as two wipers intermittently swiped over to dismiss the mizzle. 'It's days like these that surveillance in a dry car seems like bliss.'

'Yeh, those poor buggers are going to be soaked through.'

Mantel relieved that her boss had calmed down continued to stare out of the window. 'Comes with the territory I suppose.'

Ahead of Griffin and Mantel the Fun Fair had come to town, albeit at this stage looking like a half completed oversized Meccano set in a dodgy caravan park. They looked on as the weather failed to inhibit the determination to get the show on the road. A well-oiled machine coupled with well-rehearsed procedures resulting in swift progress.

'They certainly earn their crust,' Griffin said with cup in hand also gazing ahead, knowing that although they were in an unmarked car their presence would have been clocked, as he hoped.

Parked in an adjoining car park that belonged to the pay-as-you-play golf course that threaded through the forest, the detectives had a panoramic view of the soon to be fairground. This site on the edge of the forest had been a venue for circuses and funfairs for as long as anyone can remember. In recent years a tarmacked site, a car park for forest visitors the rest of the year, ensuring that the rain was not a concern, many a summer's festivities previously ruined by a quagmire. This piece of the forest was at one end of a large open plain, where history had it that in the late 1500s Queen Elizabeth came to watch hunting. A lodge was built on the hill for her to view the activities; memories are patchy as to whether she made an appearance. Tourists still visited the Hunting Lodge and model aircraft enthusiasts and fans of drones, rather than hunters made use of the plain.

One could only be impressed by the industriousness of the travellers, shirking certainly not on the agenda. 'I take it the youngsters have moved their home tutoring to be able to give a hand,' Griffin said dryly.

'Would you believe this, someone was telling me that just a couple of years back they saw elephants out there when a circus came to town,' Mantel said getting a little bored.

With the mention of elephants, having finished his coffee, Griffin sparked into action pulling his seat belt across. 'Right, enough of here for now. They're here. We know they're here and they know we know. Let's see how it goes. Probably serenely, without even a caution,' Griffin said pointing towards the sky out of his windscreen. 'Hey, look that's not a remote-controlled plane it's one of your flying elephants.'

Mantel drained the last of her soya milk. 'Here we go boss, look who's turned up,'

A battered white transit deposited Richards senior and his three boys into the middle of the site, the four of them immediately embraced by workers they were obviously familiar with. 'They haven't wasted any time. We'll leave them to it. Make sure that uniform are aware that they've made an early appearance.'

'Will do. Tell you what boss, it might cause too much aggro, but wouldn't it be worth a look round the caravans. If Nash was looking for a hiding place. Well...'

'Great minds Luce,' Griffin replied starting the engine.' I've only once before instigated a search of a fair ground camp and it was a complete nightmare. Sticking a stick into a hornet's nest would have been more pleasant. We need to think of a subtle way to approach it if we do. At the moment we've no tangible reason and they will let us know that. As you know they are some of the savviest people you'd meet. We need a link, a reason, something to justify a search. Although if I'm honest I don't think this lot would house a convicted rapist, at least knowingly and I don't think Nash would fancy being found by them.'

*

The sun had won over the drizzle in their morning struggle. It was now a wonderful warm and still day. The River Thames didn't appear to acknowledge this as it flowed powerfully through central London. At its source in England's deepest glorious countryside you would not believe that it could turn into this roaring, uncontrollable torrent, making its way impatiently towards the North Sea. Baring its teeth in the capital where it was never a millpond. The closest it got to being placated was when parts of it froze over in Victorian times.

Sat in an up-market restaurant right beside this intriguing beast of nature, Veronica and her brother watched the people on or around it. Their view was from the South Bank, the still towering St Pauls Cathedral dominating the vista, framed by two of the many elegant road bridges that spanned the river. Walking to the restaurant they had passed a myriad of attractions, food vendors with cuisines from around the world, mime artists and jugglers, and down on the riverbank a tussle between sand artists as to who should get the best pitch. With the shared lamb dish ordered Veronica and Stephen enjoyed their gin and tonics and the crusty bread with a balsamic dip. The tables edging onto the tow path and the river beyond were well bid and the envy of the passers-by and were themselves an attraction. A more eclectic mix of humans on the planet you would be unlikely to find passed them by. Tourists, businesspeople and locals; it was hard to differentiate, the pace of their stride possibly the only indicator.

'This is wonderful, there's not enough places like it right on the Thames,' Veronica said. 'You've obviously been before.'

Stephen gave his shades a wipe on his white linen napkin. 'A couple of times.'

'You're certainly not going to be starved of people watching and St Pauls looks majestic.'

'Sort of place Dan would have loved. He'd have been in his element out here.'

'Absolutely,' Veronica replied allowing herself thoughts of her late father. Dan was their dad, well sort of. No, he wasn't an 'uncle', a friend of the family sort of acquaintance. He was their adopted father, once removed. Veronica as a toddler, and Stephen were adopted. Sadly, their adopted father died young. A few years passed and along came a replacement in the guise of Dan Hawkins. A man with no children that he admitted to or knew of. Veronica and Stephen were either in or approaching their informative years, and far from being awkward, a great guy entered their lives, someone they respected and who would be a positive influence. He was funny, caring and generous, even if he was absent a fair amount. Showering them with gifts and taking them on trips, all of which were great fun. They never wanted for anything. A real plus was he always had a cool car. Potentially sensitive moments when growing up were always handled in the right way. Boyfriends did not bring the anguish that could be expected. In Veronica and Stephen's case this applied to both of them. Dan being a man of staunch right wing opinions, Stephen had severe reservations about 'coming out'. He need not have worried, the whole transition, simply slotted into normal day to day life. Their great relationship continued, if not thrived. Stephen's partners were welcomed the same as Veronica's. In fact, in a couple of cases better, as even Veronica admitted that she did date some dodgy geezers. As they moved into adulthood and became a little more perceptive, they came to realise that Dan, as they called him, did not hold down a run of the mill, nine to five job. However, whatever direction his careers adviser at school had pointed him in it was a lucrative one. It was not for them to question where he worked nor what he did. When the time came he supported them in their chosen jobs; Veronica working in several pubs across the county, and Stephen developing a niche in multi-media marketing, never being anything but encouraging.

A decade ago, life changed. A boozy family Sunday lunch interrupted by the police. Dan was taken away and never returned. Initially on remand and then committed for a variety of offences. The trial exposed him as a modern-day gangster; robbery, corruption, GBH, you name it he did it. This time he was sent down for a lengthy stretch. Foreshortened a few years back when he suffered a fatal heart attack, dying in prison. Their adopted mother continued to enjoy a healthy lifestyle, albeit continually glancing over her shoulder as to when their assets may be seized.

Allegedly Dan Hawkins was a fence in the gold heist at the Spanish bank and he found a way to tip off Veronica and her brother as to its whereabouts. These details proved to be extremely dubious, the gold proving elusive, although not before Veronica had established herself as the landlady of The Cobblers. As no association between Hawkins and Veronica was ever made, Veronica could have moved away from The Cobblers without any questions being asked, however, having put down some roots, she enjoyed running the pub and there was her then fledgling relationship with Griffin to consider, so she decided to continue as Veronica Edwards, an adopted persona. Her background was and still is unknown to all, including Griffin, her CV being a little sketchy on the personal detail front.

Veronica could visualise her adopted playboy father taking a seat, removing his Panama hat, ordering a strong drink and thoroughly enjoying this wonderful table on a terrace overlooking the Thames. She retained fond memories, despite him being an absolute rogue.

'I reckon he'd have had the dover sole,' Stephen said.

'Off the bone.'

'Absolutely. We should order a good French wine in his memory.'

'Good idea, maybe a Chateau Neuf du Pape and get these topped up while you're about it,' Veronica said holding up an empty glass. 'You've got fingers in all sorts of tech pies Stephen and know a lot of people in those fields.'

'Yep, suppose so. Why?'

'Well this Andy Nash. Chatting with Mike over breakfast this morning he was all excited because his tech guys were going to tell him where Andy featured in this dark web thing. He then called me on the way up here to say that they'd found nothing, he was extremely pissed off, probably as much as I've ever heard him.'

Stephen ordered a couple of drinks and the wine list from an attentive waiter. 'That's surprising The police are regarded as some of the best in that field. Usually there's something on everyone with a conviction, especially as bad his.'

'So, you reckon there could, or in fact should be something?'

Stephen held his hands up. 'Look sis, I don't know, it's a weird place to go especially if you go a bit deeper. The first level is becoming the norm as more and more people access it. You need to delve much, much deeper these days.'

'What like Mickey Flannagan when he's going on a proper night out, he goes, out, out?'

'Quite.'

'Could you have a look for me? I'd owe you one.'

'No promises but leave it with me. I'll need some more information though.'

'I haven't mentioned it yet, but I'm sure Mike will be up for it. He's tearing his hair out at the moment and I don't want that, I mean, what would I run my fingers through.'

'Please sis far too much detail.'

'And his boss is nagging him.'

'As I said, leave it with me. Right, let's order this wine.'

*

'That was superb Stephen. Thank you,' said a well lubricated Veronica under the refurbished Blackfriars Station. 'Need to make up a bed for Lily, it's our first night protecting each other. And you will look into that dark, dark web stuff for me please.'

'Sis, as I said, leave it with me. Safe journey and love to Lily, must go my train's due.' Stephen pecked his sister on her cheek and tottered up the steps to his platform, cursing himself. Why had he led his sister to believe that he was such a computer guru? Yes, he was successful in media marketing, but the dark, dark web, was a no, no, no. He was just a normal guy, within a world where he was perfectly happy. He couldn't let her down, but where to start. This task was so alien to him. He boarded his busy train, standing room only. Gazing at his fellow passengers, he was no different to any of them, so why had he promoted himself beyond his station. Who was he to be advising his sister on matters that frankly he had little or no knowledge of. Social media, home shopping, streaming and music that was about his limit. Oh, and spread sheets, train timetables, and restaurant searches, but not convicted rapists and their chums posting lurid details. The thought alone churned his stomach. He scrolled his contacts. Who will know about this dark, dark web? Who could he trust? Bobby? Now he was broad minded, filthy at times, harmless banter though. No, he was far too nice. Richie, no, or did he?

Frankie, unknown but reliable when asked for anything. Would she be offended if asked? What if they were all on it? Was he the black sheep? Nothing new in that. Discreet, anonymous forums, they're the answer. But wait, get into those and can you get out? Questions breeding questions. Would he need a new identity; e-mail, social media accounts, one of those phones that you cannot be traced to. Those that are on every cop show. A 'burner' that's it. Stephen's mind raced along a tangent, reinventing himself as a private detective, a super sleuth. Would Amazon sell Deerstalker hats? The train rumbled on through the suburbs. Perhaps rather than covert he should go overt? Raise it as a normal question down the pub. 'Anyone been on the dark, dark web recently?' 'Oh yeh, do all my shopping there.' He looked around the carriage where his fellow passengers gazed at their phones. Were they on the dark, dark web? He needed to come clean with his sister. He was a fraud. He couldn't though. His pride and ego, two traits that he did have, must be upheld. As must his relationship with his sister, the only person in the world that he really trusted and loved, and of course his adopted mum. He had to delve into this murky world. He would devise a plan. He needed to sober out and get his act together. He could not let his sister down. He would start as soon as he got home. Maybe after a nap.

CHAPTER THIRTEEN

A trip into the inner sanctuary at St Vincent's was a recent addition in the Blue Skies House's social diary, initiated by the Rev. Mandy Jarvis as part of her drive to make the church more inclusive. She regarded the efforts of the previous incumbent, Henry Wilton-Brook, if that was his real name, as somewhat tardy. In her opinion, during his ten years he had let St Vincent's slip. Now de-robed, so his title withdrawn, Wilton-Brook appeared to have used the facilities; church, vicarage, and village hall, to fulfil personal preferences, rather than in a manner expected of him. Congregation numbers had remained reasonably healthy and this kept his superiors at bay, however, scrutiny had since revealed that this was largely down to free wine, coke, fizzy variety, and crisps at the Sunday Services. More of the budget was spent at the local wine merchant than on much required maintenance, ensuring that his personal cellar in the vicarage was well stocked. Mandy more than thankful of his decision to leave this when he made his hasty, unexplained departure.

Other than Sundays the church and its adjoining hall were rarely used, of most surprising was the lack of wedding services. A 200-year-old picturesque church in a leafy surround, an idyllic setting for any photo album, should be in demand. It appeared that Wilton-Brook regarded weddings as too much hassle and if anything discouraged them. What he had developed, in fact re-introduced, was a key cutting service. Repairing and bringing back to life a hundred and twenty-year-old piece of machinery housed in the crypt, he offered free key cutting to parishioners. On Mandy's arrival she discovered a smart cupboard with a vast selection of what she assumed to be duplicate keys, and a large quantity of a fine single malt whisky. Not one for unnecessary paperwork, she disclosed neither, the keys dumped and the whisky, the source of which remained a mystery, she would share with her flock. As key cutting did not float her boat, the service was closed, the machine redundant in the crypt.

Whereas Wilton-Brook kept the church locked up, it would be open-house during the new vicar's tenure. Encouraging the locals to pop in, making herself available when not otherwise engaged. Regular coffee mornings and school visits were proposed. These would include brass-rubbing and a history of the church. Mandy had already worked on an enlightening script that would keep the students interested. Weddings were actively sought; a couple of bookings already taken. Her sermons were upbeat and popular, only cheerful hymns were sung. The free refreshments on Sunday's had ceased, obeying an order from above that she had to stop turning the budget into wine. The stash of scotch and the overflowing supplies of wine in the vicarage meant that Mandy was still able to entertain freely. A popular friendly addition to the parish, Mandy's arrival was regarded as a positive move. A fresh honest face, her initial ideas enthusiastically received, and her future plans eagerly anticipated. Rumours of her past adding to her alluring character.

Today Mandy was supplementing the brass-rubbing with a couple of tots of the malt and a brief history of those laid to rest in the crypt. 'So, ladies and gentlemen gather round please,' Mandy announced in her best Cassock, a robe that she liked to wear over her naked body, along with her favourite just over the knee black leather boots. Assembled ahead of her four residents, plus Prisha chaperoning and the now ever-present discreet security, ex-SAS Eddie once again on duty. Mandy and Prisha had struck up quite a friendship in the short time the vicar had been in residence. Regularly meeting up, Prisha fascinated with Mandy's previous career. The reverend deciding that after the visit from the police it was bound to be common knowledge sooner rather than later. The fact that Prisha's best friend, Nimra, was one of those who called made it a no-brainer. The three of them enjoying sharing their dalliances over a bottle or two from the cellar. 'So, as I believe you are all aware this is our largest and oldest tomb, Lord Hall's, the prominent landowner back in the 1800s. He who built Blue Skies House. It was in part his family money that got the church built, so it's the Hall family who I should be thankful to for this job. At the time they had the foresight to have this crypt built or Lord Hall won't have had a place for his impressive tomb. And it was his family that had the secret tunnel built which I will tell you more about later. Now who's next?'

'Is that where you and your copper had a shag?' Prisha whispered standing close to Mandy nodding towards Lord Hall's resting place. Mandy smiled and moved on to the next tomb.

The party progressed around the expansive crypt built into the hill upon where St Vincent's majestically stood, Mandy thriving on delivering these tales of the past that Google had so kindly provided.

'Now ladies, and gentleman, our last tomb,' Mandy said with a personal smile in Eddie's direction, as they reached the furthest corner. 'This is Egbert Penn, the church's very first Warden, who apparently still inspects the church on Saturday nights to ensure...' The already limited light dimmed. A door could be heard slamming somewhere above them. There was a gasp and even ex-SAS Eddie at the back of the gathering, felt a little uneasy.

'Anyone got a 50p for the meter?' Mandy joked turning back to the tomb as the lighting dropped another notch. 'Now as I was saying, our Egbert...'

The lid of the tomb started to lift. Everyone froze. Ex-SAS Eddie blurted out, 'fucking hell'. The ladies screamed.

The haunting laughter of Vincent Price in Michael Jackson's Thriller emanated from the tomb. Faces changed from horror to disbelief. Mandy burst into laughter as the lights slowly returned to normal.

'Oh Mandy, you devil,' Margaret said laughing. 'I nearly wet myself.'

'Don't think you were the only one Margaret. You should have seen Eddie at the back, his face was a picture. I wish I'd taken one. Don't think his SAS training covered this. You okay Eddie?'

Eddie smiled, raising an embarrassed hand.

'You are such a tease,' Prisha said. 'There could have been a heart attack.'

'Oh shit, I didn't think of that. That would have taken the edge off it?'

'All's fine though, so come on we all want to know how you did it?' Nimra asked with everyone looking intently at the vicar.

Mandy explained her love for practical jokes, particularly when she could use the skills gained getting a First in Electrical Engineering. This was going to be her chosen career; electrics not practical jokes, before being lured into the lucrative world of up-market prostitution. She showed them the wi-fi device she had been holding that controlled the lights, sounds and the raising of the lid, Mandy's piece de resistance. Extending her skill set to carpentry and the hinged bit of plywood was particularly rewarding.

'So, as you can see, all pretty simple stuff, I'm so glad you enjoyed it,' the Vicar concluded still smiling. 'Sorry, but you were my guinea pigs. I now intend to use it on school visits. But I must ask you if, like the ending of The Mousetrap, to please keep it a secret. I'm going to be asking this of everyone, although asking school kids to keep stum, well, we'll see. Enough of our Egbert Penn, now for the secret tunnel, this way please.'

'Does he haunt the church?'

'You'll have to take a visit to the nave on a Saturday night to find that out.'...

CHAPTER FOURTEEN

Griffin's office had shrunk, at least it appeared that way as his enlarged team arrived for the morning briefing. Normally an incremental body would not have made this sort of difference, however, even a smarmy estate agent would struggle with the term 'spacious' when you wheel in the equivalent of a port-a-loo in the form of DC Kevin Henshall, who, like many big lumps, was conscious of his size in enclosed spaces. Nicking a blagger or in a scrum on the rugby field his size had many plus points, Griffin considered whether this was the true meaning of the phrase, 'an elephant in the room' as his new DC slipped into a corner of his office beside a grey filing cabinet hoping to not be so noticeable, an impossible task.

'Okay, let's get going with this. I'm not expecting too much,' Griffin announced turning from his desk. 'Off you go Nimra,'

'Okay, well it was an interesting trip.'

'I bet it was,' Mantel smiled.

Nimra resisted a grin, flicking open her notebook. Henshall doing likewise, leaning his pad on top of the tall cabinet. 'As you say whether we gleaned anything new I'm not so sure, let's start with Andy Nash. First thing I've got written down here is cute.'

'Did you say cute or...'

'Yes Luce you heard right,' Nimra continued. 'A pretty universal view. Obviously, they all knew what he'd done and they sort of have to brush that to one-side. They take that as read. This is their opinion within the confines of their workplace. They saw cute as a reference to how he probably committed his crimes.'

'Yeh, yeh, replace cute with conniving bastard. He wasn't just cute though, was he? More appropriate is what Lucy thought she'd heard you say,' an agitated Griffin responded. 'What a load of do-goody crap trap. What else did they say?'

Nimra scoured her notes. 'Pathetic also came up a few times. And more poignantly, little remorse, if any.'

'Self-egotistical one of them called him,' Henshall chipped in. 'Which from reading his file seemed to sum him up.'

'Yes, interestingly, most felt that he was absolutely no threat to them,' Nimra continued. 'Which they regarded as pretty normal.'

'Yeh, just as Prisha didn't see the bastard as a threat at Blue Skies House. You've got to be so careful with blokes like him.' Mantel had venom in her voice. 'What he says bears absolutely no relation to his thoughts or actions.'

'Quite, but, there's a but.'

Griffin now eager to press on. 'And the but is?'

'They felt he was always hiding something. That they weren't getting the whole Andy Nash. Even the way he would patronizingly say thank you for everything. Now many of those we questioned were on the side-lines, no direct involvement. Others though, were primed to observe, and they have regular observation meetings, as they call them. Now we didn't meet with Roberts nor Swift, but we heard that Roberts certainly valued these observations.'

'Well at least that makes some sense,' Mantel responded. 'See if they are any different when off camera, away from the counselling, with their guard down.'

'When you say hiding something,' Griffin probed, intrigued. 'Literally or emotionally?'

'Both,' Henshall replied. 'That he was always in second gear and that there was more to come.'

'It sounds like they believe he has something left in the tank.'

'Certainly sounded that way to us,' Henshall replied glancing for Nimra's agreement.

'Agreed, they felt he was playing the game and saying what he was expected to say.'

'Well that follows on from his statement, where there was little remorse. He apportioned blame elsewhere where convenient. So, in conclusion their opinion of Andy Nash was?' Griffin asked looking towards Nimra and Henshall.

'A cunning fucking nutter,' Henshall replied to which Griffin and Mantel showed surprise. 'Sorry, their views, although I do share them.'

'Yep, as Kevin says, those were their words,' Nimra continued. 'Most of those we spoke with were great to chat to, very open and forthright. Remember they work in a very specific, difficult environment. There are no prizes for not saying how they see it, especially when asked in confidence by police officers. So yep, as you've said many times sir, they thought he was a fucking nutter.'

'So not as leftie as I thought, perhaps I done them a disservice. I hope their honesty continued in a similar vein when they gave you their views on Roberts and our Iain Swift,' Griffin responded. 'Before that, to conclude, Andy Nash, there was nothing different to what we already knew? No other tasty bits of gossip you'd like to share, like a postcode where he's holding out?'

'Fraid not sir.'

Yearning for some caffeine Griffin realised that the meeting was bereft of any refreshments but decided against interrupting the flow. 'Onto the boss then, Jenny Roberts. What did they make of her?'

'Wet,' Henshall said. 'Some acknowledged that she was a good psychiatric nurse, but certainly not all of them.'

'Meaning?'

'A fucking shit manager,' Nimra interjected. Henshall unable to suppress a smile as Nimra held up her notepad. 'Again their words.'

'Hey, you two have really hit it off, I like the dovetailing, quite a double act, you rehearse this? You could be the force's answer to Little and Large,' Griffin smiled. 'I know you wouldn't Nimra, but it's good to see you not sitting on the fence Kevin.'

'We're just quoting what they said sir,' Nimra said continuing to point at her notepad. 'Only Romero, her PA, was not quite as damning.'

'Understandable.'

'By the way sir, who are Little and Large?' Nimra enquired.

'Seventies comedy act,' Henshall said. ' The Ant and Dec of their time.'

'Thank you Kevin, although very different in my book.'

'Was there anything else said about Roberts?' Mantel asked. 'I never shone to her, a bit of a two faced bitch in my book.'

'Not really,' Henshall said. 'Most felt that the place was an administrative disaster. Pissed off with her failure to deal with the issues that had an impact on their own roles. Couldn't see how she ever got the job.'

'The plus for them, it seemed to us, was that although they had no respect for her as a manager, they weren't going to complain and upset what was a very cosy lifestyle. We took a look at the attendance records and you would think that Rotherfield was the epi-centre for flu.'

'Did you get the feeling that they blamed Roberts for Nash absconding?

'Not directly, but they weren't surprised. Got many comments about how ludicrous security was the day me and Luce visited, compared to the norm. Some saying that they thought a patient doing a bunk was inevitable what with the lack of security and poor management.'

'Did you get to question the blond bombshell?' Mantel enquired. 'Doubt whether a big strong boy like him gets flu. And what was Romero like.'

'Romero was disappointing, the voice not matching the expectation.'

'Nimra needed a cold flannel after our chat with Anton, your blond bombshell,' Henshall responded.

'Moving on,' Griffin said shaking his head. 'Right, our friend, Mr Iain Swift. Please proceed my dynamic duo.'

The two detectives smiled, looked at each other and nodded. During their trip they had struck up a friendship, intrigued by their contrasting backgrounds before becoming police officers. 'I don't think that I've ever heard someone so disliked and it was across the board,' Nimra said. 'And Romero, well he virtually spat his words out.'

'Confirming that he's not a very nice person,' Griffin responded. 'Something that I think we'd already ascertained.'

'Well yes, but this view was from everyone. How he is so open with the porn is what really upset a lot of them. And that's both sexes,' Henshall said. 'He doesn't seem to have any respect for the unit or those who work there.'

'They all hope that he gets moved on soon.'

'What about his relationship with Nash?' Griffin asked, not sure what was being gained by the ongoing character assignation of someone they all agreed to be a bit of a wanker.

'Unprofessional, was a pretty universal feeling,' Nimra replied.

Henshall shifted uneasily feeling a little discomfort at being wedged in the corner. 'They would certainly not trust him.'

'What in his job, as a line manager or as a psychiatric nurse?'

'All of those and they all seemed to find him far too self-assured and as I said not to be trusted.'

*

Ellie Richmond slumped onto one of the two very comfy black leather sofas in their apartment, having slipped off her jacket and kitten heels. 'Phew-wee,'

'Cuppa?'

'Yes please. And a biccy?'

'Coming up.'

'That was fun.'

'Yes, and you looked great. Bump, what bump?'

'Not so bad yourself.'

'I'll rustle up some 50s dance music to keep the mood going.'

'Only if you don't expect me to dance anymore.'

Ellie and Rod had spent the previous afternoon rummaging in the local charity shops in search of dance hall gear for this afternoon's dance at Blue Skies House. Residents donning their original outfits where waistlines permitted. Flared skirts and pencil ties. Beehives, although not a duck's arse in sight. Prisha ensured that the ballroom looked the part. With the heavy drapes pulled tight to block out the afternoon sun, the lighting and glitterball stored in the basement for such occasions really set it off. Pete, generally known as a local artist, brought his own decks and a vast collection of 45s. Long Tall Sally, Mack the Knife, All Shook Up and many more rocked the retirement home. With staff encouraged to join in, a party was had. The licensed bar ensured that any stiff limbs were quickly loosened. Once again Robbie, the chef, proved the catch of the afternoon. Belying his physical stature with a jive that brought the house down. He was one of the few males with enough hair for a bouffant. Sally the Sous Chef's turn with Trevor in his immaculate teddy boy outfit, would have received maximum marks.

Ellie and Rod cut the mustard and despite being heavily pregnant, Ellie covered the floor with some style. In her official capacity as Head of Nursing and unofficially, the shoulder to cry on, Ellie was probably the favourite of most in Blue Skies. Affectionately known as Matron, Ellie had been at the Home since it opened its doors. Previously a top nurse at the local A&E, this was a dream move, the perfect time to move away from mainstream nursing. Never married, devoting herself to her nursing career, Ellie had just passed the big four zero. The journey to here was not without pitfalls. A few months back a series of events nearly jeopardized her position. Some of which became very public and difficult to handle. Ironically, in reflection, aspects of this period brought her considerable sympathy. Being a private lady, Ellie had found many of the emotions hard to cope with and still harboured many memories. In particular, for Benny 'BJ' Johnson, the previous owner with whom she had an out of character affair, wooed by his considerable charms. Only for this to be literally blown to bits when BJ was killed in the catastrophic explosion. As a consequence it was revealed that she was not alone in being a mistress of his. Worse was that this was disclosed to her by his widow, Julie, who found it in her heart to forgive and forget. Ending in tears for the shallow Julie Johnson when she was arrested for her part in the blast and the killing of her husband, along with a catalogue of other misdemeanours. She now resided on a remand wing awaiting her trial at the Old Bailey alongside ex-DCI Countney, one of her many bi-sexual conquests. For Ellie, this unwanted upheaval of her life led to her liaison with Rod. The rest as they say is history. With the new owner on board tranquillity had returned to Blue Skies House. Although for Ellie some difficult memories remained, possibly scarring her for life.

'Tell you what, that new vicar, Mandy isn't it, she's certainly getting around, as they say. Bit of a mover.'

'Yes, she's very popular. I really like her,' Ellie replied. 'It's great that were filming Alice and Robbie doing their jive. I didn't see that coming from Alice, she's normally so straight laced. Put it on YouTube and it will go viral.'

'Viral? Sounds nasty.'

'Oh, you dinosaur. That means millions would have watched it. Could earn a few bob.'

'Well if I tried what Robbie did you'd need smelling salts and a crane to get me up,' Rod said grimacing then smiling, having served Ellie tea and biscuits, he prised off his winkle pickers. 'That's better. Wonder of modern science how Robbie managed it with his gut.'

'You're just jealous. Anyway, you didn't do so bad yourself,' Ellie replied dunking a digestive. 'I need to pop back to the house later for a meeting.'

What Ellie, Rod and their fellow be-boppers had failed to notice was a face at a window watching the dancing.

*

'Fuck the good weather,' Griffin said hands thrust in his trousers pockets.

'Sorry boss?' Mantel asked beside her DI.

'If it was pissing down, even freezing cold, none of this would have happened.'

'Oh, I see,' Mantel replied her arms crossed. 'Fair weather yobs.'

'I wonder what they do when it's pissing down?' Nimra pondered.

'Wanking probably,' Griffin retorted. 'Whilst looking at that deep dark fucking web.'

'The guys will be happy,' Mantel continued. 'Hasn't been a lot of double bubble for a while.'

'Well worth it,' Griffin replied cynically. 'It's no tea party out there having a fucking Molotov lobbed at you.'

'Does this happen every year sir, don't remember it last year. I mean I'd have been in the thick of it,' Nimra pondered. 'Maybe I was away.'

'I assume you didn't go to Southend Nimra?'

'Ayia Napa actually. Why Southend?'

'Sorry a bit of reminiscing. Southend-on-Sea, on the Thames estuary with a dodgy view of the North Kent refineries. Home to the world's longest pier. And here's a bit of trivia, they used to run old tube trains up and down the pier.'

'I'll remember to make a note of that boss for Ronni's next quiz,' Mantel replied looking curiously at her DI. 'But with due respect, what the fuck has Southend got to do with this?'

'Mods and rockers. Before my time, definitely yours, been in loads of films and plenty of books. And it wasn't just Southend, Margate and Brighton also suffered, mainly on Bank Holidays for some reason.'

'I know the mods, they used to go round on scooters, like the ones that are trendy now,' Nimra remarked pleased to have recently read a book that mentioned them.

'Correct, top of the class. Good to see someone with a bit of historical knowledge. The very same ones that are being used for raids around the posh streets of London's West End. But yes, there were massive gang rivalries. In Southend they used to meet near the Kursal on the front.'

'The Kursal?'

'Ironically, a funfair in Southend. An old mate of mine, his dad owned it, told a tale of someone with a machete in his head wandering up the promenade on a Friday night.'

'Lovely.'

'Legendary those mods and rockers,' Griffin replied. 'Unlike these wimps.'

Ahead of the three detectives their uniformed colleagues, in full riot gear, attempted to placate those involved in the fisty-cuffs that had inexplicably broken out at the funfair. At least fifty officers had arrived in mini-buses, having been on stand-by in nearby streets since late afternoon, responding to intelligence that there may be trouble in the pipeline.

Low-life from the estates decided that a teatime trip out to antagonize easily wound-up fairground workers would be fun. Tooling themselves with petrol laden cocktails. Griffin always wondered where they got these from, they're not something you kept in your larder in anticipation of a riot, or did you? Many highly flammable cuddly toys had already been destroyed in the fracas. Keeping a safe distance, Griffin, Mantel and Nimra looked on as the confrontation played out in front of them. Many of those involved were well past their youthful days. Remnants of the good old football hooligans from the late seventies who you would have hoped to have matured with age. The footage from the police cameras would be a thugs 'who's who' from all our yesterday's. There wouldn't be many surprises in the custody suite. The Richards family had been spotted having their version of a good time helping out the fairground workers. The only members of the general public left were those rubbernecking, many filming in the hope that the media may pick it up.

'So boss, what's next?' Mantel asked. 'Doesn't look like there's much for us here.'

'Where's Kevin?' Griffin enquired.

Nimra got out her phone. 'He went to have a closer look, I'll give him a call, bollocks no signal. Oh here he is.'

A stressed DC came to a halt after running over from the fair. 'You should come with me boss.'

*

A cordon had been formed around the coconut shy. The fighting easing as the 'Black Mariahs' as Griffin fondly remembered them, carted off those they could collar. The four detectives were at the back, behind the coconuts that remained firmly wedged into their stands. The brown hessian, military style fabric sheeting that formed a backdrop cocooning them. Amongst the folds the body of a young lady.

'Who found her?' Griffin asked crouching. 'I doubt whether their CCTV would have picked up anything, but who knows. And that's if she was here in the first place, which I very much doubt. I reckon whoever did this wanted her found, they like the publicity. Who knows, let's wait for forensics.'

'A dog found her, some sort of terrier, its owner was filming the fighting, trying to get some different angles whilst keeping out of the way. He's in the bus over there,' Henshall replied pointing to one of the many fortified police mini-buses. 'He came and found a uniform who I happened to be talking to.'

'I'm taking it you rang it in?'

'Yep, I was on it straight away. In fact here they are,' A couple of heads and two hands brandishing warrant cards appeared round the sheeting...

...'The real bummer with this is that there will be even more of the murder boys and girls taking over the station. And worse, the Old Stool's going to be rammed,' Griffin said referring to the station's local, as he walked with his team back to their cars, a police helicopter hovering overhead and a media one buzzing around. The disturbance had been quelled when heavy-handed, no-nonsense tactics were deployed as soon as it became a murder scene. An enormous police presence now swarmed over the fair and its surroundings. Vans taking some away, others awaiting questioning. The pathologists and forensics going about their tasks, the serious crime unit taking charge.

'Don't envy those guys trying to get statements from that lot,' Mantel said alongside her DI. 'And yeh, suggestions for another boozer for the debrief boss? I reckon you're right about steering clear of the station for the time being. I suppose we could go to The Cobblers.'

'Do you think this one will be Nash's work sir?' Nimra asked.

'Could be Nimra, looked like the MO of the other one the way she was. Let's hope they get some DNA from this one,' Griffin said looking at his DC, wondering whether the penny had finally dropped as to how fortunate she appeared to have been. 'But two murders means it's getting serious. I'm already having to fight to keep you three with me, they're on the hunt for additional resources. We need to find Nash quick...'

*

Bob wailed away at a respectable and pleasant level, filling Mantel's first floor flat with the cool sounds of the Caribbean. She believed that if you listened carefully you could hear the waves lapping at the seashore. Reggae was tonight's choice, on another night Motown or when the mood cried out for it, Rock Anthems. Mantel's choice of music was eclectic, driven by circumstances rather than fashion. Tonight's was reflective, a portion of Bob Marley, Jamaica's finest provided the perfect soothing backdrop as she sat on the sole large sofa in her spacious chic apartment above the Bookies, having finally made it home after earlier events at the funfair. She reflected on her new title, one that she loved it. Detective Sergeant carried so much more clout and kudos than Detective Constable. She knew it was only a stepping-stone and had to carry on proving herself. Police life marched on, some would say monotonously. Mantel knew that this was partially true and certainly not the lifestyle portrayed in the TV dramas. It was her chosen career though, and she loved most aspects of it. Today had been another tough day, the finding of a corpse never got any easier.

*

Lily, on tip toe, placed the whisky bottles back on the highest glass shelf having given it a wipe. With closing time approaching a few little jobs helped the hands on the clock move faster on quiet nights such as this, the fun fair having closer pubs for the media to frequent. Just two punters remained; Jock, unusually in a sober mood, in conversation with his mate Richard, an occasional customer, sat on stools at the bar from where Lily was able to take in snippets of their conversation as she passed; footie and women, in no particular order. Pretty par for the course, The Cobblers was not an offshoot of the Oxbridge Debating Society, but it did have its fair share of lively discussions. Sport and sex closely followed by politics. Tabloid in content rather than broadsheet. Lily loved it, always striving to hear the views on the day's news, the exchanges were proper pub banter, part of the pub's fabric. At the moment, The Cobblers was more than her place of work, it was a place to rest her head, eagerly accepting Veronica's suggestion to move in while Andy Nash was at large, this latest murder justifying her decision. Veronica had nipped off upstairs half an hour earlier with it being so quiet, leaving Lily with the chucking out and locking up duties. At a table in the corner, Greg the discreet security, glanced at his watch, with Lily hoping that glass of cold Pinot Grigio would be waiting for her in a few minutes time.

*

The Reverend Mandy Jarvis reflected that they were a very nice couple and hoped that marriage would suit them, delighted figuratively to be cracking the bottle of bubbly on the hull as they launched their new life, hoping that they would avoid the icebergs. The request for this late meeting in the church to discuss the service and add-ons was not a problem. Modern lives meant modern timekeeping. They had gushed with details of the lavish reception and the exotic honeymoon, leaving Mandy to consider that a small percentage of these would be far more lucrative than the fee she would get for the choir and organist. The reading of the Banns and that they should attend took a lot of explaining, and she still wasn't convinced that they had really got it. It was obvious that they regarded St Vincent's as an attractive, but not significant ingredient of the whole cocktail. The Church, its C of E beliefs and the blessing by the Lord Almighty, nothing more than a tick-box exercise that an expensive limo could deliver them to and whisk them away from. They left hand in hand

110

happy and contented, especially when told that confetti throwing was allowed. Mandy stood inside the door at the back of the church having waved them off and tried to imagine what it would be like to be standing here and to hear the 'Bridal March' start playing.

*

Mantel was surrounded. To her left on the couch her personal black laptop and private mobile. On the other side the last two years black A5 diaries. Ahead on the modern glass, black and chrome coffee table a large glass of chilled Chenin Blanc, not the cheapest on the shelf but inexpensive and quaffable, alongside a bowl of sweet potato crisps. A free-standing chrome lamp swung over her head to provide subtle lighting. Looking through the diaries memories of the past couple of years and her fling with Glenn Friar, co-owner of The Cobblers, flooded back. In particular, the grand a month a clothing allowance that was no more. Was it that or the significant downturn in sex that concerned her most? They both had there pluses. It had been a very convenient and enjoyable relationship. Fine restaurants and top hotels; plenty of sex and a happy bank balance. If she had allowed it to run Mantel had no doubt that it would have ended in tears. She hadn't wanted anything to jeopardise her police career, it was her choice to end the affair amicably when her promotion came through, pleased that she had squirrelled away a little of the incremental income. Mantel reflected that her apartment was lovely, the area charming and she had a great bunch of workmates. But she was a city girl, at one with the grime and crowds of people, plus, some would say considerably more stress, a view that Mantel disagreed with.

*

Lily pondered whether she loved the pub or Veronica the most? It had to be her boss. A wonderful person, so caring but with an intriguing mysterious aura, attractive and flirty, whilst always appearing in control. Lily didn't want to appear ungrateful, nights up in the flat were fun, always hugely enjoyable. She wouldn't want it to become permanent though. Home was her first-floor apartment, over the Estate Agents, bought by her parents, a space that she had nurtured. It was hers, the hub of her social life. She had an address book of friends that she struggled to keep in touch with, even with social media. Relationships as and when she wanted them. As she cleared out the till, she reflected that the affair with Inspector Hargreaves was the only slightly dark cloud. His increasing emotional heaviness still not outweighing the considerable pluses, but was it wearing thin on her part? 'Come on guys, I know that you've got homes to go to. And so has Greg.'

*

Mandy had strolled down the aisle and sat on the front pew, on the bride's side. She looked around. What a fabulous church and a congregation that brought her joy and other biblical nouns of happiness. This first gig flying solo as a vicar was going well; wasn't it? Her sermons, if a little offbeat, appeared to be well received. There were a lot of smiles on the faces of those she greeted when out and about. But the vicarage and church were both huge and much of the time she was alone in them. A stark contrast to her earlier frenetic life, a change in direction that she chose. Could she blend a bit of the past into the new career? She intended to give it a good go. She was no Mother Teresa, more a sexed up version of the Vicar of Dibley. Top of her to do list was to get rid of the Superintendent, he was past his sell-by date by some margin, a relic of her past and he didn't fit into her future plans. That would be an easy tick. Then there was the ladies night at the vicarage that needed her attention, if only to get a date in the diary. Should she invite Suzanne Holder MP? Perhaps not.

*

Mantel had replied to all she wanted to, deleted or filed the rest of the messages in her various personal files, whether e-mail, text or social media. A question remained; should she go with the girls to Ibiza? Probably. She needed to get on to it and book the leave. She was finding previously unknown tardiness creeping into her personal life since being in the sticks and out of the mainstream action. She knew that her promotion to sergeant would probably see her hanging around for at least another year. Could she last that long with such little social life? There was netball, which was fun when the job didn't interfere. Thankfully the job was fulfilling, and she had a great boss in Griffin. Her mind was made up though, as soon as was credible she would seek a transfer back into town. In the meantime, Andy Nash? Having become friendly with Prisha,

Mantel hoped that the opportunity would arise for some personal time with the bastard to relieve her of unprofessional pent up anger.

*

Doors bolted, takings in the safe, lights off, alarm on, Lily climbed the old wooden staircase. Strange day, with another murder less than a mile away. Judging by Mike Griffin and his colleagues who came in earlier, they were no closer to solving these nor finding Andy Nash, all of which was a worry.

'White wine Lils?' was the welcoming call from above.

'You bet, large one.'

Being friends with Prisha, Lily had clear ideas as to what she would do to Nash given the opportunity.

*

Mandy rose from the pew and walked to the door, she was pleased with the friendships she had struck up in the area. Meeting many good people and intriguing characters. On the downside, the couple of murders in the locality were more than a concern. Her thoughts went out to Prisha and her horrifying ordeal at the hands of Andy Nash. Given time with him in the crypt she knew how she would put the collection of ancient torture instruments stored down`` 8there to good use. With this thought buoying her it was time for a whisky. Did she have any peanuts stashed away? She hoped so as supper had been a swift sarnie ahead of the pre-nuptial meeting.

CHAPTER FIFTEEN

'That's how it is Detective Inspector and to be honest I've enough on my plate to be arsed with arguing the point. I can only go with what the experts say, and these murders need resources. I'm sorry if it disappoints you,' a stressed DCI Fairmead instructed Griffin from behind her desk, having delivered directives that he was not happy with.

'Understood Ma'am, even if not pleased. I'll go and convey the news to the team.'

'You just do that Inspector,' Fairmead replied returning to her computer.

A frustrated and dispirited Griffin left his boss's office and trotted down the stairs. He put his head round the door of the crammed CID office and noted that his team were absent, a DC on the murder squad passed on a message prompting him to continue his journey onto the staff canteen.

'Morning guys,' Griffin said as positive as possible as he pulled out a chair and joined the three detectives in the bustling, recently renamed, 'The Forest Café'. With the cuts, how could the cost be justified, was the universal question? Deciding to seek refuge in the canteen whilst awaiting news of their DI's urgent summons to the upper echelons, Mantel, Nimra and Henshall looked at him in anticipation.

'So, come on,' Mantel prompted taking the lead, her warm soya milk held in both hands, looking her boss directly in the eye. 'What did the DCI have to say?'

'Well, pretty much as usual when summonsed,' Griffin replied his hands clasped in front of him. 'A mixed bag, some good, some not so good, and the rest disappointing depending how you look at it.'

'What does that mean sir?' Nimra asked giving her DI a frustrated look as Henshall leant back in his chair to reduce his presence, meagre crumbs of a bacon butty with lashings of ketchup on a plate ahead of him.

Griffin sifted his news into an order to promote the positives. 'Okay, in no particular order, the DNA is back...'

'And there's no proof it's Nash,' chipped in Nimra.

Griffin pointed at his DC. 'Correct, you're getting good at these, unfortunately no DNA as before. So, two murders and the attack on you Nimra, that we know about that is, all with no DNA,' Griffin said with obvious frustration in his voice. 'With have a name for our first victim.'

'Local?' Mantel asked.

'No, a little vague, an illegal Latvian immigrant, 23 years old, of no fixed abode.'

'Her name?' enquired Henshall.

'Ilma Kalnana, pretty common in that part of the world so I'm told. The powers that be are on to it. Nothing on the second one yet, although it is early.'

'So sad,' Nimra said. 'Let's hope they can track down her family.'

'I agree,' Griffin responded clasping his hands again on the white laminate table, deciding to get what he guessed would piss his team off out there for all to digest. 'The official word, not mine, is it that Nash is not around here and may never have been. Central intelligence that looks at escapees, I never knew that there was such a department, well, they think that he's probably long out of the country. They don't think he's the murderer, that's MIT's view. They reckon that the MO is too different from anything Nash done in the past, wearing a condom appears to have swung it. It also means they don't think the flasher was him either. Some mumbo jumbo psycho stuff that the lady he flashed wanted to believe it was Nash, so convinced herself it was. Couldn't see the woods for the trees sort of stuff. Not sure how they got to that, but I had my doubts anyway...'

'That's bollocks,' Mantel exclaimed in a tone that no one would question. 'Someone's out there flashing their bits and there's a murderer who could very well be a convicted rapist on the loose, fact. Have they proof that Nash has left the country? If that's their opinion so be it, but I think it's crap. I have an opinion that the gold bars are long gone and are now bling, no-one believes me on that me, but it's my opinion. Their opinions end up as directives even though he's not been caught.'

'Many do believe you Luce, but you're not the braided bunch. I can't ignore them, well not officially,' Griffin ventured hoping to lift the mood.

'So, what are you saying boss?' Henshall asked from his laid-back position, fingering a crumb.

'All investigations into Nash are being eased back to concentrate on finding the murderer. Resources are stretched.'

'No,' Nimra responded in frustration. 'As Lucy says, Nash is still out there. What proof have they got that he's not the murderer?'

'None and don't worry it's not a total shut down and there are some positives to this,' Griffin replied seeing his team visibly deflate, Nash was as personal as could be allowed in an investigation. Griffin could not let morale drop any further. He hoped that his finale would keep them motivated but didn't hold out too much hope.

Mantel scrunched her carboard mug. 'So, the good news is? Don't tell me, she said to give us all a pat on the back for all our hard work. Sometimes you do wonder who is making these decisions and what they want of us. Do they live in the real world, they certainly don't live round here.'

Griffin choose to not reply to his DS's tirade mainly because he totally agreed with her sentiments, but didn't want to dwell on the subject, he needed to move on. 'As I said, the Nash file is still very much open, just officially downgraded. In my eyes it is still top of the pile. The positive is that you're not, nor am I being moved to the murders, we now have responsibility for everything else.'

'Everything,' Mantel asked a little confused. 'What do you mean?'

'Well, whilst the murders are taking up so much, we are the lead on anything else that comes in that's not uniform's responsibility, nor what can be transferred to another division or unit. A big task but, in my view, better than being a very small cog in a much bigger investigation. I can assure you that if we'd been moved, we would not have been at the sharp end despite them being on our patch. I guess it would have been surveillance,' Griffin said scraping back his chair and getting to his feet, deciding enough was said. 'So come on, there's more than plenty to get on with. Nash to the fore but without a song and dance. Unless you want to see Fairmead having my balls for breakfast.'

'Now that's tempting,' Mantel replied, Griffin shooting her a glance and wry smile. 'You could sell tickets for that, perhaps for charity. You're right boss, let's find the bastard and prove them wrong.'

'Exactly, let the results do the talking,' Griffin said relieved to be ending with his DS behind him, hoping that Nimra and Henshall would follow her lead. 'You still okay for rugby later Kevin?'

'You bet. Looking forward to it boss.'

*

If they were at Cruft's it would have been a Great Dane standing next to a Bulldog, as this was the edge of a rugby field, they were the archetypal back row forward and scrum half. One in their prime, the other seeking to maintain a level of fitness as he drifted into retirement, occasionally turning out for the 'stiffs'. Henshall and Griffin in traditional shorts and rugger tops from the days before polyester, stood with their hands-on hips as the under sixteens trudged towards the changing room, a demanding training session completed. Their fellow coaches collecting the multitude of cones, bibs and other training accessories strewn across the pitch.

'Loads of potential there, Bobby Given really stood out. Great hands and awareness, and Jordan's a big lump for his age, caught me right in the bollocks when we were demonstrating tackling techniques,' Henshall said giving his tackle a soothing squeeze.

'Yeh, Bobby's already in the national under sixteen's squad. Most, including Jordan are in or knocking on the county door.'

'These are superb grounds, no floodlights though?'

'You have to remember that this is a school. They play their matches on Saturday mornings. If they need lights during the winter for Thursday training, they use the all-weather facility,' Griffin replied pointing towards the fenced area in the distance in amongst the hundred acres of sports fields that the Burlingham School boasted. 'I went to a school with similar grounds in New Zealand, but space wasn't at a premium out there. We had to shoo the sheep off and all that comes with that. Just look at this.' Griffin swept his arm across the vista that included London's distinctive skyline just a few miles away.

'It's certainly quite a place. I had nothing like this. Didn't play rugby at school, football only and not much of that. But my dad was a member of the local rugby club. I must have been a toddler when I first went.'

'Can't imagine you being a toddler.'

'Is there boarding here?'

'Yes, mixed with day pupils. Some parts of the school date back some five hundred plus years.'

'Wow. Bet the digs here are better than in the police house,' Henshall said referring to the limited but adequate rooms that he was allocated to get him over the first few weeks. 'You're not local, are you?'

'No, nor is Lucy. Nimra's your local girl if it's where to get a flat. Pricey.'

'I bet but need to get it sorted and quick. A proper big bed is the priority,' Henshall said admiring the school buildings. 'Tell you what boss.'

'Mike please, at least here.'

'Okay. Mike. This place is closed for the summer, yes?'

'Yep. A few summer camps and training like us. Some staff are always in, but, yes, largely empty. Why do you ask?' Griffin enquired looking up at his towering DC.

'Well. I was just thinking that if Nash knew this, it's not a bad place to hide is it? I mean security was pretty well non-existent when we arrived.'

'Kevin, you may be onto something there,' Griffin said scanning the buildings and thinking that it was a plausible notion, pleased that Henshall remained switched on, even when off duty. 'I'd struggle to get any additional resources for a search, but the four of us could pay a visit in the morning and have a little mooch. I know the Head's PA, I'll give her a call and clear it. We'll keep it very discreet. I don't want to set off any unnecessary alarm bells or to get a warrant. Good thinking Kev.'

'It's a long shot but you never know,' Henshall replied chuffed to have his idea so enthusiastically accepted. 'So, what happens now?'

'Shower, few beers with the guys, then possibly a ruby. You up for it?'

CHAPTER SIXTEEN

'Whilst we're waiting sir, there's something I think you should know, well everyone really.'

Griffin was amused that Mantel, Nimra and Henshall were all sat up straight whilst waiting for the Headmaster's PA to come down from her office on eclectic antique chairs and a studded padded bench beneath a slightly wonky sash window in Burlingham School's traditional wood panelled reception within the oldest part of the building, dating back to 1539. Many framed photographs, memorabilia and trophies portrayed the school's history, there was even a distinctive aroma that nobody could put a finger on. 'What's that Nimra, not pregnant are you?' Griffin replied flicking through a substantial prospectus without looking up.

'Most definitely not and I'm not sure that you can ask that,' Nimra responded with an indignant smile.

'Pleased to hear it.'

'It's just that there's a growing feeling out there that what we're saying isn't totally true.'

Griffin put the glossy brochure back on the polished walnut table and looked up at his DC. 'What do you mean by not telling the truth?'

'They think it's all propaganda and that the murderer is Andy Nash.'

'That's ridiculous. Surely you've been able to convince Prisha.'

'Even she's swinging both ways. Says it's too much of a coincidence.'

'Oh, what a load of bollocks,' Griffin exclaimed. 'Oohps sorry.'

Ruth, the school receptionist glanced in the DI's direction in a manner that suggested that he may be sent outside if there was a repeat of such language, before breaking out into a broad smile and wagging a finger in jest.

'What should we do, post the DNA results in the local paper?' Mantel suggested in a hushed voice. 'Get someone with a sandwich board ringing a bell, oh-ye, oh-ye...'

'Well I thought you'd like to...'

A brightly dressed Afro-Caribbean lady appeared through a door to the side of the reception. 'Good morning Mike how are you?'

'Patricia, good morning. Thank you for seeing us,' Griffin responded hurriedly getting to his feet to shake hands with the Headmaster's PA, a lady who had proved to be a useful resource. Burlingham School attracted the offspring's of some of the area's wealthiest families, and as had been the case since time began, wealth wasn't always acquired through legitimate ways. Burlingham's parent profile was a cross-section of society, some more successful than others. A mixture of means to pay the fees each term; old school, inheritance, worked hard for it and a small number by other methods, the latter being of most interested to Griffin. Plus, where there's money drugs seem to follow. The sharing of information was a two-way street, Patricia having a fast track for police advice, asking Griffin to speak about drugs and crime at a number of assemblies. 'This is Lucy Mantel, Nimra Shimra and Kevin Henshall,' Griffin continued deciding to keep introductions informal.

'Pleased to meet you,' Patricia replied smiling. 'Ah, here she is.' A confident looking slim young lady dressed in jeans and t-shirt entered the reception and smiled at the visitors.

'Mike, this is Imogen Hart, our Head of School for the forthcoming year. Imogen, this is Detective Inspector Mike Griffin and his colleagues. Imogen was in school this morning so I thought she may be useful in showing you around and she kindly agreed to help. I'd be useless at it. Imogen will be able to show you the parts that only the students know about.'

'Thank you, that will be most useful,' Griffin replied inwardly disappointed that he wasn't being given a free rein. Perhaps he should not have been so low key when he asked Patricia if they could take a look around. Citing information gathering rather than anything criminal to avoid alarming her and, although he didn't think she would, requesting a search warrant. Now frustrated that his call first thing had been a little rushed and not thought through, he needed to come up with a compromise strategy that would not offend. 'Can I make a suggestion?'

'Certainly Mike, always open to ideas.'

'That we split up. Lucy and Nimra go with Imogen and she can take them around the buildings. And as I have seen those perhaps Kevin and I can take a look around the grounds and other areas? We can then share our thoughts.'

'Your call Mike. That sounds fine by me,' replied Patricia thinking nothing of it, she had pressing admin to deal with. 'Mick, our Head Groundsman is out there somewhere should you wish to ask him anything. Are you okay with this Imogen?'

'Whatever works best,' smiled Imogen.

'And please when you are finished let Ruth know and I'll come and join for some refreshments in the dining hall.'

'That would be great, thank you Patricia,' Griffin said. 'Okay team, ready? And we'll continue with Nimra's point later.'...

...'Maybe it wasn't such a good idea boss,' Henshall said hands on hips. 'It's such a vast area, unless we were able to do a thorough search we'd have to get very lucky if he was here somewhere.'

'I have to agree Kev, but I don't think it was a bad idea. In fact there are many sites like this that I hadn't thought about that he could get into,' Griffin said standing beside his DC in the middle of a netball court looking back towards the buildings. These were grouped in one corner of the site with a multitude of entrances, joined together by a web of walkways. Each block differing in size. To hide would be easy as it would be to escape, especially as the school was virtually empty. 'We'd struggle with the element of surprise even if he was here, but as you mentioned if he has been here at all it might help to flush him out and at least give us a chance of finding him.'

'We could look at those,' Henshall said pointing up at the numerous cameras fixed to the walls.

'Good point, you volunteering? Good luck if you are. Surely he'd get out the back though, through the grounds then over the fields. Doubt whether he'd pop out to stretch his legs under the gaze of those. Who knows though, reckon you've just talked yourself into a job Kev. See you are full of good ideas,' Griffin said patting his DC on his back and making his way to the gate. 'Right let's see if Lucy and Nimra have had any better luck. I'll go and find them while you go and dig out the footage, with any luck you'll be able to access it from your desk. After that, there's all the other sites he could be hiding in that have cameras. You'll be busy.'...

...'Ssshhh. What's in there Imogen?' Mantel whispered pointing at a door to the side of the senior Art Room where muffled noises could be heard from within.

'Just a store cupboard,' Imogen replied in a hushed concerned voice, disturbed to see both Mantel and Nimra instinctively draw their extendable batons.

'You go outside Imogen, right out of the building, okay.'

'Yeh, sure.' Sensing that something was wrong Imogen was only too pleased to follow Mantel's instruction and slipped out of the building.

'Do we call it in?' Nimra asked.

'I reckon we take a look, probably mice.'

'Fucking big mice. You sure?'

'Yeh, the element of surprise. You ready, back me up. I bang, give a shout, then hopefully, if it's not locked, pull open the door.'

'Okay,' said Nimra taking a deep breath and raising her baton.

'Police,' Mantel shouted banging on the door and pulling on the handle, moving slightly to one side.

There was a sound of hurried movement as the door opened. Mantel and Nimra braced themselves. Inside a young lady and an even younger man, both in a state of undress amongst easels and art supplies, attempted to cover up.

'Freeze, hands above your heads.'

The terrified couple, to their personal embarrassment, readily obliged...

...'Well Patricia, over to you,' Griffin said with a mischievous glint in his eye. 'I don't suppose you envisaged this when you came in this morning?' Mantel, Nimra and Henshall looked on in anticipation, how would the Headmaster's Personal Assistant handle this delicate scenario?

'Thank you Mike, yes an interesting one,' Patricia responded smiling. 'It appears that their preparations for the forthcoming art term got a little carried away.'

His team and the PA were sat with refreshments served by the skeleton brigade in the state-of-the-art kitchen in the somewhat disappointing to those who hadn't seen it before, albeit a stunning newly opened modern dining hall, having hoped for something similar to Hogwarts. Imogen, thanked for her assistance, had returned to her House Common Room, aware of who had been discovered, unaware of their compromising position, although she was neither stupid nor naive.

Griffin took a bourbon from the selection of biscuits. 'Lisa and Tom, are they both classroom assistants?'

'Tom is, Lisa is one of our junior school art teachers,' a composed Patricia replied. 'Both are single, and I believe very creative people.'

'Well there was certainly some creativity going on in that storeroom,' Mantel observed unable to resist the comment helping herself to a jammy dodger.

'Quite,' Patricia said still smiling. 'I suppose we were all young once.'

'Will you have to make it an official issue? Have they done anything wrong?' Griffin asked.

'Technically I suppose not with the school being closed. What would be your judgement Mike?'

'A tricky one,' Griffin replied looking at his team. 'Well with Kevin I can't think of a big enough cupboard at the station.'

'Quite, there are certainly plenty of those around here.'

'Where are they now?'

'Back working in the art room, rather sheepishly I would expect. Look, they were unlucky that four police officers were scouring the site. I'm just pleased that Imogen doesn't have the full facts. Can you imagine social media if she did,' Patricia replied sipping her coffee.

'So Patricia your decision is? There is certainly nothing to concern us.'

'Of course I'll have to tell the Head and he'll probably have a word with them. In fact, I'm sure he will. But knowing him that will be as far as it goes.'

'Well it certainly won't go any further from us,' Griffin said glancing round his team for reassurance. 'Lucky for them we weren't wearing our head cams.'...

*

'Well you never know what a day will bring. Wish I'd been there when you opened that door, and you know you should have called it in,' Griffin said giving Mantel a knowing look, having reconvened to his office. 'They were certainly a bit Procal Harum when I arrived.'

'Sir?' Nimra questioned once again stumped by her DI's remarks.

'Whiter shade of pale,' Henshall interjected, the rookie already more in tune with the boss's humour. 'A band and song from back in the day, 1960s I think.'

'No, still not sure what you mean, but moving on,' Nimra said with a quizzical look. 'By the way I had a look on social media and our Head girl has put two and two together, it's starting to trend.'

'My final comment on the matter boss,' Mantel said. 'I don't think he was wearing any protection.'

'Thanks for that Luce, as always giving the subject an intellectual, decisive edge, fully utilizing your acute detecting skills,' Griffin replied. 'Okay, let's move on. Nimra's observations that we are not telling the truth about Nash is a worry.'

'I didn't want to alarm anyone, but I thought it should be raised,' Nimra said folding her arms.

'No. You were more than right to. It's a real worry. Confused messages never help. Conveying the truth is tricky and apart from the mask that you're not sure about, we don't have a description. Then the official line is that Nash has done a bunk, but we're still pursuing him, because we're not totally convinced that the murderer's not Nash.'

'No mixed messages there boss,' Mantel said. 'And don't forget the flasher. Quite a potful, and as we know the level of truth on Social Media is pretty low.'

'Quite, I mean the flasher could be the murderer, we can't totally discount that. The witness has come up with very little apart from the description of the coat and hat. I mean it could be Nash. My reckoning is that he's just your run-of-the-mill flasher that the forest seems to attract. It was just too harmless in relative terms.'

'Still leaves a very confused message boss,' Henshall said, sore from the low blow at last night's training, not helped being uncomfortably wedged in the corner beside the filing cabinet.

'Agreed, what we need is some clarity, a clear message. Problem is the murders aren't our responsibility, but the community is and we need the public on our side. They don't want to know the procedural side of it, they just want facts. The rumours and their scepticism will help no one.'

'So, with it being as clear as mud boss, what's the plan?' Mantel asked.

Griffin pointed towards the wipe board with Nash's photo and little else. 'The cupboard of ideas remains bare Luce. Answers on a postcard please?'

'Old saying Nim,' Henshall nipped in seeing Nimra's quizzical look. 'Before mobiles you would send your answers in to quizzes on a postcard.'

'All we can do is keep making sure that our messages are as clear as they can be and continue pursuing what we've got on Nash. Clear up all the other stuff that comes in and hope for a lead. Kev you work on the CCTV footage. Don't think the school's the answer, but there may be somewhere else with a similar makeup with redundant space that has cameras where he may have hidden. If you see anything of interest then follow it up with a visit, take some uniform if you can find any. Nimra, you keep on Iain Swift, as much as you can on him please. And Jenny Roberts, you never know. Luce, you've got the open brief, lateral thinking, revisit old friends. Me? Well I've got a fucking two-day seminar up town, not even an overnighter, so a commute. Complete waste of fucking time but it's a three-line whip.'

*

'So Glenn, are you going to expand upon your latest extra marital activities?' Freddie Bone asked as he and his business partner, Glenn Friar, got out of his gleaming white, top of the range, Range Rover, after pulling into one of the many free bays outside The Bootmaker's Arms, aka The Cobblers, part of 'Snouts in the Trough Ltd' the company they were the sole directors of. These were two Eastend guys made good. Always smartly turned out, freshly laundered Oxford shirts, chinos and loafers, occasionally a whistle if they had a meeting of significance. Today it was smart casual, together with their tablets, an appendage like the Queen's handbag. 'Snouts in the Trough' a name derived from the time when Glenn and Freddie made considerable profits on the money markets in The City of London. Quitting The City to develop a hotel, the building that has since become Blue Skies House. A project that remains unknown to the locals as it was pre-'Snouts', their names not appearing on any of the planning documents. They abandoned this for reasons never disclosed and purchased a mini chain of four localish pubs. The Queen & Groom, the Pig & Shovel and the Cock and Bull, all successful pub/kitchen public houses, and the black sheep of the four, The Cobblers. After fighting the planning authorities for years they hoped that their plans would soon be coming to fruition. 'The Bootmakers Bar and Brasserie' would offer boutique rooms and become their long-awaited flagship. All construction work had been suspended after the owners discovered that their bank account haemorrhaged a large amount to their previously reliable builder. He went rogue in a serious way. The theft of sizeable funds small fry compared to the murder of a young journalist, caught snooping whilst pretending to be a labourer. Unfortunately for the journo his undercover exploits coincided with the builder's complete breakdown, his drug addiction spiralling out of control.

'Not much to say really. Anyhow, that's not for now. Come on, let's give the ladies this news shall we, I'm sure they are going to be delighted,'

Glenn replied grinning as he attempted to open the rickety side door. 'And this will be the first on the fucking skip.'

'Afternoon ladies,' Freddie said as the owners approached the bar. 'Good lunch?'

'Hi guys,' Veronica replied with a beaming smile. 'Not too shoddy, usual crowd and some ramblers tucked into the crisps and nuts. They didn't have any booze though.'

'Soon to be a thing of the past.'

'What ramblers?'

'No nuts and crisps being our fine dining option.'

'Hopefully we'll still get the ramblers. So, you have news? What will you have?'

'Half of IPA please, let's sit over there shall we.'

'Come on then,' Veronica said impatiently as the ladies eagerly took their seats, hoping to hear some positive news after so many false starts. 'We've brushed our hair and put on some lippy for this meeting, so it had better be good news.'

'Wouldn't have noticed,' Glenn responded. 'You both always look so beautiful.'

'That's sexist Glenn, I'll report you to HR.' Lily blushed at the slightly slimmer of the two's comment.

'I think you are HR Lils,' Veronica quipped. 'Now, enough of the flirting.'

'Well like so many solutions it was staring us straight in the face,' Freddie said, his Oxford shirt pale blue today.

'I take it that you mean the builder problem?'

Freddie pointed out of the window in the direction of Blue Skies House, partially hidden by a line of fine horse chestnut trees. 'What is the most successful local redevelopment in recent times?'

'Blue Skies House,' Lily answered. 'You've signed up Rod.'

'Correct Lily. Once again we see where the brains of this operation are.'

'Ha-ha.' Veronica said with a smile. 'Really, Rod has agreed to run the building works? That's great news. Thought he was looking to retire and look after the sprog.'

'Maybe that's why he accepted our proposition. He'll be managing it for us, the amount of hands-on stuff is his call.'

Veronica excitedly clapped her hands with the thought of real progress. 'Excellent. When does he start?'

'Tomorrow morning. We've already been through the plans and he's been recruiting, and of course, he knows the pub pretty well.'

*

'Well, well, your ears must have been burning young man,' Veronica said, having only just waved goodbye to her bosses, for them to be replaced by their new builder.

'Hi Ronni, has someone been talking about me then?'

'Too right Rod. I'm led to believe that we'll be working together.'

'Well yes,' Rod Nash replied settling onto Geoff's stool. 'But I won't be pulling pints.'

'What'll it be, on the house as you're joining us,' Veronica said buzzing with thoughts of the building works restarting and that her apartment may finally get its facelift. 'Not your usual time?'

'No. I mean yes please, a pint please. Just thought I'd take a look around ahead of tomorrow. It sounds like you've heard about it,' Rod said looking around the bar through different eyes. 'I was after a favour.'

'A favour?'

'I was wondering whether I could take a look upstairs?'

'Rodney, I never thought you'd ask.'

*

Much anticipation filled Blue Skies House's sumptuous lounge. The chintzy armchairs and sofas had been rearranged to form a mini indoor amphitheatre. The focal point a large HD television. The room was full to the brim. Residents in the box seats, the odd sherry or something stronger poured. All staff given special dispensation to attend, the gardeners abandoning their hoes and soiled boots. The kitchen brigade stationed at the rear. Michelle the junior commi-chef left to oversee the simmering pots. Even Mr Patel had left his office and Reverend Jarvis made an appearance. A hum of excited conversation preceded the teatime television programme.

The chatting ceased as the opening credits and theme tune for Ready, Steady, Cook took over. The rave from the grave was back on our screens and Robbie James had been invited to be one of the celebrity chefs. In the studio audience were four lucky residents, the tickets randomly drawn. With the show having been recorded some time ago, Robbie looked on from the back of the room, blushing at the ooohs and aaahs as he was introduced on screen.

'You look pretty good with make-up chef,' whispered Sally the Sous Chef next to her boss.

Hushed comments from those who were at the recording offering insights as to what was going on off screen, sworn to secrecy as to the outcome of the culinary contest. Robbie had filmed another three episodes on the day, impressing to such an extent that he was told he would be invited back should the show be recommissioned, expected to be a formality, leaving Robbie to consider whether he should employ an agent.

With the cooking completed the cameras turned to the audience to see how they marked the cook-off, bragging rights awarded to the resident with the most nanoseconds on screen.

Spontaneous applause breaking out in the room as the closing titles rolled and Prisha asked their Head Chef to take a bow. Robbie agreeing before hastily retreating to his haven.

With debate now in full swing as to whether the voting had been right or wrong, many incredulous that Robbie didn't win, nobody noticed the face at the window.

'It won't be long Lils before we'll be sitting in our boutique apartment,' Veronica said with a glass of Rioja, legs tucked under her at one end of the largest sofa in the flat above the pub. 'I've got a feeling that it's going to happen this time.'

'Colour schemes?' Lily enquired from the other end of the couch, legs similarly tucked up, Pinot Grigio her tipple, with the Best of Motown playing. On the coffee table a Pyrex bowl half full of cheese and onion crisps, their reward for a busy shift.

'Not sure, never got to that stage before. Always appeared to be other distractions. We'll have to go online, maybe visit some showrooms.'

'I like the we, I'd love to help you.'

'Absolutely, my on-trend consultant, whoops,' Veronica exclaimed nearly toppling off the sofa as she leant forward for a handful of crisps.

'Careful, you've only had a couple of sips. So, what's the plan for this new pad of yours,' Lily asked spreading her arms to embrace the lounge.

'Decorated throughout. Keep this as it is. Losing the third bedroom. Expand the kitchen to have more sitting space and I've agreed that will become the staffroom as there will be a few more staff, the bedrooms and here will be out of bounds.'

'How many more staff?'

'Not totally decided yet; kitchen, waiting, housekeeping.'

'I'll still have a room if I need it?'

'Of course. There'll be two bedrooms both en-suite and a separate loo, sort of a staff one, with basin. Still thinking about a shower in it.'

'It sounds so exciting and that's just up here, the rest is going to be fantastic,' Lily said leaning back and sipping her wine. 'How long do you reckon?'

'Four months is what the guys are aiming for. They reckon that a lot of the donkey work has been done. Still a bit optimistic in my book, we'll see.'

'Well you've got to start planning, I don't reckon that Rod will let them down like Buddy.'

'They didn't think Buddy would. But yes, it is all very exciting, especially at a time when there's a cloud over the area.'

'So, they start first thing tomorrow?'

'Yes, and we've got to get our stuff out in the bar before opening.'

'That won't take long. It should be a right laugh,' Lily replied referring to the charity no swearing day. 'I'll put the jars around the bar, blu-tac up some posters and dot Stairway's brochures around. That should do it.'

'I was doing a fag packet calculation and I stopped at a thousand.'

'What a thousand swear words all day, I'd go all over that,' Lily said raising her hand to indicate more.

'Well let's have a thousand as a target to aim for. With it being a pound a swear word a few were saying that they're going to put in a twenty as they walk through the door and then top it up.'

'Yeh, someone like Jock might as well put it on a card,' Lily said of their most foul mouthed customer, although this accolade would be a close run thing. 'So, let's get it straight, it runs from when the doors open until when?'

'Nine o'clock, then we'll count up. Julian's going to come down to help with the counting. Big announcement at nine thirty, although I doubt if many will be here then.'

'Who knows, doesn't matter though,' Lily shrugged finishing her wine. 'I'm going to try to donate nothing,'

'No bleeding chance of that,' Veronica replied laughing. 'Local rag said they'd send someone down with a photographer, it's caught the imagination. Perhaps we should have a prize for the top swearer.'

'They won't need any fucking encouragement. By the way I'm using mine up tonight, Mother fucking Teresa tomorrow,' Lily exclaimed. 'It's going to be great fun winding the guys up. I can't fucking wait.'

CHAPTER SEVENTEEN

'Thank you Nimra, appreciated,' Griffin said taking a double espresso from his DC as the rest of his team slowly filed in. 'I know it's tight in here but there isn't an inch spare around the whole station. Well, apart from the cells that is. At least in here it's private, apart from the bugs of course.'

'We're not being bugged are we?' Nimra asked with a concerned look.

'Hopefully only the crawly sort. It was meant to be a joke Nimra.'

'Oh, sorry.'

'Let's hope they solve these frigging murders and do it quickly."

'Ah, boss, is this for me?' Henshall asked looking at a red plastic bar stool.

'Don't ever say I'm not caring,' Griffin said as Henshall sat on the stool neatly slotted in beside the filing cabinet. 'Not a word eh. Slipped it out of the canteen this morning under the nose of the cleaners. Flashed my warrant card and told them to stay stum. I'm sure it's a disciplinary case if anyone finds out, and if anyone does ask, give it the 'what stool?' response. Kev needs it more than they do.'

'Who would ever call you not caring boss?' Mantel asked trying to be endearing. 'You're a fucking cuddly teddy bear below that grumpy exterior. Anyway, I thought you said you were on a course.'

'Pound please, you were lucky with frigging.'

'What?'

'The Cobblers are having a no swearing day for the Hospice and I told Ronni that I'd extend it to here,' Griffin replied looking around his office. 'Got a text at 1.41 this morning saying that the course was postponed, hopefully for ever, left it a bit late though, but that's HR for you.'

'This all sounds a good idea boss, but thanks for the fucking warning,' Mantel said with a theatrical glare. 'I'd have put a different tongue in.'

'Two pounds, we need a jar,' responded her DI smiling, continuing to look round his office for something suitable to collect the fines. 'Right as we're all here, let's have a run through as to where we are.'

'I don't have any change boss,' Mantel said. 'I left my purse at home.'

'I'll keep a tally,' Henshall responded from his new perch motioning his pen over his notebook.

'Goody fucking two shoes, just because he got you a fucking stool.'

'Absolutely,' Henshall replied. 'That's four now.'

'Oh bollocks. And yes I know, that's a fiver.'

'Okay. Proper policing stuff now, let's see what came in overnight, before we get onto all the new stuff I know you've got for me on Nash,' Griffin said sipping his coffee knowing that the last comment was pie in the sky. 'No biscuits Nimra, so you can start.'

'Sorry sir, none around, I did look,' Nimra replied flicking over the pages of her pad. 'Okay, the Councillor and his car lot, well his empty car lot.'

'Ah yes, Cathal's Cars, that has got to be an inside job.'

'I hear that the cameras weren't working, what surprise,' Mantel said. 'Can't think that insurance will pay out. Don't think his status will wash with them.'

'How many cars was it?' Griffin enquired, no fan of the jovial Irishman Cathal Byrne, proprietor of Cathal Cars and a vocal Councillor.

'Fifteen.'

'What, they just vanished from the car lot overnight? Henshall asked.

'Yep and not a trace yet. Office trashed and keys taken. Not sure if it's Kosher or not,' Nimra said consulting her notes. 'Forensics are on it. As you can imagine Councillor Byrne is making his views heard. Parroting that if there were more coppers on the beat and all that'

'Acting like that suggests to me that he is guilty,' Mantel said. 'If not, he should keep quiet, does he really think that anyone is going to believe him. I mean everyone knows that he's such an upstanding character.'

'Until proven sergeant, until proven, who are we to doubt the version of events from such an upstanding citizen. Keep on it Nimra and please try not to involve me. I can't stand the wanker.'

'Pound please boss. I'll mark it down.'

'Wanker's a swear word?'

'Yep, two pounds. Remember, this is your idea.'

'Oh bollo...moving on. Right Kev, cows? Heffing cows.'

'No, not Heffers, English Longhorns to be precise,' Henshall said dryly, turning over his notebook. 'Two of them, weighing about 950kg each. Worth a good few thousand guineas.'

'Guineas?' Nimra asked.

'Twenty-one shillings.'

'Fucking hell Kev, we've been decimal for a while now,' Mantel exclaimed. 'Or hasn't it reached up north yet?'

'Twenty shillings please,' replied Henshall smiling. 'Actually, we're still using groats. A guinea Nimra, is a twentieth more than a pound; one pound and five pence in decimal to be exact.'

'Thank you, I'll use that when my Mastermind application gets accepted,' Nimra said pretending to write it down.

'Two of these Longhorns have disappeared from the forest and I'll tell you what,' Henshall proclaimed looking around his colleagues brandishing his biro. 'This Epping Forest's quite a place isn't it, far worse than the Yorkshire Moors, I've only been around here a short while and we've had all sorts and from what I've read it's not unusual.'

'As our Tom would say,' Griffin interjected receiving two blank looks and a smile from Henshall.

'Right the cows,' Henshall continued. 'As you probably know farmers can let herds graze there at certain times. Well Arnott's farm did just that. Got all the licences from the City of London Authority who run it. Then, when

Tom Arnott went to pick up his dozen bulls there were only ten to be found. Two had been rustled.'

'Well the funfair has gone, so we can't blame them,' Mantel said.

'You'd better get onto the specialist unit Kev, I hear it's a frequent occurrence round the country. They'll know what's what when it comes to nicking cows. Difficult one to police in the forest, with there being no cameras. I suppose drones may be the answer. There's so many places for a suitable truck to pull into. But, yes, use the official cowboys and get them to earn their spurs.'

'That's good boss, nearly funny and you didn't swear,' Mantel quipped, Griffin giving her a wry look in return.

'Okay boss, I'll get onto it. I'm visiting Arnott's later and I'll keep you up to speed.'

'Well don't milk it eh. Right, that's the two most pressing. Anything else that I need to know about?'

'Don't think so boss,' Mantel said. 'Any news on the Chas situation?'

Chas Faggan, now retired, previously Mantel's DS, whose large brogues she stepped into, scooped over five hundred grand on the lottery, understandably taking early retirement when offered. Nipping off down the A30 and across Dartmoor to his holiday home on the coast in picturesque Cornwall. Only for it to emerge, from a Cornish police snitch, that this bolt hole was a seven-figure villa overlooking the Atlantic Ocean. Prompting an investigation as to how he achieved this on his pay grade, with no apparent inheritance to bolster his bank balance.

'Well, having no official involvement this is just hearsay. Word is that nothing untoward has come to light, that's not saying that it's been dropped. Again, not officially, and you know the complaints team, they are not prepared to let it go. So, watch this space.'

'Sounds promising for Chas though. Just can't see him taking backhanders he was just so M&S, if you know what I mean,' Mantel said. 'Have you had any personal contact with him? I haven't, I'm waiting for the all clear. Don't want them snooping round me'

'Again, not officially,' Griffin said. 'But he's doing absolutely fine. With the investigation being official he hasn't been allowed to leave the country. But, in Chas's words, he is having it large and is pretty confident of being cleared.'

'So, unofficially, watch this space,' Mantel responded. 'And please say hello, unofficially.'

'Right next. I've been told that the tech guys will have something in the next few days. I've been banging on the door, quite literally, but they are full to the brim with the murders,' said Griffin obviously frustrated. 'I've got them looking into any links between Nash and Swift, in fact, any links at all. But I'm afraid we'll have to wait and see on that one. Off the record Ronni's brother is meant to be a bit of a web wizard and she's asked him to have a look into those deep dark places. That's also not official, and just for your ears.'

'Worth a try boss, anything's worth a try,' Mantel said. 'I do feel a bit pissed off though, yes I know a pound.' As Henshall motioned with his pen. 'But we're being treated like we don't belong here. We're right at the bottom of the pile when we ask for any help.'

'Agreed Luce, but that's how it is, the murders are top priority.'

'And, whilst I'm on it another bugbear, all these extra guys knocking about and not a decent one in sight,' Mantel sighed. 'Are they any closer to nabbing anyone?'

'A point of order on your first point,' Henshall interjected. 'The women aren't great either.'

'I'll leave you two to argue over that. On the murders, do they have any suspects, is that what you mean?' Griffin said leaning back. 'Well, from what I hear, no, they have absolutely zilch. At least it means that the shit is hitting their fan, not mine.'

Henshall pointed his biro at his boss. 'I'll let you have that one boss, it was used in a particular context, not as an expletive.'

'Well thank you Kevin Henshall, so generous,' Griffin said leaning forward again. 'Any new news about Swift, Nimra?'

'Nope, sorry sir. Going through the list of his affiliations. He's definitely an activist.'

'Yep, he's certainly one of those. And I assume that no one has any other new news on the Nash front. We just need him to turn up somewhere. To be honest Monte Carlo would do, it would be disappointing to not nab him, but at least it would be something concrete,' Griffin said slowly closing the file on his desk.

'We still out tonight boss?' Henshall asked.

'Too fucking right…yes, I know,' Griffin replied wondering if he was going to regret introducing the swear box. 'And it's not Chutney Ali's. Lucy has booked the Meze. Seven thirty meet in the 'Terrible Influence', if that's okay. Look thanks guys, please just keep going, it's appreciated. At the moment it's all the 'c's; cars, cows and crap. And, like the crap, stick at it.'

*

The Reverend Mandy Jarvis sat at her desk in the opulent study, one of the plethora of reception rooms in the vast vicarage, a building originally built to house a Bishop, hence its size. Mandy scoffed at her employer's PR people constantly pleading poverty. Short of money? Oh yeh, with assets like these. Then there are the secretive donations that nobody will ever get to the root of. Religion and money could only be spoken about in hushed tones. The plates by the doors at the Sunday Services certainly did not generate enough to cover the running costs of the church. Mandy considered whether if water could be turned into wine, did the Church's Director of Finance have the skills to turn fivers into seven figure bank drafts. Who was she to scoff though? Good salary, nice accommodation, decent expenses, mileage allowance, uniform, phone and a fast internet connection. Plus. the unexpected well stocked wine cellar.

Barefoot, dressed in trackies and purple t-shirt, it was not the company phone that Mandy stared at quizzically on the desk, it was her personal, guarded, smart phone with a surprise text on its screen.

can we meet later pls i can come 2 u @ 10

Why? Wondered Mandy, this was out of the blue. Mandy fully recognised her past and her failings and that she needed the huge antique wardrobe

139

in the vicarage to house her skeletons. She was not naive enough to think that she could brush everything under the study's fine Indian silk rug without some residue. Mandy knew that the sender of the text was in a similar position and may be finding it difficult to balance scales that could easily topple. With these thoughts she thumbed her reply.

ok park side vicarage cum 2 back door

*

'I like it in here,' Mantel said above a robust southern European tune that engulfed the room. 'Probably the one restaurant with a real buzz. Great food as well.'

'Clever concept,' Griffin replied. 'A Mediterranean feel, with a menu that transports you back to your holidays. Sun, sea and shagging, with a kebab thrown in.' The quartet of detectives had downed a couple of rounds before making the short trip from the Terrible Influence Inn next door to its sister Meze restaurant. Both places into their second year and showing no sign of slowing down. The Terrible Influence Inn was previously an out of favour town centre pub called the Princess Louise, that the new owners stripped it back to its bare boards, introduced craft beers and an extensive gin menu. No food, that box ticked by the Meze, a refurbished gone bust French Bistro, once again going for the basics. Exposed lighting and wiring plus a huge griddle. Tables packed in and a simple Med menu featuring a choice of kebabs.

'There's not one of these on the Yorkshire Moors,' Henshall said.

'So, you're first experience then?' Mantel asked.

'Yep, doesn't look too complicated though,' Henshall replied, menu in one hand, bottle of Tuborg in the other. 'This beer's a first as well.'

'Complicated. You're dead right, there is nothing complicated about the Meze concept Kev,' Griffin replied also with a Turkish beer in front of him, the ladies hitting the cocktail list. 'Grilled meat, salad and rice. Not cheap, nor expensive. Massive margins. Fast and furious and that's just the till.'

'Not a fan then boss?' Henshall suggested.

'Look don't get me wrong, they're okay. As Lucy said they've got an atmosphere, which is something round here. The money laundering guys have got an eye on them, as have the drugs squad.'

'Really.'

'Yeh, not all of them but a few. Intelligence has it that there is much untoward activity, as we know cash is king when they claim to not accept cards yet. Probably why law-abiding Yorkshire has yet to see them.'

'There's a few in the bigger cities and towns, and law-abiding Yorkshire. I'm not so sure about that.'

'Right, I reckon it's the lamb kebab for me,' Griffin said.

Nimra finished sucking at a garish drink through a coloured straw. 'A fish one for me,'

'A bit of meat for me,' Mantel said glancing around. 'At least the view is better in here.'

'An improvement on the station, present company excluded, obviously,' Henshall said narrowly avoiding the hole he was about to inadvertently dig. 'The mixed grill for me.'

'Don't worry, I'll leave you young bucks to it after we've eaten. You can spoof for who pays, I'll sign it off. I said I'd pop in and see how Ronni got on with her no swear day. How did we get on Kev?'

*

Mandy had returned to the study to await her meeting. A lasagne from the freezer and a glass of Merlot fortifying her, she now contemplated her strategy. Two options were clear to her, offensive or defensive?

The former would have to be all out attack, taking no prisoners. As much as she had known Suzanne Holder for a long time, sharing many experiences, reality was that they were competitors in the field of top-drawer prostitution. Vying to be the top dog, so to speak, in a seedy underworld of drink, drugs and sex. Involving 'names', many of them far nastier than their public personas. If push came to shove tonight it would inevitably be dog eat dog. Mandy needed to be prepared, be on the front foot. Aim for her Achilles heel and follow it through. Leave Suzanne in no doubt who was boss. Mandy sipped the large malt she had poured as a digestive. What was the MP's Achilles? Easy question; alcohol. Spike a soft drink then lay out the rules of engagement. Treat it as a military exercise. If her career was plummeting Suzanne was coming to play rough and threaten to expose Mandy and their address books, then Mandy saw no reason to be holding her hand on the way down.

The impressive Napoleonic Grandmother clock in the hallway struck ten, taking another sip this prompted Mandy to reconsider her strategy. Suzie would be here any minute. Why was she having these thoughts? Surely her old friend, was coming to ask for help and not to drag Mandy, her one-time accomplice, through the dirt with her. Mandy poured herself another couple of fingers of the malt from a crystal decanter on the walnut dresser and returned to the desk. Suzanne was coming for help and support. Mandy was probably the only person that she could turn to. An ally who knew the truth. If Suzanne was seeking protection then Mandy reflected that she should provide it. Why had she even considered retribution? Reconciled Mandy leant back. She would listen and, hopefully, provide support and guidance, even refuge if matters had progressed that far.

'Hello. Hello. Mandy.' A voice Mandy that instantly recognized from the hall.

'Hi, in here,' Mandy called out getting to her feet having taken a swift gulp of whisky as Suzanne Holder appeared in the doorway. Not looking like the politician driven by the media to power dress at all times. Nor the sassy girl from the streets. Tonight, stripped of make-up, dressed largely in black, hair tucked up into a baseball cap, it was an attempt at the incognito look.

'Mandy, oh thank you so much for this,' Suzanne gushed moving swiftly across the room to give her old chum a hug.

'Good to see you Suzie,' Mandy replied. 'New look?'

'They're on to me Mandy.'

'Who are?' Mandy asked trying to appear naïve to the obvious scenario. Thinking, how long did Suzanne, the savvy street wise lady, really believe that the press would give her an easy ride.

'The fucking press. I'm finished.'

Mandy considered that a scotch would in most circumstances have been a good idea, not here though. 'Don't be so hasty, you're not finished. Let me get you a cup of tea.'

'I don't want another cup of fucking tea. I'd prefer one of those,' said Suzanne standing back and pointing at the crystal tumbler on the desk.

'Not a good idea. But I can appreciate your views on tea. Come on take a seat and tell me all.'

Suzanne took off her cap and slumped onto the Chesterfield sofa. Mandy grasped the tumbler and turned a chair to face her, unsure as to where this was going and where truthfully Suzanne wanted it to go. Many questions raced through Mandy's mind. Had the housekeeper kept the second bedroom up to speed? Was Suzanne hungry? Did she bring a toothbrush? If the press had shaken the tree had her name come up? 'So, other than this, how are you keeping?' Mandy asked trying to appear nonchalant when struggling to know what to say.

'What,' replied an incredulous, possibly soon to be ex-Member of Parliament.

'You never seem to be off the box at the moment. I knew those photogenic looks would hold you in good stead.'

'What the fuck Mandy. This is fucking serious. I've had a call from a journalist wanting an exclusive. Saying that this was the best way as it will come out anyway and that this way I can be far away when it breaks.'

'That's good of them. Man or woman?'

'Sounded like a woman. Yeh, pretty sure it was. Didn't recognize them though.'

'So?' Mandy asked ineffectually, now desperate to know whether her name had come up.

'So Mandy. So what the fuck do I do, what the fuck do I do?'

'To be honest Suzanne you always knew this was a strong possibility. If you don't mind me asking, how much they are offering?'

'It's still to be finalised, but they started at seven fifty. I reckon I could get them up to a mill,' Suzanne replied letting her front drop. 'They stressed though that it had to be an exclusive and the cheeky cow said that it had to be from the horse's mouth.'

'No one likes a slimy journalist trying to be funny. Big money though,' Mandy said wondering what her story was worth and that there were going to be a few high-profile individuals having to explain themselves when inevitably it all came out. 'Look, you've been a real success since you got into Parliament. I'm sure that you will be in demand whatever happens. What price your memoir? And Celebrity whatever will be knocking on your door before you know it.'

'Yeh, yeh, you're right, as you always were. But it's still a fucking mess and fucking difficult to deal with.'

'It was never going to be a walk in the park, and that it could get messy. This needs to be handled carefully...Shit who's that?' Mandy exclaimed getting to her feet, responding to the grand chime of the doorbell. 'Sorry, I'm going to have to get that, comes with the job being open all hours.'

Suzanne said nothing as Mandy left the room, thought about Mandy's scotch but rejected it, she had enough to deal with. She heard the front door opening and a muffled male voice that Mandy didn't appear to welcome. A discussion ensued, seemingly on the doorstep as no one appeared.

'For fuck's sake,' Mandy exclaimed quietly to herself as she closed the heavy oak front door, having dismissed a reporter who was asking about the murders with not a mention of the MP. She told him abruptly that it was too late to be door stepping and that she was in a meeting with her ultimate boss, which either impressed or confused. She wandered back down the hallway to the study pondering what she could do to help Suzanne apart from offering to carry her bags to wherever she chose to do a bunk to. Deciding to not mention that it was a journalist at the door. 'Sorry about that, parishioners eh. Now where were we...'

There was no reply because the MP was not in the study. A car could be heard pulling away, not the journo as he had parked up the road. Mandy hurried to the window and caught a glance of Suzanne driving her Range Rover out of the drive. What Mandy didn't notice was a shadowy figure amongst the laurel bushes.

CHAPTER EIGHTEEN

Cheerful exchanges, the clatter of pans, along with the tantalizing aroma of a frying bacon had not disturbed Lily. Not even Rod and his boys getting the day's building work underway beneath her bedroom window appeared to have raised her from her slumber.

'Good to hear Rod down there, he'll do a good job,' Griffin said having stayed over after a small celebration to mark the success of 'No Swearing Day'.

'Yeh, I like Rod. I'll tell you what, that old Julian lets his hair down when he wants to, doesn't he? A dark horse that one,' Veronica said standing at the small stove in the kitchenette, serving up from a full frying pan.

'Raising just over £2,600 was worth celebrating,' Griffin reflected. 'I suppose if we ran a children's hospice we'd want the occasional distraction.'

'Couldn't do it myself. Here you go.' Veronica placed a plate with two fried eggs, two rashers of crispy back bacon and a pork sausage in front of the DI, the toast already on the table. 'He's had a couple of good weeks, what with the quiz night.'

'Thank you, majestic as always.' Griffin grabbed the brown sauce and squirted it all over as Veronica joined him with a matching plateful.

'Remember last night when I asked you to remind me to tell you about Stephen?'

'Ah yes. Stephen. You wanted me to remind you.'

Veronica waved a speared piece of sausage in Griffin's direction. 'Thank you, I might have forgotten. Well he'd like a word with you.'

'Got something of interest has he?'

'He ran it past me and I immediately said that he needed to speak with you directly, I'll leave it to him to tell you more.'

'Interesting, I'll call him later. Shall I use the personal number you gave me?'

'Yep. He also had a proposition for both of us.'

'I'm all ears,' Griffin said his plate emptying fast.

'I'm up for it, but it might be a little lastminute.com for you,' Veronica continued also making healthy progress. 'His company's got a box at Ascot tomorrow. Not Royal Ascot so don't worry, you won't need a top hat, it's just a normal meeting. And like so much corporate stuff these days they've had a few call off. So Stephen's got a couple of spare tickets and wondered if we'd like to go.'

'That's very thoughtful of him and sounds like a cracking idea, a day at the GGs, not been for a long time,' Griffin replied picking up his phone to check his diary. 'I need a change of environment and there's nothing in here to stop me, and I keep getting pestered to take some leave, so you're on.'

Veronica wiped her fingers on a tea towel before picking up her phone. 'Excellent. I'll text him to let him know and that you're going to call him.'

A bleary-eyed Lily in a pink towelling robe appeared at the door, en-route to the bathroom. 'Morning all, that smells so nice.'

*

Mandy sat at her desk, a strong black coffee and her phones ahead of her, the couple of paracetamols yet to kick in, pondering that perhaps the couple of malts after Suzanne's departure were not such a good idea. Her attempts to contact the MP had proved fruitless and her office weren't expecting to see her today. Being told on the phone by a helpful and pleasant young male voice that her work diary stated that she was out, written in bold capitals and underlined, and that she had given no explanation as to why or where.

*

Griffin left the daily murder squad briefing that he attended on most days, with no new information. The murders continued to baffle all involved. The truth was that they had not progressed at all, hitting a substantial brick wall. Yes, they were following up leads and their statement to the press would be upbeat to not alarm. The truth was that their enquiries regarding the dead ladies had divulged very little, which in itself was extremely sad. Phone records offered nothing, the few so called friends knew little about them. The refuge they stayed in drew a blank. Neither had been in the country more than a couple of months. There was an unusual aspect to the case that puzzled all. The two murdered ladies had similar backgrounds, both prostitutes and illegal immigrants from Latvia, the assumption being that they knew each and may have travelled over together, although as yet there was no proof. A connection could be made as far the motive and a possible profile of the murderer if it was just them, which in this instance would be a sick bastard preying on the vulnerable. It was the apparent randomness of Nimra's attack if it was the same perpetrator as was widely believed, although without evidence, even circumstantial information was thin on the ground, that could not be fathomed out. This made the investigation much more difficult. What was the link between illegal immigrant prostitutes and a serving police officer? Even if you ignored Nimra's job, she was miles away as far as being a match. The only semi-plausible argument to date being mistaken identity. Feasible apart from the fact that it was in her flat. This, the mask and the apparent wearing of a condom when he carried out the murders ruling Nash out of their thoughts. They had not established where the murders took place, but what they did know was that it was not at the refuge. History showed that murderers who do not have a pattern to their actions were considerably harder to apprehend, anticipation of their next move rendered virtually impossible. A small hope was that the murderer was running parallel lists. In this case the prostitutes were easy pickings to satisfy some basic urge alongside a harder target to offer a greater challenge. This was at the very best, clutching at straws. If this was a pattern then who would he target next? Griffin left the large top floor meeting room with the majority of the officers scratching their heads. He could sense that the mood was downbeat with a definite need for some motivation, positive news would not go amiss. Not too different to where he found himself with Nash's disappearance. As he went down the stairs to his office, he reflected on the one considerable failing of the supposedly all-conquering DNA; if they weren't on the database it was worth little, if nothing to those trying to find them. Worse in this case where, as yet they don't have any to find a match to.

Flinging his jacket onto the back of his chair, Griffin sat and once again considered not just those poor young ladies who had been savagely murdered, but DCI Angela Christy, the SIO on the case, a colleague he admired, who he knew would be getting serious grief. Remembering what Veronica had said at breakfast he brought up Stephen's number on his phone and called it, hoping that he would have something positive to say.

'Hello.'

'Stephen. Mike Griffin.'

'Yeh, hi Mike.'

'Is it convenient? Your sister said to call.'

'Yeh, just let me go to somewhere a bit quieter.'

'By the way, thanks for the invite to Ascot, really looking forward to it.'

'No problem. It should be a great craic. Right that's better.'

'Ronni said you had some information.'

'Possibly, but don't get your hopes up too much.'

'Go on, I'll take anything.'

'Okay, I managed to pull up a list of those in the UK using the site that you'd given to sis that Iain Swift was on. Obviously, a pretty big list, but with it being so specialist it's manageableish. Not sure what I've done is legal or not, what with data protection and all that comes with that.'

'Don't worry about that.'

'The list meant nothing to me when I first looked at it, until one name sprung out. Now you must remember that this was a very deep dig, many levels below any normal search. Those on it didn't fill out an application form with Joe Bloggs from Arcadia Avenue @gmail.com.'

'I appreciate that. So, this name?' Griffin asked willing Stephen to cut to the chase.

'Glenn Friar.'

'What, as in one of the City Slickers that own the pub, your sister's boss?'

'Apparently the very same. I'll send you the list, but I'd like to do it encrypted and to a safe address.'

'Yes, of course,' Griffin replied his mind racing with this new revelation. 'I'll speak to our guys as to where to send it and come back to you.'

'Okay, no problem.'

'And Stephen, thanks.'

*

'Okay, a smidgeon, it may just be village gossip and nothing to do with Nash, but it may stir something up.'

'Spill it out then boss,' Mantel said, the team having gathered in the DI's office.

'A source has disclosed that a certain Glenn Friar subscribes to the same deep dark porn site that Iain Swift does.'

'Really,' Mantel replied surprised and a little baffled. Her liaison with Friar, for what was well over a year, would not have raised any suspicions that the owner of The Cobblers was anything but classical in his approach to sex. Never having the time nor desire for any deviation, certainly not as depicted in the sites on Swift's hard drive.

'Who's Glenn Friar?' Henshall asked from his still unclaimed stool beside the filing cabinet. Nobody noticing Nimra's shocked face. She had only the other night said to Prisha that their sessions with Friar had moved on and were far more risqué, for want of a better phrase.

Nimra discreetly texted Prisha.

meet hr green tree café

Prisha responding immediately.

ok

'He's one of the two City Slickers as the boss likes to call them that own The Cobblers, Queen & Groom, Pig & Shovel and the Cock & Bull,' Mantel explained. 'Implicated in the gold fiasco but nothing was proven. They made their millions in The City a decade ago when the shit was hitting the fan for most. And of course, he is Ronni's boss, the boss's...'

'Yes, thank you Luce, too much information,' Griffin interjected with a wry smile knowing Mantel's own association with Friar. 'He's someone, or should I say one of two that I have always had my doubts about. Just too squeaky clean in my book. In fact Kev, this one is for you. You've no history there, you can look at it through fresh eyes, get what you can on this guy, any links between Friar and Andy Nash, don't think we've ever looked at that. Come to think of it Rod, Andy's uncle is working for Friar, a little digging around there might be interesting. Lucy will fill you in with what we've got.' Mantel returned the wry smile.

'I'm on it boss,' Henshall replied sensing that this might be a bit meatier than cattle rustling.

'Luce, when the full list comes through, and it might be a biggun, I want you all over it. Who knows who else we might find?'

'Okay boss,' Lucy replied trying not to show her disappointment, knowing that this would see her chained to her desk, her least favourite aspect of the job.

'Nimra, I want more on Swift now there's some sort of connection locally.'

*

'So, what's so urgent?' Prisha enquired sat at a table in the corner at right angles to her friend.

'Glenn has turned up on a porno search that the governor has done.'

'Doesn't really surprise me, as you know he is a consenting adult. You said the other day that he was, what did you say, getting kinkier every time. Very quaint,' replied Prisha glancing around the attractive café. It's chicness meant a few extra pennies on their prices for the latest snacks. Very much on-trend, but not necessarily young mums, nor dads. A national daily had carried the story of the Green Tree's buggy ban. Babies were fine, but their transport simply cluttered the place. It caused a bit of a hullaballoo locally.

'Well, he has been pushing the boundaries and I'm not sure that I'm liking it as much,' Nimra replied slightly embarrassed as Prisha sipped her Macchiato, Nimra having chosen the less calorie conscientious Mocha.

'I'll be honest with you Nim, I totally agree with you.'

'And there's more. This ain't top shelf stuff, this is very, very hard core. Trust me, I've seen some of it and I can assure you, you wouldn't want your parents to see it.'

'Urgh,' Prisha responded with a disgusted look. 'Well that decides it then, we finish with him.'

'No, not so quick.'

'Why?'

'Well, I have a bit of a dilemma.'

'What's that? Surely we simply dump the pervert.'

'But from a policing point of view I might have a chance of a unique insight into him.'

'That's one way of putting it.'

'No seriously. Who knows what we might gleam?'

'What happens though if he gets heavy?'

'We'd just have to deal with that at the time, but against the two of us I doubt he'd try anything. You know the agreement, it's together until you say otherwise. Look it's too good an opportunity for me to miss, what with possibly being connected to the Andy Nash case.'

Prisha leant in. 'For fucks sake Nim that changes it all, you know it does. You know I'd do anything to get at anyone connected with that bastard.'

'So, you're in then?'

'Of course I'm in, so long as we've got the pepper spray and your expanding baton close at hand.'

'Absolutely.'

'But don't leave me alone with him.'

'And you with me,' Nimra replied, a cocktail of nervousness and excited anticipation running through her veins. 'Now I'm not promising that this leads to Nash'.

CHAPTER NINETEEN

The Reverend had not slept at all well. Tossing and turning, thoughts of Suzanne Holder engulfing her. When she did drift off, dreams of parties flooded her mind, faces from her past close up and fiendishly grinning. Enough was enough, Mandy decided that this was doing her no good at all and got up early, she needed to get busy. Suzie was a big girl. For God's sake she was an elected Member of Parliament. There should be others out there looking out for her, although Mandy did wonder how many true friends Suzanne Holder had that she could turn to.

Showered, a large brew and a couple of slices of Marmite on toast, and she was ready to go. First task was to modify the tomb lid. Bookings were some weeks off, but this needed to be spot on. The dummy run had been good, very good, the reaction would stay with her forever, but improvements were possible. With Prisha sworn to secrecy, she planned to make a visit to the crypt her party piece at the forthcoming ladies night. A date for which was finally in the diary. Egbert Penn's mysterious past and his tomb would be great fun after a few drinks.

As always, Mandy marvelled at the crypt, so much larger than the footprint of the church, spreading out beneath the village hall. If she saw out her days at St Vincent's would she be entombed down here? A nice thought to have, a future vicar recounting her achievements, more likely her notoriety. If the latter would she be afforded such a prestigious resting place?

These thoughts of little substance filled here mind as the lid went up and down. For theatrical purposes a little too smoothly, preferring a slight judder as if it was being forced open. To date she could not find a solution, Google and YouTube not coming up trumps on this one. The vicar did wonder if anybody else had searched for, 'how to make a tomb lid judder?'

Deciding that the lid's action needed greater thought Mandy wandered around. The brass, gold and silver glinted in the subdued light, there was always something new to see and today was no exception. A gold candlestick in an alcove caught her eye, it could look pretty good in her bedroom, a room that needed a personal touch. It was a quite stunning piece, probably only eighty or so years old, with an art deco look, standing out amongst items of greater age. Mandy decided that it would be a talking point in her boudoir, if anyone visited. Were there any rules and regs for moving of items from the crypt? Who would know if she moved the candlestick? No doubt Health and Safety should be informed, and a risk assessment carried out. Obviously bodies could not be moved, but this was here for cosmetic reasons, and her bedroom was part of the church.

With her decision made Mandy stepped forward to complete the deed, clasping the candlestick with both hands, around twenty inches tall it was weighty but not too heavy. To her horror its plinth came away and remained on the stone slab. Mandy's stomach done a cartwheel; she'd broken one of the church's treasures, her entombment may come quicker than she had planned. Thankfully, there was no bolt of lightning. What to do? She looked around for a suitable place to put the candlestick. To be honest did it really need a plinth, it looked good on its own. She stood back and decided that it was an add-on and that she preferred it without. She needed to find somewhere to store it out of sight. An empty plinth would be like the opening credits of a detective drama where a spotlight shone where the priceless item had once been. Before hiding the plinth, the tomb needed closing. Now that would be a good opening scene of a murder mystery, the lid of the tomb of some nobleman opening, with a judder. With the lid shut, Mandy spotted a suitable place for the plinth and bent over to pick it up, surprised that it was heavier than the candlestick. There was an engraving on it, in fact quite a lot of them. With the light too dim to see them clearly Mandy decided that it deserved further investigation and carried the plinth up to the nave, placing it on the front pew. The sunlight through the majestic, stained windows, that had survived Hitler's best efforts, lit it up. It had something about it that she recognized but could not put her finger on what it was. Taking a couple of photos Mandy considered who would know anything about something like this. Then it clicked, renowned antiques dealer and anything else that he could make a few bob from, William Carter-Stoop, or Billy Stoop as she knew him, a childhood friend who had reinvented himself from humble beginnings into a successful posh boy, he would know. Despite being somewhat of a fraud, Billy knew his stuff when it came to old things.

hi do u know wot this is

With photos of the plinth attached, Mandy left it on the pew and went back to get the candlestick. As she came back up the stairs her phone pinged. Placing the candlestick beside the plinth she read the text.

fm

Earth Wind & Fire's September filled the church as her phone rang out. 'Billy, hi, you sounded surprised by my text, it's a gold plinth for a candlestick, but I forgot to put the candlestick in the photo, I was going to do that now.'

'Mandy, if it's what I think it is then that's no plinth, that's a fucking gold bar. What size it?'

'Ah, that's what it is, blimey, never seen one of those in the flesh before. It's sort of the size of a proper fruit and nut chocolate bar, not one of those massive supermarket ones.'

'You're fucking joking.'

'So what's a gold bar worth Bill? I guess a fair bit, a thousand?'

'I'd need to look it up Mand to see today's prices, but I reckon it would be somewhere nearer half a mill.'

'Fucking hell.'

'Where did you find it?'

'In the crypt.'

'Look, put it somewhere safe. I'll be with you in about an hour.'...

...'Mandy, this is James who I mentioned, a very old friend and an expert on all things gold.'

'Pleased to meet you,' Mandy said greeting Billy and James, a computer bag slung over his shoulder. She had taken the opportunity to scrub up a little after Billy had texted to say he would be bringing someone else, deciding against religious attire, opting for jeans, a neutral blue blouse and a little lippy. She showed them into the study where the gold bar held centre stage on the desk. 'It's a beauty Mand, but Jesus,' Billy said, a chap of medium build, looking dapper in a blue suit, appropriate shirt and tie and a red hanky protruding from the jacket's top pocket, moving swiftly over to the bar. 'I said to put it somewhere safe.'

'O ye of little faith,' Mandy replied smiling. 'So come on, is it kosher?'

James shaped to pick up the bar. 'May I?'

'Of course, I know where you live,' Mandy replied putting a finger to her mouth. 'Actually I don't. But still, please go ahead.'

Silence ensued as James studied the gold bar. Returning it to the desk, unpacking his laptop and firing it up.

'Well?' Mandy enquired, unable to keep stum any longer.

'Well it's definitely a real one,' James replied tapping away. 'You obviously saw the markings; well they will give us the bar's history. If you'll give me a moment I should be able to give you chapter and verse, plus, hopefully a little bit more.'

Mandy smiled at Billy with a little shrug, sitting opposite James as he beavered away in the Captain's chair with a furrowed brow. Mandy was too excited to think about offering refreshments and stared at the handsome, slightly overweight chap in a smart blue jacket, that she guessed to be linen and an open neck pale yellow shirt, double cuffed with neat cufflinks. Many thoughts swam around, the one most reoccurring being; 'why was there a gold bar in the crypt?' She leant forward with a hand on each knee in expectation of his next words.

'Right,' James said leaning back. 'Where to start?'

'The beginning's usually a good place,' Billy responded looking decidedly more relaxed than Mandy.

'This gold bar has history. Are you the only one who knows about this Mandy, other than us two?'

'Well, yes. As far as I know'

'That's a good starting point.'

'Why's that?' Billy asked leaning forward, sensing that his chum had found out something interesting.

'And you found it in the crypt under that candlestick?' James continued pointing at the candlestick on a side table.

'Yes again. Has the candlestick anything to do with it then?' Mandy asked still believing that it would look good in her bedroom. 'I didn't think they were one of the same.'

'As far as I can ascertain at this point, I agree, it has absolutely nothing to do with it. In fact, if I was a detective, I'd say the bar was being hidden underneath it.'

'Hidden?'

'Well yes.'

'So how long do you think it's been down there, aren't all gold bars old?' Mandy asked believing the bar to be considerably older than the candlestick.

'Not necessarily. I don't have an exact date yet but from its unique markings I should be able to quite easily,' James said pointing first at the bar then at his screen. 'What I can tell you is that this bar was part of a heist in The City of London a dozen years ago when sixteen of these were stolen from the vaults of a Spanish bank called Banco Catalan,'

'I remember it well, an audacious raid and the gold was never recovered,' Billy said.

'Correct.'

'Bloody hell,' Mandy exclaimed. 'So this is stolen?'

'Correct again.'

'Should we call the police?'

'We should,' James replied glancing at Billy, who in turn glanced at Mandy.

'Definitely only the three of us who know about this Mand, and you're absolutely sure of that?' Billy probed. 'And are there any cameras in or around the church?'

'Yes, as I've said, and no cameras. What are you thinking Billy?'

*

Nimra and Henshall sat at a window table in the Cobblers with a couple of soft drinks.

'The guy talking with Lily,' Nimra said. 'He has got to be a crisps rep. Definitely not from Slimming World. Did you see the number of crisp bags he had in that case?'

'So that's Lily is it?' Henshall said admiring the Assistant Manageress that he had heard much about, as she listened to a besuited chap with an old-fashioned black travelling rep's suitcase full of crisps opened on the bar.

'You've not met Lil's then? Nimra asked. 'Great girl, you'll like her.'

'I hope so.'

'Easy, she's quite choosy.'

'I'm not sure how to take that.'

Nimra smiled and sipped at her diet coke. They were here to chat with Lily on official business, a tick the box exercise, making enquiries into cars and cows, leaving Mantel ploughing through the deep dark porno web site list. Getting out of the station deemed a wise move as the DS's mood deepened with each entry she checked.

'Ah, here we go,' Nimra said as Lily approached with the rep packing away his wares.

'Don't suppose I'm meant to hug and kiss when it's official,' Lily said hugging and kissing Nimra. 'And hello Kevin, we've yet to be introduced.'

Henshall stood, smiled and shook Lily's hand.

'All very formal Lils thought you might have given him a snog,' Nimra said.

'Please Nimra, some decorum, if that's the right word,' Lily replied with the rep departing out to his Vauxhall in the car park.

'Who was that you were talking to, there's something familiar about him?'

'That's Les the creepy crisp. You don't want to know him. He gives me the shudders. Always seems to come in when Ronni's out. Everything's a double innuendo, he always tries to get too close. That's why I put the bar between us. And boy does he shovel on the cheap aftershave.'

'You've got the hots for him then?' Nimra enquired.

'Oh yeh, just my sort, just like our Kevin here,' Lily replied smiling at a blushing Henshall. 'Apparently he's happily married, but I tell you what I reckon there's history. You should look him up on your computer.'

'We can't just do that,' Nimra replied flicking open her notepad. 'What's his name?'

'Les Chandler. I think he's fairly local, not round here but not far, Hertfordshire I think. He's from Bartwell Crisps. He's always trying to flog us a flavour that would cause a mutiny. Last time it was 'crushed avocado on toast'. Today was one for the vegans so he said, 'Pulse, Pea & Parsnip', all very green.'

'Pulses, parsnips and peas, you're kidding,' Henshall said. 'Wouldn't go down well in Yorkshire.'

'It's the truth, needless to say I didn't place an order, can you imagine it. But yeh, look him up, I'd like to know what the slime bag has in that suitcase other than crisps.'

Nimra scribbled a note. 'On it.'

'So what do you want to ask me?' Lily enquired, the pub ticking along in the background. 'I'm all ears.'

'It's just whether there's been any mentions of some stolen goods?' Henshall asked getting out his notepad.

'Bleeding hell Kev, what in here, stolen goods, how dare you. The Cobblers, straighter than a twelve bob note. Home only to law abiding citizens. Stolen goods. You should wash your mouth out young man.'

Nimra laughed at Lily as Henshall blushed again and then dug a deeper hole. 'Cars or cows?'

'I'll check out the back Kev,' Lily replied laughing. 'See if anyone sneaked one in when my back was turned, maybe I'll find a cow in the back of a cabriolet.'

'Come on Lil, give him a chance,' Nimra said. 'Cathal's Cars and Arnott's cows, I know that you'd let us know if you did hear anything, just thought we'd pop in and ask.'

'And it's very nice to see you both, what with both our bosses away grafting in a hospitality box at the races. To be honest Nim, Cathal Byrne has caused a bit of a laugh in here. I mean the councillor is not the most popular guy. Word is that his missus is off and seeking a huge settlement, hence the insurance scam,' Lily said tapping a beer mat. 'And the rustling, well they're just milking that.'

'So the regulars think it's an insurance scam like we suspected, now that is interesting,' Nimra said making a note.

'Absolutely and a bad one. Shoddy criminal activity is frowned upon around here I can tell you,' Lily replied waving the beer mat.

'So, there's nothing been mooooted about the cows,' Henshall asked. Lily and Nimra looked at each other and shook their heads as Henshall blushed, instantly regretting what he said.

*

The smattering of customers was pretty normal for a midweek lunchtime in The Meze. The owners good to their pledge to only close on Monday's, calculating that the cost to open the rest of the week was relatively small, and who knows new big spenders could walk through the door at any time. One of today's tables possibly proving the point. Two smart looking gents, accompanied by an attractive lady, were going through the card.

'We don't need anything in writing for this, do we?' Billy asked.

161

James leant back holding a glass of Merlot having enjoyed the lamb kebab. 'I'd prefer not, what about you Mandy?'

'Gentleman's handshake suits me,' Mandy replied immediately glancing at Billy. 'And no smutty remarks please Billy.'

'As if,' Billy responded also enjoying what was the second bottle of the red wine, this one on-the-house, following large gin and tonics with the pitta bread and humus. 'So James the next step is yours. But you're confident, yes?'

'It'll be a cinch, trust me. There's nothing that can go wrong,' James replied. 'Just need to negotiate a price and it will be done. Of course, you'll need to trust me on that one.'

'With my mother's life,' Billy replied smiling.

'Thought she died at least a decade ago?' Mandy said with a smile, pleased to be somewhere where she was not recognized by either the owner or the other four customers.

'Detail, Mandy, detail. Look unless we trust each other this deal will go tits up and that's no good for any of us.' Earlier, discussions at the Vicarage had started cagey whilst trust was established, all three scratching the ground to establish their territory. Any potential impasse being overcome when Mandy uttered what will become legendary in terms of this deal: 'Oh bollocks, what the fuck, let's just do it'. With the ice well and truly broken, a deal was quickly brokered, and a plan assembled. Lunch at The Meze was agreed to be the perfect way to sign off the proceedings, Billy generously offering to pick up the tab.

'Okay, we'll touch base tomorrow afternoon when I should have news,' James concluded as the owner arrived with complimentary Ouzos.

*

'Well that was cracking,' Stephen said perched on a stool in the hospitality box.

'Was for some. Gary cleaned up, I take it he's off picking up more winnings,' Veronica replied her heels slipped off, the rest of the chosen outfit holding up well.

'Yeh, he had a cracking day, but it's not all about the winning.'

'What a load of bollocks.'

'Okay you're right, lucky bastard. Oh, and before I forget sis and this stuff takes over completely.' Stephen held up a half full champagne flute as around them the box swiftly emptied with the last race over. The concourse of Ascot racecourse way below them also clearing and leaving the tell-tale remains from a typical day at the races, hundreds of expired losing betting slips strewn across the tarmac that a team with brooms were starting to tackle. A few lucky punters remained collecting their winnings from the line-up of bookies, themselves packing up, eager to get off home.

'What's that Stephen? Veronica asked a near empty flute ahead of her on a small table.

'The Reverend Mandy Jarvis, you asked me to look into her.'

'Blimey Stephen, that was yonks ago.'

'I know, I know, sorry, but Mike's web stuff sort of took over and I forgot to tell you.'

'Well, fire away then, I probably know most of it now.'

'Okay, here goes. Ex high class prostitute, with an interesting address book?'

'Yep.'

'Centre fold?'

'Sort of.'

'First in mechanical engineering at uni?'

'Yep, but I thought it was electrical engineering. You got anything new?'

'Yellow belt in Karate?'

'Karate or karaoke?'

'Ha, ha, nope definitely Karate.'

'That's a new one on me and interesting. Suppose it could prove useful in the prostitute game. Next, you're getting better.'

'Friends with Suzanne Holder, your MP.'

'Now that's a goodie. Didn't have a Scooby on that one. When from?'

'Not sure, I'll have to come back to you on that,' Stephen replied pleased by his sister's positive response. 'And finally, she's having an affair with a Superintendent Hawes from my neck of the woods.'

'Yes to that one, but I'm not supposed to know and for your files, I believe from a reliable source that it should read 'had'. I hear it's all over, but that might need verification,' Veronica said as Griffin and Gary, Stephen's partner, returned to the box together. The Inspector having had a pee, the latter with an enormous grin waving a few twenty-pound notes.

'Beginners luck Gary,' Stephen said putting his arm round him.

'Cops day out,' Griffin said picking up his beer from the table. 'Just bumped into Superintendent James Hawes from the Hertfordshire force and surprise, surprise, it wasn't his wife that he was arm in arm with, and I certainly doubt whether it was his niece who he introduced me to, as he made out she was.'

*

Mandy hadn't been so buoyant for a long while, not since her ordination. Singing along in the kitchen to the music on her phone, a 'party mix'. The adrenalin was flowing so much that she had decided to bake cookies for her congregation, not her usual evening pastime. Occasionally patting the flour covered gold bar on the large oak table, en-route back to the crypt, deemed by consensus to be the safest place for it over the next few days. Regrettably, Mandy had to agree that it should once again act as a plinth for the candlestick, it was also waiting to be taken back down, her bedroom would have to wait. Sifting yet more flour she reflected that his was the life she wanted; a commitment to the church and her community, plus a bit of raw excitement, although she did admit that this may be a little extreme as a starting point.

Mandy, Billy and James had discussed at length the potential consequences. In truth they all knew that they should hand it in and wait for it not to be claimed before they could be called its rightful owners. That idea sucked though, if James could ascertain where it derived from by a few taps on his keyboard, then that option was a no-go. The decision was made to cash it in, James entrusted with negotiating the best price. Mandy was realistic and savvy enough to know that it would fall well short of the market value, as she understood it this was the nature of wheeler-dealing in the under-world. Her research since lunch had established that gold was trading at around one thousand six hundred per ounce, so their little beauty could be worth north of five hundred and fifty grand. Worst case scenario she reckoned to be one hundred and sixty each. This was far from ambitious and inwardly she hoped for at least ten to twenty more. Whatever James achieved it could not be sniffed at, although she did recognize that she was entrusting a guy she had only met less than twelve hours previously. She needed both James and Billy to keep to their word. Her security being that she had possession of the bar. Once melted down all chances of the gold being identified would disappear. Of course, whoever James did the deal with was a liability, but wasn't that the norm in the criminal world. The cogs would grind to a halt if there was no trust. Weren't the majority of transactions all below board? In no time at all the gold would seep out into the market either round peoples necks or on their fingers, making a lot of people happy, including her.

As she pottered merrily around the large kitchen, she regretted, in parts, giving the Superintendent the elbow; a session with him now would be the icing on the cake. Passing by the gold bar once again she gave it a little polish with her apron, imparting more flour on it. Any thoughts of Suzanne Holder largely forgotten. Billy was going to advise her on the best bank account to place the deposit; Switzerland, the Channel Islands or even Monaco, all nice places to pay a visit to the bank manager. A windfall like this would come in very useful, Mandy wondered whether someone was smiling down on her.

Without warning an arm was thrust round her neck, a knife in a gloved hand, held at her throat. Aggressively, without a word, she was pulled from the flour covered, cluttered worktop back to the table and forced face down onto it. Mandy tried to remain calm, to think clearly, not to say a word. When attacked like this on a previous occasion, when much younger, she had lashed out without thinking and suffered for it, only being saved by good fortune, not her actions, a little composure was required. An arm held her down as the knife slashed at her clothing. Surreally she caught a glimpse of the gold bar and the candlestick and hoped that her attacker would be too obsessed with her to notice them. Mandy doubted he would think that she would have half a million pounds worth of gold on the kitchen table. Enough, what the fuck, a deep breath and as composed as she could be, Mandy unleashed her pent-up anger, forcing herself up with all the strength she could find within herself. The element of surprise knocked the would-be rapist back, she had a nano-second to react. Swinging her left foot viciously and with considerable power catching him square in the bollocks, a vasectomy would not be required. He screamed with the pain, her yellow belt in karate proving its worth. With her clothing still relatively intact, Mandy turned to face the masked intruder.

'You fucking bastard, you're dead,' Mandy yelled kicking out with her right foot as desperately he lunged with the knife obviously still in considerable pain from the blow to his groin. Her kick was not as successful, the knife plunged into her. She yelled out in agony. He pulled the knife out and thrust again. Mandy reached out to her right and grabbed the candlestick. The second incision more painful than the first, blood gushed from the wounds. With all the strength she could muster Mandy swung the candlestick with venom, connecting a sickening blow on his skull, blood spewing around and over them. He went down like a pack of cards. With the knife still protruding Mandy made for her phone on the worktop, her assailant not moving. Managing just one small step before she collapsed beside him into the puddles of their blood that were forming on the flagstone floor.

CHAPTER TWENTY

'God, this place is really getting on my tits,' Mantel exclaimed as she slumped into a chair in her DI's office for the 8.00am briefing. 'When the fuck are they going to solve them and get the fuck out of here?'

'Morning Luce, nice to see you as well,' Griffin said turning from his desk as Nimra took the other chair and Henshall slipped onto his stool, all three detectives with the de rigueur cardboard mugs. 'And of course, morning to you all. I've got a feeling that today's going to be an interesting one. Take it you've all read about the local MP?'

'Nope what's that?' Nimra replied moving across to her boss's desk and peering at the newspaper headline on his screen.

EXCLUSIVE

MP'S BOOZING & BONKING SKELETONS

COME OUT OF THE HOME OFFICE CUPBOARD

'Does it really dig the dirt?' Mantel asked. 'Not worth reading otherwise.'

'Not read it all yet,' Griffin replied as Nimra returned to her seat. 'But I did note that our local vicar gets a mention, so probably worth a read. Because she's our MP we get the heads up if there's anything of potential consequence from a security angle. From what I'm allowed to be told at my pay grade, they reckon that Suzanne Holder has done a bunk out of the country. No doubt it will bring the press back sniffing around here for more.'

'Do you reckon she's done a bunk to the same place as Andy Nash?' Mantel said cynically. 'How was the racing?'

'A cracking day out thanks. Ronni's brother's partner, Gary, cleaned up. Count on a couple of fingers the winners the rest of us had, but it was great, and the hospitality box was the bollocks. Great food and drink and a fantastic view of the course and I suppose Royal Berkshire beyond,' Griffin said, himself with a large espresso in a cardboard cup. 'Talking of the vicar, saw Superintendent James Hawes there with some bimbo on his arm.'

'Bimbo?'

'Thought that was still used…?'

'A good-looking lass, with not a lot between their ears,' Henshall said.

'Lass?' Griffin laughed. 'Don't get many of those round here, plenty of Lassies.'

'Very funny boss. So do you reckon the MP will resign?' Mantel asked.

'Reckon so or forced out. I mean a Tory MP and a booze, drugs and sex scandal, what is the world coming to,' replied a buoyant smiling Griffin, the away-day having done him the world of good. 'Right Luce, let's get on to this list.'

'Yes boss, the fucking list,' Mantel replied with a wry smile opening her laptop. 'Well I'm through it and it's thrown up a few semi-interesting names, as well as Glenn Friar.'

'Go on then, will they help to find Nash?' Griffin asked without any real expectation.

'Fucking hell,' exclaimed Nimra.

'Sorry Nim, you with us?'

'Sorry sir, just that the MP's really opened a can of worms,' Nimra responded reading the article on her phone. 'They'll be some explaining to do at the homes of the great and good at the Home Office and New Scotland Yard. She ain't held back. Bet she got paid a fortune for this. It'll run and run.'

'Does the boss get a mention?' Mantel asked.

'Ha bloody ha. Thank you Nimra for your observations, you can look forward to policing the by-election.' Nimra smiling at her DI's veiled threat of a return to uniform.

'Right the list Luce.'

'Don't think the ones I've found will be of much use,' Mantel continued. 'Rod Nash is first up.'

'That doesn't completely surprise me. Like uncle like nephew, that's the phrase, isn't it? And he's a bloke,' Griffin said.

'A bloke. Makes it okay then?' Nimra enquired indignantly.

'Look, he had some lonely nights to fill after his wife died. It's interesting, but we've been all over him and he seemed clean to me, no signs of anything like this.'

'Not something you leave around the lounge.'

'Quite. He'll always be on our radar because he's family, but I reckon he subscribes to all sorts. Interesting, but. Next.'

'Old man Richards.'

'Now there's a surprise. Or should I say I'd be surprised if he wasn't. Don't suppose the boys were brought up with Blue Peter on the television. Unless any of you know anything different I don't have the Richards involved with Nash.'

'Nope, agreed,' Mantel said closing her laptop. 'And finally, and this one made me smile, our prominent GP, Theo Shapiro.'

'Well, well,' Griffin said grinning. 'They call him 'Little Fatty Arbuckle' down at the rugby club. He'd be in the First XV if there was a non-playing members drinking team. Regarded as a bit of a snob. Outspoken but harmless in my view. Another who doesn't surprise me.'

'He's been my GP since I moved here,' Mantel said. 'This will make me look at him in a different light, although I've yet to visit him.'

'Think he does the whole station, got some kind of contract for all the medicals, emergencies and the like and anything else that's needed, if the in-house's not available.'

'He's mine to, been the family doctor for years,' Nimra said. 'Bit too smug and sweaty for my liking.'

'Well that's Theo for you, no doubt you'll meet him Kev. So that's it is it for the whole fucking list?' Griffin said with a blank look towards his DS. 'Well I suppose this at least this gives us the excuse to get Friar's and

Rod's DNA, we've probably got a bucket load of Larry Richards already. As for our doctor, he done a demonstration of taking the test to his staff, even recorded it, you can find it on YouTube. Getting the results was all part of the exercise, so I'm sure they're on file somewhere.'

'Oh, and Nimra asked me to check out a Les Chandler and he's on there.'

'Les who?'

'Les the Creepy Crisp, as Lily at The Cobblers calls him,' Nimra replied.

'Sorry, what the fuck's Lily got to do with the price of fish.'

'Sorry?'

'An old phrase,' Henshall interjected having previously been quietly absorbing information about locals he had yet to encounter. 'Think it dates back to the 19th century...'

'Thank you, Britannica.'

'Les Chandler is the crisp rep at the pub and Lily said that he was really creepy, so I thought he was worth a look at. He was in The Cobblers when we were there asking some questions and he does look, well, you know., dodgy suit and matching shirt and tie,' Nimra explained. 'Not got a police record as such, but back in the day a couple of cautions when parents of the junior football teams he looked after complained about his behaviour, but nothing like what we're after and nothing since. He's moved around a bit, but I guess sales guys do. Family man, but that counts for nothing. He might be on the radar for other things perve related and he did come up on the list and do you know what, he just looks familiar.'

'Worth a stab Nim, worth a stab, we have fuck all else. Could be our flasher? But you don't think that he's involved with Nash?'

'Don't think so sir, I'll follow up a couple of things before I draw a line though.'

'He doesn't sound worth bringing in,' Griffin said turning to Henshall. 'Okay, fine. Anything on Friar Kev?'

'As you said boss, squeaky clean, which could be a front. As we've got this on him, I'll continue digging. And yeh, an excuse to check his DNA, I'll think of a reason, no one likes the thought of being exposed and being associated with anything like this.'

'Yes please, good to get that on his file. There must be something on him. Right, I want Iain Swift's apartments searched, I'm getting the warrants,' Griffin continued. His team sitting up with the boss's unexpected proactive initiative. 'He's hiding something, who knows it could be Nash, although we'd look fucking stupid if he is, but I very much doubt it. My call continues to be that Swift is just a slimy little bastard. It'll just be the four of us, resources and all that, so we'll draw straws who goes with who and to which apartment,'

Griffin's phone rang out. 'You're fucking joking. Yes, right we'll be there. Take it the DCIs know...Good'

'What is it boss?' Mantel enquired sitting forward. 'It sounded serious.'

'There's been a fatal stabbing at St Vincent's vicarage.'

*

Only for those who like things a little macabre did St Vincent's church and its surrounds still look picturesque. The inevitable blue and white tape had been applied around the outer rim of the grounds, beyond the graveyard. Police and medic vehicles a little incongruous in the car park. Professionals going about their tasks, those in white overalls in and out of the vicarage.

Griffin stood between DCIs Angela Christy and Nicola Fairmead in the vicarage's kitchen, all bedecked in their white overalls. The carnage that resulted from the attack and Mandy's attempt at baking cookies remained untouched. Little numbered yellow bollards dotted around the evidence. The candlestick on its side on the floor where Mandy had dropped it. The bloodied, floury, gold ingot sat undetected on the table and hadn't even warranted its own little marker. The two bodies being attended to by a mixture of forensics and medics were blocked from the detectives views, although it had been confirmed that one of them was the Reverend Mandy Jarvis.

'Well it looks like we might have found our killer Mike,' DCI Christy said in a matter of fact way.

'Certainly looks that way ma'am,' Griffin replied.

'Any thoughts Nicola?'

'We get the station back and everybody stops moaning, in particular your Lucy Mantel,' the forthright Lancastrian quipped without looking at Griffin.

'Hear on the grapevine that you won't be around much longer Nicola, back up north I hear.' Christy, said with Griffin's ears pricking up.

'Aye, but who knows when HR get involved.'

'The vicar was pretty new, wasn't she Mike?' Christy asked dressed in a smart blue business suit and flat shoes, standing rigidly as all around bustled.

'Just a few months. Very popular from what I know. So sad. Did you see that she was in the papers this morning?'

'Mandy Jarvis, in the papers this morning?' Fairmead enquired. 'What for?'

'She was mentioned in the Suzanne Holder exposé.'

'I saw that, I got a call from HQ forewarning me of it, didn't read it all though. That's going to be another bleeding election to police.'

'Yeh, should have bought shares in stubby pencils, these elections seem to be coming round every few months,' Griffin replied in a matter of fact way.

'Do we know who chummy is then Mike?' Christy asked, not bothered about local policing issues. 'Told that it's not Nash.'

'Heard that but not yet had a chance to get a look at him, assuming it's a him,' Griffin said, now in no hurry; the deed had been done, nothing to rush for, no one else would be. Pleased, like so many, that this should see the end of Serious Crime's tenancy at the station.

'Suppose with her being connected to the MP we'll get another media scrum,' Fairmead said. 'Look, if there's nothing else for me here I've got a full in-tray to deal with, so if you'll excuse me. Let me know when he's identified.'

'No problem Nicola.'

Griffin looked on as his boss made to leave, the crowd around the corpses thinning to reveal Mandy, knife still protruding, and an average looking male with a dishevelled mask and a badly smashed head laying on the stone floor. 'Hang on, I know him.' Fairmead stopped in her tracks and turned back towards her colleagues. 'That's Iain Swift, assistant psychiatric nurse at Rotherfield where Nash escaped from. I've just got warrants to search his properties. That's a waste of a warrant request, still it saves on the journeys I suppose.'

'Also saves me some time,' Christy said cheerfully. 'We've no doubt got something on him somewhere, but I take it that you'll have plenty more on him. I'll send one of the team to get all that you've got. That's a result in itself.'

'Yes, of course. But fuck me, this is a turn-up for the books,' Griffin said hands on hips looking down at Swift. 'There was a possibility that he was involved in helping Nash abscond, but we didn't really have anything to prove that. Yes, we've got plenty of info on him, he was one of those who irritated and made you want to find some dirt to bring him in. Strange guy, a complete wanker in my book, but I didn't think he'd have the balls for murder. Actually thought he would be standing to be a MP sometime soon, had that way about him. Just shows how wrong I was. It's one of those occasions where it would be good to get some answers from him as to what his motive was, especially the randomness of it all.'

'Always a problem when a murderer dies,' Christy said standing over Swift's body. 'Unless you're into seances, but I don't see you as that sort Mike. Anyway we can't always get it right like they do on the tele.'

'The shrinks will have a field day,' Fairmead observed joining them and looking down at Swift. 'All sorts of theories I'm sure.'

'Doubt if they will come up with the real reason though,' Griffin retorted.

'So your theory would be what Mike?' Christy probed.

'Simple. Fucking nutter with a screw loose.'

'Can't go wrong with that in my book,' Christy said now starting to look around the kitchen.

'Hang on what's that?'

'A candlestick,' said Christy looking at it on the floor. 'Think it done the damage, not a dent on it though, must be good quality, I quite like it, art deco would you say?'

'Not that, this,' Griffin said pointing at the flour and blood covered rectangular block on the table.

'Not sure, a chocolate bar that was going to be used in the baking? offered Christy. 'It should have a marker whatever it is.'

'That's no chocolate bar,' Griffin replied taking gloves from his pocket and slipping them on. Removing a pen from inside his jacket and giving the object a poke. 'This is a fucking gold bar.'

*

'Okay, this is a sad day for us all,' Ravi Patel said at the head of the large chrome and glass table in the ground floor meeting room in Blue Skies House. A table that required a twice daily shine from the Home's ever-present cleaners. Ahead of him his management team, convened for a scheduled meeting, all in sombre mood. The news of the vicar's murder and the demise of the multi-murderer had now spread far and wide. Although Swift's identity had yet to be released, Mandy's relationship with the apparently disgraced Member of Parliament, coupled with a lack of other news, had brought the media scrum back into the town with a vengeance. The whirr of the news helicopter returned and the Constablesque duck pond opposite the church was home to the communication trucks. The ducks would go hungry today, the usually ever-present Heron nowhere to be seen. 'I know that many of you had become very friendly with Mandy in her short time at St Vincent's.'

Ivan Coltham, Finance Director, looked on, aimlessly stirring his fine bone china cup. He'd had little to do with Mandy but couldn't fathom out how the peaceful area that that he was born and bred in had become a magnet for such horrid events in recent times. Matron Ellie and Prisha Khatri, here to give a marketing brief that had been postponed, sipped at their drinks, peering through red eyes. Rod Nash looked on twirling his biro. Chef Robbie sat quietly having broken the news to his brigade prior to the meeting.

'I'll keep this as brief as possible. The Spa development in the basement should be re-starting soon. The coins that were found in the grounds turned out to be a marketing promotion for the Lord of the Rings film not Roman. Why it took them so long to realise this I really don't know, I suspect they were forgotten and put away in someone's drawer,' Ravi said tapping his fountain pen on his pad. The space below Blue Skies House was a huge mish-mash of random rooms. Currently mainly storage space for the kitchen. Plus, a couple of emergency, largely redundant staff bedrooms, an expansive laundry room and a home for the engine room; boilers, pumps and fuse boxes. The plan was a total revamp and to open a Spa, accessible to residents and an exclusive members only club, access for which would be through an existing separate entrance that completely avoided the residents areas. Planning had sailed through when the explosion, and the spurious claim of ancient treasure being found in the grounds put it all on hold. 'So, on a sad day, this is positive news, I'll keep you informed. And as you know, I have finally appointed Stella Hadden as General Manager. She comes from the hotel industry with quite a track record and highly regarded. I'm sure you'll like her; it will enable me to be less hands-on. She will be starting next week, and I'll introduce you to her individually. Okay, that's it for today. Any news I get I'll let you all know, as I hope you will do likewise. Thank you.'

They gathered their phones, pads, pens and cups from the table and quietly left the room. Normally news such as this would cause a buzz and they would be rushing off to share it with others, not today though

*

'Boss, can I make a suggestion?' Henshall asked having found his DI in the vicarage's neat garden.

'Of course Kevin, what is it?'

'Now we know what Swift was capable of I reckon that we should still search his properties and quickly, before this lot go in,' the burly DC said glancing round at the MIT officers assembled around the building. 'Especially as you've got the warrants sorted, let's get in their while it's all fresh, I mean he probably stayed in one of the places yesterday before coming here. And whilst we're about it take a look at his office. If he was involved with Nash, he may have left something, thinking he was going back. It's too good an opportunity to miss.'

'You're totally right Kev. Absolutely spot on, this makes me think that he's involved with Nash even more, too much of a coincidence in my book. Yes, the warrants have been issued, let's use them before anyone thinks of withdrawing them, although they'll now be crime scenes so don't really need them, but it gives us a bit of cover, technically it's not ours. Tell you what, let's see if we can have a word with Jenny Roberts while we're there. Nothing to lose.'

'Totally agree boss.'

'Come on then, we're done here. You get the girls, we'll convene back at the station to get our ducks in order and then get on it. Great stuff Kev.' Griffin slapped Henshall on his shoulder. 'You never know we might find Nash tied up in a cupboard and have him back in custody by teatime.'

'Ever the optimist boss.'

*

'All okay Luce?' Griffin asked looking at his laptop. 'How's Cambridgeshire?'

'Yep, fine boss, journey wasn't too bad. You?' Mantel asked looking at Griffin on her laptop.

'We've only just arrived. Parking, what the fuck is going on in central London?'

'Tell you what boss,' Mantel said picking up her computer and slowly panning it around Swift's out-of-town pad. 'Not what I expected, it's very chic and expensive looking. Tidy, clean lines, like a magazine shoot. The bathroom and kitchen are spick and span. Clean towels and sheets.'

'Same here,' Griffin replied as he did likewise with his computer. 'See. Money, that's what it is. I reckon that as well as being a wanker and a complete fucking nutter, he was also a spoilt arsehole. Bet he's got a couple of housekeepers; they'll be in for a shock.'

'Couldn't agree more. Right, Kev's already got started, I'll keep you informed.'

'Yep, Nimra's a bit of a concern though, this has really got to her. Daren't say a word.'

'Understandable boss, isn't it? She was probably attacked by him and she became quite friendly with Mandy. You have to remember boss that although she'd only been at the church for a relatively short while Mandy had become very popular, there is going to be a lot of grieving for her. I don't think the newspaper stories are going to have a negative impact. To be honest most knew something about her past and it probably endeared her to them,' Mantel said setting her laptop down. 'Keep a look out for Nim boss, she'll need it even if she doesn't say so herself. Right, I'll keep you posted.'

'Same here and I will Luce,' Griffin said preparing to search Swift's city apartment which he reckoned to be worth multiple millions. Reconfirming that mummy and daddy must have made a fortune as barristers specialising in getting criminals off. If not, Swift had an extremely lucrative side-line.

The boy, girl teams for the searches had been decided back at the station, with Nimra's idea of a live video stream enthusiastically adopted, potentially offering extra sets of eyes at both apartments. They had all expected to find an element of chaos from their albeit limited knowledge of Swift, reality was that they could not have been more wrong. As both pairs of detectives worked their respective ways through his homes it became apparent to all of them that order represented control, enabling him to present randomness in his actions. Creating confusion for others. The murder guys would struggle to find any incremental clues at either place. The apartments, in one of Griffin's favourite terms, were squeaky clean. Two things were missing though, Nash and a personal computer. Swift appeared to be a control freak. Having the police running in circles would have sated his ego. To find his laptop could provide answers to so much, in particular, his motives and any involvement with Andy Nash. The complete lack of paperwork at either of the homes indicated that all he needed was stored elsewhere, probably in some cloud. Griffin suspecting that it may be a deep, dark cloud. Despite all this self-control, Swift appeared to let the red mist cloud his actions when the pressure was on, the wheels appeared to come off at the crucial point. If he did attack Nimra it had pantomime aspects to it. Yesterday's visit to the vicarage looked to be an uncontrolled frenzied attack, where all the best laid plans had been left at the front door. The prostitutes were easy targets to bring some order and probably had little meaning to him. He had bigger fish to fry, but he had failed. Why Nimra and the vicar though? They would never know, and would they unearth others? Griffin and his team were unanimous that here was a classic psychopath whose story should be told to students of the condition, as it clearly demonstrated how unpredictable psychopaths were.

'Hey boss, look at this,' Mantel said holding the camera in front of an open wardrobe. Clothes either neatly hung or folded. Tailored items, and a fair share of what you would wear at a rally or demonstration. 'I wonder if they're colour coded to suit the cause. Suppose you'd call it socialist chic. I'll tell you what boss, I'm finding it all pretty creepy. Are you?'

'Pretty much the same, it's mirrored here. All fucking weird. Two properties kitted out the same, just yours is worth a nano-fraction of this one. Look, without his personal computer we're not going to get much more. You take a look at the offices, although I don't hold out much hope of anything there, then we'll chat tomorrow. We mustn't forget that it is Nash that we're after.'

'Agreed. Kev and I are done here. Yep, we'll give the offices the once over and try to get a word with Jenny Roberts. I think you're right that we should revisit her with all the new information. Don't think she's involved, too fucking wet, but worth getting in there before the murder guys,' Mantel said. 'Then Kev can buy me a drink on the way home.'

'Enjoy.'

*

'That Jenny Roberts, is she for real, thanks?' Mantel asked, shades on, sat in the beer garden of an attractive country pub on the Cambridgeshire, Essex border as Henshall placed a beer in front of her and lobbed a couple of packets of crisps and nuts onto the table. 'Thanks, is this the northern equivalent of a cream tea?'

'Ha, ha, Betty's tearoom in Harrogate is renowned for their cream teas I'll have you know. But yes, Jenny Roberts is a confusion in my book,' Henshall replied supping at his pint with one hand, the other grabbing a packet. 'Detached from reality. How on earth she can have opinions on others and their state of mind totally beats me.'

Mantel looked admiringly at her rugged, handsome colleague. 'That's the way of the world Kev, do as I say not as I do. Let's take the positives from it though, she agreed to see us and let us look at Swift's office. We had no warrants, no nothing, and that's exactly what we found, nothing'

'It was oh so gracious, she's away with the fairies. Obviously pleased to see the back of Swift, whatever the circumstances, you could sense it in her voice. Gets back her cushy life.'

'Yep, but we got fuck all else. His office was quite obviously bereft of anything for a reason. Probably another tease, knowing that we would take a look at some stage.'

'I must admit that I'd expected a little more than that, but there was nowt,' Henshall said shifting his backside on the uncomfortable wooden bench.

'And ridiculously it appeared that Roberts had chosen to completely forget the Nash debacle, although she can't have. She was so non-plussed about it. I reckon her bosses have moved on, it's been swept under a non-existent carpet. The initial heat is off, so they all move on despite the fact that he is still out there, still a fucking nutter and nobody appears to have a clue as to where he is. Washed her hands of all responsibility after appearing so concerned in the days after it happened when the pressure was on. I'll tell you what, she's in for a reality check now as the shit returns and hits the fan with Swift being revealed, they'll jump all over her with questions as to why she didn't notice anything. God, some people are so frustrating. And we still have no idea where the fuck Nash is.'

'And he wasn't in a cupboard as the boss had hoped for. Look, what about this as an idea?' Henshall said hoping to lighten the discussion and find out a little more about his attractive colleague.

'Go on, I'm all ears, it had better be more fun than we've already had today. Will it help to find Nash?'

'No, in fact the plan has nothing to do with him really.'

'Well that's a promising start.'

'If you fancy it, have these, then get back on the road and drop the motor off. Couple of drinks locally, then some food in that Meze place. That's if you're not busy?''

'Nope, the red carpet film premier is later in the week. So you're on.'

*

'Surprisingly quiet Ron,' Griffin said as he sat on Geoff's stool at one end of the bar.

'Hi, yeh, all clocked off or gone to that suspected terror attack in Birmingham that's probably gone to the top of their agenda. Pint?' Veronica asked, a straight pint glass already in hand hovering under a pump. 'How's it been?'

Griffin fumbled with a beer mat looking round a near empty bar, reflecting on the day's events, nodding at Greg in the corner. 'Yes please. A sad and strange day. Here?'

'Same really. Extremely sad, with a huge ironic sigh of relief that the killer is no more,' Veronica said not bothering to take any money as she handed over the pint. 'The big thing is that it can't be forgotten that Andy Nash still remains at large.'

'At large, I like that, a bit Dickensian. And despite our best efforts there's no news on that front. How's Lily been? I know that she had got quite friendly with the vicar.'

'Very reflective, a little tearful. Kept herself busy. A few of the journos don't know how close they were to a slap with some of their inappropriate comments.'

'Tough for her, I know Nimra was pretty much the same,' Griffin said. 'A little bit of a somewhat sad twist was that there was a text message on the vicar's phone from Suzanne Holder, probably sunning herself somewhere sent what we can only assume was just after the attack, when the paper published the story, simply saying, 'sorry'.'

'I wonder if she's heard that Mandy's been murdered?' Veronica mused taking the stool next to Griffin. 'From what I read she doesn't sound quite as nice as the public profile she had in Westminster and round here. Although if I'm honest I knew very little about her.'

'I'm sure her PR people would have informed her,' Griffin said having made short work of his pint and holding up the empty glass. 'You not working then?'

'Cheeky sod. Thirsty eh?'

'There's another angle to this that hasn't made the news.'

'Oh yes, what's that,' Veronica asked having scuttled back round the bar.

'We discovered a gold bar.'

'You're kidding,' Veronica exclaimed allowing the beer to overflow. 'Shit, where?'

'On the kitchen table in the vicarage. It was just sitting there,' Griffin replied oblivious to Veronica's reaction.

'What was a gold bar doing in the vicarage?' Veronica quizzed composing herself and wiping up the spillage. Griffin never had and still not did not have any idea that Veronica ever had any interest in the gold. Totally unaware that her late adopted father was a modern-day gangster with connections with the original heist. Secrets that she intended to keep.

'Well for me it might provide some answers and I reckon that it further implicates young Geoffrey,' said Griffin looking down at the fugitives stool.

'What, so you think it's part of that gold malarkey that caused you so much stress?' Veronica probed without wishing to sound too interested.

'Yep, it's one of the sixteen that I've been looking for over the past decade. So with my limited maths I reckon that in another 150 years I'll have them all. Obviously, this is just between you and me, just thought you may be interested,' Griffin said mulling over the case in his mind. 'But the fact that the dodgy old vicar and Geoff were sighted running a bar in Thailand becomes a little more poignant. But then how do you explain five hundred grand's worth of gold sitting covered in flour, blood and bits of skull on a kitchen table.'

'Oh please Mike, too much information.'

'And where does Mandy Jarvis fits into this? Who knows and will we ever know? I didn't think she knew the old vicar, let alone Geoff. Forensics have been all over St Vincent's this afternoon with two briefs, gold and murder. Doubt if that combination in a church comes up often. It'll be interesting what they come up with.'

'As you say, you'll just have to wait and see. Fancy a curry? Lils can lock up here, I'll just have a word with her. And I promised to give Stephen a call,' Veronica said taking her phone from her back pocket and disappearing out the back, not being able to contain herself, needing to share the news.

*

'What do you know about this gold bar that has so excited the boss?' Henshall asked dipping Pitta bread in a small bowl of hummus. 'I got the file up when I knew of my posting here, but only skimmed through it, it's enormous, must have been quite a case.'

'Well, from all accounts, and I've only had a brief word with the boss, sitting on the kitchen table amongst the carnage in the vicarage, covered in blood, bits of Swift's brains and flour was one of the gold bars from the Spanish bank vault robbery,' Mantel said, relaxed and enjoying Henshall's company, mellowed by the red wine and earlier drinks.

'Does this solve anything then? You finished with the hummus?' Henshall asked about to clean out the dip.

'I'm done. Doesn't solve anything really. I still think that the other fifteen bars are bling. But it does point more of a finger at the previous vicar, a really dodgy sort who done a bunk, and Geoff, a regular at The Cobblers, who we think both slipped off to Thailand.'

'The boss seemed very animated by it.'

'He's had it round his neck for over a decade now and perhaps he thinks that this is progress. Who knows, watch this space. No doubt we'll get a progress report in the morning. Ah, here come the kebabs.'

*

The news channel on a television in the bar of a swish west London hotel reported on the closure of the hunt for the 'Forest Fiend' the killer of two immigrant prostitutes and now responsible for sad death of a young vicar; Mandy Jarvis, murdered in the kitchen of her vicarage whilst baking cookies. The identity of the killer had yet to be released. William Carter-Stoop and James Charwell stared at the screen in disbelief, having learnt of the tragedy independently around lunchtime, urgently organizing to meet.

'Well I certainly hadn't factored this in,' James said holding the remains of a large Jack Daniels.

'Poor, poor Mandy,' Billy replied. 'Do you think they were after the gold?'

'I very much doubt it, but who knows.'

'If she had put it back in the crypt as agreed then who'd have known it was there?'

'It looks like a very sad coincidence William,' James replied motioning to the waiter for a replenishment of their glasses. 'I just can't believe that I knew her for less than twenty four hours. Just think what's occurred in that time, you couldn't make it up.'

'She certainly led a life as I told you on the way to St Vincent's, she didn't deserve it to end in this way. And what with the newspaper. Did you read the Suzanne Holder story?' Billy asked.

'Sorry, no, why? Heard about it. Should I?

'Mandy was included in the revelations. Not as a main player but certainly an integral part of the MP's past.'

'When was this article?'

'Just this morning, that's what's so incredible. She'd only told me a few weeks back that she didn't want to go into her shell when she got ordained. Wanted to bring life and a fresh spirit to her role and her community. To be a breath of fresh air in the church,' Billy said finishing his bourbon. 'It's so sad. I will truly miss her, she was fun. It was going to be the start of a new era. I've known her since we were kids.'

'Look Billy, as sad as all this is, and it is, and in no way do I wish to diminish it,' James said as their drinks were served. 'But, the gold could very well still be there in the crypt, just waiting for us to collect it.'

'It's not a problem James and you're right,' Billy said taking a large swig to suppress the sad thoughts of his old friend. 'Mandy said she would put it straight back where she found it as soon as she got back.'

'So, how do you fancy a trip back to St Vincent's?

*

Two trim, naked attractive females groped and fondled each other on the king size bed in a superior room in The Foresters Arms pub.

'Prish this is so much better.'

'Oh yes Nim, yes it is.'

'Glenn is finished.'

'Definitely. Let me get your champagne.'

The ladies pulled themselves apart. Nimra shifted to the side of the bed and grasped the two champagne flutes. They were making the most of Glenn Friar's generosity when he'd cancelled their proposed rendezvous at the last minute, citing undisclosed personal reasons. Nimra wondering whether Henshall's phone call with him regarding the web had set off alarm bells, perhaps leading to him reconsidering his extramarital activities with a copper. Or did he have someone else? Unlikely as he had offered the pre-paid room and champagne to Nimra and Prisha as an apology. His parting shot to Prisha, 'enjoy', which they certainly were. It was their first experience of bedding each other alone and would not be their last, proving to be the perfect antidote for the very sad death of their friend.

'To Mandy.' Nimra sat up and chinked Prisha's glass.

'To Mandy.'

*

'Oh my god Kevin,' Mantel exclaimed with Henshall thrusting hard. 'That is so, so good.'

Henshall kept quiet more than enjoying screwing his DS on her bed, thinking that life down south wasn't so bad.

'Yes, yes, more, more please Kevin.' Their naked bodies rubbing against each other, Henshall's large frame engulfing Mantel's slender toned body.

'Yes Kevin, yes, yes, yes...'

*

'Well Inspector you've certainly earned your full English once again.' Griffin rolled to one side and slumped back onto the bed as Veronica pulled the duvet over herself.

'You'll never let me forget that, will you?' Griffin smiled in response to the breakfast comment, an in-joke between the two of them. Their first venture between the sheets had not hit the mark, Veronica retaliating by not offering a cooked breakfast, an occurrence that to date, had never been repeated.

CHAPTER TWENTY ONE

'Morning all. Trust we all had a good night.' Griffin greeted his little jaded detectives at the 8.00am briefing. 'Let's hope for a better day today. A few things to discuss. The only result in, so far, is confirmation that it was Swift who attacked Nimra and murdered the other two, and who knows there could be more, so no surprises there. Don't know about you guys, but I didn't see him having the balls to murder. Had him down as just some gobby prat. But there you go, can't get them right all the time. Our trips yesterday generated fuck all as far as Nash is concerned, so a complete waste of time.' Neither Griffin nor Nimra noticed Mantel and Henshall sharing a sneaky glance. 'So, what else and where is Nash?'

'Tell you what boss,' Mantel said. 'No mention of the Merc. We didn't see it at his flat or office. Did you?'

'Very true Luce. Nope, not sure where he'd park it up town. Don't think it matters now, but interesting, it'll turn up somewhere.'

'So where do we go now sir?' Nimra asked.

'Good question Nimra. Does Prisha say much about Nash?'

'Not a lot. All I know is that she'd have his gonads off given half the chance, but little else. To be honest she doesn't seem that traumatised by it all.'

'Okay, well it affects everyone differently. As you know all Nash's victims, including Prisha have got uniform keeping an eye out for them should he ever surface. Don't know about you but I find it fucking baffling, absolutely fucking baffling, maybe the experts have got it right and he has left the country.' Griffin leant back with his hands behind his head. 'Oh, and for what it's worth I've got another name from Stephen, Ronni's brother, from the list, someone who has local knowledge. He flagged it up with Ronni.'

'Go on,' Mantel asked without any particular interest, believing that this deep dark web was yet another red herring in the search for Nash, especially now that Swift was no longer on the scene.

'Told me over breakfast; full English, bacon, eggs, tomatoes, fried bread,' Griffin said tantalisingly, guessing that the others would not have experienced such a culinary delight. He was right, Henshall had rushed back to the Police House to get changed. Nimra simply did not leave herself enough time to indulge in the fayre that was included in the deal, preferring to indulge in other ways. Only Mantel had found time for a small banana after Henshall had obliged once again before making haste. 'Bob, the quizmaster.'

'What, the big guy who got pissed at the charity gig?' Nimra asked.

'That's him, and the one that Ronnie sacked after that. From all accounts he'd left porn up on his laptop in the pub a couple of weeks earlier, so she wasn't surprised that his name cropped up. You still keeping an eye on the site Luce now you can easily access it?'

'Yep, for what it's worth. I'll cross check him and run some other checks, do you have his surname?'

'Err, Quizmaster?'

'Thanks, I'll give Ronni a ring.'

'Tell you what I'll give you Stephen's number then you can link directly with him if you need to.'

'Good idea boss always wondered how you made Inspector,' Mantel said with a sly smile that was returned. 'The one thing I will say is the site's so dodgy it must be very close to be breaking a few laws.'

'Need to know who's behind it first. Always been one of the many grey areas on the world wide web, which in my book it was built with too many stable doors.'

'Stable doors?' Nimra enquired as always inquisitive.

'Closing the stable door after the horse has bolted,' Henshall interjected. 'Trying to sort it out after you've fucked up.'

'Exactly, thank you Kev. It was the same before the internet, the worst in my memory were the snuff videos, we could never tell whether they were real or not, nasty buggers. So nothing has really changed, just that these days they are supposedly far easier to access, which is a load of bollocks in my book. So, in answer to your question Luce, it's the same as so much in this job, you need proof. We'd have to catch them at it and then what laws are they breaking? They'd plead private property and amongst friends? All bollocks again I know, but with resources stretched it's unlikely to figure high on anyone's agenda. Keep at it, I'm with you though, with Swift gone it's probably not going to give us anything apart from being able to have a quiet word with some individuals and to get their DNA, which of course we will then destroy,' said Griffin looking innocently at Mantel for a response, with none forthcoming he turned to Nimra. 'Nim could you delve into Swift's finances please. I'm still not convinced that he wasn't involved with Nash in some way. You never know there may be a payment that shines out from an 'A. Nash'. Or a payment to a hotel where he's having it large. Ferry booking maybe. Who knows?'

'I'll see who owns the flats and maybe have a look at mummy and daddy's finances.'

'Good idea but tread carefully on two counts. One, the murder boys won't take kindly to you interfering. By the way did you see that the first caravans have rolled out of town?'

'Fucking great result in my book,' Mantel replied. 'We'll be able to get a drink in the pub.'

'And two sir?' asked Nimra.

'Sorry yes, two, remember mummy and daddy were barristers who took pride in looking after number one and won't be too pleased if they thought we were digging around and they may be grieving. Right, Kevin. What about Friar? What did he say when you spoke with him on the phone?'

'A bit spluttery before he regained his composure,' Henshall said from his perch. 'He tried to brush it off until I said it had come up in our enquiries. Don't think he liked the idea of being exposed. Asked what it was, but I said it was an ongoing matter and left him hanging.'

'Excellent, make him stew,' Griffin said pleased to have one of his City Slickers feeling the pressure. 'Did you mention the DNA test?'

'Yep. He asked why, I said procedure and I'm seeing him at nine thirty at the Cock & Bull. Wants to appear helpful, but I could tell that he was reluctant.'

'The redevelopment of the Cobblers is precious to him and he knows that I'm seeing Ronni, so won't want to rock the boat. Good work, I'll be interested to hear how he is when you swab him. I'm doing the same with Rod Nash later. Mentioned the deep dark web site on the landing outside the lift, very neighbourly and, like you, I said that the test was just procedure. He even suggested a beer when I pop in with it. Very accommodating. Wasn't fazed at all. Seems a nice bloke.'

'Don't suppose it's long before Ellie drops,' Mantel said. 'He'll have his hands full then, although the deep dark web as you refer to it so affectionately may be a godsend when he's up with the sprog in the middle of the night.'

'Quite Luce, as always so forensically put,' Griffin replied with a smile. 'Is it worth me having another chat with Jenny Roberts? After what you said about how she was when you visited, I'm not so sure.'

'I'd just keep an eye on her boss,' Mantel said. 'Don't think she worth investing too much time in.'

'Okay, I'll go with that, but like all the names we've got, we must keep probing. Oh, and we have got Larry Richards DNA from his last misdemeanour and from each of the boys. Come to think of it we haven't heard anything of the Richards family for a bit. Now that is a worry.'

'Commentators curse boss,' Henshall said.

'Sorry?'

'It's something they say in sports commentaries Nim. The commentator says something like it's looking easy for a football team or cricket batsman, then as soon as they've said it, the opposition scores or the batsman's out.'

'Thank you Kev, I actually understood that,' Nimra replied with an appreciative smile. 'You're better than Google, we should call you Alexa.'

'Then there's the gold,' Griffin continued closing the Nash file. 'Leave that with me. I can't wait for the prints and forensics to get back. I'll keep you all informed. Okay that's it, unless you've anything else. I take it there's no sign of the cars or cows?'

Nimra and Henshall shook their heads as they made to leave.

'Thanks guys and keep going, he's out there somewhere. We just don't know where.'

*

'Higher, higher,' the audience had shouted with great enthusiasm throughout the afternoon. Ernie aka Brucie, was centre stage with the victorious Janice, flanked by two 'Dolly Dealers'. Janice simply couldn't believe her luck, an enormous fan of TV games shows, so to be the winner was more than her wildest dreams. The £20 wine voucher she had just won was of little consequence. By popular demand 'Play Your Cards Right' had returned to Blue Skies House. Ernie, a veteran of the old peoples home circuit, a Brucie impersonator, was the perfect host. His two female assistants performing the glamorous dealing roles were like ducks to water, pleased with the cash and a welcome distraction from their jobs on the check-outs at the local Hyper-Market. The stars of the show though, had been the residents, ably cheered on by members of the staff, including the owner Ravi Patel, and a rare appearance from his wife Amoli, a Challenge TV addict.

'That was just fantastic Prisha,' Veronica said at the back of the room, Prisha having asked her to pop in. 'Thanks for inviting me, it's so good to see these events. They're so uplifting.'

'Thanks for coming. Look, I just wanted to ask you something.'

'Go on,' Veronica said guessing that there was an ulterior motive to the invite.

'Well Nimra says that they're no closer to finding Andy and as much as I want to believe her and I know that she wouldn't lie to me, I also know it must be difficult for her. And I was just wondering whether Mike had said anything off the record to you and if they were any closer to tracking him down. Sorry if you think I shouldn't ask.'

'Look Prisha it's totally understandable for you to be concerned,' Veronica said turning and looking directly at Prisha. 'And I don't mind you asking, but I'm afraid what Nimra's saying is right as far as I know. They really don't have a clue and it is very frustrating for them. Mike keeps saying that there's no news, and that he appears to have vanished. I'm sure that you will be the first to know.'

'Thanks Ronni, that's appreciated. I owe you. Look, I hope you don't mind but I need to get clearing away.'

With the euphoria of the show's climax subsiding and the residents dispersing, Margaret sidled over to Prisha. 'When you're done here Prisha a quick drink in my room?' Margaret asked. 'The entertainment committee's got much to talk about.'

'Yes, of course Margaret, I shouldn't be long.'

'It was great, such fun. Janice is beside herself.'

'Thanks, it looked like everyone enjoyed themselves.'

Margaret lifted the bottle gift bag she held in one hand. 'Where's Ernie? I've got him a little gift.'

'Last I saw of him he was going into his dressing room with his Dolly Dealers'

'Oh I see, perhaps I won't disturb him then. I'll leave this at reception for him.'

'I don't know what you're insinuating Margaret.'

'Well you know. Anyway I'll see you in a bit, I'll just go and get Ellie.'

Prisha smiled to herself as she packed away the oversized playing cards and considered Margaret's liking of Ernie, pondering what was on the Committee's agenda.

*

'You heard the news boss? So much for keeping Swift's name out of the press,' Mantel said as the DI entered a less rammed CID room, those who remained re-ignited by the latest development.

'No, but it seems to have got this lot going,' Griffin replied pausing at his DS's desk, his blue jacket over his shoulder. 'What's happened?'

'Swift's places have been torched, the psychic unit razed to the ground and they've found the Merc burnt out in a car park on the outskirts of Rotherfield,' Mantel said pointing at her screen. 'Certainly fuels the fire, so to speak, that there was more to our Iain Swift than what we knew.'

'Well, well. Any injuries?'

'Thankfully, no. They managed to get everyone out at the unit. One went walkabout but she's been recaptured. As you say it's got this lot hopping around again. Just hope they all don't move back in.'

'As always so caring, I doubt it though, they're too only pleased to be shot of you,' Griffin said with an exchange of glances. 'Just when the DCI thought it was a neat open and shut case.'

'Early call is some militant group, but I find it all a bit strange what with him being dead, certainly a different way of making a statement,' Mantel continued tapping on her keyboard. 'I'd be surprised if it has nothing to do with the murders, but as I said curious timing.'

'Agreed. If someone does put their hand up check whether Nash has any links. I doubt it, he doesn't seem a political animal. My two penneth about the fire bombings for what it's worth, would be that they're all to do with that deep, deep dark web,' Griffin said nonchalantly making for his office. 'Has anything about Swift been posted on that?'

'I haven't actually looked boss. I'll have a look now, you're obsessed with it.'

'You just do that, it's become my latest itch,' Griffin called from his office. 'Ever heard of a TV show called Play Your Cards Right?'

'No. Why?'

'Oh, just that Ronni phoned to say she'd been to see a version of it at Blue Skies House. Hadn't a clue what she was talking about, anyway her main reason for phoning was that Prisha had a word with her. Checking that we'd got nothing on Nash. Might be worth a word with Nim. Get her to have a word with Prisha to reassure her that she will be the first to know when we've caught him.'

'Will do boss.'

'And please, do let me know if Swift features on my lovely deep dark web.'

*

'You ever heard of 'Play Your Cards Right?'

'Wow, yeh, it's a cult game show with Brucie,' Stephen replied from his study, the box room prior to the advent of the computer, in his compact, neat, newly built terraced house on an estate in the Stevenage suburbs. 'Use his phrases all the time in my blog. Why?'

'The old peoples home put on a version of it on this afternoon and I popped over, great fun,' Veronica said wandering around the woods adjacent to The Cobblers. 'How is your 'Lighter Shade of Pink' blog doing?

'Well, as you're asking, very well indeed. In fact, we are in demand.'

'Oh yes.'

'Advertisers scrambling to be on it, well three. Contacted an agency the other day looking to monetarise it, and within twenty four hours they had three national brands queuing up.'

'Excellent. I'll take a look, nice little earner.'

'Hope so and please do. These three go live tomorrow morning. It's all very exciting. Over 25,000 views daily and growing. In fact, I was working on it when you called.'

'Does Gary help you?'

'Bit of a sore point that one sis.'

'Oh, why's that?'

'Oh, you know, lovers tiff. Put it this way, we're having a cooling off period.'

'I see. Hope it works out for you.'

'Look, I'm pleased you called. I was having a chat with my dark web guru...'

'I thought it was you, so who is this guru? Is it a he or she?'

'Let's stick with guru.'

'Oh, okay, secret squirrel stuff eh? So what did they say?'

'Well they, my guru, was saying that from what she can ascertain...'

'Ah ha, a she.'

'Okay, she's a she. Happy?'

'Made my day Stephen. Go on.'

'Well this site that Mike's interested in is very exclusive.'

'What does that mean?' Veronica asked glancing at her watch, thinking that she should be getting back to the pub.

'The site gets its content by invitation only. From what I'm told, it's quite prestigious in those circles to extract extreme stuff.'

'From the very little that I saw of it, I'd say it's just extreme yuk and not very nice yuk.'

'Well yes and that's being kind. From all accounts it's a badge of honour to get something published on it.'

'It's a strange world out there Stephen when you can get an accolade for that sort of stuff.'

'But my guru was suggesting...'

'She.'

'Yes, sorry, she was suggesting, that she could go a little deeper and find out how you submit material. She says that it is extremely well hidden, making it an achievement to submit anything, let alone get it published.'

'Well why not? I'm sure Mike would be interested,' Veronica said angling back towards the pub. 'Your guru, she's doing this for free isn't she?'

'Well yes, she's a student.'

'Oh, I see.'

'A very clever one. She's at Uni, she's no schoolgirl. She would really like to take this further, enjoys that fact that she's doing it for someone else, i gives her a little protection, it's not the nicest subject. She's doing it as part of her course.'

'I see, so as well as very being clever, she's obviously very broad minded, as must be her lecturer.'

'Definitely, I can assure you, she is.'

'Oh, I see. I don't think I'll go any further there. Well at least not at the moment, that's one for over a late night glass of wine'

'Look, I'll get her to find out more, you never know, it could lead to finding out who's responsible for the whole thing.'

'Well that would be a Brucie Bonus. I'll let Mike know what you're up to. But I don't see why not? Anything to help find Nash has to be worth a shot. It will stop my Inspector from becoming Mr Grumpy and that has to be a good reason for doing it,' Veronica said turning around. 'Look I have to go. Two reasons, Lily needs my help and there are cows approaching fast. So, bye, love you and please keep me informed.'

CHAPTER TWENTY TWO

With the knock on his door Doctor Theo Shapiro hastily closed his personal laptop and placed it on a cabinet beside his desk, rubbing his hand through his thick black curly hair to compose himself.

'Come in,' Theo announced getting to his feet, the chair creaking, his stature not changing a great deal as he lifted his large 5'4" frame. 'Ah, Rod, good to see you.'

'Theo, thanks for seeing me so early,' Rod Nash replied in his freshly laundered building gear, Ellie would have had kittens, let alone a baby if she thought of him visiting the surgery in soiled clothing. He shook the doctor's outstretched hand in the opulent consultancy room. A style reflected throughout the surgery. There was much envy locally if your postcode did not match the registration criteria for Dr Shapiro's surgery, despite many admitting to not being fans of his bedside manner, preferring to see one of his colleagues. There was an unaccountable kudos about being registered at Dr Shapiro's.

'No problem Rod, please take a seat, this shouldn't take long.'

Theo Shapiro had been the principal GP in this practice for over 20 years and was an established personality in the area. Known as an outspoken, some would say obnoxious character, he was proud of his position within the community. Combining his NHS role with lucrative private work at the nearby pay-as-you're-treated hospital, giving him unprecedented access to the private lives of many of the local population. Married to Louise, with two children, one of each, his reputation was one of being a socialite. As a non-playing member and unofficial medic at the rugby and cricket clubs, Theo was often found at the bar discussing matters of the day. A staunch right-winger he was not afraid to air his views. His popularity heightened by his willingness to sign off whatever a patient put in front of him in if it enabled them to navigate bureaucracy, something he loathed, never technically breaking any rules, at times stretching the spirit of them. Assisted at the practice by three junior GPs, plus two extremely popular and hardworking practice nurses and three ladies rotating duties on the reception. Not forgetting the ever faithful Amy and her daughter, his trusted cleaners. There was no Practice Manger, Theo never wanted to hear on the social grapevine of an Ayatollah running his surgery behind his back from the front desk, he was no dictator though. Turnover of staff was miniscule. Doctors only moving on to further careers, all remaining friends and grateful for the experience. Theo liked to think he ran a tight, happy ship both here and at home.

Rod rummaged in a pocket as he sat down, producing a small sample bottle. 'Right, here's what you asked for.'

'Excellent,' Theo replied instinctively grabbing a small polythene bag from a drawer and handing it across his desk. 'Pop that in there, good you've marked it up.'

'And you said bloods,' Rod said placing the capsule carefully into the bag.

Theo got to his feet and swept his arm in the direction of a small tray of a the medical equipment required to extract a blood sample. 'Yes, I'm all se to go. Not a Hancock armful just a large malt. Left arm I assume, roll up your sleeve please Rod. Not bothered by this old boy are you? Just that the colour drained from your cheeks.'

'Let's just get on with it shall we,' Rod responded rolling up his sleeve, more than a little squirmy about giving his own blood.

'Okay, it's only a little prick and you seem to have a good set of possible targets here,' Theo said tapping at the veins on Rod's arm.

'Pleased to hear it.'

'I was thinking about you last night,' Theo said as he inserted the needle and drew out a decent amount of claret, or quite possibly Merlot.

'Oh yes,' Rod replied not looking at the incision, preferring to stare out of a large sash window.

'More your nephew. Is there any news about Andy? It is strange how he's just disappeared.'

'I reckon he's left the country. Mike Griffin's the chap to talk to on that front, catch him at the rugby club over a pint and he might divulge all. But from what I hear Andy's not been seen. Now that the murderer's been caught there's even more reason to believe that he's done a bunk, which will be the best for everyone. Apart from him being locked up of course.'

'Quite, but that poor vicar. It sounded so terrible. Hold that there could you please,' Theo said placing a bit of lint over the slightly bloody tiny hole in Rod's arm. 'So, so sad.'

'Did you know her?'

'No, but from what I read in the paper she was known by quite a few. Seemed very popular from what Lou said. Looks like we need a new vicar and a new Member of Parliament.'

'Never a quiet moment round here.'

'Could you just enlighten me on one thing.'

'I'll try,' Rod replied his finger pressed on the lint.

'I was looking at Andy's records the other day, as I'm bound to be asked about him at some time for some reason or another, did he have any tattoos on his body?'

'I honestly don't know, I seem to remember he wasn't a fan,' Rod said checking that there was no bleeding and pulling his sleeve down. 'Why?'

'It's just that I remember that he had a large birthmark on his back and what with tattoos being so fashionable, I wondered whether he may have had one to cover it up.'

'As I said Theo, I don't think so, but don't actually know,' Rod replied placing both hands on the arms of his chair to push himself up, relieved that taking his blood was over. 'Five days for the results?'

'Crossed fingers and a following wind. Could be quicker'

*

'Good of you to join us Kevin,' Griffin said wishing to appear serious whilst suppressing a smile as Henshall sloped into the DI's office.

'Bastards,' Henshall replied resting rather than sitting on the edge of his stool beside the filing cabinet, arms firmly crossed. 'Sorry boss.'

'Anything important?' Griffin asked looking towards the other two detectives in his office, all here for the daily morning briefing. The three of them in the loop as to why Henshall was urgently summoned to the front office. 'Is it worth sharing?'

'You're in on it, aren't you?' Henshall probed looking round his DI's office at three faces fit to burst.

'What's that Kev?' Mantel asked trying to be nonchalant.

'The new lead for Arnott's cows, that I was urgently called down to the front desk for.'

'Tell us mooore,' Nimra replied giving up the cause and laughing.

'Was it helpful?' enquired Mantel hand over her mouth.

'What a milk urn with a fillet steak on top, with Frank on the desk pronouncing that as I took so long coming down things appeared to have moooved on, but they'll be udder leads. I mean it wasn't even funny. I should have guessed something was up when there were so many at the front desk. I suppose I should take it as a belated initiation and that I am now part of the team.'

'There's on big question Kev,' Griffin said sipping at his espresso.

'What's that boss?'

'Where's the fillet steak?'

'Eff off, it wasn't even real, and I didn't get a coffee. Life's a bummer.' A smile appeared on Henshall's face.

'Ah poor Kevin,' Mantel said with a none too sympathetic look. 'Oh boss, before we go on, can I share my dream?'

'Only if it's mucky.'

'Please, what sort of girl do you take me for? And don't answer that,' Mantel replied adjusting herself in her chair. 'It was really weird. I was in a car, one of Cathal's cars. I know that because it still had one of those boards on top of it. Well, we went to a drive in burger place, don't think it was a Mac's...'

'We?'

'Not sure who with, you know how it is, but I wasn't alone,' Mantel replied to her captivated audience. 'Anyway serving this huge burger was Andy Nash wearing absolutely tonnes of bling, then we pulled away eating this enormous burger and then I woke up.'

'Well you certainly took your work home with that one,' Henshall said now relaxed on his stool. 'All wrapped up in one dream; stolen cars, missing cattle turning up as burgers, gold into bling and Nash.'

'Well, all I can say Luce,' Griffin said ruefully. 'It wasn't me in the car with you because I had pizza last night.'

'Ha, bloody, ha,' Mantel replied. 'It's no surprise that I had a nightmare after looking at that web site. It's fucking gruesome, why do they do it? No, don't answer that, we've done that.'

'On that front I have potential news,' Griffin said. 'Stephen, Ronni's brother is, and this is totally off the record, going to try to establish who is hosting this site. Whether it leads to Nash, I very much doubt, But I for one would certainly be very interested to find out more about how these things operate.'

'My guess would be some scruffy back street house with a perve at the keyboard. Probably works in IT at the council,' Henshall suggested.

'I reckon it's not even in the UK,' Nimra offered. 'Probably one of my distant cousins, probably not that distant back in Delhi.'

'Nah,' Mantel said dismissively. 'A hidden part of one of the big corporations in the States. It's big money and provides access to so much personal information.'

'Well no promises, but once again, worth a stab even if I don't think it will lead us to Nash,' Griffin said attempting to lob his empty cup into the bin, giving a little celebratory punch as it dropped in off the rim. 'I'll let you know what he comes up with, if anything. Think I'd prefer the trip to Delhi out of those. Tell you what, whoever's right gets to go and talk to them. As for Nash, just the one sighting then.'

'A sighting, now that is news, where and when boss?' His detectives sat up in expectation.

'Serving at that burger joint. You just told me, it's as good as we've got,' the DI replied with a straight face. 'Right, now for something interesting, the prints from the gold are in.'

'Goldfinger,' Henshall quipped in an attempt to mimic the Bond theme tune, his colleagues looking at him in amusement.

'Yes Kevin, the very same,' Griffin replied. 'Didn't have you down as a singer and I still don't. Well, the vicar's are on it, no surprises there. Then we have three sets that were very feint, but once again the guys have come up trumps. The old Reverend, Wilton-Brook, perhaps expected as it was in the vicarage.'

'Always top of my list,' Mantel said. 'Right dodgy.'

'Agreed. Then our Geoff from the Cobblers, which goes some way to answering our hunch over his bunk with Wilton-Brook out to Thailand. Then, of a bit more interest, Mike Curtis.'

'Curtis, the old governor at the Cobblers before Ronni?' Mantel asked.

'The very same, lucky that we had his prints. No idea where they'll start to find him, but very interesting. Then there's two others.'

'A bit like Wetherspoons,' said Nimra.

'Was that a joke Nim?' Mantel asked.

'A busy bar, get it?'

'I'd stick to police work.'

'How they got all these off of that bar is beyond me. I'm sure that Kevin will be able to tell us all about the history of fingerprinting,' Griffin continued with a glance at his DC.

'Bit complex that one, many scientists since the late eighteen hundreds stake claims...'

'Okay, thank you Kevin, we'll save that for a rainy day. These other two are new to me. A William Carter-Stoop, from all accounts generally known as Billy, and a James Charwell. Do any of you know them?' Three heads shook. 'Well Billy is a wheeler dealer into all sorts of stuff, he's had dealings with us in the past, a few stolen items. Nothing serious. Charwell is a little more interesting, a gold trader, who spent some time inside a decade ago for an insurance fraud. From what I could deduce after getting this late last night, is that they are a couple of Raffles style characters.'

'Raffles, I thought that was a bar in Singapore?' Nimra queried. 'The one where Bogart said, 'Play it again Sam'.'

'That was Rick's Bar in Casablanca,' Henshall replied. 'I think the boss is referring to a TV thief called Raffles back in the 70s who liked cricket, played by Anthony Valentine...'

'Thank you Kevin, spot on, I think.' Griffin once again confounded by his DC's range of knowledge, from absolute crap to the semi-useful. 'The Yard are handling it and they're tracking down the Thailand two, so there won't be any jollies for us up for grabs. And they'll try to locate Mike Curtis, good luck to them with that. I'm off up town straight after this to sit in on the interviews. Billy and James have agreed to come in which should be interesting. I'll keep you informed. Anything else?'

'Well, I'm off to Blue Skies House to do some DNAing,' Nimra said. 'A bit of community stuff, it's all being paid for, the tests that is, not me.'

'Couldn't afford you Nim,' Henshall quipped.

'Absolutely Kevin,' Nimra replied blushing slightly. 'They've got some genealogy chap, meant to be an expert who's been coming in regularly for their family trees and all that, and they thought that getting their DNAs would be fun. Not sure why, but it'll add a few more to the database.'

'Good to be proactive Nim,' Mantel said. 'Means we'll be ready when Michael Caine recruits for his next heist.'

'Well enjoy it Nimra, is it staff as well?'

'Anyone who wants to join in.'

'Drive-in free public DNA testing, now there's an idea. I mean it only takes a minute, DNAs R Us,' Griffin said grabbing his jacket. 'Enough. Right, I'm off prospecting for gold.'

*

Dr Theo Shapiro sat back and stared at the paused image on his personal laptop. His last patient had been and gone half an hour ago and with it being half day at the surgery it was only him and Maggie on reception left in the building. Today his diary was clear, no private appointments. A crystal tumbler with a large splash of scotch in one hand as he contemplated what to do next. Frustrated that his text to Mike Griffin had not been answered. He had hoped to take up Rod's idea of a meeting with the Inspector for a pint at the rugby club later, an idea now on hold until he got a reply. Patience was not a strong attribute of the GP.

He closed his laptop in frustration and put it in its leather case, downed the whisky and decided to await Griffin's reply at home.

*

'This is a really great idea Prish,' Nimra said standing beside her friend as residents and staff queued in Blue Skies House's 'ballroom' to have their DNA extracted. Gary, the genealogy expert was administering the tests under the guidance of the ready to drop Matron, being only days before the due date. They were assisted by Alisha, the Area Manager from the DNA kit company, there to help promote her product and apparently herself. Margaret, as Margaret always did, marshalled the line-up. 'I need to have a word with Alisha.'

'What about her outfit?' Prisha asked. 'Or are the force running out of DNA kits?'

'Ha, ha. No, just that I'm under orders to try and get a copy of the results.'

'Isn't that a bit sneaky, even illegal?'

'Using ones initiative I'd prefer to call it, but yes it probably is. I reckon if I offer to promote these sort of events on my travels, that should do it. She looks the sort who's easily bought.'

'Bitchy. Although the killer heels, which must be killing her, and the cleavage have certainly got her noticed,' Prisha said referring to the rep's flirty attire a little out of sync with a retirement home.

'Quite, she's certainly out to make an impression.'

'Ellie's got the defib on stand-by for a couple of the gentlemen residents and she's certainly turned up the heat in the kitchen.'

'Great turnout, chefs, gardeners, concierge, although I didn't see Mr Patel, or did I miss him?'

'No, he's out today, but Stella our new boss has had hers taken. Suppose she feels she should join in and make an early impression.'

'I was introduced to her earlier, seems nice to me.'

''Yes, first impressions, I like her. Word is she's a bit of a girl. Background in hotels and hospitality. Hope to get her out for a drink soon. Talking of which, are you free after this?

CHAPTER TWENTY THREE

'Ray, good to see you,' Griffin shook DI Ray Pyke's hand in his compact, highly personalised office in the Curtis Green Building on the banks of the River Thames, just along from Westminster, the home to New Scotland Yard and the Met.

'Mike, looking good,' Pyke replied.

Tucked behind the door, the other person in the room got to their feet. 'Arnie, good to see you,' Griffin said turning to greet his old friend DS Arnie Smith. With Griffin, fit and stocky, standing at just 5'9", Smith, a lived-life, carrying a few extra pounds six footer and Pyke, a 6'5" beanpole, they made a contrasting trio, linked by blue business suits and their devotion to the force.

'Good to see you back at the sharp end Mike,' Smith responded in a thick south of the river accent, shaking hands with appreciative venom. 'Didn't get a nosebleed then, coming in from the sticks?'

'Fuck off, probably more action out there than you get in here,' Griffin replied taking a seat along with his colleagues.

'Okay, we've not got long Mike, we've already shown them into interview rooms and given them refreshments. I wanted to make sure you got the update first and to get our strategy straight,' Pyke said sitting very upright behind his desk, with his sticky out ears Griffin could not help but think he looked like a giraffe in a shirt and tie. 'Thought we'd go down memory lane with this one and let you and Arnie loose on it.'

'What, to see if we fuck up again,' Griffin replied with a smile. 'Sounds good to me, let's look at what we've got then.'

'Plenty,' Smith responded delighted to be reunited with his old mucker, Griffin was his DS when he was a wet behind the ears DC, belatedly fresh out of uniform on the original gold heist.

'You have the details on the prints and who planted them. We're actively pursuing the Thai angle and we reckon we've already tracked down Curtis albeit to Guadalajara in Mexico,' Pyke said flicking through some papers.

'Good work.'

20

'The wonders of ye-olde computer. As you know Geoff Rous and Wilton-Brook were always on the radar, but never enough to warrant a trip out there.'

'So, some lucky bastards have now got an expenses paid trip to Thailand, eh?'

'Correct,' Pyke replied, Smith grinning overtly.

'It'll be tough Arnie, don't forget to pack the factor 50 and some condoms. Who's got the short straw to go with you?'

'Cassa,' Smith replied still smiling, referring to DC Caroline Stickland a stalwart of the force, with a reserved seat in front of the disciplinary panel. 'They won't know what's hit them Mike, not just Rouse and Wilton-Brook, Thailand full stop. First time out there for me, looking forward to it.'

'Blimey, you sure Ray. It might be cheap out there, but these two, well. I wish I has an exs budget like that.'

'Decided that it needed a bit of old-fashioned policing,' Pyke replied, who like Griffin and Smith had put in the hard years and collected the badges and bruises to prove it. 'No poncing about, I reckon they'll be four of them on the plane back.'

'Confident stuff, I like it. So who's off to Mexico?'

'To be decided...'

'Ah, it's my ball is it. One of the perks Ray, you don't need to justify it to me. Just hope they've got a sombrero in your size. And don't tell me DC Maddie Clarke has been asked if her passport's up to date,' Griffin said with a mischievous smile.

'Chosen on merit Mike,' Pyke replied. DCs Maddie Clarke and Cassa Stickland were peas in a pod. Should Maddie and Cassa suggest a quick one down the pub after a shift, you knew to put on your drinking boots and line up the paracetamol for the morning.

'So I'm left with interviewing a couple of wannabe hoorays well above their stations,' Griffin said mockingly shaking his head at his two oldest friends in the Met. 'I read what you sent me on the train. By the way, please note, I'm on the train, so I'm expecting a little lubrication after this.'

'A given,' Smith replied. 'So as you've seen, William Carter-Stoop had known the Reverend Mandy Jarvis since schooldays when he was plain ol Billy Stoop. Now a player in the top end of the second-hand market or antiques as the snobs call it. From the chat I had with him when they checked in, he obviously enjoys playing the posh card judging by the flowing hanky out of his top pocket. I've already got him down as really shallow. You thought the same didn't you Ray?'

'Yeh, nothing of substance would be my call, bit like what he buys and sells I'd imagine,' Pyke said consulting the open manilla file on his desk in front of him. 'Reckon he'll spurt out everything if we use the tactics you texted. Likewise with Charwell. We can't find any links between him and the vicar, so can only surmise that this was their first meeting. Taken along for the ride by Billy boy. He might be a little harder to crack, but I don't see him being too brave and he should collapse like Arnie trying to shuffle a pack of cards with a little discreet pressure.'

'We've got them down as a couple of small-time chancers who thought three cherries had come up only to see them disappear as quickly as they arrived,' Smith said with the knowing look of a seasoned detective.

'So, run it past me how you see it,' Griffin said leaning forward.

'Right,' Pyke said with purpose. 'Obviously, there is nothing proven.'

'Nothing is, until it is Ray, but go on, your instincts are usually right.'

'Our vicar found the gold bar in the crypt completely by chance.'

'The crypt?

'Forensics, they're fucking clever but a strange lot, tracked it back to where there was a gap, how I don't know, the wonders of modern science, they believe that it had been down there under the candlestick, one of the murder weapons, for a few months. Obviously having her phone must have helped them. So the vicar's contacted her old mate Billy Now what we will never know is whether Jarvis knew anything about gold bars. We don't have any links previously. We think that it was just a lucky find, so to speak.'

'Okay, I'm with that. So she takes it to the vicarage and calls Billy for his advice. What next?' Griffin asked.

'We have Jarvis's phone records that prove that contact was made on the morning of Jarvis's attack and I sure that it will be verified when we get into Billy's mobile,' Smith said.

'So Billy graciously offers to come and take a look, being the good Samaritan he is,' Pyke continued. 'Remember Jarvis has sent him photos of the gold bar, so he's well aware of what he's going to see.'

'And his mate James goes with him. Billy takes him along with the view to him setting up the sale, what with his connections and in their excitement they both grab hold of the bar and leave their grubby mitts all over it, and all round the study and hallway,' Griffin said animatedly. 'Or, were they planning to hand it in to us at the station as soon as they found a gap in their diaries?'

'Exactly. You're good at this,' Pyke responded. 'I reckon Charwell went off to find a buyer and no doubt his phone will reveal something. Would you believe they kindly handed their phones in when they arrived, didn't have to, but I asked, and they did.'

'Didn't happen to mention anything about a murder then?'

'May have let it slip. They'll be putty in your hands Mike. I doubt they had the foresight to delete anything off their phones, we're downloading them as we speak. So with Charwell off finding a buyer, the vicar and Billy were left playing the waiting game.'

'I don't think the vicar was supposed to leave it on the kitchen table and chuck flour all over it though.'

'I don't think she envisaged what happened to happen,' Smith responded. 'We can find absolutely no connection between the two events. Absolutely nothing to put Swift and the gold together. Now we may be wrong, but we don't think he went there on the off chance there'd be an ingot up for grabs on the kitchen table. The bastard had gone there with the sole intention of raping the vicar and probably to murder her.'

'Sadly, I'm with you on that one Arnie,' Griffin said with a downbeat look. 'What a fucking psycho, probably the worst I've come across.'

'He doesn't sound very pleasant and I know that you met him so have first-hand experience,' Pyke said. 'Right, back to Billy and Charwell, apart from literally handling stolen goods we don't think they've done anything wrong. Another twenty four hours and it may have been so different. Unless they've left some incriminating evidence to the contrary on their phones, they're only in for a caution. Although it's worth giving them a grilling, whilst they're not the Krays, they're obviously no angels.'

'So let me clarify. Absolutely no connection with these two and Rous, Wilton-Brook or Curtis?' Griffin asked.

'Correct, absolutely zero and I'd put money on it,' Pyke replied. 'And you know me, that's not easily said.'

'Okay I'm happy with that, I don't think that the coincidence theory come into play here, it was just a freak sequence of events,' Griffin said leaning back and placing his hands behind his head. 'Right, so what we want is chapter and verse as to what happened and make sure that their stories stack up, all the time putting the shit up them to warn them not to be naughty boys again.'

'Correct again,' Pyke said. 'That's unless they cough to anything else. You ready then?'

'Yep.'

'Are we having a bet as to who topples first and how long they last?' Smith asked.

'It's Billy for me in ten seconds flat,' said Pyke.

'What I reckon we won't get is a confession that the schneisters were planning to go back and see if the bar was still there after they heard that Jarvis had been murdered, which I reckon the bastards would have been thinking.'

With the relative pleasantries and the official stuff completed by Smith, Griffin, previously observing silently, leant forward and rested on his arms on the fixed table in Interview Room 6. 'So, Billy or William, what do you prefer?' Griffin asked in a comforting tone.

'William will do fine Inspector.'

'Okay William as you know you're here in connection with the murder of Reverend Mandy Jarvis in the Vicarage at St Vincent's church.'

'I've nothing to do with that.'

'Your fresh prints were found in the kitchen, and all over the house where Mandy was discovered stabbed to death,' said Griffin failing to add that the prints were only on the gold bar and in the study and not found anywhere else in the kitchen, guessing that with such a strong opening statement Billy would be oblivious to the finer detail.

'As I've said, I've nothing to do with Mandy's murder.'

'Oh, sorry, do you deny going to the vicarage on the day of the vicar's murder?'

'I was there, I admit that, but I didn't murder Mandy, she was an old friend,' Billy answered struggling to keep his emotions under control. 'I had gone to see her that morning about a business matter.'

'And what was that? Did you have a falling out over this business matter,' Griffin asked continuing to lean forward. 'Because at the moment William, we have you at the scene of a murder.'

'No. Wait. As I said I was there in the morning and Mandy was fine,' Billy responded now not thinking straight, forgetting all about the lunch at the Meze restaurant.

'So what was this business you were discussing with the vicar? Remember Billy that if you tell us the truth we may be able to eliminate you from the murder enquiry and concentrate on the gold bar.'

Billy froze, any composure left in him evaporated. He stared at the Inspector, then the DS, the nano -second of relief that a murder charge could be dropped instantly replaced with a new concern. The accusations hurled at him by the calm and calculating DI, had completely scuppered any pre-planned thoughts of denying knowledge of the gold bar. Rapidly calculating that to spill the beans on the ingot and how innocent he was regarding the murder could see him walk out of New Scotland Yard a free man, not a murder suspect. To not divulge anything of note on the gold could see the old bill implicating him in a murder where his prints were all over the crime scene.

'Okay Inspector,' Billy said taking a deep breath. 'Let me tell you what happened that morning.'

'Please, go-ahead,' Griffin replied with his best understanding face.

'Well I got a text from Mandy...'

*

Dr Theo Shapiro strode, well little more than waddled, down his tree-lined road past fine houses of a similar size to his, all of contrasting architecture. His destination the rugby club at the end of the road, a mere three minutes downhill on the way there, possibly fifteen if staggering back. He was frustrated. It was a rarity that a personal message went unanswered. Of course, there was a chance that the technology had failed and that the Inspector would be sitting on a stool with a foaming pint of cask ale awaiting his arrival. Mike Griffin, a respected pillar of the community, a Detective Inspector, regarded as a jolly good sort at the club was unlikely to ignore such an important request to meet for a chat with the prominent health professional in the area.

Theo pondered that perhaps he should have given a clue as to what it was about as he pushed open the oak door to the bar. A near empty bar, completely empty if you didn't include Stan, the bar manager reading a copy of the London Standard, everybody else out on the pitches training.

'Evening Doc,' Stan said putting his paper down. 'Pint?'

'Please Stan. Mike Griffin not been in?'

The Queens, a renowned boozer round the back of New Scotland Yard was heaving with civil service types of all genders. Whether nine-to-five, flexitime, hot desking or other variations on that theme, when the home time bell tolled The Queens was the ideal place to vent the issues of the day. Maybe to slag off your boss, or even initiate an office romance before the commute home. At five thirty a seat was hard to find. Griffin looked at his phone catching up on his messages as Pyke got the drinks and snacks in, and Smith took a call outside. Of particular intrigue was a rare text from Dr Theo Shapiro, a guy he knew through professional circles and had chatted to a couple of times at the bar down the rugby club, but Griffin could not recall ever having a request to meet him for a beer. He glanced at his watch, there was no way that he was going to make it tonight so thumbed a reply.

sorry only just seen this stuck up town another time perhaps unless its urgent

Griffin tucked his phone away as the beers, snacks and his colleagues arrived at the tiny table with equally small stools.

'Well, that's those two sorted then. Cheers,' Pyke said raising his glass before taking a serious glug.

'Perhaps not ten seconds.' Smith grabbed a bag of nuts form the table. 'But not far off it. You could tell neither of them considered being implicated in the murder. You certainly caught them off balance with that Mike.'

'The shame is I don't think they've got much else to offer or they wouldn't have offered up their mobiles so easily, but it's always good to see the smugness disappear,' Pyke said looking like a parent at a teachers meeting in a kindergarten classroom on a stool that was no higher than his ankles. 'They were certainly floundering.'

'Bricking it springs to mind,' Griffin said feeling satisfied with an enjoyable afternoon's work. Such had been the outpouring by both of them that they had curtailed the interviews when it was decided that there was nothing more of interest to be gleaned. Proceedings concluded with DNA tests and a promise that they would be in touch. 'Despite being half a mil down, I bet they're in some fancy cocktail bar celebrating swerving the murder charges. As I said, fear plays mind games, and they were genuinely worried.'

'And you were right Mike, the only question they both clammed up on and sort of denied, was whether they intended to re-visit St Vincent's.'

*

'Is it urgent?' Theo pondered as he stared into his whisky having read Griffin's text for the umpteenth time. It was semi-urgent. It was also a dilemma, Hippocratic oath versus personal reputation? As this wasn't his first scotch the climb back home may take a little longer. Even Theo couldn't justify a cab for six hundred yards. With the bar now busy there maybe someone going his way and could drop him off?...

CHAPTER TWENTY FOUR

'Morning all.' Griffin greeted his team. 'Don't suppose that Nash has turned up overnight?'

'Ha, fucking ha,' Mantel replied sipping her soya milk. 'So he wasn't in a cell at the Yard and they'd forgotten to give us a call?'

'Fraid not, although it was an enjoyable afternoon. Fucking envious though, Arnie's off to Thailand to speak with Geoff and the old vicar, and they've located Mike Curtis in Mexico, so Ray's going out there. I was hoping that Nash had turned up in Barbados and needed accompanying back.'

'Two hopes there boss, and one's dead,' Mantel quipped.

'Lost me again,' Nimra said.

'Kev?' Griffin looked towards his huge DC with an encyclopaedic mind to match his physical stature, for him to explain this remark to his colleague.

'Sorry, but I don't know that one.'

'But Kevin, you know everything,' Nimra exclaimed. 'Luce?'

'One hope is the late American comedian Bob Hope...'

'Who was actually English,' Henshall chipped in.

'Sorry Kev, you had your chance. The other is no, as in no hope.'

'Ah, I get it, I think,' Nimra replied still looking a little perplexed. 'Sorry sir, you were saying that you had a good time at the Yard?'

'Yeh, I interviewed the two chancers who had met Mandy at the vicarage on the morning of the stabbing and boy did they shit themselves, believing that we had them on her murder. I'll tell you more over a beer sometime, it was amusing though. At least we thought so, we had some fun with them.'

Mantel wagged a finger at her boss. 'Boys will be boys,'

'What time is the media appeal?' Nimra asked.

'Pretty much all day,' Mantel replied having coordinated this latest appeal, the most extensive to date, the content as hard hitting and raw as the regulators would permit before the watershed. 'We're posting it on social media from ten and throughout the day, right across the board. Local radio has been briefed. The BBC stations will carry it on their lunchtime and teatime bulletins, the independents, well it's up to them. Obviously, we hope the local ones will carry it. We hope to make it the story of the day and to trend on social media. The press office will be monitoring the coverage.'

'And TV?' Henshall asked.

'Again the BBC local station has all pledged to carry it at lunchtime and or their early evening news. Pending the news of the day we may get a national shout. Then there's the World service, which could throw something up and the rolling 24 hour news channels are always looking for something to fill the time. We also got promises from ITV, Channel 4, Sky and 5, so fingers crossed there.'

'You're under selling yourself Luce, this is a big step up by going national with the appeal,' Griffin said. 'Topped off tonight with it being on Crimewatch, you've done a fucking great job.'

'Thank you boss,' Mantel replied shifting uneasily with the praise. 'But without the fantastic support of the press office I'd have got nowhere. They've pulled out all the stops, I think it's hit a nerve with a few of them. Rapists are the lowest of the low.'

'There are a couple of consequences we should be prepared for. It's nationwide so will, hopefully, increase the number of sightings, many of which will be false, most in good faith, others though will be from those with nothing better to do. This in turn could become an irritant, not to us but around the country, there'll be some of our colleagues who will get pissed off being asked to follow-up the crap,' said Griffin panning round his team. 'So it's best behaviour today, please be as polite as possible with everyone, we need their help. Look since Nash absconded we've had a murderer round here, many might have forgotten about Nash. Obviously not the victims, nor those with any involvement. But for many a murderer on the loose was top of their agenda. This is our chance to reignite everyone's concerns. We need the eyes and ears of everyone. I suggest we reconvene at lunchtime to take stock and then regularly throughout the day. We've got the backing of upstairs on this one, so let's make it count. Anything else Luce? You've done a fantastic job.'

'Nope, that's it boss, fingers crossed.'

'Yep, Nash under lock and key by lunchtime and the Crimewatch slot cancelled would be a satisfactory outcome,' Griffin said tapping his biro. 'I do have some interesting news to share on a different matter.'

'Swift and the timed devices?' Henshall suggested.

'Ah, so the news has spread like the fires,' Griffin said a little disappointed to have his exclusive quashed.

'Just something about incendiary devices with timers, they were very excited,' Nimra said turning her head towards the main office where a few of the murder team remained.

'So it appears that Swift, as well as being a fucking pyscho, was a devious bastard. Once again forensics have achieved miracles, this time the fire boys. Somehow they discovered two incendiary devices, with links to timers at the seat of the fires in the Unit and at his London flat. So much for militant groups being behind it, it looks like Swift was covering his own tracks, eradicating all evidence, whilst being able to defuse the devices remotely once he done his deed and not been caught. Been watching too much Spooks in my book.'

'Yeh, I doubt the fucker was contemplating dying though,' Mantel replied cynically.

'Must have had a reasonable lag on the timer though,' Henshall said shifting forward on his perch.

'Agreed Kevin. They reckon he gave himself thirty six hours from leaving wherever he left from. Why thirty six hours? Who knows, but that's their rough calculation at this stage.'

'That's what I was getting at boss,' Henshall continued having done the maths in his head. 'We got lucky that he didn't set it for shorter.'

'What for us not to be frazzled?' Mantel said.

'Exactly,' Griffin said. 'Although of little consequence as we didn't find anything, not even the devices, which in itself is a little embarrassing. Thankfully, I don't think he'd factored in us in being so quick off the mark for what it was worth.'

'So do you think he calculated there being people, like the guys out there searching his homes?'

'Could well have done Nim, which would have been very nasty. And they were lucky, so to speak at the unit. From what I heard it was so well hidden that smoke was seen before it took hold, so they were alerted to it early enough to clear the building. Personally, I think he was just intent in destroying everything, any strand of evidence if he was still alive and being interrogated, which of course he wasn't. A laptop was recovered from the Merc, but as that was the most intense fire of the four, they reckon there's zero chance of recovering anything from it.'

'This is going to sound macabre sir,' Nimra said. 'But to have had the chance to examine inside his brain, to get an idea of his thinking would have been fascinating, don't you think?'

'I know and I agree. It's what I said to Angela and Nicola at the time, that the frustration with a murderer dying is that it leaves so many unanswered questions.'

'I reckon that's what it was,' Henshall interjected. 'His brain was just so big and gnarled that it imploded. Some nutters can pull it off, some can't'

'No sympathy here for the bastard,' Griffin said. 'And it doesn't help us to find Nash, which I hope this appeal does. It does draw a line under Swift, at least for us, even if he was involved or did know something, we'll never know.'

'Not quite boss,' Mantel said.

'Sorry, have I missed something?'

'It's Mandy's funeral tomorrow,' Nimra said quietly.

'Oh yes, sorry. I hadn't forgotten.'

'I take it we're attending boss.'

'Absolutely Kevin.'

'From what you've said, it will be interesting to see who discreetly turns up to pay their respects,' Mantel said with a mischievous look.

*

'Come in Prisha, make yourself at home,' Margaret said answering the Head of Marketing's knock on her door with her ever present smile. 'Just in time, it's about to start. Fancy a tipple? You look nice.'

'Thank you. No thanks, saving myself, I'm out later,' Prisha replied taking a seat, dressed for the pub and her rendezvous with friends at the Terrible Influence Inn after watching the programme. Margaret, being Margaret, would have loved to have joined them for a drink or two. Often reminiscing with Prisha about her antics when she was her age.

'Don't mind if I do, do you?' Margaret asked opening her drinks cabinet.

'Please go ahead. Right here we go,' Prisha said as the preliminaries for Crimewatch appeared on Margaret's proportionately sized state-of-the-art television. Each and every room in Blue Skies House benefited from the latest technology and a super-fast, fibre broadband connection.

'Ellie's late,' Margaret said pouring herself a generous gin and tonic, and a slice from a small pot prepared by the kitchen. 'She so wanted to see this.'

'You haven't heard?'

'What, oh no, it's not bad news is it?'

'No, all's fine Margaret. She went in for a check-up this afternoon and with it being so imminent they asked her to stay in. To be honest they've been keeping a close eye on her throughout. Rod's with her.'

'That's because of her age?' Margaret said taking her favourite chair as the programme began. 'How old is she, late thirties?'

'Forty, but she looks good for it doesn't she? Her we go, let's talk about Ellie after this,' Prisha said as the programme opened with the presenter

introducing the appeal as to the whereabouts of the convicted rapist And
Nash, who continued to be on the run.

*

The wife was out, the kids were out, again, he should have a word, and
Theo decided that his brain was decidedly out of sync. At least not
functioning as he would have liked it to. Ahead of him on the mahogany
coffee table in the lounge of his spacious detached house was a half full
glass and bottle of his favourite red wine. French, of course, and burgund
at that. A 2014 Gevry-Chambertin, in the distant past he seemed to recall
James Bond quaffing it, if Ian Fleming deemed it a fine wine then that wa
good enough for Theo. A little expensive for his pocket, if not his tastes, it
would certainly not appear on the family Sunday lunch table where it
would not be appreciated, a decent Languedoc would suffice for that.
There had been no further communication with Detective Inspector
Griffin, leaving Theo undecided when, or even whether to contact him
again. Crimewatch played out on the television in front of him with
delightful images of the town he lived in and adored so much.

*

'Pint please wench?' Griffin demanded as he slid onto Geoff's stool at the
end of the bar and loosened his tie and nodded towards Greg in the
corner.

'Enough of that,' Veronica replied whipping her tea towel in the direction
of her favourite DI. The only other punter in The Cobblers not looking up
from his pint and the smart phone he was engrossed in.

'Quiet tonight?'

'Yeh, it's late, and now the re-dev is back underway they've started
drifting off again, a few in earlier. Still it won't be long before it's all
finished and we'll be complaining that we're rushed off our feet.'

'Did you watch it?

'Crimewatch you mean. Yes, you?'

'We got a preview of it an hour before screening.'

'We had it on because I was interested,' Veronica said pouring the pint. 'Don't think it would have been appropriate if we had the usual crowd in. It's one thing bragging about being on some TV game show, not quite the same seeing your mate's mug on Crimewatch, don't think it's a must watch.'

'What did you think though?'

'It was good, very much to the point, and pretty hard-hitting. Has it got a response?'

'Early vibes have been good, although there's always the usual initial surge. Don't think people watch television these days unless there's a number to call. Good job we shipped in some civilian help as we've got plenty to follow-up from everything else during the day. The power of social media globally is quite frightening. I now know all the Commonwealth countries because they've all had a sighting of Nash.'

'Really, here you go,' Veronica said handing over the pint.

'Thanks. And if you name a town in the UK I bet he's also been seen there.'

'So how do you follow them all up?'

'Well we listen to them all. Any chance of some nuts, dry roasted?'

'Fucking hell Inspector, I didn't know that I'd be wining and dining you tonight,' Veronica said lobbing over a bag, the other customer grinning to himself at their banter.

'So, yes we have our automated response system. I say automated, a person takes down details and asks some poignant questions, like did they have two legs or arms. If they tick eight out ten boxes, which is very rare, then it's put into a pile for a proper police follow-up. Nothing beats the pen and paper, although every single call is logged on the computer. We'd be given an urgent shout if a call was of particular interest. Our biggest fear is letting the real sighting get away. Like that guy who turned The Beatles down.'

'Not quite the same, but I get what you mean. I probably couldn't remember who's been in tonight, let alone last week.'

'I can help with tonight,' Griffin replied looking around the bar. 'No one. I don't think it's necessarily tonight that we'll get a positive sighting. Now we've re-planted the seed, he's got nowhere to go that someone hasn't seen the appeal. We can start to sift what we've got, although I remain pessimistic. For instance, Kuala Lumpur, the sighting was just too tall, Cape Town was a black man and we've had countless women, whereas one of the sightings from Brighton does have some merit.'

'All very scientific Mike.'

'The computer is fantastic at times, but old fashioned legwork is required here. We'll see, for now a pint and your delightful company is all I yearn for,' Griffin said, with Veronica responding by sticking two fingers in her mouth. 'You on your own? No Lily?'

'Off shagging your mate,' Veronica said, a comment that made the customer down the bar show a small amount of interest. 'And no point getting any of the others in. Just means keeping ones legs crossed.'

'Ah, good point. I'll keep an eye if you want to go.'

'Not a bad idea. You going to the funeral tomorrow I take it.'

'Yeh, are you?'

'Yes,' came a shouted reply from the direction of the ladies. With this, the chap with his phone glanced in Griffin's direction.

'Which rag do you write for? Griffin asked of the casually dressed, unshaven guy, sensing a journo was in the camp.

'Freelance, how did you guess?'

'You stand out even more than we do.'

'You mean coppers?'

'See,' Griffin said finishing his pint. 'Treat it sensitively tomorrow please. This area's taken an unfair bashing. They don't need any more bad press.'

'I'll just tell it how it is.'

CHAPTER TWENTY FIVE

'Respectful eyes and ears today please guys.' Griffin greets hi troops his appetite satisfied by another of Veronica's full English breakfast's. 'Obviously pay your respects, but from the professional viewpoint I'm expecting quite a turnout and don't want to be caught unawares having not spotted something or someone.'

'So who's on your 'who's, who' list?' Henshall asked, the team assembled in Griffin's office for the early briefing, all respectively turned out in black, there being no alternative directive.

'Across the board Kev. Word is the Bishop's presiding.'

'That'll be the Bishop of Essex. I read recently that there are 108 Bishops in England.' Henshall replied. 'So, who else do you think will turn up?'

'Well there's her client list,' Griffin said, Henshall having been bought up to speed with Mandy's colourful past, including the prominent figures in the force who had indulged in her services. 'There could be a few of those flirting round the edges not wishing to be clocked. Problem is they'll probably bump into the Spooks.'

'The Spooks, as in MI5?' Mantel enquired becoming intrigued.

'Wouldn't surprise me Luce. Look out for the Ray-Bans and a bulge in their pocket.'

'Too much info boss.'

'There's no way that with an address book like hers that they weren't all over it, and now they'll want to make sure that she is firmly laid to rest.'

'Oh, please boss,' Mantel retorted, her mind racing ahead of her boss's thoughts.

'Then of course, there's always Nash.'

'He wouldn't be there, would he?' Nimra asked with a concerned look. 'He's no reason to, Mandy wasn't even round here.'

'I agree Nim, but he is an unpredictable nutter, I haven't been privy to the guest list, so as they say keep em Peeled', Griffin said attempting a gesture involving his fingers and eyes and failing. 'Away from the funeral Ronni tells me that Stephen's hoping to have the host's details for that site later, from all accounts he has made significant progress.'

*

'Perfect,' Veronica said as Lily appeared in the bar dressed in a respectful black dress with a sexy slant. 'Exactly how Mandy would have wanted.'

'You to Ron,' Lily replied admiring her boss's designer outfit.

'Twenty quid I think. One of the last things I got out of Geoff's bag before he done his bunk. Never worn it as the funerals dried up,' Veronica said smoothing down the dress and adjusting the hat. 'Hat; yes or no?'

'Your call Ron. I'm not a fan, so I'm not.'

'Ah, here they are.' Freddie Bone's gleaming white Range Rover pulled up outside the window. 'You're right Lils, I'll go without, they don't suit me either.'

'Morning ladies,' Freddie said, as immaculately turned out as always. 'You both look respectfully lovely.'

'Morning Freddie and thank you,' Veronica responded giving a twirl pleased to receive a compliment from a someone with obvious good taste. 'Where's your Siamese twin?'

'No idea, all a bit strange,' Freddie responded shrugging his shoulders and glancing at his watch. 'Didn't arrive at the office this morning and his phone goes to voicemail.'

'Home?'

'I'll leave that a bit, don't want to set off any unnecessary alarm bells. No one wants a domestic. He's often stayed away but is always around in the morning.'

'Will you be okay on your own Freddie?' Lily asked cheekily to which Freddie gave her a playful, indignant glance. 'I take it that's a yes then.'

'Georgie and Marti, sorry Angie, will be here soon, so all is set. We'll be back as soon as it's appropriate I reckon there'll be another media circus. I've stocked up on crisps.'

*

'Nice service,' Mantel said nonchalantly as the four detectives gathered near the gravestones, not wishing to be the first in the vicarage for the wake. 'Great turnout, but word has it that there was zero family. Some very glamourous sorts though, a real contrast with her congregation.'

'Is that one? Nimra asked.

'One what?' Griffin replied.

'A Spook,' Nimra said trying to be as discreet as possible in pointing out a bloke in shades and a dark suit on the other side of the graveyard.

'I don't know Nim, ask him to turn round and then we can see if he's got 'Spook' printed on his back,' Griffin quipped as the person in question removed his sunglasses. 'No, in fact that's George Batho and he's a Commander at the Yard, in charge of firearms and quick response. He must have dabbled.'

'Do you think any Spooks turned up?'

Griffin put his hand on his DC's shoulder. 'Nimra, they're spies, not Z list celebrities seeking publicity.' His phone bleeped as Veronica sidled up. 'Hi Ron, it went well do you think?'

'Hi. Yes. Have you heard?'

'Heard what?' Griffin replied as he scrolled through his messages.

'Glenn is in intensive care, having been shot up town in the early hours,' Veronica said.

'Blimey. No run of the mill shooting either,' Griffin replied with a concerned look having read the news on his phone. 'Ironically, it was George's team, some sort of vice raid that went pear shaped. Sounds like a biggun. At some smart hotel. He's lucky, there's two dead, plus three more in intensive. Thankfully, none of ours though. Culmination of something serious it looks to me. So what was our City Slicker doing to be caught up in that?'

Both Nimra and Mantel remained quiet, listening intently. 'Well he was on that web list,' Henshall added. 'There may be a connection?'

'Oh shit,' Veronica exclaimed looking away from her screen, putting her other hand over her mouth.

'What is it?'

'He's died.'

*

A media frenzy presided at The Cobblers. The funeral of the murdered local vicar, herself an ex-socialite call-girl. Plus the shooting dead of a successful businessman, the owner of this pub by a police marksman in a vice-raid in London's West End, provided an intriguing cocktail of suspicion and gossip for the journos. Griffin was already hearing official rumours of very murky business dealings that Glenn Friar was involved in. From all accounts his home was already crawling with police officers.

The pub had a contrasting atmosphere, fevered excitement out front, sombre behind the bar. Despite the pub's notorious reputation, and the trials and tribulations regarding the redevelopment, Freddie and Glenn, together with Veronica's considerable input, had ensured that the Cobblers was a relatively friendly place to visit, and more importantly a happy place to go to work in. The owners were tireless in their efforts to ensure job satisfaction, any night where takings exceeded expectations a extra few bob, tax-free, would be in the pay packet. They came as a pair and were largely inseparable in business and had been for years, since they first met at the money brokers, Merter's way back. It was no secret though, that their personal lives had evolved quite differently. Freddie having matured from the archetypal City yuppie to the caring husband and father. Glenn, despite marriage and family had never shed his desire to party. He never mixed business with pleasure though, well as much as possible, the gap narrowing in recent times. His affair with the then DC Lucy Mantel and, more recently, being seen with DC Nimra Shimra and Prisha Khatri, from Blue Skies House, to name just two extramarital outings, added to the growing concerns that Freddie had of his business partner. He had hoped that bringing the building work back on track would re-focus him. Initial reports that Freddie had ascertained from the shooting indicated that Glenn was caught up in something big and ugly that he had no inkling of.

'Oh my god Mike,' Veronica said pausing from serving, still in her black dress, Freddie having left her to it. 'What a fucking place this is.'

'Certainly never a dull moment. Only the other day my mate Arnie was suggesting that I'd left the sharp end for a cosy life in the sticks,' Griffin said clasping a near empty pint glass. 'At times, the goings on round her make the OK Corral seem like a Lyon's Tea House.'

'Well there's an analogy,' Veronica replied looking round the bar. 'This lot make you laugh, communication professionals. The right hand doesn't know what the left is doing. You've got two reporters from the same station sitting over there.'

'Well, finding the positives, good for trade and your bonus.' Griffin lifted his empty glass for Veronica to refill. 'Thank you.'

'Yep you're right, look for the positives. He was such a nice guy. A right flirt and a mucky sense of humour, but a good laugh and a very fair boss. If there's a biography written it'll be well worth a read. Here you go,' said Veronica handing over the beer. 'Right better help out. Oh, Stephen said he'd call at six, hopefully he's got some positive news.'

*

'Nim, can I ask you something?' Prisha asked curled at one end of the comfy sofa in Nimra's small flat. On the coffee table foil containers with the remnants of the curry collected from Chutney Ali's, along with one empty and one half full bottle of Prosecco.

'Of course, what is it?' Nimra replied from the other end of the sofa, which didn't leave a lot of space in between, their bare toes touching. Both returning to their jobs after attending the sad drinks that followed the funeral, before calling it a day. Texting and deciding that their new friend would approve of curry and wine as a perfect send off.

'Are you really bitter towards Andy Nash; I mean really angry.'

'You bet, you know that,' Nimra responded looking a little surprised. 'You don't need to even ask, why?'

'Oh, it's just, well I just wanted to be sure.'

'I know that I can never feel like you. But when Swift tried to attack me I got a sense of how it must have been and the anger it generated and still does, even with him dead. All rapists are just a complete waste of space in my book.'

'How far would you go?'

'As far as it takes.'

'What murder?'

'Good question. I'm not sure, but I think I would,' Nimra replied leaning forward and topping up the two glasses. 'Look, this is going to come out wrong, but I'll say it. Yes, I want to see him dead and I want to do it, that' if you don't get there first. But why should I then spend the rest of my life locked up for just doing what everyone wants to see done. Why should I lose my freedom?'

'That doesn't sound wrong at all. Retribution for something like this need to be recognized as a special case, not as a callous murder,' Prisha said picking up her glass. 'But the do-goody leftie liberals would not see it that way.'

'Best scenario would be for him to die and for you to know that you'd done it, without anyone being able to prove it, but you could still celebrate it.' Nimra tensing up with thoughts of Nash taking a sip of Prosecco.

'And for him to suffer?'

'Absolutely, that's what I think I want most. Problem again is that if you left him disabled, with a gaping hole where his manhood should be, he'd be cared for while you're banged up.'

'So, let me get this right, your perfect scenario would be to see him suffer, perhaps even tortured, then murdered and you walk away completely innocent, with no case to answer?'

'You're speaking like me when I'm being a police lady,' Nimra replied giggling. 'But yes, spot on. What do you have a plan?

'I've got many Nim, just need to decide on which one would be the best given the opportunity.'

*

'Stuffed,' Lily exclaimed putting her empty plate down on the coffee table strewn with foil containers, none completely emptied, spoons protruding.

'Me to.' Veronica placed her plate on the table that also had glasses and bottles of Merlot and Pinot Grigio vying for space.

'Excellent as usual though,' Griffin said mopping up the last of his sauce with a piece of naan bread.

The pub had closed a couple of hours early. Veronica's decision readily approved by Freddie, who told her he was up to his eyes in it. The 'it' very much sounding like shit, which she thought was probably more appropriate. The journalists had drifted off, realizing that they would nothing of interest from the staff. With the bar cleared and Georgie and Angie packed off home, they had climbed the stairs to the refuge of the lounge. Sanctuary after another strange day. Lily had sorted the drinks, while Griffin ordered the works for delivery from Chutney Ali's. Veronica had taken the opportunity to change out of her black dress, deciding to drop it off at the Hospice's shop tomorrow as it held sad memories.

'Do you think they'll continue with the building works?' Lily asked topping up her glass.

'Don't know Lils, I hope so.'

'It seems a bit of a poisoned chalice.'

'I agree. I'll take this in the kitchen,' said Veronica in response to her phone ringing out. 'It's Stephen.'

'About fucking time, better late than never I suppose,' Griffin said recovering his phone to look at a message, adding his plate to the table.

'I'll start on these,' Lily said collecting up the debris.

Griffin looked at his message from Dr Theo Shapiro:

can we meet please

Intrigued by his persistence Griffin replied:

6 rugby club tomorrow

Theo's response immediately pinging back.

ok

'Good news for once,' Veronica said returning. 'Stephen reckons he's cracked it.'

'Excellent.'

'He's going to send it to you as he says there's bits that are a little complicated but reckons your guys will know what it's all about. Whateve the fuck that all means, I'm just the messenger. Oh thanks Lils, I'll help.'

'Sounds promising, I'll take a look in the morning, I'm just not up for it now.'

CHAPTER TWENTY SIX

'They've had a boy sir, just got the call from Prisha.'

'Sorry Nimra?' Griffin asked having breezed into the main office ready to impart his news, only for his DC to usurp him and steal his thunder.

'Ellie and Rod.'

'Ah yes, excellent. Hope all are well?'

'Sounds like it.'

'Good. Right, I also have news.'

'Fire away boss,' Mantel said turning from her screen, baby talk not floating her boat..

'Looks like we've identified where the host of the deep dark web site is.'

'Do you realize that you lower your voice when you say, 'deep dark' boss?' Mantel remarked. 'It's quite sexy, you should use it with Ronni.'

'If we could convene in my office then I'll go through the plan,' Griffin said heading for his office, ignoring, but noting Mantel's comment. 'Whoever fancies getting the coffees in could be in for a a trip. To give you a clue it begins with W, so that could be Wellington, Washington even Walthamstow?'

'Walsall?' Henshall asked following his boss.

'The West Indies,' Nimra chipped in hopefully.

'Fucking hell, hold the front page, has Lucy gone for the coffees?' Griffin said chucking his jacket over the back of his chair. 'Never known her to be this keen, hope she's not going to be disappointed.

'Probably gone for her passport boss.'

'Better not be Walthamstow then,' Nimra said smiling.

'In the meantime, while we're waiting for Luce, I believe you have some news Kevin,' Griffin said looking towards Henshall. 'In fact news that I didn't think I'd hear.'

'Yes boss,' Henshall responded from his still to be reclaimed stool, the consensus being that they must have legal rights if the Café came looking for it. 'I have received word that old farmer Arnott is going to be very happy with, because our farming unit…'

'The Tractor Boys,' Griffin interjected leaning back both hands behind his head.

'They have found his cows.'

'Operation Steak and Chips.'

''Sorry?' Nimra asked once again confused by what was being said. That's right isn't it Kev, that's what they called it?'

'That's right boss. The cows had been chipped and that led to them being found in a cattle market in Yorkshire. Ironically on my old patch.'

'What have I missed?' Mantel asked appearing with refreshments.

'Steak and chips apparently,' Nimra replied.

'Sorry?'

'We've found the stolen cattle through their chips,' Henshall said feeling pleased with himself.

'Well that will please the farmer, Tom what's his name,' Mantel said not the least bit interested in Henshall's cow coup, dishing out the drinks.

'I reckon he'll be over the moooon,' Nimra offered.

'So boss, where are we off to?' Henshall drummed his fingers on top of the filing cabinet building the anticipation.

'Wallingford.'

'How did they manage trace it to wherever that is sir?' Nimra asked a little put out with the lack of appreciation for her joke.

'Fuck knows; strangulation, triangulation, it's all quite amazing to me,' Griffin replied shrugging his shoulders. 'I've swung this as being part of the Nash case. I still believe that Swift had something to do with it and this website plays the there's no such thing as a coincidence card for me.

We know that Swift had been letting Nash have access to it, so it's far from being a speculative finger in the wind. I'll let the Vice guys know about what we've found, but I thought there would be no harm in us paying a visit first.'

'Where and what is this Wallingford?' Mantel asked.

'A village in Oxfordshire, south of Oxford, near Henley-on-Thames, home to the famous rowing regatta,' Henshall replied. 'Never been to either, but Wallingford's meant to be a traditional country town. Lots of old thatched cottages.'

'Yes, that's what we've got, an old cottage on the edge of town, owned by a retired civil servant and his wife. Of course it may not be them, could be a rogue teenager or lodger tucked up in a disused barn, who knows.'

'Bit like a rural version of Cluedo sir?'

'Exactly Nimra. Who knows what we will find. I'm asking for back up just in case they come at us with pitch forks.'

'That's one for your Cluedo Nim,' Henshall said tapping his pad. 'The farmer with the pitchfork in the barn.'

'All sounds lovely,' Mantel said not at all enthused by the news. 'I'll put my passport away then.'

'Come on Luce, the English countryside and all that fresh air.'

'More fucking cows more like,' Mantel retorted. 'When are you thinking of going as I may be washing my hair?'

'Asap, just getting it cleared with the local guys. So finish your soya Luce, powder your nose and I'll fire up the combined harvester.'

*

The maternity ward was a mixture of euphoria and concern, mixed with pragmatism and for some terror as to what may lay ahead. Emotions that the nurses took in their stride, this was their version of a production line, albeit producing a delicate and extremely precious commodity. For some of the parents it was a once in a lifetime experience after months of waiting, possibly with considerable pain, possibly both emotional and physical. Others eager to get on with nurturing their growing families taking it all in their stride, yearning to get away from the hospital.

'Okay El, everything's packed,' Rod said patting Ellie's purple leather holdall.

'Excellent, thank you Rod,' Ellie replied holding tiny baby Jonny, named after Rod's late brother, cradling him with the care she would give to a fine crystal vase. After a smooth birth Ellie had been given the green light to return home. Mother and baby were relaxed and healthy. Jonny having already willingly located his mother's nipples. Rod was a little more stressed, paperwork completed, he now prepared for what is generally regarded as the most frightening drive that any adult ever makes. Negotiating traffic with the most valuable, fragile cargo on board.

'I'll take this down and get the car round,' Rod said, still not convinced that he had done everything he needed to. In preparation the apartment had received a deep clean from Maria, their loyal cleaner. The hastily arranged grocery delivery taken in, as had the numerous bouquets and two floaty, helium filled blue balloons. Envelopes collected from the door mat and piled on the dining table. 'Oohps, the cards, nearly forgot them.'

'Mr Nash,' said one of the friendly senior nurses approaching the bed with Rod scooping up the cards. 'Could you come over to the nurses station please.'

'See, I told you that there was something else. I'll just see what they want and then we'll be off.' Ellie watched her partner stride over to the nurses station a little concerned that he was greeted by a besuited gentleman and an officious oriental looking lady.

'Mr Nash?'

'Yes.'

'DI Kwan, and this is my colleague DC Castle.' The lady brandished her warrant card at the builder, with the nurses nearby discreetly listening in 'We'd like you to come with us to answer some questions.'

'Sorry, there must be some mistake. My partner's just given birth and this is a maternity ward.'

'I'm afraid we must insist. I'll come with you over to Ms Richmond to say goodbye, but we need to go now,' DI Kwan said trying to show compassion that didn't come naturally, instructed by her DCI to show some sensitivity towards mother and baby and the rest of the maternity ward. 'We don't want any fuss do we?'

'What is this about though?'

'All will be revealed at the station. But I don't think they'll be any surprises Mr Nash.'

'Okay,' Rod replied the colour draining from his cheeks as the reality of the situation kicked in. They hadn't needed to say that they were from the Vice Squad, he had been receiving text updates regarding the situation since the raid up town and Glenn Friar's shooting, hoping to avoid the inevitable, especially here and now.

'Sorry Ellie,' Rod said kissing his partner then baby Jonny, with the eyes of the ward on them. 'But something urgent has come up and I need to answer some questions. I'll get them to ring Prisha to pick you up. I won't be long.'

'But Rod,' Ellie exclaimed as Rod turned and walked away with the slim, unsmiling lady, who had not been introduced that Ellie guessed to be a police officer.'

*

'Ash how are you?' Griffin asked greeting DI Ash Tabbing with a firm handshake, another old chum from The Met. 'No police stations out here?'

'Hi Mike, correct,' replied the burly six feet plus bearded Thames Valley Detective Inspector. 'And this is?'

'DS Lucy Mantel please meet Ash Tabbing, best centre the force has ever had,' Griffin said referring to Tabbing's rugby prowess. They were in a quiet corner of the otherwise busy car park at the M40 service station at junction 8A, Tabbing's requested meeting point.

'Pleased to meet you Lucy. Lucky lady to have this guy as your boss, there's only a few of us good guys left in the force,' Tabbing said shaking distracted Mantel's hand.

'Hi. Sorry, I need to take this,' Mantel said responding to her phone and moving away, having asked Nimra to call in response to her surprising an disturbing text.

'You reckon the cuts are deep down with you,' Tabbing continued leaning against his car. 'The only stations round here now are Oxford, High Wycombe and Reading, not even a satellite. Logistically I can tell you it can be fucking tricky, but hey, why let policing get in the way of politics. Anyway enough of that, it's good to see you sober after the last time. I took a look at what you sent. I can tell you it's some of the worst porn I'v seen. I'm not sure that they were all even alive, are you? And animals totally disgust me.'

'Agreed, as it stands the site may not have technically broken any laws. But as I said on the phone, I'm after something else,' Griffin replied looking around for his DS. 'So are we set, or is it a coffee first?'

'We should push on, afters maybe,' Tabbing replied gingerly pushing himself up off the car, an old rugby back injury flaring up as he brushed h teeth earlier. 'I've got four uniforms meeting us there and my DC, Tommy you'll like him. Right rural sort, cracking rugby player. Scrum half like you Plus I put an armed response unit on stand-by.'

'Fucking hell Ash, a bit over the top. I thought you said there were cuts and it's a retired couple we're going to talk to not some drugged up oiks a ghetto.'

'Better safe than sorry, it might be all a front. Anyhow, it caused a bit of excitement when I shared the site, and intrigue, apparently these two are pillars of the local community. Look it keeps my guys busy, now there's a specialist ag team we've lost a lot of cases. Anyway, are you one hundred percent sure about your info?'

'As sure as I can be Ash, you saw it. They weren't difficult to pinpoint, it's not like they're holed up in a flat in a block on some estate,' Griffin said. 'Right, so, I'll follow you there. I'll do the knocking on the door and see th lie of the land. Don't deploy the big red key or storm the building unless I say so.'

'And there was I looking forward to a rooftop chase across the thatches.'

'With your back? Right, here's Luce, let's go,'

*

'That was Nimra on the phone boss,' Mantel said glancing across at Griffin as he pulled out of the services following Tabbing onto an A road.

'Anything interesting? Keep an eye on Ash's motor, we don't want to lose him.'

'No problem, I've got him. Rod Nash has been arrested, they picked him up in the maternity ward just when Ellie was about to go home.'

'Fucking hell. Who did and why wasn't I told? When?'

'Couple of hours ago, the Vice Squad.'

'That explains one thing.'

'What?'

'Why I didn't get a call, world of their fucking own that lot, unless they want a favour or some cooperation. Nim say anything else?'

'Word is that it's in connection with what Glenn Friar was caught up with when he was shot up town.'

'Now that is interesting. I need to have a word with Ronnie and see what's being said at the Cobblers. Weren't both Rod and Friar on our web subscription list?'

*

Griffin and Tabbing holding mugs with humorous slogans filled with tea, sat on a leather sofa in a smart lounge. Opposite them, perched on fashionable large relining armchairs, were Mr and Mrs Tucker, a hospitable welcoming, middle class, stereotypical middle England couple. There cottage was not shabby chic, nor classically furnished from the local flea market, more M&S and John Lewis, definitely not IKEA. Maintained to the highest level, immaculately clean. A sizeable, beautifully kept garden lapped around the property. No signs of teenagers nor lodgers. Mantel and her new friend, DC Tommy Crab, a personable attractive young man, despite being an inch shorter than Mantel in her stockinged feet, usually no-go, were sifting through the study bagging evidence. The armed response unit had been stood down. The greeting they received from Mr and Mrs Tucker, now Roy and Tina, certainly did not warrant a swat team's assistance. Griffin remained sceptical, wary of a scam, thoughts that receded with every minute that passed.

Net curtains in the proximity had twitched as Griffin, Tabbing and Mantel had made their way through the white picket fence, up the dainty tiled front path lined with marigolds just twenty minutes earlier.

'Mrs Tucker?'

'Yes.'

'DI Griffin, and this is DI Tabbing and DS Mantel, can we come in please?' Griffin asked, as they showed their credentials, with a search warrant tucked in his pocket, that was not asked for.

'Certainly, would you mind taking your shoes off please,' the unconventional reply. At which point the interrogation became more of a cosy chat.

'It was a nice little earner,' Tina Tucker had said, smartly dressed in a cross between country casual and top end High Street. In her late fifties, that both Griffin and Tabbing could sense she believed to be the new forties, a lady who would be very much at home having lunch in the latest on-trend country pub.

'Think it's pretty disgusting myself, but who am I to argue with those prepared to pay handsomely for it,' Roy said, retired after thirty years plus at the Home Office having reached a grade that gave him his own office.

'It all got a bit carried away,' Tina said, her neat bob hairstyle nothing like the image of Tina Turner that sprung to Griffin's mind when he first heard the name. 'As it all got more and more popular it seemed to get more extreme.'

'It was a bit like one of those runaway trains in one of those black and white films with Buster Keaton,' Roy continued in jeans and crisply ironed sky blue oxford shirt. 'It paid for some nice holidays, a nice supplement to my pension. Anyway, I expect you would like to see it all, it's in the study. Will we have to close it down? I didn't think it was illegal, although if I'm honest I think it should be.'

'It depends on what we find Roy,' Griffin replied struggling to think of a chapter in the police manual that dealt with a scenario such as this. 'But, yes, if you could show us everything we will take it from there.'

'I'll get the kettle on,' Tina said. 'Do your colleagues outside want some tea?'

*

It had taken a few hours to go through everything, a meticulously run business that Ray and Tina were more than willing to help and explain all aspects of. For Mantel their organised filing system, both on the computer and the paperwork was somewhat therapeutic. In the same strange way that Griffin had found it a pleasure dealing with the polite couple. The sandwiches made with fresh granary bread from the local bakery were delicious, as was the home-made lemonade that accompanied the late lunch-cum-afternoon tea served on the patio.

Griffin conferred extensively with Tabbing throughout as how best to proceed in these unusual circumstances. Both agreed that Mr and Mrs Tucker did not present a threat to national security and reluctantly concluded that this would probably be the end of the Tucker cottage porn industry. They sensed that the couple may be relieved to have the pressure removed, looking forward to a return to previously tranquil country lives. Although amusingly both appeared to have come to enjoy how lucrative peddling porn could be. Griffin looked forward to studying the accounts of their trading company, details of which, like everything, were provided without a quibble. What had been missing was a valid explanation as to how they became embroiled in such a sordid business in the first place. Neither of them wishing to divulge anything of its origins.

*

'Well fuck me, that was a first,' Griffin said following the signs for the M4 and the M25 having bade farewell to DI Tabbing and DC Crab; Mantel having secured Tommy's number should there be anything else to discus

With a boot full of goodies to examine back at the station, Griffin and Mantel had pulled away from Marigold Cottage with a cheery wave from the arm in arm couple, no doubt eager to pull a cork or twist a cap, or perhaps something a little stronger to reflect on an interesting day.

'All very surreal boss,' Mantel said. 'Such a delightful couple'

'Are we being hoodwinked Luce?'

'I don't think so on this one boss, but I've had similar thoughts,' Mantel conceded. 'Can you imagine the local grapevine. The village's Facebook page will be on fire. It'll be interesting to see if the real reason for the police spending half a day at Marigold Cottage leaks out. It could only come from them or the local guys.'

'Who knows, they may be publicity seekers and leak it themselves. You have to remember there will be neighbours and friends who will have ha their favourite porn site closed, not knowing that it was Roy and Tina wh ran it.'

'We'll have to pass it all onto Vice won't we?' Mantel asked.

'Not until we've had a good look to see if there's anything linking to Nash This will be a priority Luce, we need to move quickly, our trip here will nc stay a secret for long and the Vice boys will be all over us. But it could tur out a win, win, if we get something then hand it all over.'

'But as you say, only if it helps to find Nash.'

'Absolutely. Like you, I still can't get over the surrealness of it all. Roy anc Tina Tucker hosting such a disgusting website and earning a small fortune out of it. We're in the wrong game Luce,' Griffin said. 'I need to get some juice before the motorway, fuck is it five thirty?'

'Yep, why?'

'Meant to be meeting Dr Theo at six, bollocks. I've got a feeling that he might have something for us. If not, why be so persistent? I'll text him when we stop.'

*

Griffin glanced at his watch as he hurried across the rugby club's carpark. 7.45, one hour forty five minutes late. Thankfully, Theo had responded to his text. Would it be worth all the trouble? The stationary traffic on the M25 had not helped his mood, at least a pint beckoned. Being a non-training evening the bar was almost deserted, the exceptions, a committee meeting in one corner and Theo propping up the bar.

'Pint Mike?' Stan asked from behind the ramp.

'Please Stan. Hi Theo, what can I get you, sorry I'm so late.'

'Oh hi Inspector,' Theo slurred. 'Same again please.'

Stan passed over the pint, raised an eyebrow in Theo's direction and turned towards the optics.

'So how can I be of help Theo?' Griffin asked leaning against the bar next to the doctor.

'We can't talk here, let's take a seat. Hippocratic Oath and all that,' Theo said pointing across the room as he slid his considerable frame off the stool, standing a little uneasily, pouring his old scotch into the new glass.

'So all this is just between me and you, Mike,' said Theo taking his seat.

'What is?' Griffin enquired realizing that Theo was considerably more pissed than he first thought.

'All this Nash business.'

Griffin didn't reply as Theo sipped his scotch and he took a satisfying gulp of his extremely well kept pint, considering the two points that Theo had uttered, or should it be spluttered, the Hippocratic Oath and Nash. Did he want to receive news, possibly a confession or even tittle-tattle, that potentially broke client confidentiality from Theo in this state? This was not some faceless informer in a back street alley, he would have to deal with the doctor in a professional capacity in the future. To receive information that Theo may not even remember, could compromise everything and be tricky to deal with. Griffin decided that it would be best to conduct this discussion when Theo was totally coherent, in full control of his faculties. Calculating that what he had to say could wait a further few hours?

'Can I make a suggestion Theo?' Griffin asked looking Theo straight in the eye. 'That we have this chat in the morning, perhaps after a full English and a strong coffee.'

'Are you suggesting that I am pissed Inspector?'

'Yes Theo I am, because you are,' Griffin replied. Theo gave him a surprised look. 'Look, let me take you home. Then in the morning I can pop over to meet you when it's convenient and I promise I won't be late.'...

...Griffin helped Theo out of the passenger seat and assisted him across h drive towards his front door.

'Do you have keys Theo?'

'Of course I've got fucking keys,' replied an indignant doctor as he rummaged through his suit's pockets with no success as the front door opened. Griffin had never met Mrs Shapiro before and was somewhat surprised to see an attractive lady, late forties 'blond' with a figure show off in a vibrant tight fitting pink and black gym outfit.

'Oh Theo darling, have you had one too many?'

'Hello Lou.'

'Mrs Shapiro?' Griffin asked unsure whether she was taking the mickey.

'Louise please, sorry I don't think we've met.'

'Mike Griffin. I thought it was best to drop Theo off.'

'Thank you so much Mike. Is that Inspector Mike Griffin?'

'Yes.'

'Oh I'm so pleased that you met with Theo, he was worrying about the meeting all day.'

'Was he? Well we need to continue it in the morning, perhaps you could remind him,' Griffin said still supporting Theo, who was grinning at his wife. 'I arrived late so we didn't get to chat as much as we wanted.'

'Oh, I see. Here let me take him,' Louise said taking her husband's arm. 'I'll get him a coffee.'

Griffin watched as Louise helped Theo into the house as he returned to his car, thinking that she appeared extremely understanding, although who knew what may be said behind closed doors? And that she must be pretty strong to handle Theo's bulk in the way she did. Griffin reflected whether Dr Theo Shapiro may be about to provide much needed positive information with regard to their search for Andy Nash. Deciding a chat with Ronni at the Bootmaker's about the day's developments and a pint or two, having had his earlier one scuppered, would tick the box.

*

'That's right boss. The cows had been chipped and that led to them being found in a cattle market in Yorkshire. Ironically on my old patch.'

Griffin perched himself on Geoff's Stool and ordered a pint from Georgie. The day to had been an emotional mixture of promise and concern. Ellie Richmond was probably in the apartment across the landing from his. Possibly alone with her baby. Her joy severely dented, to say the least, by Rod's arrest, or did she know anything about his business? His overnight detainment now confirmed. Then there was Ronni. The pub promised so much for her personally and yet at point of delivery it appeared that she may be thwarted once again. Her expression as she served and chatted at the far end of the bar did not convey her usual free spirit, Griffin deciding to use his best negotiating skills as she wandered back towards him.

'Hi Ron. Looks like rain.'

'Oh fuck off Mike, that wasn't even funny.'

'Sorry, been shit has it?'

'Strange I'd say. Can't stop thinking about poor Ellie and the baby.'

'Surely someone's with her?' Griffin asked hopefully.

'Yeh, Margaret and Prisha from Blues Skies have been with her, and Lily's just popped over, not a lot of consolation though, is it?' Veronica said aimlessly wiping around the bar with a bar towel. 'Then there's here. You heard any more?'

'I'm probably no further ahead on the rumour mill than you are. All I've heard is that if it sticks Rod is on pretty sticky ground and may be away for some time.'

'Oh my god, what a bleeding mess. So what's he done, is it as everyone says all to do with sex and porn and that he was in this with Glenn?'

'I believe so. Has Freddie said anymore?' Griffin asked probing to see if the co-owner knew anything of this, although his gut feeling was that he didn't or he would have been collared by now.

'Hardly spoken to him and haven't seen him. Just said that Glenn's wife had gone away with the kids. He didn't know where and suspected that she might not attend her husband's funeral. Seems that as much as she knew that he was no angel, she didn't have a clue that he was into anything like this. Around the bar they're pretty surprised with Glenn but not shocked. Rod though, although a bit of a boy back in the day, most thought that was well behind him and that he was looking forward to becoming a father. Everyone's hoping that they've got the wrong Nash.'

'Nice to think so Ron, but I don't think so. It would be intriguing to know how Rod and Friar's paths crossed.'

'I was thinking that. When Rod came on board for the building stuff it was like they had hardly ever met. Do you reckon that was a lie?'

'Don't know Ron, I'm really not in the loop. It does seem that they go back further. I'm afraid all I can offer is watch this space. Whilst you're there, I'll have another pint please,' Griffin said handing over his glass.

'Crisps, nuts?'

'Salt and vinegar please, that'll be my supper tonight.'

'Cheese and onion al dente for me later.' Veronica replied her smile re-appearing. 'I'm fearful for the re-development now. It's obviously on hold, and Freddie hasn't said anything yet, don't like to ask at the moment.'

'Another watch this space, thanks,' Griffin said taking his pint. 'Oh and by the way a big thank you to Stephen. We tracked down the hosts of that site, that ironically both Friar and Rod subscribed to.'

'Is it connected?'

'I suppose there's a chance. I wouldn't bank on it, but it could be. It'll be checked out just in case. Anyway this couple that hosted the site out in Oxfordshire, they were not what you'd expect. They were your classic Daily Mail early retired couple out in the sticks. It was a different sort of raid, a first for me. A few hours that'll I'll share with you later. But your Stephen's a real tech guru, you should be proud of him.'

'I am,' replied Veronica deciding that this was not the time to reveal that her brother was not the brains behind it and that those belonged to a twenty year old student.

'Oh, on another point, what do you know of Doctor Theo Shapiro?'

'He's my doctor, don't think he's ever been in here.'

'Doesn't surprise me, bit of a snob, too good for here.'

'Cheeky bastard. Bit creepy and sweaty if I'm honest,' Veronica said sipping a glass of water. 'Prefer to be seen by one of the junior doctors and I've heard the same from other ladies. But he's a bit of a medical institutional figure in these parts, isn't he? Why do you ask?'

'Nothing really. Actually that reminds me I need to change my GP; I suppose to his surgery. Must get onto that.'

'Back to this website,' Veronica said intrigued as to what her brother and his guru had exposed. 'Has Stephen's secret squirrel stuff been helpful in finding Andy Nash?'

'Well he's not locked up yet. Not sure what we've got until we've had a good look at everything we bagged this morning. If I'm honest, I doubt it, but...'

'I know, watch this space.'

CHAPTER TWENTY SEVEN

Walking through to the restaurant area of the Foresters Arms Griffin pondered Theo's choice of meeting place, a pleasant country pub on the brow of a hill to the north of Epping Forest, with stunning views over the woodland and beyond to the capital, currently the public house to be seen in. Despite it being just off his patch and a few miles away from the doctor's catchment area, Griffin was sure that it was frequented by many of Theo's patients, together with a few that he had had reason to question over the past year or so. Reckoning that Theo would hope that he would not be pestered, but that his presence may be noted. Griffin smiled, Theo's considerable physical bulk meant that he could not fail to be noticed. He had accepted Theo's invitation to join him for lunch, apparently an apology and to thank him for his assistance at the rugby club because he wanted to hear what Theo had to say. The fact that he had texted early pushed the right buttons reconfirming Griffin's belief that it might be something of substance. His wife's comment that he had been worrying about yesterday's meeting left an impression, the doctor did not come across as the sort of person to waste people's time and probably not very tolerant of those who wasted his, notwithstanding last night.

Griffin looked around the shabby chic bar area, strangely for no reason thinking that Tina and Roy Tucker would be at home here. Dating from the late 1800s the Foresters Arms was a large building offering five stylish boutique rooms, a secluded beer garden with the latest alfresco culinary kit and a reputation for the best and most friendly staff in the area. The proprietor, Annie Belling, late 50s, a society belle in her day, prided herself in running a discreet establishment, whilst accepting a nice little backhander from a Fleet Street hack for any juicy gossip. Annie's reputation was that to cross her was not a good idea, although on the occasion he had dealings with her Griffin found her both amicable and willing, even a bit of a flirt. The Foresters was no scampi in the basket establishment. Its menu did have a retro feel, but with a contemporary continental twist at top end restaurant prices. A deliberate ploy that worked, welcoming clientele from the top rung of society's ladder. The signed photos of well-known faces in the toilets testimony to this.

Theo was already in the restaurant sat at a spacious corner table, his back to the entrance, something Griffin would never contemplate. A delightful waitress with multi-coloured hair and many visible piercings and tattoos showed Griffin to the table through the crowded dining room. Noting that the doctor had a coke, he assumed without a rum or scotch, Griffin ordered a sparkling water, ice and a slice of lime. 'Hello Theo,' Griffin said pulling out his chair.

'Mike, sorry miles away,' Theo responded looking back from the window he was staring out of, contemplating what he would say to the Detective Inspector when he arrived. 'Look thanks for coming and sorry about last night.'

'No problem and it was a pleasure to meet with Louise.'

'Yes,' Theo replied somewhat sheepishly. 'I got told off and rightly so.'

'We've all been there.'

'I thought you were single?'

'Doesn't stop you from telling offs from the fairer sex. We all know how it is,' Griffin said as his drink arrived. 'It takes forever to build a pile of brownie points only for one small thing to bring them all tumbling down.'

'Too right there Mike. Look I suspect like me that you haven't got long, but I thought that this was a bit more civilised than the surgery. I'm going for the Japanese salmon with a side salad to keep in the good books. It's delicious by the way.'

'I'll go with the same then,' Griffin replied surprised to be confronted by such a contrite luncheon partner, belying the character he had previously experienced and his reputation, noting Theo's familiarity with the menu. Small talk followed as the order was taken, discussing the health benefits of Japanese cuisine and raw fish. 'So Theo, that's enough about the merit of sushi versus tempura, what is it you want to share with me?'

'Well there's a couple of things. The first is a little embarrassing, the second is a patient confidentiality matter. But I need assurances from you that there will be no comeback.'

'Look Theo we are both confronted with these sorts of scenarios on a daily basis in this politically correct world,' Griffin said sipping at his water having disposed of the straw. 'We've just got to trust each other. I'm old school. If you've not broken any laws then you should have nothing to fear.'

'Exactly, that's good to hear. It's becoming more and more difficult. We are going through a ridiculous initiative at the moment where we are finally setting up a national database for patient records. It's taking forever. I mean how long ago did they invent the computer?'

'Before I entered this world.'

'Quite. But we still can't share the information or if we do there are so many hoops to jump through that the patient's died before we get the information. I mean what's the point of a free to all database that's got private and confidential stamped all over it?'

'We have the same, the faster the computers get, the more levels of red tape are applied to slow the process down,' Griffin said agreeing with Theo's view on bureaucracy. 'Anyway, here we are, one to one, no tape recorders, what have you got?'

The waitress approached with two plates. 'Ah, here we go,' Griffin noting that the salmon smelled and looked extremely appetising, starting to wonder though whether he would ever get to hear what Theo had to share with him. 'Tell me Mike, do you subscribe to, shall we say, adult web sites?'

'No, but then I do get to see a hell of a lot of adult stuff in my work, so I'm a bit like the brewery worker who prefers tea. Do you?' Griffin replied pleased that possibly the ball had started to rolling.

'Well yes, although the one that I was going to talk about and take a screen shot for you has suddenly closed down which is a bit of a bummer.'

Griffin suppressed a grin at the doctor's choice of words as the 'there's no such thing as a coincidence' theory kicked in. 'What was on this site?'

'Adult material.'

Stating the bleeding obvious sprang to Griffin's mind. 'With a sexual angle?'

'Yes, it's a porn site.'

'Extreme?'

'Yes.'

'And what did you want to share with me about this site, which if everyone's alive and they're consenting is not illegal,' Griffin asked, knowing that the site in question had concerns on both counts, wonderir whether Louise knew of his viewing habits, perhaps she was party to them?

'Yes, obviously I wouldn't indulge in anything illegal. As I said, I was going to show you a screen saver shot of it. But as I can't it may be impossible t prove, but I know what I saw.'

'I can make my own mind up whether that's a problem or not, but I can't do that until you've told me what you saw.'

'Yes, sorry, well at first it didn't register, I mean why would it, it was pret off beat even for this site. Then the penny dropped.'

'What did Theo?' Griffin asked enjoying the salmon whilst becoming mor frustrated with Theo.

'It was Andy Nash.'

'Sorry, what was Andy Nash?' Griffin replied putting his knife and fork down and looking at the doctor.

'The chap in the video was Andy Nash.'

'What, he was smiling at the camera?'

'Far from it, in fact, the opposite.'

'Enough of the riddles Theo, how can you be sure it was Andy Nash if you didn't see his face.'

'It wasn't just the once, it was every day.'

'What?'

'They posted new material daily to this particular site.'

'Theo please give it to me straight. What was happening and how do you know that it was Nash?'

'Andy Nash has a very distinctive birthmark on his back. Large and unmissable,' Theo replied, having somehow managed to finish his meal whilst talking, wiping his mouth with his napkin. 'I'm sure that it will be mentioned on his police record.'

'I don't recall it, but I'll take your word for it,' Griffin said, thinking that when the opportunity arose he would check it out with the office, he didn't want to interrupt Theo now that he was finding his stride. 'Go on. So Nash was in a daily posting doing what?'

'Well to be honest Mike, not a lot. Fancy a dessert? That was nice but there wasn't a lot, was there?'

'I'm fine but please don't let me stop you.'

'He was being buggered,' the doctor blurted out as if a previously sealed valve had blown, taking a sip of his coke. 'This guy, who I think was Andy Nash, was shafted by a different masked man every day. Now I don't know if it really was every day, but that was what you were led to believe.'

'Really,' Griffin responded coolly wondering whether this was the breakthrough. If it was the same site he looked at he had seen some pretty awful stuff, but could not recall this particular act, he made a mental note to put this on his list when he phoned the office. 'Where did this take place?'

'He was tied to a bed in a room with subdued lighting, naked and this other guy would come in, as I said a different one every day, also naked apart from the mask and do the business, didn't last long, ten minutes max.'

'Was there any sound?'

'Actually a pretty good soundtrack, someone had good taste.'

'Any human noises?'

'Not that I can recall. Thank you, could I have the spotted dick please wit
custard,' Theo asked the waitress as she cleared away the plates. Griffin
could not resist a smile. 'There is one other thing.'

'And that is?'

'The guy on the bed, who I believe was Andy Nash, he had a cannula in h
left wrist.'

'What attached to tubes?'

'No and only one arm.'

'I suppose that's the sort of thing you'd spot,' Griffin replied absorbed by
the revelations, reflecting that this was certainly not a waste of his time,
and with a good lunch to boot. 'What was the name of this site?'

'I really couldn't tell you Mike. As I said it's been taken down and I'll be
honest I subscribe to a few, it's a bit of a weakness,' Theo replied his self
confidence returning now he had released what had been pent up inside

'Well, with your permission, if we could borrow your computer my guys
will be able to locate it,' Griffin said pretty well convinced that this was
the same site and that they probably had all that was needed back at the
station, but he could not resist the opportunity to delve into the doctor's
personal space. 'You have my assurance that your name will remain secr
and that it will be just this site that they look up. I could even get them to
come to you, home or surgery? Or I'll pick it up and bring it back within a
couple of hours.'

'I'm not particularly happy about that, but If you are sure it will not
become public.'

'Look Theo, if this can lead us to Nash, and between you and me, this wi
be the first sighting we've had. This could be a real breakthrough. Louise
won't need to know anything about it,' Griffin said probing for an Achille
Heel.

'Okay, if it will help as much as you say and lead you to find Andy Nash.
But I'm trusting you Mike and please don't involve Lou.'

'It will be fine, trust me. Now you said there was something else,' Griffin said in a reassured manner inwardly taking in what he had heard, wanting to get back to the station to see whether or not Theo had something, whilst contemplating that the next revelation could prove to be just as revealing. He looked on in expectation as the doctor tucked into the spotted dick.

'This next bit is a little more sensitive, what with the Hippocratic Oath,' Theo replied wiping custard from his mouth. 'This is really good, are you sure that you don't want some?'

'No I'm fine. If you'll excuse me I'll just take a leak while you're enjoying that.'

Griffin made his way out to the gents, taking in the photographs over the urinal, surprised that he knew a few of the supposed famous faces, before slipping out into the empty beer-cum-cigarette garden. Pulling out his phone and calling Mantel. 'Hi Luce, could you check a couple of things for me when you get the chance.'

'No problem, I'll do it now, fire away. How's it going?'

'Very interesting and possibly fruitful. Can you check Andy Nash's file and see whether it mentions any distinctive marks in his medical records.'

'Anything in particular?'

'A birthmark on his back.'

'Okay and...'

'On the site we just raided, can you search for a posting where a bloke is tied up on a bed and is fucked by a different masked man every day.'

'Lovely, actually I seem to remember that one, but as you couldn't see anyone I didn't dwell on it. The connection?'

'See whether the bloke tied up has a birthmark on his back.'

'I'm on it. I take it you're still with the doctor?'

'Yeh, we're just halfway through his revelations, he's just tucking into his spotted dick.'

'Sorry?'

'Laters.'

Griffin returned to the table, the dessert bowl already removed.

'So where were we Theo? Ah yes, the sensitive patient information. Is th connected with Nash? Coffee?'

'Absolutely, yes please Mike. Yes, both Andy and Rod, but I really am not sure if I should be saying anything, but it seems so wrong to hold back something that may be significant.'

'Perhaps if I ask you the questions, then you can choose to answer what you want, I can then gauge how far we take it,' Griffin said deploying a tactic where sharing the responsibility took some of the pressure off, at the same time considering that he had got more than expected from the meeting, and should he quit while ahead and not risk any chance of compromise muddying the waters? 'Of course if you want to change your mind Theo that's fine, we can leave it here and just enjoy the coffees. It would be a shame though to have come this far.'

'No, let's continue, it feels good to be sharing this,' Theo responded. 'Tell me Mike, how much do you trust DNA?'

'Totally, if I'm honest I think it's fantastic, how did we manage before? Of course for a match they have to be on the database, and yes, there will b the odd error, there always has been and will be in the future. You're a massive advocate aren't you? I've read a couple of your articles on it, the were very interesting.'

'Thank you. I think there's a lot more to come, but it's going to cause arguments, if not more on the domestic front.'

'We've already experienced it. The truth can be a dangerous tool. I reckon it will expose that inbreeding isn't only the pastime of aristocrats.'

'I totally agree. Sometimes things are best just left alone.'

'So how does this concern the Nashs'?'

'Well, as you know I'm Andy and Rod's GP, plus Ellie's and I've been monitoring the pregnancy very closely. Thankfully, news is that mother and baby are both doing extremely well and have gone home, but of course Rod is helping your chaps with your enquiries.'

'Where are we going with this Theo?' Griffin asked with the doctor reverting to meandering.

'Sorry, yes. I don't know if it was common knowledge, but Rod was both pleased and very surprised that Ellie was pregnant.'

'I had heard through the rumour mill that he didn't think he could.'

'Well, it's true, he can't.'

'Sorry?'

'The baby is not a little Rod.'

'I thought that they had it checked out in the womb,' Griffin replied enjoying his coffee as reality hit. 'You're not going to say what I'm thinking are you Theo?'

'Sounds like it Mike.'

'That the baby's father is Andy.'

Silence followed as they drank their coffees.

'I can only think that he raped Ellie just before he was collared,' Theo continued. 'It fits with the timeline and when Nash was at his most prolific.'

'And poor Ellie, she didn't want to say anything and then like a knight on a white charger Rod appeared at just the right time and all was sweetness and light.'

'But what wasn't factored in Mike were the advancements in DNA. Rod not being the father would have always come to light after he gave in to his suspicions as the birth approached and got tested. I've got the results back from the extensive test he had the other day and there is absolutely no way that Rod Nash could have fathered a child.'

'Blimey. Who knows?'

'Me and you. I've been looking into this subject and digging round patient files for a while now, all for medical research of course. I got Rod's result fast tracked and with the help of a chum down the lab, we got all the information together, including Andy's DNA. The rest as they say is history.'

'When you say it's only me and you that know, of course Ellie knows.'

'Sorry yes, I think she is in denial and would probably have carried on that way if Rod's test had not been so conclusive.'

'She doesn't know about the latest test and result?'

'No, and obviously nor does Rod.'

Griffin pondered that Ellie was another victim who may be seeking retribution. 'You're her doctor Theo, how do you think she will handle it all?'

'I've really no idea Mike, I mean it appears that she has been harbouring the rape for the past nine months. I've known her for over twenty years and I very much doubt if she has told anyone else. She's a very private person.'

*

'Okay, all that you've got in my office,' Griffin said bustling through the CID office, jacket coming off and tie loosened in a few paces. A quick call with Mantel after the goodbyes with Theo had ascertained that they were onto something. His team had a positivity about them as he walked past, the adrenalin was flowing. A breakthrough in any case was a detective's lifeblood.

'I've got photos from his file,' Nimra said following hard on the heels of her boss with her laptop.

'I've got him on the web,' Mantel proclaimed.

'And I'll get the drinks,' Henshall said making for the door.

'Excellent stuff, so from the top,' Griffin said, jacket flung over his chair as he perched on the edge of his desk. 'The birthmark?'

'Yep, pretty impressive,' Nimra responded twisting her laptop round for all to see. 'You'd pay a fortune for a tattoo like that.'

'And that one didn't cost anything,' Mantel chipped in.

'It looks like a lion's head, even one of those images of Che Guevara you get on t-shirts,' Griffin said looking closely at the screen.

'Good imagination boss, map of Australia sprang to my mind,' Mantel said turning her laptop. 'And here is that birthmark on the website.'

'Choice,' Nimra said looking at the images of a naked man tied face down on a bed, being buggered by a well-built guy with a face mask on.

'Not one for the family album,' Henshall said returning with the refreshments taking a look at Mantel's laptop as he passed them around.

'Having looked at it a few times I would have said that it could very well be Nash. Now with the birthmark I'd say it's a definite and I'm pretty confident,' Mantel said as her laptop moved between the team.

'The other blokes?' Griffin asked.

'No idea,' Mantel replied. 'Hired help?'

'Funny you should say that,' Henshall said returning the computer and moving back to his stool. 'It may be just a coincidence...'

'Don't do coincidences Kev.'

'Well I've done a bit of digging into what Friar and Rod Nash were involved in.'

'And?'

'Well pretty much everything that is pretty gross.'

'This better be worth it Kev.'

'Bear with me. They supplied people for extreme video shoots, where anything goes, including animals.'

'I can never get that,' Mantel said screwing up her face. 'There was some of that on this site.'

'You wouldn't have thought our Tina and Roy would have gone for that, didn't see any pets at the cottage,' Griffin replied tongue firmly in cheek.

'Quite, a drugged up guy, tied up and shafted up the jacksy, that's all fine,' Mantel retorted, her tongue in a similar position. 'But a bit of New Zealand mutton...'

'Thank you Luce, that's put me right off the lamb jalfrezi,' said Griffin pointing towards the screen. 'On the drugged up front, you can clearly see the cannula, but I wouldn't have noticed it if Theo hadn't mentioned it. This is all excellent stuff, and this gives us evidence that he may be alive...' Griffin stopped mid-sentence as DCI Fairmead entered the office carrying a Tupperware style container in gloved hands.

'I've received a gift,' she said nonchalantly. The three detectives looked on as the boss's boss put the box with a sealed blue lid on their boss's desk. 'Go on open it. Gloves on. Are they doing what I think they're doing?' Fairmead asked pointing at the laptop with the frozen image of two men having anal sex.

'Yes ma'am, potential progress in the Nash case,' Griffin said pulling a pair of disposable gloves from a drawer.

'Well this is also progress on that front.'

Griffin tentatively made to remove the lid of the container which was the size of a shoe box. 'It's cold.'

Fairmead smiled as Mantel, Nimra and Henshall looked on, intrigued both by the box and its contents, and the rare appearance of the DCI.

'Careful,' Fairmead said as Griffin popped open the lid. 'We're breaking quite a few health and safety rules here.' Necks craned as Griffin carefully placed the lid upside down on his desk, revealing a box filled with crushed ice.

'Here use this,' said Henshall handing Griffin the tray he had carried the drinks on as his boss looked around for somewhere to put the ice.

'Thanks.' Griffin carefully removed a layer. 'I take it you've already done this?' Griffin asked Fairmead who looked on with her arms folded.

'Yes and Rhea is out in the carpark getting some air,' Fairmead replied referring to her PA who had helped to unpack the parcel a few minutes earlier.

Griffin scraped off another layer of the crushed ice, revealing a severed penis with testicles intact. 'Oh fucking lovely. Recognize it Luce?'

'Not sure boss.'

'What the fuck,' Henshall exclaimed.

'Oh my god,' Nimra said putting her hand over her mouth.

'And here is the note that came with it.' Fairmead placed a previously folded sheet of A4 white paper on Griffin's desk next to the container.

'Bit old school isn't it. Not had one of these myself, thought they were only the movies,' said Griffin as he and his team lent over to read the note composed with letters cut from a newspaper.

aNDY NAsH

£100o0o cAsH

WiLl CaLL At 7

There was a knock at the door and Sergeant Art Symmons, a seasoned uniform copper with over twenty years at the station, stepped in. 'Excuse me all. Ma'am, we've got it sorted. Do you mind?' Symmons said pointing at, then sidling over to Griffin's computer, immediately tapping on the keyboard. 'Sorry Mike, needs must.'

'No problem Art, assume you got CCTV of the delivery then?'

'More than that Mike. Shit come on you bastard. Sorry about this,' Symmons replied as he tapped the keyboard in frustration. Fairmead and Griffin's phones bleeping simultaneously.

'Interesting,' Griffin said looking at the message.

'We'd better go down there Mike,' Fairmead said. 'Art, you show DS Mantel what you've got, we've got a body in the forest.'

'Nimra, you come with us. Kev you stay with Luce.' Griffin tugged his jacket from his chair.

'There you go,' Symmons said as the screen filled with a number of camera views. 'Right Luce, here you go.' Mantel and Henshall either side of the sergeant looked at the progression of video images. 'So here's matey coming into the station with a rucksack on his back. Then the front office.' Symmons pointed at the screen with a biro he picked up from the desk. 'He takes a carrier bag out of the rucksack and puts it on the counter, leaves it there without asking for anyone, then leaves, without saying a word.'

'Did it have Fairmead's name on it?' Henshall asked.

'Yeh, we've got the bag downstairs, 'For the attention of DCI Nicola Fairmead' to be precise, I know what you detectives are like for detail. So here you go, still with hood up going out of the car park. I reckon it's a male or a woman with a very flat chest.'

'Art you can't say that.' Mantel grinned and nudged the Sergeant in the ribs.

'Then he leaves the station and the carpark to where he's got a mate waiting for him in a red Corsa, a very dirty red Corsa with a reg that we can't make out. Shouldn't be a problem though. There you go, and then they drive off.'

'Is that it?' Mantel asked.

'They're working on it to see if they can pick the car up anywhere else. But it went towards the forest so not as many cameras out there. Give it time they'll track it. Right I'll leave it with you Luce. Shout if there's anything else.'

'Art you are a star, thank you,' Mantel said as Symmons left the office. 'Diamond, absolute diamond is Art, he'd be worth buying a drink to get to know a bit better if he drank, but he doesn't.'

'This whole thing doesn't look very professional to me Luce.'

'I would say chancers if it weren't for the meat and two veg, which must have taken some sorting out. And there's something about that guy's walk that's familiar. Hi Nim,' Mantel said taking a call from Nimra.

'Hi, the bosses were wanting to know if you got anything from the CCTV?'

'Plenty. We were just saying that they are not very professional. No faces, but a black hoodie, white guy, about five eight, gloves and a distinctive walk like that comedian when he does his 'out, out' sketch, oh you know him. But I reckon it was more of a limp than a Caribbean gangster's strut.'

'Mickey Flannagan,' Nimra replied.

'That's it, well done. And he got in an old red Corsa, no plate though.'

'Okay, I'll pass it on, we're just walking over to the body. Oh and they asked can you put out a nationwide request for anyone dealing with someone having their tackle removed in the last twenty four hours.'

'Why do that if it's Nash's?'

'What if it isn't, I suppose. Must go Luce, we're here.'

'They want us to put out a call for anyone knowing someone who's lost their bollocks in case it's not Nash.'

'Makes sense. Look, if the plan has been to post this everyday then with the site closing down they don't have that avenue anymore. So what do you think they'll do?' Henshall said busy studying footage from the website.

'Well if this ransom demand is bona fide, they've cut his wotsits off. Can we see if they're intact on there?'

'You can't tell without magnifying, but I still don't think you'll be able to see, he's face down.'

'Whatever, first things first we need to get this off to the lab,' Mantel said, then, much to Henshall's ongoing admiration, nonchalantly tipped the melting ice back over the evidence, slapped the lid back on and clipped it shut, giving it a little pat. 'This will perk up forensics day.'

CHAPTER TWENTY EIGHT

'Just been onto Luce sir and they've got some interesting stuff from the CCTV,' Nimra said as they approached the hastily erected tent, rustling through the woodland undergrowth, thankfully dry as the detectives footwear was not countryfied. Uniform officers scurried about making it crime scene rather than a place of natural beauty. Blue and white tape stretched from the road, around the carpark and the seventy or so yards to where the body was discovered and a similar distance beyond.

'Look forward to hearing about it, thanks Nimra. Bazzer, what have we got?' Griffin asked greeting Inspector Barry Hargreaves outside the tent.

'Ma'am, Mike. Well, you'll certainly recognize him. We haven't touched anything, apart for confirming that he was dead, which was pretty obvious.'

'Who found him?'

'Anonymous call from a public phone.'

'Fucking useful,' Griffin surmised looking around. 'So no public involved, dogwalkers?'

'Thankfully not. I would say he's not been here that long. Reckon the call was coordinated to ensure that we were first on the scene, they were very precise with where he was.'

Fairmead uncharacteristically giggling as she followed Hargreaves and Griffin into the tent, having watched Griffin nearly fall arse over tit into brambles as he put on his forensic suit. They were not in dense woodland clusters of bushes and trees spread over grassy land. Not a fashionable spot and it rarely saw visitors despite an unmade car park being nearby.

'Well it's definitely Nash. Normally say poor bastard, but this bastard deserves all that he got,' Griffin said looking at the clothed body that appeared to be standing semi-tucked away next to a bush, one of the prevalent prickly hawthorns throughout the forest, this one keeping the body upright. Nash's hands were in the pockets of a buttoned up beige mackintosh, a plain brown baseball cap on his head, top of the range white trainers finished the look. 'So as you say the call must have been from the perp or an accomplice; they didn't want him out here for long and seen by the public. Definite local knowledge.'

'We're checking all the public phone boxes and dusting them for prints,' Hargreaves responded. 'And checking any cameras near them, but I don't hold out much hope, this is a professional job.'

'Problem with the murder of scum like this is that the motivation to find the murderer is zero unless it's to give them a medal for carrying out the deed.'

'Agreed, but some poor bastard at the murder squad has to take it seriously, it's their job,' Hargreaves said crossing his arms. 'I'm with you though Mike, draw a line, go for a pint and celebrate the bastard getting his comeuppance.'

'He looks eerie,' Fairmead said breaking her silence. 'Should be in that Madame Tussauds and he looks like he's about to flash.'

'I think you're spot on with that ma'am,' Griffin replied as they all slipped on gloves and approached the corpse for closer examination.

'Could be wrong,' Griffin continued carefully undoing the mac. 'But if I'm right, I think they were out to make a statement.'

'Spot on Mike,' Fairmead said as Griffin revealed trousers, well the legs of trousers elasticated above the knee and nothing else, a gap where his manhood would have normally presided. Jagged but competent needlework in its place. 'It doesn't make sense; the ransom demand is pointless, in fact just ridiculous.'

'Agreed, and a total load of bollocks in my book. I would say that someone has tried to stitch us and Nash up good and proper.'

'Didn't have you down as a comedian Mike,' Fairmead replied. 'And, off the record, I totally agree with what you and Bazzer have been saying. Keep paperwork to a minimum and cremate the bastard as quick as possible.'

'Take the positives,' Hargreaves said. 'By the way I heard about that package, interesting twist.'

'What are those positives Bazzer?' Fairmead enquired. 'That he's dead and it looks like he suffered?'

'It draws a line for the victims.'

'Yes, sorry, I agree, that can be so important.'

'Well at least it means that we don't have to wait for the phone call. But leaves unanswered questions. Who did this, are they Nash's bollocks in the office, which I very much doubt, so whose are they? And where are his?' Griffin asked pointing at the stitched area. 'Then there's who sent the ransom note? SOCO's going to have a field day, the autopsy on this le will make an interesting read. It should show a very red arse if it's confirmed that it's Nash on the website.'

'Thanks for that Mike.' Fairmead raised an eyebrow. 'Normally I'd pull a few strings and get it all fast-tracked, but why waste resources on him. Did DC Shimra say that they'd got something from the cameras?'

'Yep, I'll get her to elaborate,' Griffin said sliding out of the tent to find h DC.

With the raincoat returned to its original position to cover over the lack evidence Nimra went through what Mantel had conveyed,.

'Okay, I'm going to get back to the station ma'am, from what Nimra has said I've got an inkling of something, but I'd like to see the images from the CCTV on a decent screen and not a phone,'

'Just one more point about here sir,' Nimra said as the bosses went to peel off their gloves. 'The guys found narrow wheel tracks from the car park to here, four of them, a trolley of some sort I suspect, but apparent it did not go back. Could have been dumped or carried back. And there's signs of deliberate wheel spinning at the car park, probably to distort an tyre tread marks being found.'

'Good work Nimra. Keep at it, you can't just dump a body like this and no leave clues. Could you hang around here for the lab guys and keep me updated.'

*

'I take it all back about coincidences Kevin,' Griffin said analysing the CCTV footage of the drop-off alongside Henshall and Mantel, who was now referring to it affectionately as 'bollockgate'.

'Why's that boss?'

'I'll put my house on...'

'Penthouse apartment boss,' Mantel interjected. 'Don't under sell it.'

'Sorry yes, I'll put my apartment on this being Davy Richards, he of the notorious Richards family. You'd have thought that one of the other members of the family would have done the courier bit, not the one with a fucking limp. And then just to make it even easier they bring the family run-around for a getaway car. Fucking idiots. What a waste of our fucking time.'

'So coincidences R us in this case boss?'

Yes, an extraordinary one, but one none the less,' Griffin replied slumping back in his chair. 'Verging on the possible, but not quite. They must have got word that Nash had disappeared, even left the country. But even they could not have foreseen, in fact, I doubt even Einstein could have, let alone the Richards, that on the same day they deliver their creative ransom note and the teaser, that Andy Nash's body would reappear strung up in the forest with the same MO, for want of something better to call it.'

'Doesn't answer how they got hold of the fresh tackle, don't suppose you can get that on eBay,' Mantel pondered chewing the end of a biro. 'A ransom note for a dead person, they get ten out of ten for originality,'

'Possibly on-line, through that deep dark web, and you know my thoughts on that,' Griffin replied glancing at his DS. 'Anyway, that's still to be answered and I'm sure that the Richards family will be full of answers.'

'Yeh, some cock and ball story,' Henshall responded.

'Very good Kev. I reckon we'll get a call pretty soon from one of our colleagues somewhere in the country on that question, I mean if that's happened on your patch you're going to welcome all the support you can get.'

'And whoever it is won't be needing a jockstrap.'

'Kevin please, you should have got out while you were ahead,' Mantel tutted. 'I mean, didn't they think we'd test it? It's not one size fits all.'

'Exactly, well put Luce. Right you two, sort out some back-up and get out to those wankers. They've obviously had a brainstorming session as to how to pay for their ciggies and came up with demanding a ransom for Nash, with one minor problem.'

'They hadn't got Nash,' Henshall replied.

'Correct, but why worry about little details like that when they can cut up a newspaper and ask for a sack full of cash in used notes. Probably demanding it be dropped behind the local bus shelter. They need to stop watching Netflix for their ideas.'

'They can't be that stupid,' Mantel said, to which Griffin raised an eyebrow. 'I mean how can you have a brainstorming without brains?'

'And getting hold of the fresh meat can't have been cheap,' Henshall quipped.

'There's another joke there if I could be bothered. They'd have thought nothing of paying a few bob for the knackers for a hundred grand return. But they're going to be out of pocket and possibly lose their spacious tax payer home. So first things first, get out there. I may be proved wrong, but I doubt it. Chuck murder charges at them, then they'll break like a bar of Kit Kat, with just a little bit of pressure,' Griffin said, pleased with his analogy as his detectives made to leave and he turned his attentions back to Mantel's laptop that was still in his office with an image of Nash frozen on the screen, pleased that finding who murdered him wouldn't be his responsibility.

*

'Party time eh?' Griffin said taking a stool, having had to squeeze past the crowds to get to the bar. Not Geoff's stool, that had a scantily clad young lady wrapped around a burly, heavily tattooed guy occupying it.

'Power of social media Mike,' Veronica replied placing a pint in front of the Inspector. The Cobblers was pretty much full with a mix of the sexes, rarity in itself. 'You can feel the relief, time to let your hair down. Lil's said that it went berserk on social media.'

'Viral?'

'Quite possibly. When news of finding Andy Nash's body in the forest came out you could sense everybody breathing out with the nightmare over.'

'Understandable. From within the police bubble you don't always appreciate how the tension's racked up out here.'

'It's been a while you know, for many a virtual lockdown, too frightened to venture out at night. What with the murders and poor Mandy, it's been ghastly and quite frightening,' Veronica said. 'Bet you've had an interesting day?'

'You could call it that. But with how it works these days,' Griffin replied sipping his pint. 'It's not like the TV and books where the hero cop sees it through then rides off into the sunset with a glamourous heroine on his arm. I'm left with dealing with the Richards family.'

'You're mixing up your cops 'n' robbers with spaghetti westerns. So, tell me more about the Richards and how they fit in. They're not in tonight, thankfully, wouldn't want them winding people up when everyone's had a few.'

'No, they won't be bothering you, I can assure you. They're paying us a visit,' Griffin replied with a knowing look.

'Oh. I see,' Veronica responded with an equally knowing look. 'Here's an idea, I'll check it out with Lil's, but all the girls are in, they all wanted to work, begged for it, wanted to be part of the celebration, so they can easily handle it down here. We can grab a drink and take it upstairs then you can give me all the details. It'll be interesting to hear real facts. The rumours that are circulating are becoming less and less believable as the evening goes on. Someone even said that you'd been sent a knob in an ice bucket.'

Griffin slumped onto the couch looking round the pub's spacious lounge, a peaceful sanctuary, putting his fresh pint on the coffee table having thrown his jacket over an armchair. Veronica following him in with a large gin and tonic. 'Good, Lil's said she'd lock up then she's going to see the li of the land. May join us, may bat on with friends, or may even go back to her flat, but thinks that will be tomorrow.'

'Normality returns. You forget how people adjusted their lives.'

'So, come on, what have the Richards family got to do with all this?' Veronica asked curling her legs up under on the sofa, cradling her drink.

Griffin recounted the tale of the container and its contents, to which Veronica's reply was plain and simple: 'Oh my god'. Then he explained h hunch and how Mantel and Henshall had found Richards senior and his three boys all stoned out of their minds. No sign of mother, Anita, or daughter Louise, nor the grandchildren. A considerable number of beer cans were strewn throughout the substantial council house. On the kitchen table it looked like an arts and crafts class, with scissors, chopped up newspapers and glue. 'So they've been brought in, but they're too ou of it to be coherent. A news channel was on their TV, that Kevin said was the hugest he's ever seen. And with the local news carrying the Nash story, we're wondering whether they realized that their game was up before it had really started and were drowning their sorrows. Whatever, that's tomorrow's task, well Lucy and Kevin's. Between you and me I thin there might be something going on between those two.'

'Really? Minor gossip Mike, of more importance, whose knob was it?'

'Ah yes, 'bollockgate' as Lucy's termed it, we've had an enquiry from the Nottinghamshire boys.'

'What, 'can we have our knob back please'?' Veronica quipped, as alway engrossed with her Inspector's tales. 'Are they sending them in a pre-pai envelope with a note on it, 'warning may contain nuts'?'

'Very good. From all accounts some paedo had been murdered on an estate just outside the city centre, one that the Richards happened to liv on before they were asked to move south. The body had had their vital organs removed.'

'What heart and lungs?'

'No, those vital to a paedo.'

'Ha, ha. Sorry shouldn't laugh. That's disgusting,' Veronica said putting her hand to her mouth to cover her smile. 'So what happens with it now?'

'Not sure if I'm honest. I would suggest that the labs will speak to each other and make an e-match,' Griffin said finishing his pint. 'Okay if I get a bottle of red and some crisps?'

'Sure. Then what do they do with it? Reunite it, give it a burial. Cremate it?

'Bar-b-q?' Griffin added returning from the kitchen with a bottle of Merlot and pouring it into two glasses. 'I suppose I should know, but I don't. I don't remember studying the return of dicks at Hendon. I'll find out for you.'

'Thanks, just don't share it when we're about to tuck into bangers 'n' mash.'

'Please. After this I'm giving up the sheikh kebabs.'

'Moving on,' Veronica said leaning forward and switching glasses. 'Cheers. Just one more question, how much does one of them cost?'

'Questions, questions and another one that I don't have the answer for. Have a look on eBay,' Griffin replied with a smile. 'I reckon that no cash will be exchanged and that it's a favour for a favour.'

'Not a contactless transaction then. So, come on, who's in the frame for Nash's murder.'

'I thought we were moving on. That's classified stuff.'

'Never stopped you before Inspector. I like your classified stuff.'

'Well, just between us, your co-owner, the onetime City Slicker and Rod Nash are definitely being mentioned in despatches and would be early favourites with the bookies if they weren't locked up or laying on a slab. They're looking very closely at all those involved with that dodgy website. Although never an innocent site, they now think it could be a lot deeper and darker than first believed. They're keeping an eye out for news of

Nash's murder appearing somewhere on it, perhaps Stephen might have some news on that front.'

*

'Right, I think that's me done, there wasn't much on there,' Roy Tucker said getting to his feet and collecting the two empty wine glasses, having watched the national and the Shires local ten o'clock news with his wife.

'Yeh, I'm bushed, it's been a bit traumatic. I didn't sleep much last night,' Tina replied turning the television off with the remote. 'Don't know about you, but I'm looking forward to the pub quiz tomorrow for a bit of normality.'

'Do you regret any of it?'

'It did get a bit extreme, I preferred it at the start.'

'I agree, but it brought in a bit of extra cash and we had some great trips out of it. I loved Barbados and New York, they're the tops for me. You?'

'The cruises were great, I know that you weren't so enamoured,' Tina said getting to her feet and puffing up the cushions. 'I wonder whether we'll ever hear from anyone, or is that it forever?'

'Don't know. I liked Rod Nash, but I was always wary of that Glenn Friar.'

'I agree with you Roy, I think it was Friar who pushed it too far. Although he was fair and upped the payments. What I'm really pleased about is getting rid all the stuff the police didn't want down the dump and having good deep clean. I feel that it's properly in the past now.'

'Me too. We'll have to find a new pastime Tina, I can't see us doing nothing.'

'Perhaps a new more gentile website?' Tina replied.

'What the...' Roy exclaimed with the sound of the front and back doors of their quaint thatched cottage crashing open as Thames Valley Police's SWAT squad plundered in.

'Armed police, everyone on the floor.'

'There's more coming out that Rod and Friar go back a long way and it's not particularly nice,' Griffin continued finishing off a bag of salt 'n' vinegar crisps and picking up his wine. 'And of course, there's Ellie and the baby.'

'What about Ellie and the baby? How are they involved?'

'Oh fuck,' Griffin exclaimed quietly thinking brain into gear before opening mouth might have been a good idea. 'I haven't seen you for a couple of nights, have I? Now this is classified and for your ears only.'

'Go on, but I'm not sure I'm going to like this.'

'It's suspected that the baby's not Rod's, and that it's Andy's.'

'Oh my god, no.'

'Still to be totally verified, but as it came from their doctor I reckon it's pretty kosher. Ellie has not been approached on it, but the timelines stack up and would indicate that Ellie may be one of his last victims before he was arrested.'

'That's fucking terrible Mike. Do you think anybody knows?'

'Not sure, Rod may have worked it out. He'd been having tests.'

'I remember you mentioned a while back that it was a surprise. So are the results conclusive?

'Fraid so.'

'Poor Ellie, but what can anyone do for her?' Veronica said visibly upset taking a long sip of her wine.

'Well, if it's what we think, then the real father's dead and the, I suppose you'd call him the adopted dad won't be around for a while.'

'Oh Mike, it's so sad. But as you say, nothing proven yet. We can only hope, although the baby's not got the greatest genes whatever the outcome.'

'You know what they say about smoke and fire. It's all moving at a pace, as these things invariably do as more and more facts materialise. But nothing is ever straight forward, my gut says that this whole scenario is going to get worse before it gets any better.'

'Another watch this space eh?' Veronica said reflectively. 'Amongst all this, I do have some good news.'

'Please share. There's not much good news about apart from finding And Nash strung up in the forest.'

'And he was without his wotsits, wasn't he?' Veronica enquired topping up their glasses. 'Seems to be a bit of a theme developing.'

'Now that wasn't on the news.'

Veronica tapped her nose. 'Have they found them, it?'

'No, and a search of the area failed to find anything. Not sure what they used as a sample for the sniffer dogs. Anyway, your good news?'

'Oh yes, sorry you've just placed a revolting image in my mind, thanks for that. Yes, my news, the redevelopment is going ahead.'

'Excellent.'

'Yep, a relief, Freddie was in earlier saying that life goes on. He's got to find a new builder, but once he does it will restart.'

'So, many reasons for a celebration. No murderers, apart from Nash's, but that doesn't count. No rapists, and the en-suite back on track.'...

CHAPTER TWENTY NINE

'Hi Stephen. Not like you to be up at the crack of dawn.'

'Hi sis, look I've got something for Mike, didn't know if this was too early, or even if I should make contact with him direct with all that's happened?'

'Well why don't you ask him yourself, he's sitting here,' Veronica replied in t-shirt and trackies enjoying a bacon butty, handing her phone over to Griffin as he tucked into a full English.

'Morning Stephen, how can I help you?' Griffin asked picking up his mug of tea, enjoying breakfast before finishing getting suited and booted for what should be a positive early briefing at the station.

'Morning Mike, sorry to bother you, but I've been looking at this web site again,' Stephen said sensing that his nose may be growing Pinocchio style as Griffin had yet to be informed that he was not the computer guru. His student's interest had strengthened, definitely not waned, with her discoveries, pestering Stephen to share her new findings to bolster her uni project.

'Okay, but you do know that there's been many developments since you tracked down the site?' Griffin replied stabbing a mushroom covered in brown sauce.

'Yes, I had a call with sis. Look, it's just that I magnified the images and in the room there was a box or similar with a Bartwell Crisps logo on it in the corner.'

'I had a pack of their salt 'n' vinegar last night,' Griffin replied chewing the mushroom.

'It was a chat that I had with my sister about their rep that sparked my interest and made me cross ref back to the list of subscribers to confirm that Les Chandler was on it.'

'Name rings a small bell.'

'The creepy Bartwell Crisp rep that sis and Lily don't like.'

'Ah yes. Let me put this on speaker. Listen to this Ron, Stephen's found something on the web, images that may have a link to your crisp rep.'

'Hi sis.'

'Hi again Stephen,' Veronica replied licking her fingers, the butty finished

'It may be nothing, but I was saying to Mike that there was a Bartwell Crisp box in the room you said Andy Nash was in.'

'I reckon our tech guys will have gone through the images with a fine tooth comb, but they wouldn't necessarily have placed any importance on a crisp box or whatever it is that you've seen, nor linked it to a subscriber so good work,' Griffin continued, his intrigue pricked. 'Could you send me over what you've seen, I know that we can do it at this end, but I'd like to see what you've seen. You can't always trust these computer images not to be altered.'

'No problem, I'll get onto it.'

'That's great Stephen. Tell you what, if you ever fancy joining the police on the IT side I'd happily put in a good word. I'll pass you back to Ronni, here you go.'

*

'Well it definitely says Bartwell Crisps and I've cross-referenced with the official company logos, look,' Mantel said pointing at her laptop and the Bartwell Crisp logo from the company's official site. The detectives compared the logo having analysed a still image on the boss's desktop of the room Nash was held in and the box in the corner. 'So it's a proper Bartwell crisp box as far as I can tell, I'm sure that forensics will confirm it.'

'Why should it be anything else?' Nimra asked.

'No reason, just to be sure.'

'I reckon it's like it is on the TV news with Zoom, Skype and all the others Not everyone's a Spielberg,' Henshall said. 'What you can spot in the background is more interesting than what's being said. I reckon it's just sloppy editing.'

'That may be, but it does make you wonder about this Les Chandler character,' Griffin said sifting the information. 'He works for Bartwell's, has a couple of cautions, albeit from way back on his file…'

'That were potentially involving under-age, and boys at that,' Nimra chipped in. 'He may have progressed.'

'Good point and he's a subscriber to the site. Plus, Ronni and Lily think he's right dodgy.'

'Reopen The Tower boss,' Mantel quipped. 'Row him down the Thames to Traitors Gate.'

'It's definitely one to pass on to the guys, if only in case they missed it or didn't know of Les Chandler, surprisingly not everyone reads the whole file as meticulously as us, it'll be interesting to hear what they say,' Griffin said believing that it may be of significance. 'Did you see Prisha last night Nim?'

'Yep,' Nimra replied inwardly blushing as she recalled their night of passion at her flat.

'I bet she was elated,' Mantel said.

'I suppose so. Although more reserved than I expected,' Nimra recalled, choosing to not mention the sex and the chilled Prosecco .

'I Suppose it's not sunk in yet. How do you react to the murder of the guy who viciously raped you, there's no right or wrong way to deal with that, she's always come across as a quite cool character,' Griffin replied turning to sit on his chair. 'Has the Richards brief turned up yet?'

'Yep, I'm just off down there, it's that bent bastard Ratty Atty,' Mantel responded making to leave. 'Richard fucking Attwood lawyer to all who disobey the law. A right QC, a Queen sized C…'

'Okay Luce, I think we all know about him and what a slime ball he is. Make sure you've got the evidence in the room with you, it should distract them all, including Atty.'

'Hope they've freshly iced it up,' Henshall said following Mantel to the door. 'Could be on the turn otherwise.'

'That's why I'm delegating it Kev, enjoy.'

*

'It's always good when you can get back for lunch Les,' Kayleigh said barefoot on the tiled floor in a flowy floral dress. 'A bite to eat then a bit of time to ourselves without the kids, perfect.'

'Does it have to be in that order?' Les Chandler enquired, jacketless having left it in the car after his morning calls at a few local pubs, grabbing his wife affectionately from behind in their expansive, designer country style, kitchen-diner in the heart of their sprawling ex-farmhouse in the Hertfordshire countryside.

'I've just put the toast on the aga, so no. Patience my little tiger,' Kayleigh replied enjoying her husband nibbling at her neck. 'You sort out the pate Will you be having a small glass of wine?'

'Absolutely,' Les responded heading to the substantial fridge freezer for bottle of Pinot Grigio and the pate. 'Ardennes, my favourite.'

'Get that Les will you,' Kayleigh said in response to the front doorbell. 'It can only be Jehovah's out here at this time of day. Give them your usual spiel.'

Les placed the wine and pate on the island and went to the front door with a bounce in his shoeless step.

'Mr Chandler, Hertfordshire Police, we have a warrant to search this property.'

*

DCI Nicola Fairmead greeted Griffin as he took a seat in front of her desk in response to her request to meet when he didn't think that there was anything in particular to discuss with much of his case load in the process of being wrapped up, racking his brains to recall if he had unwittingly done something wrong to warrant this unscheduled get together. 'Many thanks for coming up Mike.'

'No problem, how can I help you ma'am?' Griffin asked thinking that his superior's office looked more soulless than usual, if that was possible.

2

'Did you hear that they paid Les Chandler a visit at lunchtime?'

'No. They didn't hang around then.'

'Had some other intel from what I could gather, yours just accelerated things.'

'Did they have any luck?'

'Well, I was just on the phone to DCI Christy, they've arrested him, from all accounts it was very interesting and may bear fruit,' Fairmead replied keeping her gaze on her DI. 'It was a sprawling country place, well above a crisp rep's pay scale, so that needs a little look. Plus, their info was that he was a keen amateur photographer, and they found a barn kitted out as a top notch studio.'

'Interesting and...'

'Yes, boxes of Bradwell crisps, which I suppose is understandable.'

'But put the two together,' Griffin shifted in his chair liking what he was hearing but not the look his DCI was giving him, it was just too friendly. 'It means he has something to answer for?'

'Yep, and there's the usual computer equipment to look at, from all accounts a whole van load of it, she was pretty positive. So, well done to your source for spotting the crisp box, as Angela didn't say that they were already onto it I assume that they hadn't clocked it.'

'I'll pass that on ma'am,' Griffin replied genuinely pleased. Even if it was no longer his case, positive results bred a positive atmosphere, and it was always good to keep motivating the troops. He could envisage Stephen and his computer skills developing into an useful ally.

'And did you know that the Tuckers were raided late last night?'

Nope. What a proper raid?'

'Yep full on. Again some further intel with the stuff you gathered which said that they were not all they seemed on the surface. Problem is they didn't find anything, looked like the place had been deep cleaned from all accounts.'

'We've all been there, and those Thames Valley boys did seem a little trigger happy, given half a reason they'd definitely be up for some action

'Anyway there might be a compensation claim coming in, thankfully not us.'

'That'll be a bit rich considering what they were up to. A few John Lewis vouchers should keep them quiet,' Griffin replied. 'Bearing in mind there may still be questions for them to answer.'

'Those were the days Mike. A simple apology, patch it up and move on . Nowadays it keeps the desk jockeys happy, someone's going to have a whole load of paperwork to deal with.'

'Well it would have made them spill their Horlicks. I think there's a film there, they're a really intriguing couple.'

Griffin looked on, still slightly unnerved awaiting whatever warranted the meeting, the news that Fairmead had delivered was little more than CID gossip. Was it still that he was for the high jump for a long forgotten misdemeanour, although it didn't feel that like that.

Fairmead leant forward. 'So one final thing Mike, you'll be pleased to he that I'm back off up north.'

'When?'

'Tomorrow.'

'Tomorrow?'

'Yes, you probably heard about the DI getting stabbed up there yesterday.'

'Yes, terrible and the bastard got away.'

'Well that's where I was due to go to. Now they want me up there immediately to head up the case. My counterpart DCI's got too much els on his plate and this is pretty sensitive. I'm driving up in an hour or so.'

'Not wishing to see you gone before your seat's cooled ma'am, and I do wish you well, but what about your replacement?'

'That's what I wanted to talk to you about. It should have all been sorted out earlier.'

Griffin looked on trying to gauge the situation, in his mind sifting through the names he had decided that he didn't want to report to when Fairmead had first mentioned she was off at the vicar's murder. Reflecting that once again the position appeared to have passed him by.

'I've recommended you, and it's been favourably received. You are both popular and a good copper, and I like you, rare attributes.'

*

'A nice surprise Mike,' Veronica said greeting the Inspector.

'I wanted to share something with you,' Griffin replied.

'All good I hope. A pint?'

'Yes please and it could be,' Griffin responded standing at the bar, glancing round a considerably pub than the previous night.

'Here you go, bring it upstairs, I want to see Robbie from Blue Skies on the box, he's going to be on live on their big charity night. Lil's is looking after here for a few minutes; I'm recording it for her.'

'Why not put it on down here?' Griffin said pointing at a blank screen. 'I'm sure they'd like to see Robbie performing.'

'It's a rehab special all about prisons and prisoners rehabilitating. He's cooking live from a prison.'

'Ah, now I can see your reasoning, not the sort of thing your punters would chose to watch.'

'Exactly, come on.'

Veronica and Griffin settled onto the sofa in the lounge in front of the television as a celebrity in the studio handed over to another celebrity, answering to the name of Judy, in Bradwell Prison.

'Eh, Bradwell, that's where my mate's a warden,' Griffin said pointing at the screen

'Welcome to Bradwell Prison, where four inmates are going to prepare and cook supper for their fellow inmates under the watchful eye of our top chef, and everyone's favourite Robbie Jones. So what are they cooki for us tonight Robbie?'

'Hi Judy, these guys are going to produce a superb savoury 'Rehab Cobbler' in recognition of being here in Northamptonshire, home to the Cobbler, as in bootmakers and my favourite local pub The Cobblers.'

'Hey, we got a mention,' Veronica said. 'Good on you Robbie.'

'And there's my mate Rob, looking like a right prick in the background,' Griffin said getting to his feet and pointing at his mate on the screen.

'So what's in this Cobbler Robbie?'

'Meat offal Suzi.'

'Very on-trend Robbie.'

'Yes, it's important to use the whole animal and this is an excellent way doing it. Of course, we will be doing a vegetarian version which Tristram cooking.'

'Okay Robbie let's get going, you can take us through it as the guys get going.'

'Right, first thing to do is to take all these cuts and dice them up. I'll show you how then you can takeover,' said Robbie his gloved hands chopping up the meat with gusto.

'Ah, that's why Rob looks so nervous they're letting them loose with knives on live national television. Could make interesting viewing.'

'This is a bit like a mash up between MasterChef and Get Me Out Of Her eating all those bits and pieces,' Veronica joked. 'Old Robbie's a star, he' got a few drinks lined up here with that mention.'...

...'He's such a natural, hope he doesn't leave us with all this TV stuff,' Margaret said clicking off the tele with Roddie's cooking piece finished.

'Well I hope they enjoy it,' Prisha replied.

'Need to avoid those razor blades I'm sure I saw one of them slip in,' Margaret quipped smiling.

'I'd say that's the least of their problems,' Ellie replied raising a flute filled with champagne, her first drink since the birth of Jonny, who slept soundly on the bed beside them. 'Here's to a good job done.'

'Yep, deep clean done and just that box to be thrown out,' Prisha said indicating towards the Bradwell crisp box in the corner of the room. 'I'll take that with me.'

'Yes, a little toast to my nephew Les, the dirty little bastard,' Margaret responded with a steely look. 'I got a panicked call from his wet teabag of a wife Kayleigh telling me that her Les had been arrested. Just wanted to say to her get a new husband, but you can't, can you? And I thought it wasn't the right time to ask to pass on our thanks for the couple of freebie boxes of crisps.'

'Not on your Christmas card list then? Here's to Les and all that comes to him,' Ellie said raising her glass again. 'From what you've told us Margaret it sounds like it couldn't have happened to a nicer man.'

Prisha glanced round the spare en-suite bedroom in the basement of Blue Skies House. 'So the new temporary carer will be in here tomorrow. Not sure that she will have as much fun as we've had down here.'

'Quite,' Ellie replied. 'But all good things come to an end.'

'Yes, it's a shame in some respects,' Margaret said looking round the room. 'Don't forget that box Prisha.'

Margaret, Prisha and Ellie, together with baby Jonny, gathered their glasses and the half full bottle of Champagne and made to leave. Ellie double checked the bathroom for anything she may have missed and Prisha scooped up the box. Margaret fluffed up the duvet, before turning off the lights and closing the door...

POSTSCRIPT

Despite being convicted and securely under lock and key Andy Nash and his ugly legacy was etched in stone. The initial anger towards the serial rapist and how he had ripped the community apart would never subside and quite rightly so. In Blue Skies House, where he was once a well-liked colleague, he would never be forgiven nor forgotten. No one felt it more than Prisha. When details of the vicious attacks came out in court it took special resolve for her to keep it together, her determination to one day get her own back keeping her going, whilst ensuring that she got on with her own life. She found great comfort in the support she received. Margaret, the 80 year old shop steward of the residents, and Robbie the chef were always around when a shoulder was required, both went the extra mile. Like Prisha they found it difficult to keep their own anger fuelled emotions under wraps.

A matter of days after Nash's conviction Ellie asked to meet with Prisha, Margaret and Robbie. With all that had occurred they did not expect the revelation that she had been raped by Nash in her tiny office. It was a very difficult meeting, intensified when Ellie told them she was pregnant, believing the baby to be Andy's and, slightly surprisingly that she wanted to keep it. They vowed to keep this to themselves and to protect Ellie through her pregnancy, a challenge in itself.

Rod was always aware of the ghastly scenario but held out hope that the baby was his and not his nephew's. DNA testing indicated that Ellie was carrying Nash genes. Rod's previous tests did not offer any encouragement though, and they both knew this.

As the months passed, the desire for retribution remained, even intensified. During which time Ellie discovered Rod's business association with Glenn Friar and absolutely despised it. Unless he walked away from she could not have him as a father figure. With him showing no inclination to relinquish his lucrative business, Ellie needed to remove Rod from day to day parenting when the baby was born.

Although the memories remained, news of the incarcerated Andy Nash was drying up when Prisha received an out of the blue phone call from Iain Swift, Nash's psychiatric nurse, requesting a meeting. Intrigued,

Prisha agreed to meet out in Hertfordshire. With his credentials how was she to know that he was a psychopath? Prisha wrongly assumed they were going to discuss gaps in his research. Unexpectedly, Swift told her that as part of his treatment Nash would be given a version of day-release and that he wanted her to meet him. Prisha initially totally rejected this as a totally absurd idea, a load of 'care in the community' crap, threatening to walk out of the meeting and report Swift, albeit recognizing that it offered an unexpected opportunity for revenge. The persuasive qualities of a psychopath kicked in and the meeting continued convivially. Swift manipulated the facts enough for Prisha to agree to at least consider it, with the proviso that she shared his ideas with her friends at Blue Skies House. By the end of the meeting it was clear to Prisha that Swift was not normal; but what was normal in the world of psychiatric nursing? Notwithstanding this, there was absolutely no indication of his true intentions. The more Swift talked, the more the positives stacked up. Prisha did not want to accept that the chance for retribution was clouding her judgement, which it most certainly was.

Swift's plan was for Nash to be in a sedated conscious state throughout, which Prisha found surprising. Swift brushed off her concerns, saying that it was standard procedure and he would supply the prescribed daily dosage of the drugs to make sure that all was above board and closely monitored, assuring Prisha that it would be extremely safe for all parties. Swift's selling point was that Prisha would be able to do as she pleased with Nash, verbally and physically, the one proviso was that he should remain alive, with no visible marks before he was returned to the unit, explaining that this was all part of ground-breaking treatment, a significant nationwide initiative. Whatever she decided to do to Nash it should be caught on camera for research purposes and would be used in Nash's therapy. With hindsight, there were many dots that didn't join up, it was not a plan that stood up to scrutiny.

Prisha returned to the group with the obscure proposal. She was excited but fully expected Swift's proposal to be laughed out of court as being too ridiculous. To her delight and considerable surprise this was not the case, it was universally thought of as an excellent way of gaining an element of retribution with no come back.

A plan was hatched. Swift brought Nash to the basement bedroom, via a discreet door, the proposed public entrance to the much discussed Spa. He had arranged for Nash's move to be at night on a shift when he was in sole charge. Justifying it that as a new method of treatment, being close scrutinized and it was specific eyes only, hence being commenced at night, and needing to be kept secret.

With news of Nash's absconding breaking the next morning it was quick confirmed that Swift's utterances were totally bull-shit. After a quick pow wow, Prisha and her friends decided to keep stum about having Nash stashed in the basement and to deny any knowledge of Swift. A tricky decision, where secrecy would be the key to success. But as they had Nash and nobody knew, they were not inclined to let him go. At no time did they think that Swift was anything other than a very strange person, who, perhaps inadvertently, was doing them a huge favour.

It was sensibly agreed that Ellie was in charge of all things medical. This saw a cannula inserted for topping up the drugs that, despite Nash's disappearance being a news item, Swift continued to supply. Once in the room Nash had been tied to the bed. Robbie took charge of that, his trussing skills invaluable, if the method was slightly different to a chicken It was what to do with him now that they had him captive that divided t group. The options were endless, like a free run in a sweet shop or choosing a parking space in an empty car park. That was until Margaret, never one to recognize the new politically correct world stepped in and suggested, in her words, 'get one of those gay boys off the street then film the buggers shafting the bastard'. After the initial shock of her directness, they all agreed that it was an excellent idea. There was a min issue though, on which street do they find these rent boys?

Ellie had the answer, Rod's shady hard core porn business, one aspect of which was supplying all sorts to carry out acts at the deep dark end of th spectrum, was perfect for their needs. She bribed him by threatening to reveal his true Jaffa status and expose the business. This would also reve his association with Glenn Friar, in most people's eyes the squeaky clear respectable and successful entrepreneur who provided jobs locally. Unbeknown to Ellie, Rod knew Swift through his porn business and the website, something that he never revealed.

All went smoothly, with a daily stream of healthy looking blokes being smuggled into Blue Skies House. Elaborate excuses were made for locking the room, a covert operation was underway. Margaret worked up a rota for the four of them to oversee it all. The 'boys' would undress in the en-suite and put on a mask for the filming. They would then earn their crust, so to speak, and depart. All payments were Rod's responsibility. The daily screening of the 'act of the day' became a sordid albeit satisfying highlight, along with Margaret's repeated comments that the chaps were not normal and must have been medically injected. Rod, sworn to secrecy, was the only other person to know of their exploits, he had too much to lose should it be exposed. Prisha found it particularly difficult to not include Nimra, especially after her attack. To see and hear the fears in the community when they knew he was stashed in the basement stretched their commitment, often finding themselves twisting the truth to those they would never have dreamed of lying to.

An unforeseen problem was that Swift had smelled blood and his previously submerged psychopath character rose to the surface. Swift became more and more frustrated at not having a day to day role, apart from the Secret Squirrel dropping off the drugs and downloading the footage for the Tucker's to publish, the innocuous couple in Oxfordshire, who answered the advert for a 'Website Administrator'. Unknown was that Swift, after making his deliveries roamed the area looking to satisfy his psychopath desires. No one knew that Swift was the murderer until his ugly exposure at the Vicarage.

Swift's demise and Mandy's horrendous murder rapidly prompted Ellie, Prisha and Robbie to search for an end game. To return Nash into secured care was dismissed as a cop out and ludicrous. A plan was hatched that provided Prisha and Ellie with the ultimate retribution. Robbie was delighted to be an integral cog and Margaret, who was having the time of her life, set about organizing what was required. In parallel she had a sub plot that became a significant part of the plan. This was to implicate Les Chandler, her nephew, a relative who had always disgusted her with his murky exploits and shady photography hobby, that her family would never expose him for fear of embarrassing them and dragging the family into it. Margaret planted the crisp box and gradually moved it into a prominent position to drop her nephew into a whole pile of shit, whilst creating a further distraction for themselves.

Ellie also worked on a separate plan. She would expose Rod and his business dealings as soon as Jonny was safely born. With Rod, in her eye stubbornly refusing to relinquish his disgusting business, Ellie felt that sh had little option but to protect baby Jonny from being exposed to such filth. A contact of Robbie's in the Vice Squad at New Scotland Yard had been very grateful for the tip off. The shooting dead of Glenn Friar, although related was an unfortunate spin-off.

The decision to separate Andy Nash from his tackle received universal agreement at a jovial meeting in Margaret's room, the schooners of sherry possibly assisting the decision making. Prisha was the only one to suggest keeping it as a trophy, Ellie quickly squashing this on health and safety grounds. The disposal on live TV was conceived by Robbie and described as 'revolting, but quite genius' by Margaret. As far as the actu surgery was concerned, Ellie administered and oversaw matters, anaesthetic deemed not needed, Robbie's butchery skills started the job then Margaret's needlework finished it off. Although her slightly shaky hands at her advanced age left her disappointed with the quality of the stitching. Old clothes were acquired and once again Margaret's skillset was used to shorten the trousers. A van was borrowed, as was a collapsible wheelchair to get Nash into the forest. Robbie carrying it bac to avoid return tracks, before having great fun wheel spinning out of the car park. After auditions Ellie's voice was deemed the most neutral for tl phone call from one of the few working public phones, heavily disguised with gloves on. Method of murder? Simple, a lethal overdose. No need f anything fancier. All conducted with military precision.

With the deed completed, all evidence was either disposed of or given a deep clean.

The day after Robbie's appearance on television Margaret called a meeting in her room to celebrate.

'Right, job done. What's next?'...

Printed in Great Britain
by Amazon